BETTY
NEELS

THE
CHRISTMAS COLLECTION

*Four heart-warming romances to
curl up with this Christmas!*

Give yourself a treat with this special
selection of seasonal delights, by time
honoured, bestselling author Betty Neels.

Betty Neels's novels are loved by millions
of readers around the world, and this classic
collection of four novellas offers a chance to
recapture the magic of some of her most
popular festive stories.

*First published in Great Britain 2003 by
Harlequin Mills & Boon Limited,
Eton House, 18-24 Paradise Road,
Richmond, Surrey, TW9 1SR*

BETTY NEELS: THE CHRISTMAS COLLECTION
© Harlequin Enterprises II B.V. 2003

A Christmas Romance © Betty Neels 1999
The Proposal © Betty Neels 1993
Dearest Eulalia © Betty Neels 2000
A Christmas Proposal © Betty Neels 1996

ISBN 0 263 83684 3

062-1203

*Printed and bound in Spain
by Litografia Rosés S.A., Barcelona*

BETTY NEELS

THE CHRISTMAS COLLECTION

A CHRISTMAS ROMANCE

THE PROPOSAL

DEAREST EULALIA

A CHRISTMAS PROPOSAL

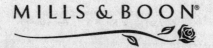

MILLS & BOON®

BETTY NEELS

THE CHRISTMAS COLLECTION

A CHRISTMAS ROMANCE   5

THE PROPOSAL   105

DEAREST EULALIA   213

A CHRISTMAS PROPOSAL   341

A CHRISTMAS ROMANCE
by
Betty Neels

CHAPTER ONE

THEODOSIA CHAPMAN, climbing the first of the four flights which led to her bed-sitter—or, as her landlady called it, her studio flat—reviewed her day with a jaundiced eye. Miss Prescott, the senior dietician at St Alwyn's hospital, an acidulated spinster of an uncertain age, had found fault with everyone and everything. As Theodosia, working in a temporary capacity as her personal assistant, had been with her for most of the day, she'd had more than her share of grumbles. And it was only Monday; there was a whole week before Saturday and Sunday...

She reached the narrow landing at the top of the house, unlocked her door and closed it behind her with a sigh of contentment. The room was quite large with a sloping ceiling and a small window opening onto the flat roof of the room below hers. There was a small gas stove in one corner with shelves and a cupboard and a gas fire against the wall opposite the window.

The table and chairs were shabby but there were bright cushions, plants in pots and some pleasant pictures on the walls. There was a divan along the end wall, with a bright cover, and a small bedside table

5

close by with a pretty lamp. Sitting upright in the centre of the divan was a large and handsome ginger cat. He got down as Theodosia went in, trotted to meet her and she picked him up to perch him on her shoulder.

'I've had a beastly day, Gustavus. We must make up for it—we'll have supper early. You go for a breath of air while I open a tin.'

She took him to the window and he slipped out onto the roof to prowl among the tubs and pots she had arranged there. She watched him pottering for a moment. It was dark and cold, only to be expected since it was a mere five weeks to Christmas, but the lamplight was cheerful. As soon as he came in she would close the window and the curtains and light the gas fire.

She took off her coat and hung it on the hook behind the curtain where she kept her clothes and peered at her face in the small square mirror over the chest of drawers. Her reflection stared back at her—not pretty, perhaps, but almost so, for she had large, long-lashed eyes, which were grey and not at all to her taste, but they went well with her ginger hair, which was straight and long and worn in a neat topknot. Her mouth was too large but its corners turned up and her nose was just a nose, although it had a tilt at its tip.

She turned away, a girl of middle height with a pretty figure and nice legs and a lack of conceit about her person. Moreover, she was possessed of a practical nature which allowed her to accept her rather dull life at least with tolerance, interlarded with a strong desire to change it if she saw the opportunity to do so. And that for the moment didn't seem very likely.

She had no special qualifications; she could type and take shorthand, cope adequately with a word processor and a computer and could be relied upon, but none of these added up to much. Really, it was just as well that Miss Prescott used her for most of the day to run errands, answer the phone and act as go-between for that lady and any member of the medical or nursing staff who dared to query her decisions about a diet.

Once Mrs Taylor returned from sick leave then Theodosia supposed that she would return to the typing pool. She didn't like that very much either but, as she reminded herself with her usual good sense, beggars couldn't be choosers. She managed on her salary although the last few days of the month were always dicey and there was very little chance to save.

Her mother and father had died within a few weeks of each other, victims of flu, several years ago. She had been nineteen, on the point of starting to train as a physiotherapist, but there hadn't been enough money to see her through the training. She had taken a business course and their doctor had heard of a job in the typing pool at St Alwyn's. It had been a lifeline, but unless she could acquire more skills she knew that she had little chance of leaving the job. She would be twenty-five on her next birthday...

She had friends, girls like herself, and from time to time she had been out with one or other of the young doctors, but she encountered them so seldom that friendships died for lack of meetings. She had family, too—two great-aunts, her father's aunts—who lived in a comfortable red-brick cottage at Finchingfield. She spent her Christmases with them, and an occasional weekend, but although they were kind to her she sensed that she interfered with their lives and was only asked to stay from a sense of duty.

She would be going there for Christmas, she had received their invitation that morning, written in the fine spiky writing of their youth.

Gustavus came in then and she shut the window and drew the curtains against the dark outside and set about getting their suppers. That done and eaten, the pair of them curled up in the largest of the two shabby chairs by the gas fire and while Gustavus dozed Theodosia read her library book. The music on the radio was soothing and the room with its pink lampshades looked cosy. She glanced round her.

'At least we have a very nice home,' she told Gustavus, who twitched a sleepy whisker in reply.

Perhaps Miss Prescott would be in a more cheerful mood, thought Theodosia, trotting along the wet pavements to work in the morning. At least she didn't have to catch a bus; her bed-sitter might not be fashionable but it was handy...

The hospital loomed large before her, red-brick with a great many Victorian embellishments. It had a grand entrance, rows and rows of windows and a modern section built onto one side where the Emergency and Casualty departments were housed.

Miss Prescott had her office on the top floor, a large room lined with shelves piled high with reference books, diet sheets and files. She sat at an important-looking desk, with a computer, two telephones and a large open notebook filled with the lore of her profession, and she looked as important as her desk. She was a big woman with commanding features and a formidable bosom—a combination of attributes which aided her to triumph over any person daring to have a difference of opinion with her.

Theodosia had a much smaller desk in a kind of cubby-hole with its door open so that Miss Prescott could demand her services at a moment's notice. Which one must admit were very frequent. Theodosia might not do anything important—like making out diet sheets for several hundreds of people, many of them different—but she did her share, typing endless lists, menus, diet sheets, and rude letters to ward sisters if they complained. In a word, Miss Prescott held the hospital's stomach in the hollow of her hand.

She was at her desk as Theodosia reached her office.

'You're late.'

'Two minutes, Miss Prescott,' said Theodosia cheerfully. 'The lift's not working and I had five flights of stairs to climb.'

'At your age that should be an easy matter. Get the post opened, if you please.' Miss Prescott drew a deep indignant breath which made her corsets creak. 'I am having trouble with the Women's Medical ward sister. She has the impertinence to disagree with the diet I have formulated for that patient with diabetes and kidney failure. I have spoken to her on the telephone and when I have rewritten the diet sheet you will take it down to her. She is to keep to my instructions on it. You may tell her that.'

Theodosia began to open the post, viewing without relish the prospect of being the bearer of unwelcome news. Miss Prescott, she had quickly learned, seldom confronted any of those who had the temerity to disagree with her. Accordingly, some half an hour later she took the diet sheet and began her journey to Women's Medical on the other side of the hospital and two floors down.

Sister was in her office, a tall, slender, good-looking woman in her early thirties. She looked up and smiled as Theodosia knocked.

'Don't tell me, that woman's sent you down with another diet sheet. We had words…!'

'Yes, she mentioned that, Sister. Shall I wait should you want to write a reply?'

'Did she give you a message as well?'

'Well, yes, but I don't think I need to give it to you. I mean, I think she's already said it all...'

Sister laughed. 'Let's see what she says this time...'

She was reading it when the door opened and she glanced up and got to her feet. 'Oh, sir, you're early...'

The man who entered was very large and very tall so that Sister's office became half its size. His hair was a pale brown, greying at the temples, and he was handsome, with heavy-lidded eyes and a high-bridged nose upon which was perched a pair of half glasses. All of which Theodosia noticed with an interested eye. She would have taken a longer look only she caught his eye—blue and rather cold—and looked the other way.

He wished Sister good morning and raised one eyebrow at Theodosia. 'I'm interrupting something?' he asked pleasantly.

'No, no, sir. Miss Prescott and I are at odds about Mrs Bennett's diet. They sent Theodosia down with the diet sheet she insists is the right one...'

He held out a hand and took the paper from her and read it.

'You do right to query it, Sister. I think that I had better have a word with Miss Prescott. I will do so now and return here in a short while.'

He looked at Theodosia and opened the door.

'Miss—er—Theodosia shall return with me and see fair play.'

She went with him since it was expected of her, though she wasn't sure about the fair play; Miss Prescott usually made mincemeat of anyone disagreeing with her, but she fancied that this man, whoever he was, might not take kindly to such treatment.

Theodosia, skipping along beside him to keep up, glanced up at his impassive face. 'You work here too?' she asked, wanting only to be friendly. 'This is such a big place I hardly ever meet the same person twice, if you see what I mean. I expect you're a doctor—well, a senior doctor, I suppose. I expect you've met Miss Prescott before?'

There were climbing the stairs at a great rate. 'You'll have to slow down,' said Theodosia, 'if you want me to be there at the same time as you.'

He paused to look down at her. 'My apologies, young lady, but I have no time to waste loitering on a staircase.'

Which she considered was a rather unkind remark. She said tartly, 'Well, I haven't any time to waste either.'

They reached Miss Prescott's office in silence and he opened the door for her. Miss Prescott didn't look up.

'You took your time. I shall be glad when Mrs Taylor returns. What had Sister to say this time?'

She looked up then and went slowly red. 'Oh—you need my advice, sir?'

He walked up to her desk, tore the diet sheet he held into several pieces and laid them on the blotter before her. He said quietly, 'Miss Prescott, I have no time to waste with people who go against my orders. The diet is to be exactly as I have asked for. You are a dietician, but you have no powers to overrule the medical staff's requests for a special diet. Be so good as to remember that.'

He went quietly out of the room, leaving Miss Prescott gobbling with silent rage. Theodosia studied her alarmingly puce complexion. 'Shall I make a cup of tea?'

'No—yes. I'm upset. That man…'

'I thought he was rather nice,' said Theodosia, 'and he was very polite.'

Miss Prescott ground her teeth. 'Do you know who he is?'

Theodosia, putting teabags into the teapot, said that no, she didn't.

'Professor Bendinck. He's senior consultant on the medical side, is on the board of governers, has an enormous private practice and is an authority on most medical conditions.'

'Quite a lad!' said Theodosia cheerfully. 'Don't you like him?'

Miss Prescott snorted. 'Like him? Why should I like him? He could get me the sack today if he wanted to.' She snapped her mouth shut; she had said too much already.

'I shouldn't worry,' said Theodosia quietly. She didn't like Miss Prescott, but it was obvious that she had had a nasty shock. 'I'm sure he's not mean enough to do that.'

'You don't know anything about him,' snapped Miss Prescott, and took the proffered cup of tea without saying thank you. Theodosia, pouring herself a cup, reflected that she would rather like to know more about him...

The day was rather worse than Monday had been, and, letting herself into her bed-sitter that evening, she heaved a sigh of relief. A quiet evening with Gustavus for company...

There was another letter from her aunts. She was invited to spend the following weekend with them. They had read in their newspaper that the air in London had become very polluted—a day or two in the country air would be good for her. She was expected for lunch on Saturday. It was more of a command than an invitation and Theodosia, although she didn't particulary want to go, knew that she would, for the aunts were all the family she had now.

The week, which had begun badly, showed no signs of improving; Miss Prescott, taking a jaundiced view of life, made sure that everyone around her should feel the same. As the weekend approached Theodosia wished that she could have spent it quietly getting up

late and eating when she felt like it, lolling around
with the papers. A weekend with the great-aunts was
hardly restful. Gustavus hated it—the indignity of the
basket, the tiresome journey by bus and train and then
another bus; and, when they did arrive, he was only
too aware that he wasn't really welcome, only
Theodosia had made it plain that if she spent her
weekends with her great-aunts then he must go too...

It was Friday morning when, racing round the hospital collecting diet sheets from the wards, Theodosia
ran full tilt into the professor, or rather his waistcoat.
He fielded her neatly, collected the shower of diet
sheets and handed them back to her.

'So sorry,' said Theodosia. 'Wasn't looking where
I was going, was I?'

Her ginger head caught fire from a stray shaft of
winter sunshine and the professor admired it silently.
She was like a spring morning in the middle of winter,
he reflected, and frowned at the nonsensical thought.

'Such a rush,' said Theodosia chattily. 'It's always
the same on a Friday.'

The professor adjusted the spectacles on his nose
and asked, 'Why is that?'

'Oh, the weekend, you know, patients going home
and Sister's weekend, too, on a lot of the wards.'

'Oh, yes, I see.' The professor didn't see at all, but
he had a wish to stay talking to this friendly girl who
treated him like a human being and not like the im-

portant man he was. He asked casually, 'And you, miss…er… Do you also go home for the weekend?'

'Well, not exactly. What I mean is, I do have the weekend off, but I haven't got a home with a family, if that's what you mean. I've got quite a nice bed-sitter.'

'No family?'

'Two great-aunts; they have me for weekends sometimes. I'm going there tomorrow.'

'And where is "there"?' He had a quiet, rather deliberate voice, the kind of voice one felt compelled to answer.

'Finchingfield. That's in Essex.'

'You drive yourself there?'

Theodosia laughed. 'Me? Drive? Though I can ride a bike, I haven't a car. But it's quite easy—bus to the station, train to Braintree and then the local bus. I quite enjoy it, only Gustavus hates it.'

'Gustavus?'

'My cat. He dislikes buses and trains. Well, of course, he would, wouldn't he?'

The professor agreed gravely. He said slowly, 'It so happens that I am going to Braintree tomorrow. I'd be glad to give you and Gustavus a lift.'

'You are? Well, what a coincidence; that would be…' She stopped and blushed vividly. 'I didn't mean to cadge a lift off you. You're very kind to offer but I think I'd better not.'

'I'm quite safe,' said the professor mildly, 'and

since you didn't know that I would be going to Braintree in the morning you could hardly be accused of cadging.'

'Well, if you don't mind—I would be grateful...'

'Good.' He smiled then and walked away and she, remembering the rest of the diet sheets, raced off to the men's ward... It was only as she handed over the rest of the diet sheets to Miss Prescott that she remembered that he hadn't asked her where she lived nor had he said at what time he would pick her up. So that's that, reflected Theodosia, scarcely listening to Miss Prescott's cross voice.

If she had hoped for a message from him during the day she was to be disappointed. Five o'clock came and half an hour later—for, of course, Miss Prescott always found something else for her to do just as she was leaving—Theodosia raced through the hospital, intent on getting home, and was brought up short by the head porter hailing her from his lodge in the entrance hall.

'Message for you, miss. You're to be ready by ten o'clock. You'll be fetched from where you live.'

He peered at her over his spectacles. 'That's what Professor Bendinck said.'

Theodosia had slithered to a halt. 'Oh, thank you, Bowden,' she said, and added, 'He's giving me a lift.'

The head porter liked her. She was always cheerful and friendly. 'And very nice too, miss,' he said. 'Better than them trains and buses.'

* * *

Theodosia, explaining to Gustavus that they would be travelling in comfort instead of by the public transport he so disliked, wondered what kind of car the professor would have. Something rather staid, suitable for his dignified calling, she supposed. She packed her overnight bag, washed her hair and polished her shoes. Her winter coat was by no means new but it had been good when she had bought it and she consoled herself with the thought that winter coats didn't change their style too much. It would have to be the green jersey dress...

At ten o'clock the next morning she went down to the front door with Gustavus in his basket and her overnight bag over her shoulder. She would give him ten minutes, she had decided, and if he didn't turn up she would get a bus to Liverpool Street Station.

He was on the doorstep, talking to Mrs Towzer, who had a head crammed with pink plastic curlers and a feather duster in one hand. When she saw Theodosia she said, 'There you are, ducks; I was just telling your gentleman friend here that you was a good tenant. A real lady—don't leave the landing lights on all night and leaves the bath clean...'

Theodosia tried to think of something clever to say. She would have been grateful if the floor had opened and swallowed her. She said, 'Good morning, Mrs Towzer—Professor.'

'Professor, are you?' asked the irrepressible Mrs Towzer. 'Well, I never...'

Theodosia had to admire the way he handled Mrs Towzer with a grave courtesy which left that lady preening herself and allowed him to stuff Theodosia into the car, put her bag in the boot, settle Gustavus on the back seat with a speed which took her breath and then drive off with a wave of the hand to her landlady.

Theodosia said tartly, 'It would have been much better if I had gone to the hospital and met you there.'

He said gently, 'You are ashamed of your landlady?'

'Heavens, no! She's kind-hearted and good-natured, only there really wasn't any need to tell you about turning off the lights...'

'And cleaning the bath!' To his credit the professor adopted a matter-of-fact manner. 'I believe she was paying you a compliment.'

Theodosia laughed, then said, 'Perhaps you are right. This is a very comfortable car.'

It was a Bentley, dark grey, with its leather uphol-stery a shade lighter.

'I expect you need a comfortable car,' she went on chattily. 'I mean, you can't have much time to catch buses and things.'

'A car is a necessity for my job. You're warm enough? I thought we might stop for coffee presently. At what time do your great-aunts expect you?'

'If I don't miss the bus at Braintree I'm there in time for lunch. But I'll catch it today; I don't expect it takes long to drive there.'

He was driving north-east out of the city. 'If you will direct me I will take you to Finchingfield; it is only a few miles out of my way.'

She looked at his calm profile uncertainly; without his specs he was really very handsome… 'You're very kind but I'm putting you out.'

'If that were the case I would not have suggested it,' he told her. A remark which she felt had put her in her place. She said meekly, 'Thank you,' and didn't see him smile.

Clear out of the city at last, he drove to Bishop's Stortford and turned off for Great Dunmow, and stopped there for coffee. They had made good time and Theodosia, enjoying his company, wished that their journey were not almost at an end. Finchingfield was only a few miles away and all too soon he stopped in front of the great-aunts' house.

It stood a little way from the centre of the village, in a narrow lane with no other houses nearby; it was a red-brick house, too large to be called a cottage, with a plain face and a narrow brick path leading from the gate to its front door. The professor got out, opened Theodosia's door, collected her bag and Gustavus in his basket and opened the gate and followed her up the path. He put the bag and the basket down.

'I'll call for you at about half past six tomorrow, if that isn't too early for you?'

'You'll drive me back? You're sure it's not disturbing your weekend?'

'Quite sure. I hope you enjoy your visit, Theodosia.'

He went back to the car and got in, and sat waiting until she had banged the door knocker and the door was opened. And then he had gone.

Mrs Trickey, the aunt's daily housekeeper, opened the door. She was a tall, thin woman, middle-aged, with a weather-beaten face, wearing an old-fashioned pinny and a battered hat.

'You're early.' She craned her neck around Theodosia and watched the tail-end of the car disappear down the lane. ''Oo's that, then?'

Mrs Trickey had been looking after the aunts for as long as Theodosia could remember and considered herself one of the household. Theodosia said cheerfully, 'Hello, Mrs Trickey; how nice to see you. I was given a lift by someone from the hospital.'

The housekeeper stood aside to let her enter and then went ahead of her down the narrow, rather dark hall. She opened a door at its end, saying, 'Go on in; your aunts are expecting you.'

The room was quite large, with a big window overlooking the garden at the back of the house. It was lofty-ceilinged, with a rather hideous wallpaper, and the furniture was mostly heavy and dark, mid-

Victorian, and there was far too much of it. Rather surprisingly, here and there, were delicate Regency pieces, very beautiful and quite out of place.

The two old ladies got up from their places as Theodosia went in. They were tall and thin with ramrod backs and white-haired, but there the resemblance ended.

Great-Aunt Jessica was the elder, a once handsome woman with a sweet smile, her hair arranged in what looked like a bird's nest and wearing a high-necked blouse under a cardigan and a skirt which would have been fashionable at the turn of the century. It was of good material and well made and Theodosia couldn't imagine her aunt wearing anything else.

Great-Aunt Mary bore little resemblance to her elder sister; her hair was drawn back from her face into a neat coil on top of her head and although she must have been pretty when she was young her narrow face, with its thin nose and thin mouth, held little warmth.

Theodosia kissed their proffered cheeks, explained that she had been driven from London by an acquaintance at the hospital and would be called for on the following evening, and then enquired about the old ladies' health.

They were well, they told her, and who exactly was this acquaintance?

Theodosia explained a little more, just enough to satisfy them and nip any idea that Mrs Trickey might have had in the bud. The fact that the professor was a professor helped; her aunts had had a brother, be-whiskered and stern, who had been a professor of something or other and it was obvious that the title conferred respectability onto anyone who possessed it. She was sent away to go to her room and tidy herself and Gustavus was settled in the kitchen in his basket. He didn't like the aunts' house; no one was unkind to him but no one talked to him except Theodosia. Only at night, when everyone was in bed, she crept down and carried him back to spend the night with her.

Lunch was eaten in the dining room, smaller than the drawing room and gloomy by nature of the one small window shrouded in dark red curtains and the massive mahogany sideboard which took up too much space. The old ladies still maintained the style of their youth; the table was covered with a starched white linen cloth, the silver was old and well polished and the meal was served on china which had belonged to their parents. The food didn't live up to the table appointments, however; the aunts didn't cook and Mrs Trickey's culinary skill was limited. Theodosia ate underdone beef, potatoes and cabbage, and Stilton cheese and biscuits, and answered her aunts' questions...

After lunch, sitting in the drawing room between them, she did her best to tell them of her days. Aunt Jessica's questions were always kind but Aunt Mary sometimes had a sharp tongue. She was fond of them both; they had always been kind although she felt that it was from a sense of duty. At length their questions came to an end and the subject of Christmas was introduced.

'Of course, you will spend it here with us, my dear,' said Great-Aunt Jessica. 'Mrs Trickey will prepare everything for us on Christmas Eve as she usually does and I have ordered the turkey from Mr Greenhorn. We shall make the puddings next week...'

'We are so fortunate,' observed Great-Aunt Mary. 'When one thinks of the many young girls who are forced to spend Christmas alone...' Which Theodosia rightly deduced was a remark intended to remind her how lucky she was to have the festive season in the bosom of her family.

At half past four exactly she helped Mrs Trickey bring in the tea tray and the three of them sat at a small table and ate cake and drank tea from delicate china teacups. After the table had been cleared, they played three-handed whist, with an interval so that they could listen to the news. There was no television; the aunts did not approve of it.

After Mrs Trickey had gone home, Theodosia went into the kitchen and got supper. A cold supper, of course, since the aunts had no wish to cook, and once that was eaten she was told quite kindly that she should go to bed; she had had a long journey and needed her rest. It was chilly upstairs, and the bathroom, converted years ago from one of the bedrooms, was far too large, with a bath in the middle of the room. The water wasn't quite hot so she didn't waste time there but jumped into bed, reminding herself that when she came at Christmas she must bring her hot-water bottle with her...

She lay awake for a while, listening to the old ladies going to their beds and thinking about the professor. What was he doing? she wondered. Did he live somewhere near Finchingfield? Did he have a wife and children with whom he would spend Christmas? She enlarged upon the idea; he would have a pretty wife, always beautifully dressed, and two or three charming children. She nodded off as she added a dog and a couple of cats to his household and woke several hours later with cold feet and thoughts of Gustavus, lonely in the kitchen.

She crept downstairs and found him sitting on one of the kitchen chairs, looking resigned. He was more than willing to return to her room with her and curl up on the bed. He was better than a hot-water bottle and she slept again until early morning, just in time to take him back downstairs before she heard her aunts stirring.

Sunday formed a well-remembered pattern: breakfast with Mrs Trickey, still in a hat, cooking scrambled eggs, and then church. The aunts wore beautifully tailored coats and skirts, made exactly as they had been for the last fifty years or so, and felt hats, identical in shape and colour, crowning their heads. Theodosia was in her winter coat and wearing the small velvet hat she kept especially for her visits to Finchingfield.

The church was beautiful and the flowers decorating it scented the chilly air. Although the congregation wasn't large, it sang the hymns tunefully. And after the service there was the slow progress to the church porch, greeting neighbours and friends and finally the rector, and then the walk back to the house.

Lunch, with the exception of the boiled vegetables, was cold. Mrs Trickey went home after breakfast on Sundays, and the afternoon was spent sitting in the drawing room reading the *Sunday Times* and commenting on the various activities in the village. Theodosia got the tea and presently cleared it away and washed the china in the great stone sink in the scullery, then laid the table for the aunts' supper. It was cold again so, unasked, she found a can of soup and put it ready to heat up.

She filled their hot-water bottles, too, and popped them into their beds. Neither of them approved of what they called the soft modern way of living—indeed, they seemed to enjoy their spartan way of living—but Theodosia's warm heart wished them to be warm at least.

The professor arrived at exactly half past six and Theodosia, admitting him, asked rather shyly if he would care to meet her aunts, and led the way to the drawing room.

Great-Aunt Jessica greeted him graciously and Great-Aunt Mary less so; there was no beard, though she could find no fault with his beautiful manners. He was offered refreshment, which he declined with the right amount of regret, then he assured the old ladies that he would drive carefully, expressed pleasure at having met them, picked up Gustavus's basket and Theodosia's bag and took his leave, sweeping her effortlessly before him.

The aunts, in total approval of him, accompanied them to the door with the wish, given in Great-Aunt Jessica's rather commanding voice, that he might visit them again. 'You will be most welcome when you come again with Theodosia,' she told him.

Theodosia wished herself anywhere but where she was, sitting beside him in his car again. After a silence which lasted too long she said, 'My aunts are getting old. I did explain that I had accepted a lift from you, that I didn't actually know you, but that you are at the hospital...'

The professor had left the village behind, making for the main road. He said impassively, 'It is only natural that they should wish to know who I am. And who knows? I might have the occasion to come this way again.'

Which somehow made everything all right again. In any case she had discovered it was hard to feel shy or awkward with him. 'Did you enjoy your weekend?' she wanted to know.

'Very much. And you? A couple of quiet days away from the hospital can be just what one needs from time to time.'

Perhaps not quite as quiet as two days with the great-aunts, reflected Theodosia, and felt ashamed for thinking it for they must find her visits tiresome, upsetting their quiet lives.

'Shall we stop for a meal?' asked the professor. 'Unless you're anxious to get back? There is a good place at Great Dunmow. I'll have to go straight to the hospital and won't have time to eat.'

'You don't have to work on a Sunday evening?' asked Theodosia, quite shocked.

'No, no, but I want to check on a patient—Mrs Bennett. It will probably be late by the time I get home.'

'Well, of course we must stop,' said Theodosia. 'You can't go without your meals, especially when you work all hours.' She added honestly, 'I'm quite hungry, too.'

'Splendid. I could hardly eat a steak while you nibbled at a lettuce leaf.'

He stopped in the market place at Great Dunmow and ushered her into the Starr restaurant. It was a pleasing place, warm and very welcoming, and the food was splendid. While the professor ate his steak, Theodosia enjoyed a grilled sole, and they both agreed that the bread and butter pudding which followed was perfection. They lingered over coffee until Theodosia said, 'We really ought to go or you'll never get to bed tonight, not if you are going to see your patient when we get back. It's after nine o'clock…'

The professor ignored the time for he was enjoying himself; Theodosia was good company. She was outspoken, which amused him, and, unlike other girls in his acquaintance, she was content with her lot and happy. And she made him laugh. It was a pity that once they got back to London he would probably not see her again; their paths were unlikely to cross.

The rest of their journey went too swiftly; he listened to Theodosia's cheerful voice giving her opinion on this, that and the other, and reflected that she hadn't once talked about herself. When they reached Mrs Towzer's house, he got out, opened her car door, collected Gustavus in his basket and her bag and followed her up the stairs to her attic. He didn't go in— she hadn't invited him anyway—but she offered a hand and thanked him for her supper and the journey. 'I enjoyed every minute of it,' she assured him, looking up at him with her gentle grey eyes. 'And I do hope you won't be too late going to bed. You need your rest.'

He smiled then, bade her a quiet goodnight, and went away, back down the stairs.

CHAPTER TWO

MONDAY morning again, and a cold one. Theodosia, going shivering to the bathroom on the floor below, envied Gustavus, curled up cosily on the divan. And there was a cold sleet falling as she went to work. A cheerful girl by nature, Theodosia was hard put to view the day ahead with any equanimity. But there was something to look forward to, she reminded herself; the hospital ball was to be held on Saturday and she was going with several of the clerical staff of the hospital.

She hadn't expected that she would be asked to go with any of the student doctors or the young men who worked in the wages department. She was on good terms with them all but there were any number of pretty girls from whom they could choose partners. All the same, when she had gone to earlier years' balls, she had had partners enough for she danced well.

She would need a new dress; she had worn the only one she had on three successive years. She pondered the problem during the day. She couldn't afford a new dress—that was quite out of the question—but someone had told her that the Oxfam shops in the more

fashionable shopping streets quite often yielded trea-
sures…

On Tuesday, she skipped her midday dinner,
begged an extra hour of Miss Prescott and took a bus
to Oxford Street.

The professor, caught in a traffic jam and inured to
delays, passed the time glancing idly around him.
There was plenty to catch his eye; shoppers thronged
the pavement and the shop windows were brilliantly
lighted. It was the sight of a gleaming ginger head of
hair which caught his attention. There surely weren't
two girls with hair that colour…?

The Oxfam lights were of the no-nonsense variety;
the shopper could see what he or she was buying.
Theodosia, plucking a dove-grey dress off the rails,
took it to the window to inspect it better and he
watched her as she examined it carefully—the label,
the price tag, the seams… It was a pity that the traffic
moved at last and he drove on, aware of an unexpected concern that she should be forced to buy someone else's dress.

Theodosia, happily unaware that she had been seen,
took the dress home that evening, tried it on and
nipped down to the bathroom where there was a full-
length mirror. It would do; she would have to take it
in here and there and the neck was too low. She
brought out her work basket, found a needle and
thread and set to. She was handy with her needle but

it took a couple of evenings' work till she was satisfied that it would pass muster.

It wasn't as though she was going with a partner,
she reminded herself. There would be a great many
people there; no one would notice her. Miss Prescott
would be going, of course, but any mention of the
ball during working hours was sternly rebuked and
when Theodosia had asked her what she would be
wearing she'd been told not to be impertinent. Theodosia, who had meant it kindly, felt hurt.

She dressed carefully on Saturday evening. The
grey dress, viewed in the bathroom looking-glass by
the low-wattage bulb, looked all right. A pity she
couldn't have afforded a pair of those strappy sandals.
Her slippers were silver kid and out of date but at
least they were comfortable. She gave Gustavus his
supper, made sure that he was warm and comfortable
on the divan, and walked to the hospital wrapped in
her winter coat and, since it was drizzling, sheltered
under her umbrella.

The hospital courtyard was packed with cars for
this was an evening when the hospital Board of Governers and their wives, the local Mayor and his wife
and those dignitaries who were in some way connected to St Alwyn's came to grace the occasion.
Theodosia slipped in through a side door, found her
friends, left her coat with theirs in a small room the
cleaners used to store their buckets and brooms and

went with them to the Assembly Hall where the ball was already under way.

It looked very festive, with paper chains and a Christmas tree in a corner of the stage where the orchestra was. There were balloons and holly and coloured lights and already there were a great many people dancing. Once there, one by one her friends were claimed and she herself was swept onto the dance floor by one of the technicians from the path lab. She didn't know him well and he was a shocking dancer but it was better than hovering on the fringe of the dancers, looking as though dancing was the last thing one wanted to do.

When the band stopped, one of the students with whom she had passed the time of day occasionally claimed her. It was a slow foxtrot and he had time to tell her about the post-mortem he had attended that morning. She listened carefully, feeling slightly sick, but aware that he was longing to talk about it to someone. There were several encores, so that it was possible for him to relate the very last of the horrid details. When the band stopped finally and he offered to fetch her a drink she accepted thankfully.

She had seen the professor at once, dancing with an elegantly dressed woman, and then again with the sister from Women's Medical and for a third time with the Mayor's wife.

And he had seen her, for there was no mistaking that gingery head of hair. When he had danced with all the ladies he was expected to dance with, he made his way round the dancers until he came upon her, eating an ice in the company of the hospital engineer.

He greeted them both pleasantly, and after a few moments of talk with the engineer swept her onto the dance floor.

'You should ask me first,' said Theodosia.

'You might have refused! Are you enjoying yourself?'

'Yes, thank you.' And she was, for he danced well and they were slow foxtrotting again. The hospital dignitaries wouldn't allow any modern dancing; there was no dignity in prancing around waving arms and flinging oneself about…but foxtrotting with a woman you liked was very satisfying, he reflected.

The professor, his eye trained to see details at a glance, had recognised the grey dress. It was pretty in a demure way but it wasn't her size. He could see the tucks she had taken on the shoulders to make a better fit and the neat seams she had taken in at the waist. It would be a pleasure to take her to a good dress shop and buy her clothes which fitted her person and which were new. He smiled at the absurd thought and asked her with impersonal kindness if she was looking forward to Christmas.

'Oh, yes, and it will be three days this year because of Sunday coming in between.' She sounded more enthusiastic than she felt; three days with the aunts wasn't a very thrilling prospect, but she reminded herself that that was ungrateful. She added, by way of apology for thinking unkindly of them, 'The great-aunts enjoy an old-fashioned Christmas.'

He could make what he liked of that; it conjured up pictures of a lighted Christmas tree, masses of food and lots of presents; with a party on Boxing Day...

She underestimated the professor's good sense; he had a very shrewd idea what her Christmas would be like. He glanced down at the ginger topknot. It would be a mistake to pity her; she had no need of that. He had never met anyone so content with life and so willing to be happy as she, but he found himself wishing that her Christmas might be different.

He resisted the urge to dance with her for the rest of the evening, handed her back to the engineer and spent the next few moments in cheerful talk before leaving her there.

It was at the end of the evening that he went looking for her amongst the milling crowd making their way out of the hospital. She was on her way out of the entrance when he found her. He touched her arm lightly.

'Come along; the car's close by.'

'There's no need... It's only a short walk... I really don't...' She could have saved her breath; she was propelled gently along away from the crowded fore-court, stuffed tidily into the car and told to fasten her seat belt. It was only as he turned out of the forecourt into the street that she tried again. 'This is quite...'

'You're wasting your breath, Theodosia.' And he had nothing more to say until they reached Mrs Towzer's house. No lights were on, of course, and the rather shabby street looked a bit scary in the dark; walking back on her own wouldn't have been very nice...

He got out, opened her door and took the key she had ready in her hand from her, opened the door silently and switched on the dim light in the hall.

Theodosia held out a hand for the key and whispered, 'Thank you for the lift. Goodnight.' And took off her shoes.

The professor closed the door without a sound, picked up her shoes and trod silently behind her as she went upstairs. She was afraid that he might make a noise but he didn't and she had to confess that it was comforting to have him there. Mrs Towzer, with an eye to economy, had installed landing lights which switched off unless one was nippy between landings.

At her own door he took her key, opened the door and switched on the light, gave her back her key and stood aside for her to pass him.

'Thank you very much,' said Theodosia, still whispering. 'Do be careful going downstairs or you'll be left in the dark, and you will shut the street door?'

The professor assured her in a voice as quiet as her own that he would be careful, and bade her goodnight, pushed her gently into the room and closed the door.

Back in his car he wondered why he hadn't kissed her; he had very much wanted to.

As for Theodosia, tumbling into bed presently, hugging a tolerant Gustavus, her sleepy head was full of a jumble of delightful thoughts, all of them concerning the professor.

Going for a brisk walk in Victoria Park the following afternoon, she told herself that he had just happened to be there and that common politeness had forced him to give her a lift back. She went home and had a good tea then went to evensong, to pray there for a happy week ahead!

She wasn't sure if it was an answer to her prayers when she received a letter from Great-Aunt Jessica in the morning. She was asked to go to Fortnum & Mason and purchase the items on the enclosed list. 'And you may bring them down next weekend,' wrote her aunt.

Theodosia studied the list: ham on the bone, Gentleman's Relish, smoked salmon, brandy butter, a Stilton cheese, Bath Oliver biscuits, *marrons glacés*, Earl Grey tea, coffee beans, peaches in brandy... Her week's wages would barely pay for them, not that she could afford to do that. She peered into the envelope in the forlorn hope of finding a cheque or at least a few bank notes but it was empty. She would have to go to the bank and draw out the small amount of money she had so painstakingly saved. If she skipped her midday dinner she would have time to go to the bank. Great-Aunt Jessica would pay her at the week-end and she could put it back into her account.

It wasn't until Wednesday that she had the opportunity to miss her dinner. There was no time to spare, so she hurtled down to the entrance, intent on getting a bus.

The professor, on his way to his car, saw her almost running across the forecourt and cut her off neatly before she could reach the street. She stopped in full flight, unable to get past his massive person.

Theodosia said, 'Hello, Professor,' and then added, 'I can't stop…'

A futile remark with his hand holding her firmly. 'If you're in a hurry, I'll drive you. You can't run to wherever you're going like that.'

'Yes, I can…'

'Where to?'

She had no need to answer his question yet she did. 'The bank and then Fortnum & Mason.'

He turned her round and walked her over to his car. Once inside he said, 'Now tell me why you are in such a hurry to do this.'

He probably used that gentle, compelling voice on his patients, and Theodosia felt compelled once more to answer him. She did so in a rather disjointed manner. 'So, you see, if you don't mind I must catch a bus…'

'I do mind. What exactly do you have to buy?'

She gave him the list. 'You see, everything on it is

rather expensive and, of course, Great-Aunt Jessica doesn't bother much about money. She'll pay me at the weekend. That's why I have to go to the bank.'

'That will take up too much time,' said the professor smoothly. 'We will go straight to Fortnum & Mason; I'll pay for these and your aunt can pay me. It just so happens,' he went on in a voice to convince a High Court judge, 'that I am going to Braintree again on Saturday. I'll give you a lift and deliver these things at the same time.'

Theodosia opened her mouth to speak, shut it again and then said, 'But isn't this your lunch hour?'

'Most fortunately, yes; now, let us get this shopping down.'

'Well, if you think it is all right?'

'Perfectly all right and sensible.'

Once there he ushered her in, handed her list over to a polite young man with the request to have the items packed up and ready within the next half an hour or so, and steered her to the restaurant.

'The food department will see to it all,' he told her. 'So much quicker and in the meantime we can have something to eat.'

Theodosia found her tongue. 'But ought I not to choose everything?'

'No, no. Leave everything to the experts; that's what they are here for. Now, what would you like? We have about half an hour. An omelette with French fries and a salad and a glass of white wine?'

It was a delicious meal and all the more delicious because it was unexpected. Theodosia, still breathless from the speed with which the professor had organised everything, and not sure if she hadn't been reckless in allowing him to take over in such a high-handed manner, decided to enjoy herself. This was a treat, something which seldom came her way.

So she ate her lunch, drank the wine and a cup of coffee and followed him back to the food hall, to find a box neatly packed and borne out to the car by the doorman. She was ushered into the car, too, and told to wait while the professor went back to pay the bill and tip the doorman .

'How much was it?' asked Theodosia anxiously as he got in beside her.

'Would it be a good idea,' suggested the professor carefully, 'if I kept this food at my house? There's not any need to unpack it; everything on the list is there and I have the receipted bill.'

'But why should you do that? It may be a great nuisance for you or your wife...'

'I'm not married, and my housekeeper will stow it safely away until Saturday.'

'Well, if it's really no trouble. And how much was it?'

'I can't remember exactly, but your aunt must have a good idea of what the food costs and the bill seemed very reasonable to me. It's in the boot with the food or I would let you have it.'

'No, no. I'm sure it's all right. And thank you very much.'

He was driving back to the hospital, taking short cuts so that she had still five minutes of her dinner hour left by the time he stopped in the forecourt. She spent two of those thanking him in a muddled speech, smiling at him, full of her delightful lunch and his kindness and worry that she had taken up too much of his time.

'A pleasure,' said the professor, resisting a wish to kiss the tip of her nose. He got out of the car and opened her door and suggested that she had better run.

Despite Miss Prescott's sharp tongue and ill temper, the rest of her day was viewed through rose-coloured spectacles by Theodosia. She wasn't sure why she felt happy; of course, it had been marvellous getting her shopping done so easily and having lunch and the prospect of being driven to the aunts' at the weekend, but it was more than that; it was because the professor had been there. And because he wasn't married.

She saw nothing of him for the rest of the week but on Friday evening as she left the hospital there was a message for her. Would she be good enough to be ready at ten o'clock in the morning? She would be fetched as before. This time there was no mistaking the twinkle in the head porter's eye as he told her. Over the years he had passed on many similar messages but never before from the professor.

'We're going to the aunts' again,' Theodosia told

Gustavus. 'In that lovely car. You'll like that, won't you?'

She spent a happy evening getting ready for the morning, washing her hair, examining her face anxiously for spots, doing her nails, and putting everything ready for breakfast in the morning. It would never do to keep the professor waiting.

She went down to the front door punctually in the morning to find him already there, leaning against Mrs Towzer's door, listening to that lady's detailed descriptions of her varicose veins with the same quiet attention he would have given any one of his private patients. Mrs Towzer, seeing Theodosia coming downstairs, paused. 'Well, I'll tell you the rest another time,' she suggested. 'You'll want to be on your way, the pair of you.'

She winked and nodded at him and Theodosia went pink as she wished them both a rather flustered good morning, trying not to see the professor's faint smile. But it was impossible to feel put out once she was sitting beside him as he drove off. Indeed she turned and waved to Mrs Towzer, for it seemed wrong to feel so happy while her landlady was left standing at her shabby front door with nothing but rows of similar shabby houses at which to look.

It was a gloomy morning and cold, with a leaden sky.

'Will it snow?' asked Theodosia.

'Probably, but not just yet. You'll be safely at your great-aunts' by then.'

He glanced at her. 'Will you be going to see them again before Christmas?'

'No, this is an unexpected visit so that I could buy all those things.' In case he was thinking that she was angling for another lift she added, 'I expect you'll be at home for Christmas?'

He agreed pleasantly in a voice which didn't invite more questions so she fell silent. When the silence became rather too long, she began to talk about the weather, that great stand-by of British conversation.

But she couldn't talk about that for ever. She said, 'I won't talk any more; I expect you want to think. You must have a lot on your mind.'

The professor debated with himself whether he should tell her that he had her on his mind, increasingly so with every day that passed. But if he did he would frighten her away. Being friendly was one thing but he sensed that she would fight shy of anything more. He was only too well aware that he was considered by her to be living on a different plane and that their paths would never meet. She was friendly because she was a girl who would be friends with anyone. It was in her nature to be kind and helpful and to like those she met and worked with. Even the redoubtable Miss Prescott.

He said now, 'There is no need to make polite conversation with you, Theodosia; do you not feel the same?'

'Well, yes, I do. I mean, it's nice to be with someone and not have to worry about whether they were wishing you weren't there.'

His rather stern mouth twitched. 'Very well put, Theodosia. Shall we have coffee at Great Dunmow?'

They sat a long while over coffee. The professor showed no signs of hurry. His questions were casual but her answers told him a great deal. She wouldn't admit to loneliness or worry about her future; her answers were cheerful and hopeful. She had no ambitions to be a career girl, only to have a steady job and security.

'You wouldn't wish to marry?'

'Oh, but I would—but not to anyone, you understand,' she assured him earnestly. 'But it would be nice to have a husband and a home; and children.'

'So many young women want a career—to be a lawyer, or a doctor, or a high-powered executive.'

She shook her head. 'Not me; I'm not clever to start with.'

'You don't need to be clever to marry?' He smiled a little.

'Not that sort of clever. But being married isn't just a job, is it? It's a way of life.'

'And I imagine a very pleasant one if one is happily married.'

He glanced at his watch. 'Perhaps we had better get on…'

At the great-aunts' house Mrs Trickey, in the same hat, admitted them and ushered them into the drawing room. Aunt Jessica got up to greet them but Aunt Mary stayed in her chair, declaring in a rather vinegary voice that the cold weather had got into her poor old bones, causing her to be something of an invalid. Theodosia kissed her aunts, sympathised with Aunt Mary and hoped that she wasn't expecting to get free medical treatment from their visitor. She had no chance to say more for the moment since Aunt Jessica was asking Theodosia if she had brought the groceries with her.

The professor greeted the two ladies with just the right amount of polite pleasure, and now he offered to fetch the box of food into the house.

'The kitchen?' he wanted to know.

'No, no. We shall unpack it here; Mrs Trickey can put it all away once that is done. You have the re-ceipted bill, Theodosia?'

'Well, actually, Professor Bendinck has it. He paid for everything. I hadn't enough money.' She could see that that wasn't enough to satisfy the aunts. 'We met going out of the hospital. I was trying to get to the bank to get some money. To save time, because it was my dinner hour, he kindly drove me to Fortnum & Mason and gave them your order and paid for it.'

Aunt Mary looked shocked. 'Really, Theodosia, a

young girl should not take any money from a gentleman.'

But Aunt Jessica only smiled. 'Well, dear, we are grateful to Professor Bendinck for his help. I'll write a cheque…'

'Perhaps you would let Theodosia have it? She can let me have it later. I shall be calling for her tomorrow evening.'

Aunt Mary was still frowning. 'I suppose you had spent all your money on clothes—young women nowadays seem to think of nothing else.'

Theodosia would have liked to tell her that it wasn't new clothes, more's the pity. It was cat food, and milk, bread and cheese, tea and the cheaper cuts of meat, and all the other necessities one needed to keep body and soul together. But she didn't say a word.

It was the professor who said blandly, 'I don't imagine that Theodosia has a great deal of money to spare—our hospital salaries are hardly generous.'

He smiled, shook hands and took his leave. At the door to the drawing room he bent his great height and kissed Theodosia's cheek. 'Until tomorrow evening.' His smile included all three ladies as he followed Mrs Trickey to the front door.

Great-Aunt Jessica might not have moved with the times—in her young days gentlemen didn't kiss young ladies with such an air, as though they had a right to do so—but she was romantic at heart and now she smiled. It was Great-Aunt Mary who spoke, her thin voice disapproving.

'I am surprised, Theodosia, that you allow a gentleman to kiss you in that manner. Casual kissing is a regrettable aspect of modern life.'

Theodosia said reasonably, 'Well, I didn't allow him, did I? I'm just as surprised as you are, Aunt Mary, but I can assure you that nowadays a kiss doesn't meant anything—it's a social greeting—or a way of saying goodbye.'

And she had enjoyed it very much.

'Shall I unpack the things you wanted?' she asked, suddenly anxious not to talk about the professor.

It was a task which took some time and successfully diverted the old ladies' attention.

The weekend was like all the others, only there was more talk of Christmas now. 'We shall expect you on Christmas Eve,' said Aunt Jessica. 'Around teatime will suit us very nicely.'

That would suit Theodosia nicely, too. She would have to work in the morning; patients still had diets even at Christmas. There would be a tremendous rush getting the diets organised for the holiday period but with luck she would be able to get a late-afternoon train. She must remember to check the times...

In bed much later that night, with Gustavus curled up beside her, she allowed herself to think about the professor. It was, of course, perfectly all right for him to kiss her, she reassured herself, just as she had reassured her aunts: it was an accepted social greeting. Only it hadn't been necessary for him to do it. He was a very nice man, she thought sleepily, only nice wasn't quite the right word to describe him.

It was very cold in church the next morning and, as usual, lunch was cold—roast beef which was underdone, beetroot and boiled potatoes. The trifle which followed was cold, too, and her offer to make coffee afterwards was rejected by the aunts, who took their accustomed seats in the drawing room, impervious to the chill. Theodosia was glad when it was time for her to get the tea, but two cups of Earl Grey, taken without milk, did little to warm her.

She was relieved when the professor arrived; he spent a short time talking to her aunts and then suggested that they should leave. He hadn't kissed her; she hadn't expected him to, but he did give her a long, thoughtful look before bidding his farewells in the nicest possible manner and sweeping her out to the car.

It must have been the delightful warmth in the car which caused Theodosia to sneeze and then shiver.

'You look like a wet hen,' said the professor, driving away from the house. 'You've caught a cold.'

She sneezed again. 'I think perhaps I have. The church was cold, but the aunts don't seem to mind the cold. I'll be perfectly all right once I'm back at Mrs Towzer's.' She added, 'I'm sorry; I do hope I won't give it to you.'

'Most unlikely. We won't stop for a meal at Great Dunmow, I'll drive you straight back.'

'Thank you.'

It was the sensible thing to do, she told herself, but at the same time she felt overwhelming disappointment. Hot soup, a sizzling omelette, piping hot coffee—any of these would have been welcome at Great Dunmow. Perhaps, despite his denial, he was anxious not to catch her cold. She muffled a sneeze and tried to blow her nose soundlessly.

By the time they reached the outskirts of London she was feeling wretched; she had the beginnings of a headache, a running nose and icy shivers down her spine. The idea of getting a meal, seeing to Gustavus and crawling down to the bathroom was far from inviting. She sneezed again and he handed her a large, very white handkerchief.

'Oh, dear,' said Theodosia. She heaved a sigh of relief at his quiet, 'We're very nearly there.'

Only he seemed to be driving the wrong way. 'This is the Embankment,' she pointed out. 'You missed the way…'

'No. You are coming home with me. You're going to have a meal and something for that cold, then I'll drive you back.'

'But that's a lot of trouble and there's Gustavus…'

'No trouble, and Gustavus can have his supper with my housekeeper.'

He had turned into a narrow street, very quiet, lined

with Regency houses, and stopped before the last one in the terrace.

Theodosia was still trying to think of a good reason for insisting on going back to Mrs Towzer's but she was given no chance to do so. She found herself out of the car and in through the handsome door and borne away by a little stout woman with grey hair and a round, cheerful face who evinced no surprise at her appearance but ushered her into a cloakroom at the back of the narrow hall, tut-tutting sympathetically as she did so.

'That's a nasty cold, miss, but the professor will have something for it and there'll be supper on the table in no time at all.'

So Theodosia washed her face and tidied her hair, feeling better already, and went back into the hall and was ushered through one of the doors there. The room was large and high-ceilinged with a bow window overlooking the street. It was furnished most comfortably, with armchairs drawn up on each side of the bright fire burning in the steel grate, a vast sofa facing it, more smaller chairs, a scattering of lamp tables and a mahogany rent table in the bow window. There were glass-fronted cabinets on either side of the fireplace and a long case clock by the door.

Theodosia was enchanted. 'Oh, what a lovely room,' she said, and smiled with delight at the professor.

'Yes, I think so, too. Come and sit down. A glass

of sherry will make you feel easier; you'll feel better when you have had a meal. I'll give you some pills later; take two when you go to bed and two more in the morning. I'll give you enough for several days.'

She drank her sherry and the housekeeper came presently to say that supper was on the table. 'And that nice cat of yours is sitting by the Aga as though he lived here, miss. Had his supper, too.'

Theodosia thanked her and the professor said, 'This is Meg, my housekeeper. She was my nanny a long time ago. Meg, this is Miss Theodosia Chapman; she works at the hospital.'

Meg smiled broadly. 'Well, now, isn't that nice?' And she shook the hand Theodosia offered.

Supper was everything she could have wished for— piping hot soup, an omelette as light as air, creamed potatoes, tiny brussels sprouts and little egg custards in brown china pots for pudding. She ate every morsel and the professor, watching the colour creep back into her cheeks, urged her to have a second cup of coffee and gave her a glass of brandy.

'I don't think I would like it...'

'Probably not. I'm giving it to you as a medicine so toss it off, but not too quickly.'

It made her choke and her eyes water, but it warmed her too, and when she had finished it he said, 'I'm going to take you back now. Go straight to bed and take your pills and I promise you that you will feel better in the morning.'

'You've been very kind; I'm very grateful. And it was a lovely supper...'

She bade Meg goodbye and thanked her, too, and with Gustavus stowed in the back of the car she was driven back to Mrs Towzer's.

The contrast was cruel as she got out of the car: the professor's house, so dignified and elegant, and Mrs Towzer's, so shabby and unwelcoming. But she wasn't a girl to whinge or complain. She had a roof over her head and a job and the added bonus of knowing the professor.

He took the key from her and went up the four flights of stairs, carrying her bag and Gustavus in his basket. Then he opened her door and switched on the light and went to light the gas fire. He put the pills on the table and then said, 'Go straight to bed, Theodosia.' He sounded like an uncle or a big brother.

She thanked him again and wished him goodnight and he went to the door. He turned round and came back to where she was standing, studying her face in a manner which disconcerted her. She knew that her nose was red and her eyes puffy; she must look a sight...

He bent and kissed her then, a gentle kiss on her mouth and quite unhurried. Then he was gone, the door shut quietly behind him.

'He'll catch my cold,' said Theodosia. 'Why ever did he do that? I'll never forgive myself if he does; I should have stopped him.'

Only she hadn't wanted to. She took Gustavus out of his basket and gave him his bedtime snack, put on the kettle for her hot-water bottle and turned the divan into a bed, doing all these things without noticing what she was doing.

'I should like him to kiss me again,' said Theodosia loudly. 'I liked it. I like him—no, I'm in love with him, aren't I? Which is very silly of me. I expect it's because I don't see many men and somehow we seem to come across each other quite often. I must stop thinking about him and feeling happy when I see him.'

After which praiseworthy speech she took her pills and, warmed by Gustavus and the hot-water bottle, presently went to sleep—but not before she had had a little weep for what might have been if life had allowed her to tread the same path as the professor.

CHAPTER THREE

THEODOSIA felt better in the morning; she had a cold, but she no longer felt—or looked—like a wet hen. She took the pills she had been given, ate her breakfast, saw to Gustavus and went to work. Miss Prescott greeted her sourly, expressed the hope that she would take care not to pass her cold on to her and gave her enough work to keep her busy for the rest of the day. Which suited Theodosia very well for she had no time to think about the professor. Something, she told herself sternly, she must stop doing at once—which didn't prevent her from hoping that she might see him as she went around the hospital. But she didn't, nor was his car in the forecourt when she went home later that day.

He must have gone away; she had heard that he was frequently asked to other hospitals for consultations, and there was no reason why he should have told her. It was during the following morning, on her rounds, that she overhead the ward sister remark to her staff nurse that he would be back for his rounds at the end of the week. It seemed that he was in Austria.

Theodosia dropped her diet sheets deliberately and

took a long time picking them up so that she could hear more.

'In Vienna,' said Sister, 'and probably Rome. Let's hope he gets back before Christmas.'

A wish Theodosia heartily endorsed; the idea of him spending Christmas anywhere but at his lovely home filled her with unease.

She was quite herself by the end of the week; happy to be free from Miss Prescott's iron hand, she did her shopping on Saturday and, since the weather was fine and cold, decided to go to Sunday's early-morning service and then go for a walk in one of the parks.

It was still not quite light when she left the house the next morning and there was a sparkle of frost on the walls and rooftops. The church was warm, though, and fragrant with the scent of chrysanthemums. There wasn't a large congregation and the simple service was soon over. She started to walk back, sorry to find that the early-morning sky was clouding over.

The streets were empty save for the occasional car and an old lady some way ahead of her. Theodosia, with ten minutes' brisk walk before her, walked faster, spurred on by the thought of breakfast.

She was still some way from the old lady when a car passed her, going much too fast and swerving from side to side of the street. The old lady hadn't a chance; the car mounted the kerb as it reached her, knocked her down and drove on.

Theodosia ran. There was no one about, the houses

on either side of the street had their curtains tightly pulled over the windows, and the street was empty; she wanted to scream but she needed her breath.

The old lady lay half on the road, half on the pavement. She looked as though someone had picked her up and tossed her down and left her in a crumpled heap. One leg was crumpled up under her and although her skirt covered it Theodosia could see that there was blood oozing from under the cloth. She was conscious, though, turning faded blue eyes on her, full of bewilderment.

Theodosia whipped off her coat, tucked it gently under the elderly head and asked gently, 'Are you in pain? Don't move; I'm going to get help.'

'Can't feel nothing, dearie—a bit dizzy, like.'

There was a lot more blood now. Theodosia lifted the skirt gently and looked at the awful mess under it. She got to her feet, filling her lungs ready to bellow for help and at the same time starting towards the nearest door.

The professor, driving himself back from Heathrow after his flight from Rome, had decided to go first to the hospital, check his patients there and then go home for the rest of the day. He didn't hurry. It was pleasant to be back in England and London—even the shabbier streets of London—was quiet and empty. His peaceful thoughts were rudely shattered at the sight

of Theodosia racing across the street, waving her arms
like a maniac.

He stopped the car smoothly, swearing softly,
something he seldom did, but he had been severely
shaken…

'Oh, do hurry, she's bleeding badly,' said
Theodosia. 'I was just going to shout for help for I'm
so glad it's you…'

He said nothing; there would be time for words
later. He got out of the car and crossed the street and
bent over the old lady.

'Get my bag from the back of the car.' He had lifted
the sodden skirt. When she had done that he said,
'There's a phone in the car. Get an ambulance. Say
that it is urgent.'

She did as she was told and went back to find him
on his haunches, a hand rummaging in his bag, while
he applied pressure with his other hand to the severed
artery.

'Find a forceps,' he told her. 'One with teeth.'

She did that too and held a second pair ready, trying
not to look at the awful mess. 'Now put the bag where
I can reach it and go and talk to her.' He didn't look
up. 'You got the ambulance?'

'Yes, I told them where to come and that it was
very urgent.'

She went and knelt by the old lady, who was still
conscious but very pale.

'Bit of bad luck,' she said in a whisper. 'I was going to me daughter for Christmas…'

'Well, you will be well again by then,' said Theodosia. 'The doctor's here now and you're going to hospital in a few minutes.'

'Proper Christmas dinner, we was going ter 'ave. Turkey and the trimmings—I like a bit of turkey…'

'Oh, yes, so do I,' said Theodosia, her ears stretched for the ambulance. 'Cranberry sauce with it…'

'And a nice bit of stuffing.' The old lady's voice was very weak. 'And plenty of gravy. Sprouts and pertaters and a good bread sauce. Plenty of onion with it.'

'Your daughter makes her own puddings?' asked Theodosia, and thought what a strange conversation this was—like a nightmare only she was already awake.

'Is there something wrong with me leg?' The blue eyes looked anxious.

'You've cut it a bit; the doctor's seeing to it. Wasn't it lucky that he was passing?'

'Don't 'ave much ter say for 'imself, does 'e?'

'Well, he is busy putting a bandage on. Do you live near here?'

'Just round the corner—Holne Road, number six. Just popped out ter get the paper.' The elderly face crumpled. 'I don't feel all that good.'

'You'll be as bright as a button in no time,' said Theodosia, and heard the ambulance at last.

Things moved fast then. The old lady, drowsy with morphia now, was connected up to oxygen and plasma while the professor tied off the torn arteries, checked her heart and with the paramedics stowed her in the ambulance.

Theodosia, making herself small against someone's gate, watched the curious faces at windows and doors and wondered if she should go.

'Get into the car; I'll drop you off. I'm going to the hospital.'

He stared down at her unhappy face. 'Hello,' he said gently, and he smiled.

He had nothing more to say and Theodosia was feeling sick. He stopped at Mrs Towzer's just long enough for her to get out and drove off quickly. She climbed the stairs and, once in her room, took off her dirty, blood-stained clothes and washed and dressed again, all the while telling Gustavus what had happened.

She supposed that she should have breakfast although she didn't really want it. She fed Gustavus and put on the kettle. A cup of tea would do.

When there was a knock on the door she called, 'Come in,' remembering too late that she shouldn't have done that before asking who was there.

The professor walked in. 'You should never open the door without checking,' he said. He turned off the gas under the kettle and the gas fire and then stowed Gustavus in his basket.

'What are you doing?' Theodosia wanted to know.

'Taking you back for breakfast—you and Gustavus. Get a coat—something warm.'

'My coat is a bit—that is, I shall have to take it to the cleaners. I've got a mac.' She should have been annoyed with him, walking in like that, but somehow she couldn't be bothered. Besides, he was badly in need of the dry cleaners, too. 'Is the old lady all right?'

'She is in theatre now, and hopefully she will recover. Now, hurry up, dear girl.'

She could refuse politely but Gustavus was already in his basket and breakfast would be very welcome. She got into her mac, pulled a woolly cap over her bright hair and accompanied him downstairs. There was no one about and the street was quiet; she got into the car when he opened the door for her, mulling over all the things she should have said if only she had had her wits about her.

As soon as they had had their breakfast she would tell him that she was having lunch with friends... She discarded the idea. To tell him fibs, even small, harmless ones, was something she found quite impossible. She supposed that was because she loved him. People who loved each other didn't have secrets. Only he didn't love her.

She glanced sideways at him. 'You've spoilt your suit.'

'And you your coat. I'm only thankful that it was you who were there. You've a sensible head under that bright hair; most people lose their wits at an accident. You were out early?'

'I'd been to church. I planned to go for a long walk. I often do on a Sunday.'

'Very sensible—especially after being cooped up in the hospital all week.'

Meg came to meet them as they went into the house. She took Theodosia's mac and cap and said firmly, 'Breakfast will be ready just as soon as you've got into some other clothes, sir. Miss Chapman can have a nice warm by the fire.'

She bustled Theodosia down the hall and into a small, cosy sitting room where there was a bright fire burning. Its window overlooked a narrow garden at the back and the round table by it was set for breakfast.

'Now just you sit quiet for a bit,' said Meg. 'I'll get Gustavus.'

The cat, freed from his basket, settled down before the fire as though he had lived there all his life.

The professor came presently in corduroys and a polo-necked sweater. Cashmere, decided Theodosia. Perhaps if she could save enough money she would buy one instead of spending a week next summer at a bed and breakfast farm.

Meg followed him in with a tray of covered dishes; Theodosia's breakfasts of cornflakes, toast and, sometimes, a boiled egg paled to oblivion beside this splendid array of bacon, eggs, tomatoes, mushrooms and kidneys.

He piled her plate. 'We must have a good breakfast if we are to go walking, too,' he observed.

She stared at him across the table. 'But it is me who is going walking…'

'You don't mind if I come, too? Besides, I need your help. I'm going to Worthing to collect a dog; he'll need a good walk before we bring him back.'

'A dog?' said Theodosia. 'Why is he at Worthing? And you don't really need me with you.'

He didn't answer at once. He said easily, 'He's a golden Labrador, three years old. He belongs to a friend of mine who has gone to Australia. He's been in a dog's home for a week or so until I was free to take him over.'

'He must be unhappy. But not any more once he's living with you. If you think it would help to make him feel more at home if I were there, too, I'd like to go with you.' She frowned. 'I forgot, I can't. Gustavus…'

'He will be quite happy with Meg, who dotes on him.' He passed her the toast. 'So that's settled. It's a splendid day to be out of doors.'

They had left London behind them and were nearing Dorking when he said, 'Do you know this part of the country? We'll leave the main road and go through Billingshurst. We can get back onto the main road just north of Worthing.'

Even in the depths of winter, the country was beautiful, still sparkling from the night frost and the sun shining from a cold blue sky. Theodosia, snug in the warmth and comfort of the car, was in seventh heaven. She couldn't expect anything as delightful as this unexpected day out to happen again, of course. It had been a kindly quirk of fate which had caused them to meet again.

She said suddenly, 'That old lady—it seems so unfair that she should be hurt and in hospital while we're having this glorious ride—' She stopped then and added awkwardly, 'What I mean is, I'm having a glorious ride.'

The professor thought of several answers he would have liked to make to that. Instead he said casually, 'It's a perfect day, isn't it? I'm enjoying it, too. Shall we stop for a cup of coffee in Billingshurst?'

When they reached Worthing, he took her to one of the splendid hotels on the seafront where, the shabby raincoat hidden out of sight in the cloakroom, she enjoyed a splendid lunch with him, unconscious of the glances of the other people there, who were intrigued by the vivid ginger of her hair.

It was early afternoon when they reached the dog's home. He was ready and waiting for them, for he recognized the professor as a friend of his master and greeted him with a dignified bark or two and a good deal of tail-wagging. He was in a pen with a small dog of such mixed parentage that it was impossible to tell exactly what he might be. He had a foxy face and bushy eyebrows, a rough coat, very short legs and a long thin tail. He sat and watched while George the Labrador was handed over and Theodosia said, 'That little dog, he looks so sad…'

The attendant laughed. 'He's been George's shadow ever since he came; can't bear to be parted from him. They eat and sleep together, too. Let's hope someone wants him. I doubt it—he came in off a rubbish dump.'

The professor was looking at Theodosia; he knew with resigned amusement that he was about to become the owner of the little dog. She wasn't going to ask, but the expression on her face was eloquent.

'Then perhaps we might have the little dog as well since they are such friends. Has he a name?'

He was rewarded by the happiness in her face. 'He may come, too?' She held out her arms for the little beast, who was shivering with excitement, and he stayed there until the professor had dealt with their payment, chosen a collar and lead for him and they had left the home.

'A brisk walk on the beach will do us all good,' said the professor. 'We must have a name,' he observed as the two dogs ran to and fro. They had got into the car without fuss and now they were savouring their freedom.

'Max,' said Theodosia promptly. 'He's such a little dog and I don't suppose he'll grow much more so he needs an important name. Maximilian—only perhaps you could call him Max?'

'I don't see why not,' agreed the professor. He turned her round and started to walk back to the car. He whistled to the dogs. 'George, Max…'

They came running and scrambled into the car looking anxious.

'It's all right, you're going home,' said Theodosia, 'and everyone will love you.' She remembered then. 'Gustavus—he's not used to dogs; he never sees them…'

'Then it will be a splendid opportunity for him to do so. We will put the three of them in the garden together.'

'We will? No, no, there's no need. If you'll give me time to pop him into his basket, I can take him with me.'

The professor was driving out of Worthing, this time taking the main road to Horsham and Dorking. The winter afternoon was already fading into dusk and Theodosia reflected on how quickly the hours flew by when one was happy.

He hadn't answered her; presumably he had agreed with her. There would be buses, but she would have to change during the journey back to her bed-sitter.

She reminded herself that on a Sunday evening with little traffic and the buses half empty she should have an easy journey.

They talked from time to time and every now and then she turned round to make sure the dogs were all right. They were sitting upright, close together, looking uncertain.

'Did you have a dog when you were a little girl?' asked the professor.

'Oh, yes, and a cat. I had a pony, too.'

'Your home was in the country?' he asked casually.

She told him about the nice old house in Wiltshire and the school she had gone to and how happy she had been, and then said suddenly, 'I'm sorry, I must be boring you. It's just that I don't get the chance to talk about it very often. Of course, I think about it whenever I like.' She glanced out of the window into the dark evening. 'Are we nearly there?'

'Yes, and you have no need to apologize; I have not been bored. I have wondered about your home before you came to London, for you are so obviously a square peg in a round hole.'

'Oh? Am I? I suppose I am, but I'm really very lucky. I mean, I have the great-aunts and a job and I know lots of people at the hospital.'

'But perhaps you would like to do some other work?'

'Well, I don't think I'm the right person to have a

career, if you mean the sort who wear those severe suits and carry briefcases...'

He laughed then, but all he said was, 'We're almost home.'

If only it were home—her home, thought Theodosia, and then told herself not to be a silly fool. She got out when he opened her door and waited while he took up the dogs' leads and ushered them to the door. When she hesitated he said, 'Come along, Theodosia. Meg will have tea waiting for us.'

Much later, lying in bed with Gustavus curled up beside her, Theodosia thought over her day, minute by minute. It had been like a lovely dream, only dreams were forgotten and she would never forget the hours she had spent with the professor. And the day had ended just as he had planned it beforehand; they had had tea by the fire with the two dogs sitting between them as though they had lived there all their lives. Although she had been a bit scared when the professor had fetched Gustavus and introduced him to the dogs, she had said nothing. After a good deal of spitting and gentle growling the three animals had settled down together.

She had said that she must go back after tea, but somehow he'd convinced her that it would be far better if she stayed for supper. 'So that Gustavus can get used to George and Max,' he had explained smoothly.

She hated leaving his house and her bed-sitter was cold and uninviting.

The professor had lighted the gas fire for her, drawn the curtains over the window and turned on the table lamp, before going to the door, smiling at her muddled thanks and wishing her goodnight in a brisk manner.

There was no reason why he should have lingered, she told herself sleepily. Perhaps she would see him at the hospital—not to talk to, just to get a glimpse of him would do, so that she knew that he was still there.

In the morning, when she woke, she told herself that any foolish ideas about him must be squashed. She couldn't pretend that she wasn't in love with him, because she was and there was nothing she could do about that, but at least she would be sensible about it.

This was made easy for her since Miss Prescott was in a bad mood. Theodosia had no time at all to think about anything but the endless jobs her superior found for her to do, but in her dinner hour she went along to the women's surgical ward and asked if she might see the old lady.

She was sitting propped up in bed, looking surprisingly cheerful. True, she was attached to a number of tubes and she looked pale, but she remembered Theodosia at once.

'I'd have been dead if you hadn't come along, you and that nice doctor. Patched me up a treat, they have!

My daughter's been to see me, too. Ever so grateful, we both are.'

'I'm glad I just happened to be there, and it was marvellous luck that Professor Bendinck should drive past...'

'Professor, is he? A very nice gentleman and ever so friendly. Came to see me this morning.'

Just to know that he had been there that morning made Theodosia feel happy. Perhaps she would see him too...

But there was no sign of him. The week slid slowly by with not so much as a glimpse of him. Friday came at last. She bade Miss Prescott a temporary and thankful goodbye and made her way through the hospital. It had been raining all day and it was cold as well. A quiet weekend, she promised herself, making for the entrance.

The professor was standing by the main door and she saw him too late to make for the side door. As she reached him she gave him a cool nod and was brought to a halt by his hand.

'There you are. I was afraid that I had missed you.'

'I've been here all this week,' said Theodosia, aware of the hand and filled with delight, yet at the same time peevish.

'Yes, so have I. I have a request to make. Would you be free on Sunday to take the dogs into the country? George is very biddable, but Max needs a personal attendant.' He added, most unfairly, 'And since you took such an interest in him…'

She felt guilty. 'Oh, dear. I should have thought… It was my fault, wasn't it? If I hadn't said anything… Ought he to go back to Worthing and find another owner?'

'Certainly not. It is merely a question of him settling down. He is so pleased to be with George that he gets carried away. They couldn't be separated.' He had walked her through the door. 'I'll drive you home…'

'There's no need.'

Which was a silly remark for it was pouring with rain, as well as dark and cold.

She allowed herself to be stowed in the car and when they got to Mrs Towzer's house he got out with her. 'I'll be here at ten o'clock on Sunday,' he told her, and didn't wait for her answer.

'Really,' said Theodosia, climbing the stairs. 'He does take me for granted.'

But she knew that wasn't true. He merely arranged circumstances in such a way that he compelled her to agree to what he suggested.

She was up early on Sunday morning, getting breakfast for herself and Gustavus, explaining to him that she would have to leave him alone. 'But you shall have something nice for supper,' she promised him. The professor hadn't said how long they would be gone, or where. She frowned. He really did take her for granted; next time she would have a good excuse...

It was just before ten o'clock when he knocked on her door. He wished her good morning in a casual manner which gave her the feeling that they had known each other all their lives. 'We'll take Gustavus, if you like. He'll be happier in the car than sitting by himself all day.'

'Well, yes, perhaps—if George and Max won't mind and it's not too long.'

'No distance.' He was settling Gustavus in his basket. 'A breath of country air will do him good.'

Mrs Towzer wasn't in the hall but her door was just a little open. As the professor opened the door he said, 'We shall be back this evening, Mrs Towzer,' just as her face appeared in the crack in the door.

'She's not being nosy,' said Theodosia as they drove away. 'She's just interested.'

She turned her head a little and found George and Max leaning against her seat, anxious to greet her and not in the least bothered by Gustavus in his basket. She was filled with happiness; it was a bright, cold morning and the winter sun shone, the car was warm and comfortable and she was sitting beside the man she loved. What more could a girl want? A great deal, of course, but Theodosia, being the girl she was, was content with what she had at the moment.

'Where are we going?' she asked presently. 'This is the way to Finchingfield.'

'Don't worry, we are not going to your great-aunts'. I have a little cottage a few miles from Saffron Walden; I thought we could go there, walk the dogs and have a picnic lunch. Meg has put something in a basket for us.'

He didn't take the motorway but turned off at Brentwood and took the secondary roads to Bishop's Stortford and after a few miles turned off again into a country road which led presently to a village. It was a small village, its narrow main street lined with small cottages before broadening into a village green ringed by larger cottages and several houses, all of them overshadowed by the church.

The professor turned into a narrow lane leading from the green and stopped, got out to open a gate in the hedge and then drove through it along a short paved driveway, with a hedge on one side of it and a fair-sized garden on the other, surrounding a reed-thatched, beetle-browed cottage with a porch and small latticed windows, its brick walls faded to a dusty pink. The same bricks had been used for the walls on either side of it which separated the front garden from the back of the house, pierced by small wooden doors.

The professor got out, opened Theodosia's door and then released the dogs.

'Gustavus…' began Theodosia.

'We will take him straight through to the garden at

the back. There's a high wall, so he'll be quite safe there and he can get into the cottage.'

He unlocked one of the small doors and urged her through with the dogs weaving themselves to and fro and she could see that it was indeed so; the garden was large, sloping down to the fields and surrounded by a high brick wall. It was an old-fashioned garden with narrow brick paths between beds which were empty now, but she had no doubt they would be filled with rows of orderly vegetables later on. Beyond the beds was a lawn with fruit bushes to one side of it and apple trees.

'Oh, how lovely—even in winter it's perfect.'

He sat Gustavus's basket down, opened it and presently Gustavus poked out a cautious head and then sidled out.

'He's not used to being out of doors,' said Theodosia anxiously, 'only on the roof outside my window. At least, not since I've had him. He was living on the streets before that, but that's not the same as being free.'

She had bent to stroke the furry head and the professor said gently, 'Shall we leave him to get used to everything? The dogs won't hurt him and we can leave the kitchen door open.'

He unlocked the door behind him and stood aside for her to go inside. The kitchen was small, with a quarry-tiled floor, pale yellow walls and an old-fashioned dresser along one wall. There was an Aga, a stout wooden table and equally stout chairs and a deep stone sink. She revolved slowly, liking what she saw; she had no doubt that the kitchen lacked nothing a housewife would need, but it was a place to sit cosily over a cup of coffee, or to come down to in the morning and drink a cup of tea by the open door...

'Through here,' said the professor, and opened a door into the hall.

It was narrow, with a polished wooden floor and cream-painted walls. There were three doors and he opened the first one. The living room took up the whole of one side of the cottage, with little windows overlooking the front garden and French windows opening onto the garden at the back. It was a delightful room with easy chairs, tables here and there and a wide inglenook. The floor was wooden here, too, but there were rugs on it, their faded colours echoing the dull reds and blues of the curtains. There were pictures on the walls but she was given no chance to look at them.

'The dining room,' said the professor as she crossed the hall. It was a small room, simply furnished with a round table, chairs and a sideboard, and all of them, she noted, genuine pieces in dark oak.

'And this is my study.' She glimpsed a small room with a desk and chair and rows of bookshelves.

The stairs were small and narrow and led to a square landing. There were three bedrooms, one quite large and the others adequate, and a bathroom. The cottage might be old but no expense had been spared here. She looked at the shelves piled with towels and all the toiletries any woman could wish for.

'Fit for a queen,' said Theodosia.

'Or a wife...'

Which brought her down to earth again. 'Oh, are you thinking of getting married?'

'Indeed, I am.'

She swallowed down the unhappiness which was so painful that it was like a physical hurt. 'Has she seen this cottage? She must love it...'

'Yes, she has seen it and I think that she has found it very much to her taste.'

She must keep on talking. 'But you won't live here? You have your house in London.'

'We shall come here whenever we can.'

'The garden is lovely. I don't suppose you have much time to work in it yourself.'

'I make time and I have a splendid old man who comes regularly, as well as Mrs Trump who comes every day when I'm here and keeps an eye on the place when I'm not.'

'How nice,' said Theodosia inanely. 'Should I go and see if Gustavus is all right?'

He was sitting by his basket looking very composed, ignoring the two dogs who were cavorting around the garden.

'It's as though he's been here all his life,' said

Theodosia. She looked at the professor. 'It's that kind of house, isn't it? Happy people have lived in it.'

'And will continue to do so. Wait here; I'll fetch the food.'

They sat at the kitchen table eating their lunch; there was soup in a Thermos; little crusty rolls filled with cream cheese and ham, miniature sausage rolls, tiny buttery croissants and piping hot coffee from another Thermos. There was food for the animals as well as a bottle of wine. Theodosia ate with the pleasure of a child, keeping up a rather feverish conversation. She was intent on being cool and casual, taking care to talk about safe subjects—the weather, Christmas, the lighter side of her work at the hospital. The professor made no effort to change the subject, listening with tender amusement to her efforts and wondering if this would be the right moment to tell her that he loved her. He decided it was not, but he hoped that she might begin to do more than like him. She was young; she might meet a younger man. A man of no conceit, he supposed that she thought of him as a man well past his first youth.

They went round the garden after lunch with Gustavus in Theodosia's arms, the dogs racing to and fro, and when the first signs of dusk showed they locked up the little house, stowed the animals in the car and began the drive back to London.

They had reached the outskirts when the professor's bleeper disturbed the comfortable silence. Whoever it was had a lot to say but at length he said, 'I'll be with you in half an hour.' Then he told Theodosia, 'I'll have to go to the hospital. I'll drop you off on the way. I'm sorry; I had hoped that you would have stayed for supper.'

'Thank you, but I think I would have refused; I have to get ready for work tomorrow—washing and ironing and so on.' She added vaguely, 'But it's kind of you to invite me. Thank you for a lovely day; we've enjoyed every minute of it!' Which wasn't quite true, for there had been no joy for her when he'd said that he was going to get married.

When they reached Mrs Towzer's she said, 'Don't get out; you mustn't waste a moment...'

He got out all the same without saying anything, opened the door for her, put Gustavus's basket in the hall and then drove away with a quick nod.

'And that is how it will be from now on,' muttered Theodosia, climbing the stairs and letting herself into her cold bed-sitter. 'He's not likely to ask me out again, but if he does I'll not go. I must let him see that we have nothing in common; it was just chance meetings and those have to stop!'

She got her supper—baked beans on toast and a pot of tea—fed a contented Gustavus and presently went to bed to cry in comfort until at last she fell asleep.

CHAPTER FOUR

THE week began badly. Theodosia overslept; Gustavus, usually so obedient, refused to come in from the roof; and the coil of ginger hair shed pins as fast as she stuck them in. She almost ran to work, to find Miss Prescott, despite the fact that it would be Christmas at the end of the week, in a worse temper than usual. And as a consequence Theodosia did nothing right. She dropped things, spilt things, muddled up diet sheets and because of that went late to her dinner.

It was cottage pie and Christmas pudding with a blindingly yellow custard—and on her way back she was to call in at Women's Medical and collect two diet sheets for the two emergencies which had been admitted. Because it was quicker, although forbidden, she took the lift to the medical floor and when it stopped peered out prudently before alighting; one never knew, a ward sister could be passing.

There was no ward sister but the professor was standing a few yards away, his arm around a woman. They had their backs to her and they were laughing and as Theodosia looked the woman stretched up and kissed his cheek. She wasn't a young woman but she was good-looking and beautifully dressed.

78

Theodosia withdrew her head and prayed hard that they would go away. Which presently they did, his arm still around the woman's shoulders, and as she watched, craning her neck, Women's Medical ward door opened, Sister came out and the three of them stood talking and presently went into the ward.

Theodosia closed the lift door and was conveyed back to Miss Prescott's office.

'Well, let me have those diet sheets,' said that lady sharply.

'I didn't get them,' said Theodosia, quite beside herself, and, engulfed in feelings she hadn't known she possessed, she felt reckless. 'I went late to dinner and I should have had an hour instead of the forty minutes you left me. Someone else can fetch them. Why don't you go yourself, Miss Prescott?'

Miss Prescott went a dangerous plum colour. 'Theodosia, can I believe my ears? Do you realise to whom you speak? Go at once and get those diet sheets.'

Theodosia sat down at her desk. There were several letters to be typed, so she inserted paper into her machine and began to type. Miss Prescott hesitated. She longed to give the girl her notice on the spot but that was beyond her powers. Besides, with all the extra work Christmas entailed she had to have help in her office. There were others working in the department, of course, but Theodosia, lowly though her job was, got on with the work she was familiar with.

'I can only assume that you are not feeling yourself,' said Miss Prescott. 'I am prepared to overlook your rudeness but do not let it occur again.'

Theodosia wasn't listening; she typed the letters perfectly while a small corner of her brain went over and over her unexpected glimpse of the professor. With the woman he was going to marry, of course. He would have been showing her round the hospital, introducing her to the ward sisters and his colleagues, and then they would leave together in his car and go to his home…

As five o'clock struck she got up, tidied her desk, wished an astonished Miss Prescott good evening and went home. The bed-sitter was cold and gloomy; she switched on the lamps, turned on the fire, fed Gustavus and made herself a pot of tea. She was sad and unhappy but giving way to self-pity wasn't going to help. Besides, she had known that he was going to marry; he had said so. But she must avoid him at the hospital…

She cooked her supper and presently went to bed. She had been happy, allowing her happiness to take over from common sense. She had no doubt that sooner or later she would be happy again; it only needed a little determination.

So now, instead of hoping to meet him as she went round the hospital, she did her rounds with extreme caution. Which took longer than usual, of course, and earned Miss Prescott's annoyance. It was two days later, sharing a table with other latecomers from the wards and offices, that the talk became animated. It was a student nurse from Women's Medical who started it, describing in detail the companion Professor Bendinck had brought to see the ward. 'She was gorgeous, not very young, but then you wouldn't expect him to be keen on a young girl, would you? He's quite old…'

Theodosia was about to say that thirty-five wasn't old—a fact she had learned from one of her dancing partners at the ball—and even when he was wearing his specs he still looked in his prime. But she held her tongue and listened.

'She was wearing a cashmere coat and a little hat which must have cost the earth, and her boots…!' The nurse rolled expressive eyes. 'And they both looked so pleased with themselves. He called her "my dear Rosie", and smiled at her. You know, he doesn't smile much when he's on his rounds. He's always very polite, but sort of reserved, if you know what I mean. I suppose we'll be asked to fork out for a wedding present.'

A peevish voice from the other end of the table said, 'Those sort of people have everything; I bet he's loaded. I wonder where he lives?'

Theodosia wondered what they would say if she told them.

'Oh, well,' observed one of the ward clerks. 'I hope they'll be happy. He's nice, you know—opens doors for you and says good morning—and his patients love him.'

Someone noticed the time and they all got up and rushed back to their work.

Two more days and it would be Christmas Eve and she would be free. Her presents for the aunts were wrapped, her best dress brushed and ready on its hanger, her case already half packed with everything she would need for the weekend, Gustavus's favourite food in her shoulder bag. She should be able to catch a late-afternoon train, and if she missed it there was another one leaving a short while later. She would be at the aunts' well before bedtime.

She was almost at the hospital entrance on her way home that evening when she saw the professor. And he had seen her, for he said something to the house doctor he was talking to and began to walk towards her.

Help, thought Theodosia. She was so happy to see him that if he spoke to her she might lose all her good sense and fling herself at him.

And help there was. One of the path lab assistants, the one who had danced with her at the ball, was hurrying past her. She caught hold of his arm and brought him to a surprised halt.

'Say something,' hissed Theodosia. 'Look pleased to see me, as though you expected to meet me.'

'Whatever for? Of course I'm pleased to see you, but I've a train to catch…'

She was still holding his sleeve firmly. The professor was very close now, not hurrying, though; she could see him out of the corner of her eye. She smiled up at her surprised companion. She said very clearly, 'I'll meet you at eight o'clock; we could go to that Chinese place.' For good measure she kissed his cheek and, since the professor was now very close, wished him good evening. He returned her greeting in his usual pleasant manner and went out to his car.

'Whatever's come over you?' demanded the young man from the path lab. 'I mean, it's all very well, but I've no intention of taking you to a Chinese restaurant. For one thing my girl wouldn't stand for it and for another I'm a bit short of cash.' He goggled at her. 'And you kissed me!'

'Don't worry, it was an emergency. I was just pretending that we were keen on each other.'

He looked relieved. 'You mean it was a kind of joke?'

'That's right.' She looked over his shoulder and caught a glimpse of the Bentley turning out of the forecourt. 'Thanks for helping me out.'

'Glad I could help. A lot of nonsense, though.'

He hurried off and Theodosia walked back to her bed-sitter, then told Gustavus all about it. 'You see,' she explained, 'if he doesn't see me or speak to me, he'll forget all about me. I shan't forget him but that's neither here nor there. I daresay he'll have a holiday at Christmas and spend it with her. She's beautiful

and elegant, you see, and they were laughing together…' Theodosia paused to give her nose a good
blow. She wasn't going to cry about it. He would be
home by now, sitting in his lovely drawing room, and
Rosie would be sitting with him.

Which is exactly what he was doing, George and Max
at his feet, his companion curled up on a sofa. They
were both reading, he scanning his post, she leafing
through a fashion magazine. Presently she closed it.
'You have no idea how delightful it is to have the
whole day to myself. I've spent a small fortune shopping and I can get up late and eat food I haven't
cooked myself. It's been heaven.'

The professor peered at her over his specs. 'And
you're longing to see James and the children…'

'Yes, I am. It won't be too much for you having
us all here? They'll give you no peace—it will be a
houseful.' She added unexpectedly, 'There's something wrong, isn't there? You're usually so calm and
contained, but it's as though something—or someone?—has stirred you up.'

'How perceptive of you, my dear. I am indeed
stirred—by a pair of grey eyes and a head of ginger
hair.'

'A girl. Is she pretty, young? One of your house
doctors? A nurse?'

'A kind of girl Friday in the diet department. She's
young—perhaps too young for me—perhaps not

pretty but I think she is beautiful. And she is gentle and kind and a delight to be with.' He smiled. 'And her hair really is ginger; she wears it in a bunch on top of her head.'

His sister had sat up, the magazine on the floor. 'You'll marry her, Hugo?'

'Yes, if she will have me. She lives in a miserable attic room with a cat and is to spend Christmas with her only family—two great-aunts. I intend to drive her there and perhaps have a chance to talk…'

'But you'll be here for Christmas?'

'Of course. Perhaps I can persuade her to spend the last day of the holiday here.'

'I want to meet her. Pour me a drink, Hugo, and tell me all about her. How did you meet?'

The following day the professor did his ward rounds, took a morning clinic, saw his private patients in the afternoon and returned to the hospital just before five o'clock. He had made no attempt to look for Theodosia during the morning—he had been too busy—but now he went in search of her. He hadn't been unduly disturbed by the sight of her talking to the young fellow from the path lab. After all, she was on nodding terms with almost everyone in the hospital, excluding the very senior staff, of course. But he had heard her saying that she would meet him that evening; moreover, she had kissed him. He had to know if she had given her heart to the man; after all, he was young and good-looking and she had never shown anything other than friendliness with himself.

He reviewed the facts with a calm logic and made his way to the floor where Theodosia worked.

She came rushing through the door then slithered to a halt because, of course, he was standing in her way. Since he was a big man she had no way of edging round him.

'Oh, hello,' said Theodosia, and then tried again. 'Good evening, Professor.'

He bade her good evening, too, in a mild voice. 'You're looking forward to Christmas? I'll drive you to Finchingfield. The trains will be packed and running late. Could you manage seven o'clock?'

She had time to steady her breath; now she clutched at the first thing that entered her head. On no account must she go with him. He was being kind again. Probably he had told his fiancée that he intended to drive her and Rosie had agreed that it would be a kindness to take the poor girl to these aunts of hers. She shrank from kindly pity.

'That's very kind of you,' said Theodosia, 'but I'm getting a lift—he's going that way, staying with friends only a few miles from Finchingfield.' She was well away now. 'I'm going to a party there—parties are such fun at Christmas, aren't they?' She added for good measure, 'He'll bring me back, too.'

She caught the professor's eye. 'He works in the path lab…'

If she had hoped to see disappointment on his face she was disappointed herself. He said pleasantly, 'Splendid. You're well organised, then.'

'Yes, I'm looking forward to it; such fun...' She was babbling now. 'I must go—someone waiting. I hope you have a very happy Christmas.'

She shot away, racing down the stairs. He made no attempt to follow her. That he was bitterly disappointed was inevitable but he was puzzled, too. Theodosia had been altogether too chatty and anxious to let him know what a splendid time she was going to have. He could have sworn that she had been making it up as she went along... On the other hand, she might have been feeling embarrassed; she had never been more than friendly but she could possibly be feeling awkward at not having mentioned the young man from the path lab.

He went back to his consulting rooms, saw his patients there and presently went home, where his manner was just as usual, asking after his sister's day, discussing the preparations for Christmas, for Rosie's husband and the two children would be arriving the next morning. And she, although she was longing to talk about Theodosia, said nothing, for it was plain that he had no intention of mentioning her.

And nor did he make any attempt to seek her out at the hospital during the following day. There was a good deal of merriment; the wards looked festive, the staff were cheerful—even those who would be on duty—and those who were able to left early. The professor, doing a late round, glanced at his watch. Theodosia would have left by now for it was almost six o'clock. He made his way to the path lab and found the young man who had been talking to Theodosia still there.

'Not gone yet?' he asked. 'You're not on duty over the weekend, are you?'

'No, sir, just finishing a job.'

'You live close by?' asked the professor idly.

'Clapham Common. I'm meeting my girlfriend and we'll go home together. I live at home but she's spending Christmas with us.'

'Ah, yes. There's nothing like a family gathering. You're planning to marry.'

'Well, as soon as Dorothy's sold her flat—her parents are dead. Once it's sold we shall put our savings together and find something around Clapham.'

'Well, I wish you the best of luck and a happy Christmas!'

The professor went on his unhurried way, leaving the young man with the impression that he wasn't such a bad old stick after all, despite his frequent requests for tests at a moment's notice.

The professor went back to his office; ten minutes' work would clear up the last odds and ends of his work for the moment. He had no idea why Theodosia had spun such a wildly imaginative set of fibs but he intended to find out. Even if she had left at five o'clock she would hardly have had the time to change and pack her bag and see to Gustavus.

He was actually at the door when he was bleeped…

Theodosia hurried home. Miss Prescott, true to form, had kept her busy until the very last minute, which meant that catching the early train was an impossibility. She would phone the aunts and say that she would be on the later train. Once in her room she fed an impatient Gustavus, changed into her second-best dress, brushed her coat, found her hat and, since she had time to spare, put on the kettle for a cup of tea. It would probably be chilly on the train and there would be a lot of waiting round for buses once she got to Braintree.

She was sipping her tea when someone knocked on the door, the knock followed by Mrs Towzer's voice. Theodosia asked her in, explaining at the same time that she was just about to leave for her train.

'Won't keep you then, love. Forgot to give you this letter—came this morning—in with my post. Don't suppose it's important. 'Ave a nice time at your auntys'. 'Aving a bit of a party this evening; must get meself poshed up. The 'ouse'll be empty, everyone off 'ome.' They exchanged mutual good wishes and Mrs Towzer puffed her way down the stairs.

The letter was in Great-Aunt Mary's spidery hand. Surely not a last-minute request to shop for some forgotten article? Unless it was something she could buy at the station there was no time for anything else.

Theodosia sat down, one eye on the clock, and opened the letter.

She read it and then read it again. Old family friends, an archdeacon and his wife, had returned to England from South America, wrote Aunt Mary. Their families were in Scotland and they did not care to make such a long journey over the holiday period.

'Your aunt Jessica and I have discussed this at some length and we have agreed that it is our duty to give these old friends the hospitality which our Christian upbringing expects of us. Christmas is a time for giving and charity,' went on Aunt Mary, and Theodosia could almost hear her vinegary voice saying it. As Theodosia knew, continued her aunt, the accommodation at the cottage was limited, and since she had no lack of friends in London who would be only too glad to have her as a guest over Christmas they knew she would understand. 'We shall, of course, miss you…'

Theodosia sat quite still for a while, letting her thoughts tumble around inside her head, trying to adjust to surprise and an overwhelming feeling that she wasn't wanted. Of course she had friends, but who, on Christmas Eve itself, would invite themselves as a guest into a family gathering?

Presently she got up, counted the money in her purse, got her shopping bag from behind the door, assured Gustavus that she would be back presently and left the house. There was no one around; Mrs Towzer was behind closed doors getting ready for the party. She walked quickly to a neighbouring street where there was a row of small shops. There was a supermarket at its end but she ignored it; there the shops would stay open for another hour or so, catching the last-minute trade. Although she had the money she had saved for her train ticket she needed to spend it carefully.

Tea, sugar, butter and a carton of milk, cheese, food for Gustavus and a bag of pasta which she didn't really like but which was filling, baked beans and a can of soup. She moved on to the butcher, and since it was getting late and he wouldn't be open again for three days he let her have a turkey leg very cheap. She bought bacon, too, and eggs, and then went next door to the greengrocer for potatoes and some apples.

Lastly she went to the little corner shop at the end of the row, where one side was given over to the selling of bread, factory-baked in plastic bags, and lurid iced cakes, the other side packed with everything one would expect to find in a bazaar.

Theodosia bought a loaf and a miniature Christmas pudding and then turned her attention to the other side of the shop. She spent the last of her money on a miniature Christmas tree, which was plastic, with a few sprigs of holly, and very lastly a small box of chocolates.

Thus burdened she went back to Mrs Towzer's. The front door was open; there were guests for the party milling about in the hall. She passed them unnoticed and climbed the stairs.

'We are going to have a happy Christmas together,' she told Gustavus. 'You'll be glad, anyway, for you'll be warm here, and I've bought you a present and you've bought me one, too.'

She unpacked everything, stowed the food away and then set the Christmas tree on the table. She had no baubles for it but at least it looked festive. So did the holly and the Christmas cards when she had arranged them around the room.

Until now she hadn't allowed her thoughts to wander but now her unhappiness took over and she wept into the can of soup she had opened for her supper. It wasn't that she minded so very much being on her own; it was knowing that the great-aunts had discarded her in the name of charity. But surely charity began at home? And she could have slept on the sofa…

She ate her soup, unpacked the weekend bag she had packed with such pleasure, and decided that she might as well go to bed. And for once, since there was no one else to dispute her claim, she would have a leisurely bath…

It was half past eight before the professor left the hospital and now that he was free to think his own thoughts he gave them his full attention. Obviously he had nothing to fear from the lad in the path lab. For reasons best known to herself, Theodosia had embarked on some rigmarole of her own devising—a ploy to warn him off? She might not love him but she liked him. A man of no conceit, he was aware of that. And there was something wrong somewhere.

He drove himself home, warned his sister and brother-in-law that he might be late back, sought out Meg in the kitchen and told her to get a room ready for a guest he might be bringing back with him. Then he got into his car, this time with George and Max on the back seat, and drove away.

His sister, at the door to see him off, turned to see Meg standing beside her.

'It'll be that nice young lady with the gingery hair,' said Meg comfortably. 'Dear knows where she is but I've no doubt he'll bring her back here.'

'Oh, I do hope so, Meg; she sounds just right for him. Should we wait for dinner any longer?'

'No, ma'am, I'll serve it now. If they're not back by midnight I'll leave something warm in the Aga.'

Once he had left the centre of the city behind, the streets were almost empty. The professor reached Bishop's Stortford in record time and turned off to Finchingfield.

There were lights shining from the windows of the

great-aunt's house. He got out with a word to the dogs and thumped the knocker.

Mrs Trickey opened the door, still in her hat. She said, 'You're a bit late to come calling; I'm off home.'

The professor said in his calm way, 'I'd like to see Miss Theodosia.'

'So would I. She's not here, only that archdeacon and his wife wanting hot water and I don't know what—a fire in their bedroom, too. You'd best come in and speak to Miss Chapman.'

She opened the door into the drawing room. 'Here's a visitor for you, Miss Chapman, and I'll be off.'

Great-Aunt Jessica had risen from her chair. 'Professor, this is unexpected. May I introduce Archdeacon Worth and Mrs Worth, spending Christmas with us…?'

The professor's manners were beautiful even when he was holding back impatience. He said all the right things and then, 'I came to see Theodosia…'

It was Aunt Mary who answered him.

'These old family friends of ours are spending Christmas with us. Having just returned from South America, they had no plans for themselves. We were delighted to be able to offer them hospitality over the festive season.'

'Theodosia?' He sounded placid.

'I wrote to her,' said Aunt Mary. 'A young gel with friends of her own age—I knew that she would understand and have no difficulty in spending Christmas with one or other of them.'

'I see. May I ask when she knew of this arrangement?'

'She would have had a letter—let me see, when did I post it? She must have had it some time today, certainly. We shall, of course, be delighted to see her— when something can be arranged.'

He said pleasantly, 'Yes, we must certainly do that once we are married. May I wish you all a happy Christmas.' He wasn't smiling. 'I'll see myself out.'

He had driven fast to Finchingfield, and now he drove back to London even faster. He was filled with a cold rage that anyone would dare to treat his Theodosia with such unkindness! He would make it up to her for the rest of her life; she should have everything she had ever wanted—clothes, jewels, and holidays in the sun... He laughed suddenly, knowing in his heart that all she would want would be a home and children and love. And he could give her those, too.

The house was quiet as Theodosia climbed the stairs from the bathroom on the floor below. All five occupants of the other bed-sitters had gone home or to friends for Christmas. Only Mrs Towzer was in her flat, entertaining friends for the evening. She could hear faint sounds of merriment as she unlocked her door.

The room looked welcoming and cheerful; the holly

and the Christmas cards covered the almost bare walls and the Christmas tree, viewed from a distance, almost looked real. The cat food, wrapped in coloured paper, and the box of chocolates were arranged on each side of it and she had put the apples in a dish on the table.

'Quite festive,' said Theodosia to Gustavus, who was washing himself in front of the gas fire. 'Now I shall have a cup of cocoa and you shall have some milk, and we'll go to bed.'

She had the saucepan in her hand when there was a knock on the door. She remembered then that Mrs Towzer had invited her to her party if she wasn't going away for Christmas. She had refused, saying that she would be away, but Mrs Towzer must have seen her coming in with the shopping and come to renew her invitation.

How kind, thought Theodosia, and opened the door. The professor, closely followed by George and Max, walked in.

'Always enquire who it is before opening your door, Theodosia,' he observed. 'I might have been some thug in a Balaclava helmet.'

She stared up at his quiet face. And even like that, she thought, I would still love him... Since he had walked past her into the room there was nothing for it but to shut the door.

'I was just going to bed...' She watched as the two

dogs sat down side by side before the fire, taking no notice of Gustavus.

'All in good time.' He was leaning against the table, smiling at her.

'How did you know I was here?' She was pleased to hear that her voice sounded almost normal, although breathing was a bit difficult.

'I went to see your aunts.'

'My aunts, this evening? Surely not…?'

'This evening. I've just come from them. They are entertaining an archdeacon and his wife.'

'Yes, I know. But why?'

'Ah, that is something that I will explain.'

He glanced around him, at the tree and the holly and the cards and then at the tin of cocoa by the sink. Then he studied her silently. The shapeless woolly garment she was wearing did nothing to enhance her appearance but she looked, he considered, beautiful; her face was fresh from soap and water, her hair hanging around her shoulders in a tangled gingery mass.

He put his hands in his pockets and said briskly, 'Put a few things in a bag, dear girl, and get dressed.'

She goggled at him. 'Things in a bag? Why?'

'You are spending Christmas with me at home.'

'I'm not. I have no intention of going anywhere.' She remembered her manners. 'Thank you for asking me, but you know as well as I that it's not possible.'

'Why not—tell me?'

She said wildly, 'I saw you at the hospital. I wasn't

spying or anything like that but I got out of the lift and saw you both standing there. You had your arm round her and she was laughing at you. How could you possibly suggest…?' She gave a great gulp. 'Oh, do go away,' she said, and then asked, 'Does she know you are here? Did she invite me, too?'

The professor managed not to smile. 'No, she doesn't but she expects you. And Meg has a room ready for you…'

'It is most kind of you,' began Theodosia, and put a hand on his arm. This was a mistake, for he took it, turned it over and kissed the palm.

'Oh, no,' said Theodosia in a small voice as he wrapped his great arms round her.

She wriggled, quite uselessly, and he said gently, 'Keep still, my darling; I'm going to kiss you.'

Which he did at some length and very thoroughly. 'I have been wanting to do that for a long time. I've been in love with you ever since we first met. I love you and there will be no reason for anything I do unless you are with me.'

Somewhere a nearby church clock struck eleven. 'Now get some clothes on, my love, and we will go home.'

Theodosia dragged herself back from heaven. 'I can't— Oh, Hugo, you know I can't.'

He kissed her gently. 'You gave me no chance to explain; indeed you flung that lad from the path lab in my face, did you not? My sister, Rosie, and her husband and children are spending Christmas with me. It was she you saw at the hospital and you allowed yourself to concoct a lot of nonsense.'

'Yes, well…' She smiled at him. 'Do you really want to marry me?'

'More than anything in the world.'

'You haven't asked me yet.'

He laughed then and caught her close again. 'Will you marry me, Theodosia?

'Yes, yes, of course I will. I did not try to fall in love with you but I did.'

'Thank heaven for that. Now find a toothbrush and take off that woolly thing you are wearing and get dressed. You can have fifteen minutes. Gustavus and the dogs and I will doze together until you are ready.'

'I can't leave him.'

'Of course not; he is coming too.'

The professor settled in a chair and closed his eyes.

It was surprising how much one could do in a short time when one was happy and excited and without a care in the word. Theodosia was dressed, her overnight bag packed after a fashion, her hair swept into a topknot and the contents of her handbag checked in something like ten minutes. She said rather shyly, 'I'm ready…'

The professor got to his feet, put Gustavus into his basket, fastened the window, turned off the gas and went to look in the small fridge. He eyed the morsel of turkey and the Christmas pudding, but said merely,

'We'll turn everything off except the fridge. We can see to it in a few days; you won't be coming back here, of course.'

'But I've nowhere else—the aunts…'

'You will stay with me, and since you are an old-fashioned girl Meg shall chaperon you until I can get a special licence and we can be married.' He gave her a swift kiss. 'Now come along.'

He swept her downstairs and as they reached the hall Mrs Towzer came to see who it was.

'Going out, Miss Chapman? At this time of night?' She eyed the professor. 'You've been here before; you seemed a nice enough gent.' She stared at him severely. 'No 'anky-panky, I 'ope.'

The professor looked down his splendid nose at her. 'Madam, I am taking my future wife to spend Christmas at my home with my sister and her family. She will not be returning here, but I will call after Christmas and settle any outstanding expenses.'

'Oh, well, in that case… 'Appy Christmas to you both.' She looked at George and Max and Gustavus's whiskery face peering from his basket. 'And all them animals.'

Stuffed gently into the car, Theodosia said, 'You sounded just like a professor, you know—a bit stern.'

'That is another aspect of me which you will discover, dear heart, although I promise I will never be stern with you.' He turned to look to her as he started the car. 'Or our children.'

She smiled and wanted to cry, too, for a moment. From happiness, she supposed. 'What a wonderful day to be in love and be loved. I'm so happy.'

As they reached his house, the first strokes of midnight sounded from the church close by, followed by other church bells ringing in Christmas Day. The professor ushered his small party out of the car and into his house. The hall was quiet and dimly lit and George and Max padded silently to the foot of the stairs where they sat like statues. He closed the door behind him, set Gustavus in his basket on the table and swept Theodosia into his arms. 'This is what I have wanted to do—to wish you a happy Christmas in my own home—your home, too, my dearest.'

Theodosia, after being kissed in a most satisfactory manner, found her breath. 'It's true, it's all true? Dearest Hugo, Happy Christmas.' She stretched up and kissed him and then kissed him again for good measure.

THE PROPOSAL
by
Betty Neels

CHAPTER ONE

THE HAZY early morning sun of September had very little warmth as yet, but it turned the trees and shrubs of the park to a tawny gold, encouraging the birds to sing too, so that even in the heart of London there was an illusion of the countryside.

The Green Park was almost empty so early in the day; indeed the only person visible was a girl, walking a Yorkshire terrier on a long lead. She was a tall girl with a tawny mane of hair and vivid blue eyes set in a pretty face, rather shabbily dressed; although her clothes were well cut they were not in the height of fashion.

She glanced at her watch; she had walked rather further than usual so Lady Mortimor, although she wouldn't be out of bed herself, would be sure to enquire of her maid if the early morning walk with Bobo had taken the exact time allowed for it. She could have walked for hours... She was on the point of turning on her heel when something large, heavy and furry cannoned into her from the back and she sat down suddenly and in a most unladylike fashion in a tangle of large dog, a hysterical Bobo and Bobo's lead. The dog put an enormous paw on her chest and grinned happily down at her before licking her cheek gently and then turning his attention to Bobo; possibly out of friendliness he kept his paw on her chest, which made getting to her feet a bit of a problem.

A problem solved by the arrival of the dog's owner—it had to be its owner, she decided...only a giant could control a beast of such size and this man, from her horizontal position, justified the thought; he was indeed large, dressed in trousers and a pullover and, even from upside-down, handsome. What was more, he was smiling...

He heaved her to her feet with one hand and began to dust her down. 'I do apologise,' he told her in a deep, rather slow voice. 'Brontes has a liking for very small dogs...'

The voice had been grave, but the smile tugging at the corners of his thin mouth annoyed her. 'If you aren't able to control your dog you should keep him on a lead,' she told him tartly, and then in sudden fright, 'Where's Bobo? If he's lost, I'll never—'

'Keep calm,' begged the man in a soothing voice which set her teeth on edge, and whistled. His dog bounded out from the bushes near by and his master said, 'Fetch,' without raising his voice and the animal bounded off again to reappear again very shortly with Bobo's lead between his teeth and Bobo trotting obediently at the other end of it.

'Good dog,' said the man quietly. 'Well, we must be on our way. You are quite sure you are not hurt?'

He added kindly, 'It is often hard to tell when one is angry as well.'

'I am not angry, nor am I hurt. It was lucky for you that I wasn't an elderly dowager with a Peke.'

'Extremely lucky. Miss…?' He smiled again, studying her still cross face from under heavy lids.

'Renier Pitt-Colwyn.' He offered a hand and engulfed hers in a firm grasp.

'Francesca Haley. I—I have to go.' Curiosity got the better of good sense. 'Your dog—that's a strange name?'

'He has one eye….'

'Oh, one of the Cyclopes. Goodbye.'

'Goodbye, Miss Haley.' He stood watching her walking away towards the Piccadilly entrance to the park. She didn't look back, and presently she broke into an easy run and, when Bobo's little legs could no longer keep up, scooped him into her arms and ran harder as far as the gate. Here she put him down and walked briskly across the road into Berkeley Street, turned into one of the elegant, narrow side-streets and went down the area steps of one of the fine houses. One of Lady Mortimor's strict rules was that she and Bobo should use the tradesmen's entrance when going for their thrice-daily outings. The magnificent entrance hall was not to be sullied by dirty paws, or for that matter Francesca's dirty shoes.

The door opened onto a dark passage with white-washed walls and a worn lino on the floor; it smelled of damp, raincoats, dog and a trace of cooked food, and after the freshness of the early morning air in the park it caused Francesca's nose to wrinkle. She opened one of the doors in the passage, hung up the lead, dried Bobo's paws and went through to the kitchen.

Lady Mortimor's breakfast tray was being prepared and her maid, Ethel, was standing by the table, squeezing orange juice. She was an angular woman with eyes set too close together in a mean face, and she glanced at the clock as Francesca went in, Bobo under one arm. Francesca, with a few minutes to spare, wished her good morning, adding cheerfully, 'Let Lady Mortimor know that Bobo has had a good run, will you, Ethel? I'm going over for my breakfast; I'll be back as usual.' She put the little dog down and the woman nodded surlily. Bobo always went to his mistress's room with her breakfast tray and that meant that Francesca had almost an hour to herself before she would begin her duties as secretary-companion to that lady. A title which hardly fitted the manifold odd jobs which filled her day.

She went back out of the side-door and round to the back of the house, past the elegant little garden to the gate which led to the mews behind the terrace of houses. Over the garage she had her rooms, rather grandly called by Lady Mortimor a flat, where she and her young sister lived. The flat was the reason for her taking the job in the first place, and she was intent on keeping it, for it made a home for the pair of them and, although Lady Mortimor made it an excuse for paying her a very small salary, at least they had a roof over their heads.

Lucy was up and dressed and getting their breakfast. She was very like her sister, although her hair was carroty instead of tawny and her nose turned up. Later on, in a few years' time, she would be as pretty as Francesca, although at fourteen she anguished over her appearance, her ambition being to grow up as quickly as possible, marry a very rich man and live in great comfort with Francesca sharing her home. An arrangement, Francesca had pointed out, which might not suit her husband. 'I hate you working for that horrid old woman,' Lucy had said fiercely.

'Well, love,' Francesca had been matter-of-fact about it, 'it's a job and we have a home of sorts and you're being educated. Only a few more years and you will have finished school and embarked on a career which will astonish the world and I shall retire.'

Now she took off her cardigan and set about laying the table in the small sitting-room with its minute alcove which housed the cooking stove and the sink.

'I had an adventure,' she said to her sister, and over the boiled eggs told her about it.

'What kind of a dog?' Lucy wanted to know.

'Well, hard to tell—he looked like a very large St Bernard from the front, but he sort of tapered off towards the tail, and that was long enough for two dogs. He was very obedient.'

'Was the man nice to him?' asked Lucy anxiously, having a soft spot for animals; indeed, at that very moment there was a stray mother cat and kittens living clandestinely in a big box under the table.

'Yes—he didn't shout and the dog looked happy. It had one eye—I didn't have time to ask why. It had a funny name, too—Brontes—that's—'

'I know—one of the Cyclopes. Could you meet the man again and ask?'

Francesca thought about it. 'Well, no, not really…'

'Was he a nice man?'

'I suppose so.' She frowned. 'He thought it was funny, me falling over.'

'I expect it was,' said Lucy. 'I'd better go or I'll miss the bus.'

After Lucy had gone she cleared away the breakfast things, tidied the room and their bedroom, and made sure that she herself was tidy too, and then she went back to the house. She was expected to lunch off a tray at midday and she seldom got back until six o'clock each evening; she arranged food for the cat, made sure that the kittens were alive and well, and locked the door.

Her employer was still in bed, sitting up against lacy pillows, reading her letters. In her youth Lady Mortimor had been a handsome woman; now in her fifties, she spent a good part of her days struggling to retain her looks. A face-lift had helped; so had the expert services of one of the best hairdressers in London and the daily massage sessions and the strict diet, but they couldn't erase the lines of discontent and petulance.

Francesca said good morning and stood listening to the woman's high-pitched voice complaining of lack of sleep, the incompetence of servants and the tiresome bills which had come in the post. When she had finished Francesca said, as she nearly always did, 'Shall I attend to the bills first, Lady Mortimor, and write the cheques and leave them for you to sign? Are there any invitations you wish me to reply to?'

Lady Mortimor tossed the pile of letters at her. 'Oh, take the lot and endeavour to deal with them—is there anything that I should know about this morning?'

'The household wages,' began Francesca, and flushed at Lady Mortimor's snide,

'Oh, to be sure you won't forget those...'

'Dr Kennedy is coming to see you at eleven o'clock. Will you see him in the morning-room?'

'Yes, I suppose so; he really must do something about my palpitations—what else?'

'A fitting for two evening gowns at Estelle, lunch with Mrs Felliton.'

'While I am lunching you can get my social diary up to date, do the flowers for the dining-room, and go along to the dry-cleaners for my suit. There will be some letters to type before you go, so don't idle away your time. Now send Ethel to me, have the cheques and wages book ready for me by half-past ten in the morning-room.' As Francesca went to the door she added, 'And don't forget little Bobo…'

'Thank you or please would be nice to hear from time to time,' muttered Francesca as she went to get the wages book, a weekly task which at least gave her the satisfaction of paying herself as well as the rest of the staff. She entered the amounts, got out the cash box from the wall safe and put it ready for Lady Mortimor, who liked to play Lady Bountiful on Fridays and pay everyone in cash. The bills took longer; she hadn't quite finished them when Maisie, the housemaid, brought her a cup of coffee. She got on well with the staff—with the exception of Ethel, of course; once they saw that she had no intention of encroaching on their ground, and was a lady to boot, with a quiet voice and manner, they accepted her for what she was.

Lady Mortimor came presently, signed the cheques, handed out the wages with the graciousness of royalty bestowing a favour and, fortified with a tray of coffee, received Dr Kennedy, which left Francesca free to tidy the muddled desk she had left behind her and take Bobo for his midday walk, a brisk twenty minutes or so before she went back to eat her lunch off a tray in the now deserted morning-room. Since the lady of the house was absent, Cook sent up what Maisie described as a nice little bit of hake with parsley sauce, and a good, wholesome baked custard to follow.

Francesca ate the lot, drank the strong tea which went with it and got ready to go to the cleaners. It wasn't far; Lady Mortimor patronised a small shop in Old Bond Street and the walk was a pleasant one. The day had turned out fine as the early morning had indicated it might and she allowed her thoughts to roam, remembering wistfully the pleasant house in Hampstead Village where they had lived when her parents had been alive. That had been four years ago now; she winced at the memory of discovering that the house had been mortgaged and the debts so large that they had swallowed up almost all the money there was. The only consolation had been the trust set aside for Lucy's education so that she had been able to stay on as a day pupil at the same well-known school.

There had been other jobs of course, after learning typing and shorthand at night-school while they lived precariously with her mother's elderly housekeeper, but she had known that she would have to find a home of their own as quickly as possible. Two years ago she had answered Lady Mortimor's advertisement and since it offered a roof over their heads and there was no objection to Lucy, provided she never entered the house, she had accepted it, aware that her wages were rather less than Maisie's and knowing that she could never ask for a rise: Lady Mortimor would point out her free rooms and all the advantages of working in a well-run household and the pleasant work.

All of which sounded all right but in practice added up to ten hours a day of taking orders with Sundays free. Well, she was going to stay until Lucy had finished school—another four years. I'll be almost thirty, thought Francesca gloomily, hurrying back with the suit; there were still the flowers to arrange and the diary to bring up to date, not to mention the letters and a last walk for Bobo.

It was pouring with rain the next morning, but that didn't stop Bobo, in a scarlet plastic coat, and Francesca, in a well-worn Burberry, now in its tenth year, going for their morning walk. With a scarf tied over her head, she left Lucy getting dressed, and led the reluctant little dog across Piccadilly and into the Green Park. Being Saturday morning, there were very few people about, only milkmen and postmen and some over-enthusiastic joggers. She always went the same way for if by any evil chance Bobo should run away and get lost, he had more chance of staying around a part of the park with which he was familiar. The park was even emptier than the streets and, even if Francesca had allowed herself to hope that she might meet the man and his great dog, common sense told her that no one in their right mind would do more than give a dog a quick walk through neighbouring streets.

They were halfway across the park, on the point of

turning back, when she heard the beast's joyful barking and a moment later he came bounding up. She
had prudently planted her feet firmly this time but he
stopped beside her, wagging his long tail and gently
nuzzling Bobo before butting her sleeve with his wet
head, his one eye gleaming with friendliness.

His master's good-morning was genial. 'Oh, hello,'
said Francesca. 'I didn't expect you to be here—the
weather's so awful.'

A remark she instantly wished unsaid; it sounded
as though she had hoped to meet him. She went pink
and looked away from him and didn't see his smile.

'Ah—but we are devoted dog owners, are we not?'
he asked easily. 'And this is a good place for them to
run freely.'

'I don't own Bobo,' said Francesca, at pains not to
mislead him. 'He belongs to Lady Mortimor; I'm her
companion.'

He said, half laughing, 'You don't look in the least
like a companion; are they not ladies who find library
books and knitting and read aloud? Surely a dying
race.'

If he only knew, she thought, but all she said cheerfully was, 'Oh, it's not as bad as all that, and I like
walking here with Bobo. I must go.'

She smiled at him from her pretty, sopping-wet
face. 'Goodbye, Mr Pitt-Colwyn.'

'*Tot ziens,* Miss Francesca Haley.'

She bent to pat Brontes. 'I wonder why he has only

one eye?' she said to herself more than to him, and then walked briskly away, with Bobo walking backwards in an effort to return to his friend. Hurrying now, because she would be late back, she wondered what he had said instead of goodbye—something foreign and, now she came to think of it, he had a funny name too; it had sounded like Rainer, but she wasn't sure any more.

It took her quite a while to dry Bobo when they got back, and Ethel, on the point of carrying Lady Mortimor's tray upstairs, looked at the kitchen clock in triumph.

Francesca saw the look. 'Tell Lady Mortimor that I'm late back, by all means,' she said in a cool voice. 'You can tell her too that we stayed out for exactly the right time but, unless she wishes Bobo to spoil everything in her bedroom, he needs to be thoroughly dried. It is raining hard.'

Ethel sent her a look of dislike and Cook, watching from her stove, said comfortably, 'There's a nice hot cup of tea for you, Miss Haley; you drink it up before you go to your breakfast. I'm sure none of us wants to go out in such weather.'

Ethel flounced away, Bobo at her heels, and Francesca drank her tea while Cook repeated all the more lurid news from the more sensational Press. 'Don't you take any notice of that Ethel, likes upsetting people, she does.'

Francesca finished her tea. 'Well, she doesn't need

to think she'll bother me, Cook, and thanks for the tea, it was lovely.'

Lucy would be home at midday since it was Saturday, and they made the shopping list together since she was the one who had to do it.

'Did you see him again?' asked Lucy.

'Who?' Francesca was counting out the housekeeping money. 'The man and his great dog? Yes, but just to say good morning.' She glanced up at her sister. 'Do you suppose I should go another way round the park? I mean, it might look as though I was wanting to meet him.'

'Well don't you?'

'He laughs at me—oh, not out loud, but behind his face.'

'I shall come with you tomorrow and see him for myself.'

On Sundays Francesca took Bobo for his morning run before being allowed the rest of the day free. 'He's not likely to be there so early on a Sunday...'

'All the same, I'll come. What shall we do tomorrow? Could we go to Regent Street and look at the shops? And have something at McDonald's?'

'All right, love. You need a winter coat...'

'So do you. Perhaps we'll find a diamond ring or a string of pearls and get a reward.'

Francesca laughed. 'The moon could turn to cheese. My coat is good for another winter—I've stopped growing but you haven't. We'll have a good look around and when I've saved enough we'll buy you a coat.'

Lady Mortimor had friends to lunch which meant that Francesca had to do the flowers again and then hover discreetly in case her employer needed anything.

'You may pour the drinks,' said Lady Mortimor graciously, when the guests had settled themselves in the drawing-room, and then in a sharp aside, 'And make sure that everyone gets what she wants.'

So Francesca went to and fro with sherry and gin and tonic and, for two of the ladies, whisky. Cool and polite, aware of being watched by critical eyes, and disliking Lady Mortimor very much for making her do something which Crow the butler should be doing. Her employer had insisted that when she had guests for lunch it should be Francesca who saw to the drinks; it was one of the spiteful gestures she made from time to time in order, Francesca guessed, to keep her in her place. Fortunately Crow was nice about it; he had a poor opinion of his mistress, the widow of a wholesale textile manufacturer who had given away enough money to be knighted, and he knew a lady born and bred when he saw Francesca, as he informed Cook.

When the guests had gone, Lady Mortimor went out herself. 'Be sure and have those letters ready for me—I shall be back in time to dress,' she told Francesca. 'And be sure and make a note in the diary—

Dr Kennedy is bringing a specialist to see me on Tuesday morning at ten o'clock. You will stay with me of course—I shall probably feel poorly.'

Francesca thought that would be very likely. Eating too much rich food and drinking a little too much as well… She hoped the specialist would prescribe a strict diet, although on second thoughts that might not do—Lady Mortimor's uncertain temper might become even more uncertain.

Sundays were wonderful days; once Bobo had been taken for his walk she was free, and even the walk was fun for Lucy went with her and they could talk. The little dog handed over to a grumpy Ethel, they had their breakfast and went out, to spend the rest of the morning and a good deal of the afternoon looking at the shops, choosing what they would buy if they had the money, eating sparingly at McDonald's and walking back in the late afternoon to tea in the little sitting-room and an evening by the gas fire with the cat and kittens in their box between them.

Monday always came too soon and this time there was no Brontes to be seen, although the morning was fine. Francesca went back to the house to find Lady Mortimor in a bad temper so that by the end of the day she wanted above all things to rush out of the house and never go back again. Her ears rang with her employer's orders for the next day. She was to be earlier than usual—if Lady Mortimor was to be ready to be seen by the specialist then she would need to get up earlier than usual, which meant that the entire household would have to get up earlier too. Francesca, getting sleepily from her bed, wished the man to Jericho.

Lady Mortimor set the scene with all the expertise of a stage manager; she had been dressed in a velvet housecoat over gossamer undies, Ethel had arranged her hair in artless curls and tied a ribbon in them, and she had made up carefully with a pale foundation. She had decided against being examined in her bedroom; the *chaise-longue* in the dressing-room adjoining would be both appropriate and convenient. By half-past nine she was lying, swathed in shawls, in an attitude of resigned long-suffering.

There was no question of morning coffee, of course, and that meant that Francesca didn't get any either. She was kept busy fetching the aids Lady Mortimor considered vital to an invalid's comfort: eau-de-Cologne, smelling salts, a glass of water...

'Mind you pay attention,' said that lady. 'I shall need assistance from time to time and probably the specialist will require things held or fetched.'

Francesca occupied herself wondering what these things might be. Lady Mortimor kept talking about a specialist, but a specialist in what? She ventured to ask and had her head bitten off with, 'A heart consultant of course, who else? The best there is—I've never been one to grudge the best in illness...'

Francesca remembered Maisie and her scalded hand

a few months previously. Lady Mortimor had dismissed the affair with a wave of the hand and told her to go to Out-patients during the hour she had off each afternoon. Her tongue, itching to give voice to her strong feelings, had to be held firmly between her teeth.

Ten o'clock came, with no sign of Dr Kennedy and his renowned colleague, and Lady Mortimor, rearranging herself once again, gave vent to a vexed tirade. 'And you, you stupid girl, might have had the sense to check with the consulting-rooms to make sure that this man has the time right. Really, you are completely useless...'

Francesca didn't say a word; she had lost her breath for the moment, for the door had opened and Dr Kennedy followed by Mr Pitt-Colwyn were standing there. They would have heard Lady Mortimor, she thought miserably, and would have labelled her as a useless female at everyone's beck and call.

'Well, can't you say something?' asked Lady Mortimor and at the same time became aware of the two men coming towards her, so that her cross face became all charm and smiles and her sharp voice softened to a gentle, 'Dr Kennedy, how good of you to come. Francesca, my dear, do go and see if Crow is bringing the coffee—'

'No coffee, thank you,' said Dr Kennedy. 'Here is Professor Pitt-Colwyn, Lady Mortimor. You insisted on the best heart specialist, and I have brought him to see you.'

Lady Mortimor put out a languid hand. 'Professor—how very kind of you to spare the time to see me. I'm sure you must be a very busy man.'

He hadn't looked at Francesca; now he said with grave courtesy, 'Yes, I am a busy man, Lady Mortimor.' He pulled up a chair and sat down. 'If you will tell me what is the trouble?'

'Oh, dear, it is so hard to begin—I have suffered poor health every day since my dear husband died. It is hard to be left alone at my age—with so much life ahead of me.' She waved a weak hand. 'I suffer from palpitations, Professor, really alarmingly so; I am convinced that I have a weak heart. Dr Kennedy assures me that I am mistaken, but you know what family doctors are, only too anxious to reassure one if one is suffering from some serious condition...'

Professor Pitt-Colwyn hadn't spoken, there was no expression upon his handsome face and Francesca, watching from her discreet corner, thought that he had no intention of speaking, not at the moment at any rate. He allowed his patient to ramble on in a faint voice, still saying nothing when she paused to say in a quite different tone, 'Get me some water, Francesca, can't you see that I am feeling faint? And hurry up, girl.'

The glass of water was within inches of her hand. Francesca handed it, quelling a powerful desire to pour its contents all over Lady Mortimor's massive bosom.

She went back to her corner from where she admired the professor's beautiful tailored dark grey suit. He had a nice head too, excellent hair—she considered the sprinkling of grey in it was distinguished—and he had nice hands. She became lost in her thoughts until her employer's voice, raised in barely suppressed temper, brought her back to her surroundings.

'My smelling salts—I pay you to look after me, not stand there daydreaming—' She remembered suddenly that she had an audience and added in a quite different voice, 'Do forgive me—I become so upset when I have one of these turns, I hardly know what I'm saying.'

Neither man answered. Francesca administered the smelling salts and the professor got to his feet. 'I will take a look at your chest, Lady Mortimor,' and he stood aside while Francesca removed the shawls and the housecoat and laid a small rug discreetly over the patient's person.

The professor had drawn up a chair, adjusted his stethoscope and begun his examination. He was very thorough and when he had done what was necessary he took her blood-pressure, sat with Lady Mortimor's hand in his, his fingers on her pulse.

Finally he asked, 'What is your weight?'

Lady Mortimor's pale make-up turned pink. 'Well,

really I'm not sure...' She looked at Francesca, who said nothing, although she could have pointed out that within the last few months a great many garments had been let out at the seams...

'You are overweight,' said the professor in measured tones, 'and that is the sole cause of your palpitations. You should lose at least two stone within the next six months, take plenty of exercise—regular walking is to be recommended—and small light meals and only moderate drinking. You will feel and look a different woman within that time, Lady Mortimor.'

'But my heart—'

'It is as sound as a bell; I can assure you that there is nothing wrong with you other than being overweight.'

He got up and shook her hand. 'If I may have a word with Dr Kennedy—perhaps this young lady can show us somewhere we can be private.'

'You are hiding something from me,' declared Lady Mortimor. 'I am convinced that you are not telling me the whole truth.'

His eyes were cold. 'I am not in the habit of lying, Lady Mortimor; I merely wish to discuss your diet with Dr Kennedy.'

Francesca had the door open and he went past her, followed by Dr Kennedy. 'The morning-room,' she told them. 'There won't be anyone there at this time in the morning.'

She led the way and ushered them inside. 'Would you like coffee?'

The professor glanced at his companion and politely declined, with a courteous uninterest which made her wonder if she had dreamed their meetings in the park. There was no reason why he shouldn't have made some acknowledgement of them—not in front of Lady Mortimor, of course. Perhaps now he had seen her here he had no further interest; he was, she gathered, an important man in his own sphere.

She went back to Lady Mortimor and endured that lady's peevish ill humour for the rest of the day. The next day would be even worse, for by then Dr Kennedy would have worked out a diet.

Of course, she told Lucy when at last she was free to go to her rooms.

'I say, what fun—was he pompous?'

'No, not in the least; you couldn't tell what he was thinking.'

'Oh, well, doctors are always poker-faced. He might have said hello.'

Francesca said crossly, 'Why should he? We haven't anything in common.' She added a little sadly, 'Only I thought he was rather nice.'

Lucy hugged her. 'Never mind, Fran, I'll find you a rich millionaire who'll adore you forever and you'll marry him and live happily ever after.'

Francesca laughed. 'Oh, what rubbish. Let's get the washing-up done.'

As she set out with Bobo the next morning, she wished that she could have taken a different route and gone at a different time, but Lady Mortimor, easy-going when it came to her own activities and indifferent as to whether they disrupted her household, prided herself on discipline among her staff; she explained this to her circle of friends as caring for their welfare, but what it actually meant was that they lived by a strict timetable and since, with the exception of Francesca, she paid them well and Cook saw to it that the food in the kitchen was good and plentiful, they abided by it. It was irksome to Francesca and she was aware that Lady Mortimor knew that; she also knew that she and Lucy needed a home and that not many people were prepared to offer one.

So Francesca wasn't surprised to see Brontes bounding to meet her, followed in a leisurely manner by his master. She was prepared for it, of course; as he drew level she wished him a cold good-morning and went on walking, towing Bobo and rather hampered by Brontes bouncing to and fro, intent on being friendly.

Professor Pitt-Colywn kept pace with her. 'Before you go off in high dudgeon, be good enough to listen to me.' He sounded courteous; he also sounded as though he was in the habit of being listened to if he wished.

'Why?' asked Francesca.

'Don't be silly. You're bristling with indignation

because I ignored you yesterday. Understandable, but typical of the female mind. No logic. Supposing I had come into the room exclaiming, ''Ah, Miss Francesca Haley, how delightful to meet you again''—and it was delightful, of course—how would your employer have reacted?' He glanced at her thoughtful face. 'Yes, exactly, I have no need to dot the *I*s or cross the *T*s. Now that that slight misunderstanding is cleared up, tell me why you work for such a tiresome woman.'

She stood still the better to look at him. 'It is really none of your business...'

He brushed that aside. 'That is definitely something I will decide for myself.' He smiled down at her. 'I'm a complete stranger to you; you can say anything you like to me and I'll forget it at once if you wish me to—'

'Oh, the Hippocratic oath.'

His rather stern mouth twitched. 'And that too. You're not happy there, are you?'

She shook her head. 'No, and it's very kind of you to—to bother, but there is really nothing to be done about it.'

'No, there isn't if you refuse to tell me what is wrong.' He glanced at his watch. 'How long do you have before you have to report back?'

'Fifteen minutes.'

'A lot can be said in that time. Brontes and I will walk back with you as far as Piccadilly.'

'Oh, will you?'

'Did I not say so?' He turned her round smartly, and whistled to Brontes. 'Now consider me your favourite uncle,' he invited.

CHAPTER TWO

AFTERWARDS Francesca wondered what had possessed her. She had told Professor Pitt-Colwyn everything. She hadn't meant to, but once she got started she had seemed unable to stop. She blushed with shame just remembering it; he must have thought her a complete fool, sorry for herself, moaning on and on about her life. That this was a gross exaggeration had nothing to do with it; she would never be able to look him in the face again. The awful thing was that she would have to unless he had the decency to walk his dog in another part of the park.

She was barely in the park before he joined her.

'A splendid morning,' he said cheerfully. 'I enjoy the autumn, don't you?' He took Bobo's lead from her and unclipped it. 'Let the poor, pampered beast run free. Brontes will look after him; he has a strong paternal instinct.'

It was difficult to be stand-offish with him. 'He's a nice dog, only he's—he's rather a mixture, isn't he?'

'Oh, decidedly so. Heaven knows where he got that tail.'

For something to say, for she was feeling suddenly shy, 'He must have been a delightful puppy.'

'I found him in a small town in Greece. Someone had poked out his eye and beaten him almost to death—he was about eight weeks old.'

'Oh, the poor little beast—how old is he now?'

'Eight months old and still growing. He's a splendid fellow and strangely enough, considering his origin, very obedient.'

'I must get back.' She looked around for Bobo, who was nowhere in sight, but in answer to her companion's whistle Brontes came trotting up with Bobo scampering beside him. The professor fastened his lead and handed it to her. His goodbye was casually kind; never once, she reflected as she walked back to the house, had he uttered a word about her beastly job. She had been a great fool to blurt out all her worries and grumbles to a complete stranger who had no interest in her anyway. She wished most heartily that there was some way in which she could avoid meeting him ever again.

She thought up several schemes during the course of the day, none of which held water, and which caused her to get absent-minded so that Lady Mortimor had the pleasure of finding fault with her, insisting that she re-type several letters because the commas were in the wrong place. It was after seven o'clock by the time Francesca got back to her room over the garage and found Lucy at her homework.

'You've had a beastly day.' Lucy slammed her books shut and got out a cloth and cutlery. 'I put some potatoes in the oven to bake; they'll be ready by now. We can open a tin of beans, too. The kettle's boiling; I'll make a cup of tea.'

'Lovely, darling, I've had a tiresome day. How's school? Did you get an A for your essay?'

'Yes. Did you see him this morning?'

'Yes, just for a moment...'

'Didn't you talk at all?'

'Only about his dog.' Francesca poured them each a cup of tea and then sat down to drink it. 'I wish I'd never told him—'

'Oh, pooh—I dare say he's forgotten already. He must have lots of patients to think about; his head must be full of people's life histories.'

Francesca opened the tin of beans. 'Yes, of course, only I wish I need never see him again.'

To her secret unacknowledged chagrin, it seemed that she was to have her wish. He wasn't there the following morning, nor for the rest of the week; she told herself that it was a great relief and said so to Lucy, who said, 'Rubbish, you know you want to see him again.'

'Well—yes, perhaps. It was nice to have someone to talk to.' Francesca went on briskly, 'I wonder if it would be a good idea to go to evening classes when they start next month?'

Lucy looked at her in horror. 'Darling, you must be crazy—you mean sit for two hours learning Spanish or how to upholster a chair? I won't let you. Don't you see the kind of people who go to evening classes are very likely like us—without friends and family? Even if you got to know any of them they'd probably moan about being lonely…'

Francesca laughed. 'You know that's not quite true,' she said, 'although I do see what you mean.'

'Good. No evening classes. Doesn't Lady Mortimor have men visitors? She's always giving dinner parties…'

Francesca mentally reviewed her employer's guests; they were all past their prime. Well-to-do, self-satisfied and loud-voiced. They either ignored her in the same way as they ignored Crow or Maisie, or they made vapid remarks like, 'How are you today, little girl?' Which, since she was all of five feet ten inches tall and splendidly built, was an extremely silly thing to say.

She said, laughing, 'I can't say I've ever fancied any of them. I shall wait until you are old enough and quite grown-up, and when you've found yourself a millionaire I shall bask in your reflected glory.' She began to clear the table. 'Let's get Mum fed while the kittens are asleep—and that's another problem…'

September remained fine until the end of the month, when wind and rain tore away the last vestiges of summer. Francesca and Bobo tramped their allotted routine each morning and returned, Bobo to be fussed over once he had been dried and brushed, Francesca to hurry to her rooms, gobble breakfast and dash back again to start on the hundred and one jobs Lady Mortimor found for her to do, which were never done to that lady's satisfaction. The strict diet to which Professor Pitt-Colwyn had restricted her might be reducing her weight, but it had increased her ill humour. Francesca, supervising the making of a salad-dressing with lemon juice to accompany the thin slices of chicken which constituted her employer's lunch, wished that he had left well alone. Let the woman be as fat as butter if she wished, she reflected savagely, chopping a head of chicory while she listened to Cook detailing the menu for the dinner party that evening. A pity the professor couldn't hear that; it was dripping with calories...

Because of the dinner party the staff lunch was cold meat and potatoes in their jackets and Francesca, knowing the extra work involved in one of Lady Mortimor's large dinner parties, had hers in the kitchen and gave a hand with the preparations.

All the guests had arrived by the time she left the house that evening; Lady Mortimor, overpoweringly regal in purple velvet, had made her rearrange the flowers in the hall, polish the glasses again, much to Maisie's rage, and then go to the kitchen to make sure that Cook had remembered how to make sweet and sour sauce, which annoyed the talented woman so much that she threatened to curdle it.

'A good thing it's Sunday tomorrow,' said Francesca, eating toasted cheese while Lucy did her homework. 'And I must think of something for the kittens.' They peered at her, snug against their mother in the cardboard box, and the very idea of finding happy homes for them worried her. How was she to know if the homes were happy and what their mother would do without them?

They went to bed presently, and she dreamt of kittens and curdled sauce and Lady Mortimor in her purple, to wake unrefreshed. At least it wasn't raining, and Lucy would go with her and Bobo, and after breakfast they would go and look at the shops, have a snack somewhere and go to evensong at St Paul's.

The house was quiet as she let herself in through the side-entrance, fastened Bobo's lead and led the little dog outside to where Lucy was waiting. There was a nip in the air, but at least it wasn't raining; they set off at a good pace, crossed into the park and took the usual path. They had reached a small clump of trees where the path curved abruptly when Bobo began to bark, and a moment later Brontes came hurtling round the corner, to leap up to greet Francesca, sniff at Lucy and turn his delighted attention to Bobo, who was yapping his small head off. They had come to a halt, not wishing to be bowled over by the warmth of the big dog's attention, which gave his master ample time to join them.

'Hello—what a pleasant morning.' He sounded as though they had met recently. Francesca knew exactly how long it had been since they had last met—ten days. She bade him good-morning in a chilly voice, and when he looked at Lucy she was forced to add, 'This is my sister, Lucy. Professor Pitt-Colwyn, Lucy.'

Lucy offered a hand. 'I hoped I'd meet you one day,' she told him, 'but of course you've been away. What do you do with your dog? Does he go with you?'

'If it's possible; otherwise he stays at home and gets spoilt. You like him?'

'He's gorgeous. We've got a cat and kittens; I expect Francesca told you that—now the kittens are getting quite big we'll have to find homes for them.' She peeped at her sister's face; she looked cross. 'I'll take Bobo for a run—will Brontes come with me?'

'He'll be delighted. We'll stroll along to meet you.'

'We should be going back,' said Francesca, still very cool.

Lucy was already darting ahead and the professor appeared not to have heard her. 'I wish to talk to you, so don't be a silly girl and put on airs—'

'Well, really—' She stopped and looked up at his bland face. 'I am not putting on airs, and there is nothing for us to talk about.'

'You're very touchy—high time you left that job.' And at her indignant gasp he added, 'Just keep quiet and listen to me.'

He took her arm and began to walk after the fast retreating Lucy and the dogs. 'You would like to leave

Lady Mortimor, would you not? I know of a job which might suit you. A close friend of mine died recently, leaving a widow and a small daughter. Eloise was an actress before she married—indeed, she has returned to the stage for short periods since their marriage—now she has the opportunity to go on tour with a play and is desperate to find someone to live in her house, run it for her and look after little Peggy while she is away. The tour is three or four months and then if it is successful they will go to a London theatre. You will have *carte blanche* and the services of a daily help in the house. No days off—but Peggy will be at school so that you should have a certain amount of free time. Peggy goes to a small day school, five minutes' walk from Cornel Mews—'

'That's near Lady Mortimor's—'

'Yes—don't interrupt. Eloise will come home for the very occasional weekend or day, but since the tour is largely in the north of England that isn't likely to be very often. The salary isn't bad…' He mentioned a sum which left Francesca's pretty mouth agape.

'That's—that's…just for a week? Are you sure? Lady Mortimor…I'm not properly trained.'

'You don't need to be.' He looked down his commanding nose at her. 'Will you consider it?'

'It's not permanent—and what about the cat and her kittens?'

He said smoothly, 'It will last for several months,

probably longer, and you will find it easy to find another similar post once you have a good reference.'

'Lady Mortimor won't give me one.'

'I am an old friend of Eloise; I imagine that my word will carry sufficient weight. As for the cat and kittens, they may come and live in my house; Brontes will love to have them.'

'Oh, but won't your—that is, anyone mind?'

'No. I shall be seeing Eloise later; may I tell her that you are willing to go and see her?'

'I would have liked time to think about it.'

'Well, you can have ten minutes while I round up the rest of the party.'

He had gone before she could protest, walking away from her with long, easy strides.

He had said 'ten minutes' and she suspected that he had meant what he had said. It sounded a nice job and the money was far beyond her wildest expectations, and she wouldn't be at anyone's beck and call.

Prudence told her that she was probably going out of the frying pan into the fire. On the other hand, nothing venture, nothing win. When he came back presently with Lucy chattering happily and a tired Bobo and a still lively Brontes in tow, she said at once, 'All right, I'll go and see this lady if you'll give me her address. Only it will have to be in the evening.'

'Seven o'clock tomorrow evening. Mrs Vincent, two, Cornel Mews. I'll let her know. I shan't be here tomorrow; I'll see you on Tuesday. You're free for the rest of the day?'

For one delighted moment she thought he was going to suggest that they should spend it together, but all he said was, 'Goodbye,' before he started to whistle to Brontes and turned on his heel, walking with the easy air of a man who had done what he had set out to do.

Lucy tucked an arm in hers. 'Now tell me everything—why are you going to see this Mrs Vincent?'

They started to walk back and by the time they had reached the house Lucy knew all about it. They took Bobo into the kitchen and went back to their rooms to make some coffee and talk it over.

'It won't matter whether Mrs Vincent is nice or not if she's not going to be there,' observed Lucy. 'Oh, Fran, won't it be heavenly to have no one there but us—and Peggy of course—I wonder how old she is?'

'I forgot to ask…'

'All that money,' said Lucy dreamily. 'Now we can easily both get winter coats.'

'Well, I must save as much as I can. Supposing I can't find another job?'

'Never cross your bridges until you get to them,' said Lucy. 'Come on, let's go and look at the shops.' She put the kittens back in their box with their mother.

'I'm glad they'll all have a good home,' Francesca said.

'Yes. I wonder where it is?'

'Somewhere suitable for a professor,' said Francesca snappily. It still rankled that he had taken leave of her so abruptly. There was no reason why he shouldn't, of course. He had done his good deed for the day: found help for his friend and enabled her to leave Lady Mortimor's house.

'I shall enjoy giving her my notice,' she told Lucy.

IT SEEMED AS THOUGH Monday would never end but it did, tardily, after a day of Lady Mortimor's deep displeasure vented upon anyone and anything which came within her range, due to an early morning visit to her hairdresser who had put the wrong coloured streaks in her hair. Francesca had been ordered to make another appointment immediately so that this might be remedied at once, but unfortunately the hairdresser had no cancellations. Francesca, relaying this unwelcome news, had the receiver snatched from her and listened to her employer demanding the instant dismissal of the girl who had done her hair that morning, a demand which was naturally enough refused and added to Lady Mortimor's wrath.

'Why not get Ethel to shampoo your hair and re-set it?' Francesca suggested, and was told not to be so stupid, and after that there was no hope of doing anything right… She was tired and a little cross by the time she got to their rooms to find Lucy ready with a pot of tea.

'You drink that up,' she told Francesca bracingly.

'Put on that brown jacket and skirt—I know they're old, but they're elegant—and do do your face.' She glanced at the clock. 'You've twenty minutes.'

It was exactly seven o'clock when she rang the bell of the charming little cottage in Cornel Mews. Its door was a rich dark red and there were bay trees in tubs on either side of it, and its one downstairs window was curtained in ruffled white net. She crossed her fingers for luck and took a deep breath as the door was opened.

The woman standing there was small and slim and as pretty as a picture. Her dark hair was in a fashionable tangle and she wore the kind of make-up it was difficult to separate from natural colouring. She wore a loose shirt over a very narrow short skirt and high-heeled suede boots and she could have been any age between twenty and thirty. She was in fact thirty-five.

'Miss Haley—do come in, Renier has told me all about you…' She ushered Francesca into a narrow hall and opened a door into a surprisingly large living-room. 'Sit down and do have a drink while we get to know each other.'

Francesca sat, took the sherry she was offered and, since for the moment she had had no chance to say a word, she stayed silent.

'Did Renier explain?' asked Mrs Vincent. 'You know what men are, they never listen.'

It was time she said something, thought Francesca. 'He told me that you were going on tour and needed someone to look after your daughter and keep house for you.'

'Bless the darling, he had it right.' Mrs Vincent curled up in a vast armchair with her drink. 'It's just the details—'

'You don't know anything about me,' protested Francesca.

'Oh, but I do, my daily woman is sister to Lady Mortimor's cook; besides, Renier said you were a sensible young woman with a sense of responsibility, and that's good enough for me. When can you come? I'm off at the end of next week.' She didn't give Francesca a chance to speak. 'Is the money all right? All the bills will go to my solicitor, who'll deal with them, and he'll send you a weekly cheque to cover household expenses and your salary. If you need advice or anything he'll deal with it.'

Francesca got a word in at last. 'Your daughter— how old is she? Can she meet me before I come? I have a sister who would have to live here with me.'

'That's fine. She's up in the nursery; I'll get her down.'

Mrs Vincent went out of the room and called up the narrow stairs, and presently a small girl came into the room. She was one of the plainest children Francesca had ever set eyes on: lank, pale hair, a long, thin face, small, dark eyes and an unhappy little mouth.

'She's six years old,' said Mrs Vincent in a detached way. 'Goes to school of course—very bright, so I've been told. Shake hands with Miss Haley, Peggy. She's coming to stay with you while I'm away.'

The child shook hands with Francesca and Francesca kept the small paw in her own for a moment. 'I shall like coming here to live with you,' she said gently. 'I've a sister, too...' She remembered something. 'Have you a cat or a dog to look after?'

The child shook her head. Her mother answered for her. 'My last nanny wouldn't have them in the house, though it's all one to me.' She laughed. 'I'm not here long enough to mind.'

'Then could I bring a kitten with me? Perhaps you would like one of your very own to look after, Peggy?'

The child smiled for the first time; there was an endearing gap in her teeth. 'For my own?' she asked.

'If your mother will allow that.'

'Oh, let the child have a pet if she wants.' Mrs Vincent added unexpectedly, 'She takes after her father.'

A remark which made everything clear to Francesca; a lovely, fragile creature like Mrs Vincent would find this plain, silent child a handicap now that she was going back on the stage. Probably she loved her dearly, but she wasn't going to let her interfere with her career. She went pink when Mrs Vincent said, 'I've been left comfortably off, but I've no intention of dwindling into a lonely widowhood,' because she might have read her thoughts. She smiled suddenly. 'I shall wait for a decent interval and get married again.'

Francesca watched Peggy's small face; it was stony with misery. She said quickly, 'I'll bring the kitten when I come, shall I? And you can choose a name for it—it's a little boy cat; he's black and white with yellow eyes.'

Peggy slipped a small hand into hers. 'Really? Will he live here with us?'

'Of course, for this will be his home, won't it?'

Eloise poured herself another drink. 'You have no idea what a relief this is—may I call you Francesca? Now when can we expect you?'

'References?' ventured Francesca.

'Renier says you're OK. That's good enough for me; I told you that.'

'I shall have to give a week's notice to Lady Mortimor. I can do that tomorrow.'

'Good. I can expect you in a week's time. Give me a ring and let me know what time of day you'll be coming and I'll make a point of being in. Now have you time to go round the cottage with me?'

It was a small place, but very comfortably furnished with a well-planned kitchen and, on the ground floor, the living-room and, on the floor above, two good-sized bedrooms and a smaller room with a small bathroom leading from it. 'This is the nursery,' said Mrs

Vincent. 'Peggy plays here—she's got masses of toys; she's quite happy to amuse herself.'

Francesca wondered about that although she said nothing. 'How long will you be away?' she asked.

'Oh, my dear, how am I to know? The tour will last three months at least, and with luck will end up at a London theatre; if it doesn't I shall get my agent to find me something else.'

'Yes, of course. Has Peggy any grandparents or cousins who may want to visit?'

'My parents are in America; Jeff's live in Wiltshire, almost Somerset, actually. We don't see much of them.' Something in her voice stopped Francesca from asking any more questions, and presently she bade Mrs Vincent goodbye, and bent to shake Peggy's hand.

'You won't forget the kitten?'

'No, I'll bring him with me, I promise.'

Back in her little sitting-room she told Lucy everything. 'It's a dear little house, you'll love it. I think Peggy is lonely—she's withdrawn—perhaps she misses her father; I don't know how long ago he died. I promised her a kitten—the black and white one. Mrs Vincent didn't mind.'

'You don't like her much, do you?' asked Lucy shrewdly.

'Well, she's charming and friendly and easy-going, but she didn't seem very interested in Peggy. Perhaps it's hard to stay at home quietly with a small child if you've been used to theatre friends, and perhaps when her husband was alive they went out a lot.'

'It'll be better than Lady Mortimor's, anyway. We had better start packing up tomorrow, and don't forget Professor Pitt-Colwyn is going to take mother cat and the other kittens. Shall you meet him tomorrow?'

'He said he would be there.' She frowned. 'I must be careful what I say about Mrs Vincent; he said he was a close friend of her husband so I expect he is a close friend of hers as well.'

'Do you suppose she's got her eye on him?'

'Don't be vulgar, Lucy. I should think it was very likely, although for all we know he's married already.'

'You'd better ask him—'

'Indeed I will not.'

He was in the park, waiting for her when she got there the next morning with Bobo. It was a bright day with more than a hint of the coming winter's chill and Francesca, an elderly cardigan over her blouse and skirt, wished she had worn something warmer.

He wasted no time on good-mornings but said, 'You're cold; why didn't you wear something sensible? We had better walk briskly.'

He marched her off at a fine pace, with Bobo keeping up with difficulty and Brontes circling around them. 'Well? You saw Eloise Vincent? Are you going to take the job?'

'Yes, I'm going to give Lady Mortimor my notice

this morning and let Mrs Vincent know when I'll be going to her.'

'You saw Peggy?'

'Yes.'

He looked down at her thoughtfully. 'And…?'

'She's a quiet little girl, isn't she? I said I would take one of our kittens there for her to look after; her mother said that I might. You will take the mother cat and the other kittens, won't you?'

'Certainly I will. When will it be convenient for me to collect them? One evening? Let me see, I'm free on Thursday after six o'clock. Where exactly do you live?'

'Well, over the garage at the back of the house. There's a side-door; there's no knocker or bell, you just have to thump.'

'Then shall we say between six o'clock and half-past six? Have you a basket?'

'No, I'll get a cardboard box from the kitchen.'

'No need. I'll bring a basket with me. You're quite happy about this job?'

'Yes, thank you. You see, it's much more money and it will be so nice not to be…that is, it will be nice to be on our own.'

'That I can well believe. Are you scared of Lady Mortimor?'

She gave his question careful thought. 'No, not in the least, but she is sometimes rather rude if anything has annoyed her. I have longed to shout back at her but I didn't dare—she would have given me the sack.'

'Well, now you can bawl her out as much as you like, though I don't suppose you will; you've been too well brought up.'

He had spoken lightly, but when she looked at him she saw the mocking little smile. He must think her a spineless creature, dwindling into a dull spinsterhood. He had been kind, but his pity angered her. After all, she hadn't asked him for help. She said in her quiet voice, 'I have to go. Thank you for your help, and we'll have mother cat and the kittens ready for you when you come.' She gave him a stiff smile. 'Goodbye, Professor Pitt-Colwyn.'

She would contrive to be out when he called on Thursday evening, she decided as she made her way back to the house.

She couldn't have chosen a worse time in which to give in her notice. Lady Mortimor had been to a bridge party on the previous day and lost money, something she couldn't bear to do, and over and above that her dressmaker had telephoned to say that the dress she had wanted delivered that morning was not finished. Francesca went into the room in time to hear her employer declaring that it was no concern of hers if the girl working on it was ill, the dress was to be delivered by two o'clock that afternoon. She glanced up when she saw Francesca. 'Better still, I'll send round a girl to collect it and it had better be ready.

'You heard that,' she snapped. 'That stupid woman having the cheek to say I can't have the dress today. I intend to wear it to the Smithers' drinks party this evening. You'll fetch it after lunch.'

She sat down at the little writing-table and glanced through the letters there. 'Bills,' she said peevishly. 'These tradespeople always wanting their money. You'd better see to them, I suppose, Francesca.' She got up. 'I've a hair appointment—see that they're ready for me when I get back.'

Francesca picked up the letters. 'Lady Mortimor, I wish to give you a week's notice as from today.' She laid an envelope on the desk. 'I have put it in writing.'

Lady Mortimor looked as though she had been hit on the head. Her eyes popped from her head, her mouth gaped. When she had her breath she said, 'What nonsense is this? You must be mad, girl. A cushy job and a flat of your own…I won't hear of it.'

'There's nothing you can do about it,' Francesca pointed out reasonably. 'It isn't a cushy job, it's very badly paid, and it surely isn't a flat—it's two small rooms with a minute kitchen and a shower which doesn't work half the time.'

'You'll have difficulty in getting work, I'll see to that. I'll not give you a reference.'

'That won't be necessary. I already have a job to go to and your reference won't be required.'

'Then you can go now, do you hear, you ungrateful girl?'

'Just as you say, Lady Mortimor. You will have to give me two weeks' wages, one in lieu of notice.' She watched her employer's complexion becoming alarmingly red. 'And whom shall I ask to arrange the dinner party for Saturday? And your lunch party on Sunday? Shall I let Ethel have the bills to check? And there will be the invitations for the charity tea party you are giving next week.'

Francesca paused for breath, astonished at herself. Really she had been most unpleasant and deserved to be thrown out of the house for rudeness. She realised that she wouldn't mind that in the least.

Lady Mortimor knew when she was worsted. 'You will remain until the following week.'

'Tuesday evening,' Francesca interpolated gently, ignoring the woman's glare.

'You will send an advertisement to the usual papers this morning. I require letters in the first instance; interviews can be arranged later to suit me.'

'Certainly, Lady Mortimor. Am I to state the salary?'

'No. The flat goes with the job, of course.' She swept to the door. 'It may interest you to know that you have ruined my day. Such ingratitude has cut me to the quick.'

Francesca forbore from saying that, for someone of

Lady Mortimor's ample, corseted figure, the cut would have to be really deep.

Naturally a kind girl and seldom critical of other people, she felt guilty once she was alone. She had been most dreadfully rude; she felt thoroughly ashamed of herself. She had almost finished the bills when Maisie came in with her coffee.

'Cor, miss, what a lark—you going away. Mr Crow was just in the hall passing as you might say and 'eard it all. He said as 'ow you gave as good as you got and good luck to you, we all says—treated you something shameful, she 'as, and you a lady and all.'

'Why, Maisie, how very kind of you all. I'm afraid I was very rude…'

'A bit of plain speaking never 'urt no one, miss. I 'opes 'owever that 'oever takes yer place is capable of a bit of talking back.'

Francesca drank her coffee, feeling cheerful again. She wasn't going to apologise, but she would behave as she always had done, however unpleasant Lady Mortimor might choose to be.

She chose to be very unpleasant. It was a good thing that there were no signs of the professor the next morning for she might have burst into tears all over him and wallowed in self-pity, but by Thursday evening she didn't care any more and allowed Lady Mortimor's ill temper and spiteful remarks to flow over her head. Heedful of her decision, she took care not to get to the rooms until well after seven o'clock, only to find the professor sitting in comfort in the only easy-chair in the place, drinking tea from a mug while Brontes brooded in a fatherly fashion over mother cat and the kittens in their box.

'There you are,' said Lucy as Francesca went in. 'We thought you'd never come. There's still tea in the pot. But Renier's eaten all the biscuits; he didn't have time for lunch. Have you had a beastly day?'

'Well, a bit sticky. I say, isn't Brontes sweet?'

The professor had got up from his chair and pushed her gently into it, and had gone to sit on the small wooden chair which creaked under his weight. He said now, 'I shall be away for the next ten days or so; I hope you settle down with Peggy.' His hooded gaze swept over her tired face. 'It's time you had a change, and I think you will find she will be much nicer to live with than your Lady Mortimor.' He got up. 'I must be going.' He scooped the cat and kittens into the basket he had brought with him, while Lucy cuddled the other kitten on her lap. 'I'll take good care of them,' he said. He smiled at them both. *'Tot ziens.'* And when Francesca made an effort to rise he said, 'No, I'll see myself out.'

The room seemed very empty once he had gone.

CHAPTER THREE

THE WEEK SEEMED never-ending, and Lady Mortimor was determined to get the last ounce of work out of Francesca before she left. There had been several answers to the advertisement, but so far the applicants had refused the job. They had turned up their noses at the so-called flat and two of them had exploded with laughter when they had been told their salary. They were, they had pointed out, secretary-companions, not dog minders or errand girls. Lady Mortimor actually had been shaken. 'You will have to remain until someone suitable can take your place,' she had said the day before Francesca was due to leave.

'That won't be possible,' said Francesca. 'I start my new job immediately I leave here. One of the agencies might have help for you, but only on a daily or weekly basis.'

Lady Mortimor glared at her. 'I am aware of that, but I have no intention of paying the exorbitant fees they ask.' She hesitated. 'I am prepared to overlook your rudeness, Francesca. I am sure that you could arrange to go to this new job, say, in a weeks' time?'

'I am very sorry, Lady Mortimor, but that is impossible.'

She watched her employer sweep out of the room in a towering rage, and went back to making out the last of the cheques for the tradesmen.

The last day was a nightmare she refused to dwell upon. Lady Mortimor gave her not a moment to herself, and when six o'clock came declared that half the things she had told Francesca to do were still not done. Francesca listened quietly, allowing the tirade to flow over her head. 'There is nothing of importance left to do,' she pointed out. 'Whoever can come in place of me can deal with anything I've overlooked. Goodbye, Lady Mortimor.'

She closed the door quietly on her erstwhile employer's angry voice. She had a happier send-off from the staff, and Crow presented her with a potted plant from them all and wished her well. 'For we're all sure you deserve it, miss,' he said solemnly.

She went to join Lucy, and, after a meal, packed the last of their belongings. A taxi would take them the short distance to Cornel Mews in the morning.

Eloise Vincent was waiting for them when they arrived mid-morning. Peggy was at school, she told them. 'My daily woman will fetch her after lunch. I'm up to my eyes packing; I'm off this evening. I've written down all the names and addresses you might need and a phone number in case you should need me urgently, but for heaven's sake don't ring unless it's something dire.' She led the way upstairs. 'You each have a room; I'll leave you to unpack.' She glanced at the cat basket Lucy was holding. 'Is this the kitten? I dare say Peggy will like having him. There's coffee in the kitchen; help yourselves, will you? Lucy's bed is made up. I'm sorry I haven't put clean sheets on the other bed; the room's been turned out, but I had to empty cupboards and drawers—you won't mind doing it?'

She smiled charmingly and went downstairs, leaving them to inspect their new quarters. The rooms were prettily furnished and to have a room of one's own would be bliss. They unpacked and hung everything away and, with the kitten still in his basket, went downstairs. Mrs Wells, the daily cleaner, was in the kitchen. She was a pleasant-faced, middle-aged woman who poured coffee for them, found a saucer of milk for the kitten and offered to do anything to help. 'I've been here quite a while, before poor Dr Vincent died, so I know all there is to know about the place. I come in the mornings—eight o'clock—and go again after lunch,' she offered biscuits, 'though I said I'd fetch Peggy from school before I go home today.'

'Can't we do that?' asked Francesca. 'We have to get to know her, and it's a chance to see where the school is.'

'Well, now, that would be nice. It's at the end of Cornel Road, just round the corner in Sefton Park Street. Mrs Vincent hoped you wouldn't mind having a snack lunch—the fridge is well stocked and you can cook this evening. She is going out to lunch with a friend, but she'll be back by two o'clock and aims to leave around six o'clock—being fetched by car.'

Francesca thought of the questions she wanted answered before Mrs Vincent left. She put down her coffee-cup. 'Perhaps I could talk to her now?'

Eloise Vincent was in the sitting-room, sitting at her desk, a telephone book before her, the receiver in her hand. She looked up and smiled as Francesca went in. 'Settling in?' she asked. 'Mrs Wells is a fount of knowledge if you've any questions.'

'Yes. She's been most helpful. Mrs Vincent, could you spare a moment? Just to tell me what time Peggy goes to bed, if there's anything she won't eat, which friends is she allowed to play with while you are away…?'

'Oh, dear, what a lot of questions. She goes to bed about seven o'clock, I suppose. She eats her dinner at school and I've been giving her tea about five o'clock. I don't know about her friends. My husband used to take her with him when he went to see his friends; they haven't been here, although on her birthday we had a party, of course—'

'May I have the names of your doctor and dentist?'

Mrs Vincent laughed. 'Oh, get Renier if anything is worrying you. He's Peggy's godfather; he's fond of her. She's never ill, anyway. Now, you really must excuse me—Mrs Wells can tell you anything else you may want to know.'

It was obvious to Francesca that Mrs Vincent had no more time for her. She went back to the kitchen and did a thorough tour of its cupboards and shelves, went through the linen cupboard with Mrs Wells and, when Mrs Vincent had left for her lunch appointment, sat down with Mrs Wells and Lucy to eat sandwiches and drink more coffee.

Peggy came out of school at three o'clock, and both of them went to fetch her since Mrs Vincent wasn't back. The children came out in twos and threes and Peggy was one of the last, walking slowly and alone.

They went to meet her and she seemed pleased to see them, walking between them, holding their hands, answering their cheerful questions about school politely. Only when Francesca said, 'The kitten's waiting for you,' did she brighten. They spent the rest of the short walk discussing suitable names for him.

Mrs Vincent was back and there was a car before the door, which was being loaded with her luggage by a tall, middle-aged man. He said, 'Hello, Peggy,' without stopping what he was doing.

She said, 'Hello, Mr Seymour,' in a small wooden voice, all her animation gone again.

'You'd better go and say goodbye to your mother,' he told her over his shoulder. 'We're off in a few minutes.'

The three of them went inside and found Mrs Vincent in the sitting-room, making a last-minute phone call. 'Darlings,' she cried in her light, pretty voice,

'I'm going now. Come and say goodbye to your old mother, Peggy, and promise to be a good girl while I'm away. I'll send you lots of postcards and when I can I will telephone to you.' She kissed her small daughter and turned to Francesca. 'I'll be trying to keep in touch,' she said. 'I'm sure you'll do a marvellous job. Let me know how you are getting on from time to time.'

She smiled, looking so pretty and appealing that Francesca smiled back, quelling the uneasy feeling that Eloise Vincent was only too delighted to be starting her theatrical career once more and couldn't wait to get away.

She was prepared for Peggy's tears once her mother had gone, but the child's face had remained impassive. 'May I have the kitten now?' she asked, almost before they were out of sight.

She and the small creature took to each other at once. She sat happily in the sitting-room with him on her small, bony knees, talking to him and stroking his head with a small, gentle hand. 'I shall call him Tom,' she told Francesca.

'That's a nice name.'

'Daddy used to read me a story about Tom Kitten…' The small voice quavered and Francesca said quickly, 'Shall we talk about your daddy? I'd like to know all about him.'

So that was the trouble, she reflected, listening to the child's rambling description of her father and the fun they had had together. Peggy had loved him dearly and there had been no one to talk to her about him. She let the child chat on, the small face animated, and then said gently, 'What nice things you have to remember about him, Peggy, and of course he'll never go away; he'll always be there inside your head.'

'I like you,' said Peggy.

It took a few days to settle into a routine. Lucy went to school each morning and Francesca took Peggy to her school shortly afterwards, going back to make the beds and shop and wash and iron while Mrs Wells gave the house what she called a good tidy up. Tom settled down without any nonsense, aware by now that he belonged to Peggy and no one else, sitting beside her chair at meals and sleeping at the foot of her bed.

There had been no news of Mrs Vincent. Francesca wasn't sure where she was, for the promised list of the various towns the company would be appearing in hadn't turned up. It was a relief that at the end of the week there was a cheque in the post with her salary and a housekeeping allowance.

It was two days later, after they had had tea and Francesca was on the floor in the kitchen, showing Peggy how to play marbles while Tom pranced around them both, that the front doorbell was rung.

'I'll go,' called Lucy, in the sitting-room with her homework, and a moment later Professor Pitt-

Colwyn's voice sent Peggy flying to the kitchen door. He caught her in his arms and kissed her soundly. 'Hello, love, I thought it was time I came to see how you were getting on...'

He watched Francesca get up off the floor and brush down her skirt. 'Marbles—am I in time for a game?' and then he added, 'Good evening, Francesca.'

She was surprised at how glad she was to see him. 'Good evening, Professor.' She scanned his face and saw that he was tired. 'Shall we go into the sitting-room? I'll make a cup of coffee while you and Peggy have a talk—she wants to show you Tom.'

He looked down at the small, earnest face staring up at him. 'A splendid idea—shall we be disturbing Lucy?'

'I've just finished,' said Lucy. 'I'll help Fran get the coffee—'

'A sandwich with it?' asked Francesca.

'That would be very nice.'

'Have you had no lunch or tea?'

'A rather busy day.' He smiled, and she could see that he wasn't going to talk about it.

She made a pot of coffee, cut a plateful of cold beef sandwiches and bore the tray into the sitting-room. Peggy was sitting on the professor's knee and Tom had curled upon her small lap. Francesca was astonished to hear the child's happy voice, talking nineteen to the dozen.

'We are talking about Peggy's father,' said the professor deliberately.

Francesca said at once, 'He must have been a marvellous dad. Peggy has told us a little about him.' She poured him a cup and gave it to him. 'You stay there, darling. Here's your milk, and take care not to spill it over your godfather's trousers.'

She passed the sandwiches too, and watched him eat the lot. 'There's a cake I made this afternoon,' she suggested.

He ate several slices of that too, listening to Peggy's chatter, knowing just when to make some remark to make her giggle. Francesca let her bedtime go by, for the little girl was really happy. It was the professor who said at last, 'It's way past your bedtime, Peggy,' and when she wound her arms round his neck he said, 'If you go to bed like the good girl you are, I'll come and take you to the zoo on Saturday afternoon.'

'Fran and Lucy too?'

'Of course. Tom can mind the house and we'll come back here and have an enormous tea.'

She slid off his knee. Kissed him goodnight then, and went to stand by Francesca's chair. 'Will we?' she asked. 'Will we, really?'

'If your godfather says so, then of course we will, and I'll make a simply enormous cake and we'll have crumpets dripping with butter.'

'Could Lucy put her to bed?' asked the professor. 'We might have a chat?'

'Of course I can.' Lucy scooped up the kitten and handed him to Peggy. 'And Fran will come and tuck you up when you're in bed.'

Peggy went happily enough, her hand in Lucy's and the kitten tucked under one arm. Francesca, suddenly shy, offered more coffee.

'Any problems?' asked the professor.

She thought before she answered. 'No, I don't think so. I should have liked to have known a bit more about Peggy before Mrs Vincent left, but there wasn't much time. Mrs Wells is a great help with things like shopping and so on. Peggy doesn't seem to have any friends...do you suppose it would be all right if I invited one or two children for tea one day? I think she is a very shy little girl.'

'She is a very unhappy little girl. She loved her father very much and she misses him; she likes to talk about him. I think that Eloise didn't understand that and the child is too small to carry so much hidden grief.' He glanced at her. 'She told me that she talks to you and Lucy about him.'

'Yes, he is still alive to her, isn't he? If you're sure that's the right thing to do?'

'Quite sure. By all means see if you can get some children round to play with her. Has she no friends at all at school?'

'Oh, one or two speak to her but she doesn't seem

to have any special friends, but I'll do my best. She has masses of toys and it would be nice if she were to share them.'

'Have you heard from Eloise?'

'Me? No. She said she would be too busy rehearsing to write for a while.'

'I'm going to Cheltenham to see the opening show next week. If you think of anything you want to know about, let me know before then.'

'Thank you. She left everything beautifully organised. I expect she's a very good actress?'

He didn't answer, and she wondered uncomfortably if she had said something about Mrs Vincent which might have annoyed him. She couldn't think of anything but if he was in love with her, and she supposed that he was, he would be touchy about her. Lucy came in then.

'Peggy's bathed and in bed; she's waiting for you to say goodnight—both of you.'

The child wreathed her arms round Francesca's neck. 'I love you, Fran.'

'Thank you, darling. I love you too, and Tom of course. Now go to sleep quickly, won't you? Because he's asleep already.'

The professor was hugged in his turn, and he was reminded of his promise to take them to the zoo on Saturday, then he was kissed goodnight. 'Now tuck me in, please, Fran.'

So she was tucked in and he stood in the little room,

leaning against the wall, watching, his eyes half closed.

Back in the sitting-room he said, 'I must be off. Thanks for the coffee and sandwiches.'

'It made Peggy very happy to see you,' Francesca said. The thought that it had made her very happy too was sternly dismissed. 'You will have a good meal before you go to bed, won't you?'

He looked as though he were going to laugh. 'Indeed I will.' He smiled at Lucy and dropped a large hand on Francesca's shoulder for a moment and went away. Lucy went to the window to watch him drive away, but Francesca busied herself with the cups and saucers.

'I shall enjoy the zoo,' said Lucy.

'Yes, it should be fun; Peggy will love it. Lucy, I must do something about finding her some friends...'

'Well, gossip around when you go to get her from school. I dare say our Eloise discouraged them—children are noisy and they make a mess...'

'You're probably right, but don't call her that, dear—we might forget and say something—I mean, I think he's in love with her, don't you? He's going all the way to Cheltenham for the opening night.'

They were in the kitchen, washing up the coffee-cups.

'That doesn't mean that he's in love with her. What shall we have for supper? It's a bit late.'

The following day Francesca made a few tentative

overtures to the mothers and nannies taking the children to school. They were friendly enough, and she made a point of letting them know that Mrs Vincent had gone away for a time and that she was looking after Peggy. She said no more than that, but it was, she thought, the thin end of the wedge...

She wasn't sure, but she thought that maybe the children had been discouraged from getting friendly with Peggy, a child too shy to assert herself with the making of friends. It might take some time, but it would be nice if she could get to know a few children while her mother was away, so that by the time she got back home Peggy would have established a circle of little friends. Already the child was livelier, learning to play the games small children played, spending long hours with Francesca or Lucy rearranging the elaborate doll's house, planning new outfits for the expensive dolls she had. 'Woollies for the winter,' explained Francesca, getting knitting needles and wool and starting on miniature sweaters and cardigans.

They all went shopping the next day, and it was apparent that Peggy had never been to Woolworth's. They spent a long time there while she trotted from one counter to the other, deciding how to spend the pocket money Francesca had given her. After the rigours of Lady Mortimor's household, life was very pleasant. Francesca, going about her chores in the little house, planning meals, playing with Peggy, sitting in the evenings sewing or knitting, with Lucy doing her homework at the table, felt that life was delightful. They had a home, well, not a permanent one, but still a home for the time being—enough money, the prospect of having some new clothes and of adding to their tiny capital at the bank. She was almost content.

The professor came for them after lunch on Saturday, bundled them briskly into his car, and drove to the zoo. It was a mild autumn day, unexpected after several days of chilly rain. Francesca, in her good suit, her burnished hair gleaming in the sunshine, sat beside him in the car making polite small talk, while Lucy and Peggy in the back giggled and chattered together. The professor, who had been up most of the night with a very ill patient, allowed the happy chatter from the back seat to flow over his tired head and listened to Francesca's pretty voice, not hearing a word she said but enjoying the sound of it.

The afternoon was a success; they wandered along, stopping to look at whatever caught their eyes, with Peggy skipping between them until she caught sight of the camels, who were padding along with their burden of small children.

The professor fished some money out of his pocket and gave it to Lucy. 'You two have a ride; Francesca and I are going to rest our feet. We'll be here when you get back.'

'You make me feel very elderly—bunions and

dropped arches and arthritic knees,' protested Francesca, laughing as they sat down on an empty bench.

'You, my dear girl, will never be elderly. That is an attitude of mind.' He spoke lightly, not looking at her. 'You have settled down quite happily, I hope?'

'Oh, yes, and Lucy and Peggy get on famously.'

'So I have noticed. And you, Francesca, you mother them both.'

She was vexed to feel her cheeks grow hot. She asked stiffly, 'How is Brontes? And mother cat and the kittens?'

'He has adopted them. You must come and see them. The children are at school during the day? You will be free for lunch one day? I'll give you a ring.'

'Is that an invitation?' asked Francesca frostily.

'Certainly it is. You want to come, don't you?'

She had no intention of saying so. 'I shall be very glad to see mother cat and the kittens again.'

His stern mouth twitched a little. 'I shall be there too; I hope you will be glad to see me.'

'Well, of course.' She opened her handbag and looked inside and closed it again for something to do. She would be very glad to see him again, only he mustn't be allowed to know that. He was merely being friendly, filling in his days until Eloise Vincent should return. She wished that she knew more about him; she voiced the wish without meaning to and instantly wanted it unsaid.

'You flatter me.' He told her blandly, 'Really there

is nothing much to tell. I work—as most men work. Perhaps I am fortunate in liking that work.'

'Do you go to a hospital every day or have a surgery?'

'I go to several hospitals and I have consulting-rooms.'

She persisted. 'If you are a professor, do you teach the students?'

'Yes. To the best of my ability!' He added gently, 'I examine them too, and from time to time I travel. Mostly to examine students in hospitals in other countries. I have a very competent secretary and a nurse to help me—'

'I'm sorry, I've been very rude; I can't think why I asked you about your work or—or anything.' She had gone pink again and she wouldn't look at him, so that the long, curling lashes, a shade darker than her hair, lay on her cheeks. She looked quite beautiful and he studied her with pleasure, saying nothing. It was a great relief to her when Lucy and Peggy came running towards them. Caught up in the excited chatter from Peggy, she forgot the awkward moment.

They went back to the little house in the Mews presently and had their tea: fairy cakes and a ginger-bread, little sandwiches and chocolate biscuits. 'It's like my birthday,' said Peggy, her small, plain face wreathed in smiles.

The professor stayed for an hour after tea, playing ludo on the floor in front of the sitting-room fire.

When he got to his feet, towering over them, he observed pleasantly, 'A very nice afternoon—we must do it again some time.' He kissed his small goddaughter, put a friendly arm around Lucy's shoulders, and went to the door with Francesca.

'I'll phone you,' was all he said, 'and thanks for the tea.'

IT WAS several days later when she had a phone call. A rather prim voice enquired if she were Miss Haley and went on to ask if she would lunch with Professor Pitt-Colwyn in two days' time. 'If it wouldn't inconvenience you,' went on the voice, 'would you go to the Regent hospital at noon and ask for the professor?'

Francesca agreed. Were they going to eat at the hospital? she wondered, and what should she wear? It would have to be the brown suit again. Her winter coat was too shabby and although there was some money now Lucy needed a coat far more than she did. She would wash her hair and do her nails, she decided, and buy a new lipstick.

The Regent hospital was in the East End. It was a hideous building, heavily embellished with fancy brickwork of the Victorian era, brooding over a network of shabby streets. Francesca got off the bus opposite its entrance and presented herself at the reception desk inside the entrance hall.

The clerk appeared to know who she was, for she

lifted the phone and spoke into it, and a moment later beckoned to one of the porters.

'If you would wait for a few minutes, Miss Haley, the porter will show you...'

Francesca followed the man, wishing that she hadn't come; she couldn't imagine the professor in this vast, echoing building. Probably he had forgotten that he had invited her and was deep in some highly urgent operation. Come to think of it, she didn't know if he was a surgeon or a physician. She sat down in a small room at the back of the entrance hall, facing a long corridor. It was empty and after a minute or two she was tempted to get up and go home, but all at once there were people in it, walking towards her: the professor, towering above the posse of people trying to keep up with him, a short, stout ward sister, two or three young men in short white coats, an older man in a long white coat, a tall, stern-looking woman with a pile of folders under one arm and, bringing up the rear, a worried-looking nurse carrying more folders.

The professor paused in the doorway of the room she was in, filling it entirely with his bulk. 'Ah, there you are,' he observed in a voice which suggested that she had been in hiding and he had just discovered her. 'Give me five minutes...'

He had gone and everyone else with him, jostling each other to keep up.

He reappeared not ten minutes later, elegant in a

dark grey suit and a silk tie which had probably cost as much as her best shoes. They had been her best for some time now, and she hardly ever wore them for they pinched abominably.

'Kind of you to come here,' he told her breezily. 'I wasn't sure of the exact time at which I could be free. Shall we go?'

She walked beside him, out to the space reserved for consultants' cars and got into the car, easing her feet surreptitiously out of her shoes. The professor, watching out of the corner of his eye, turned a chuckle into a cough and remarked upon the weather.

He drove west, weaving his way through the small side-streets until she, quite bewildered by the one-way traffic, saw that they were in Shaftesbury Avenue. But only briefly; he turned into side-streets again and ten minutes or so later turned yet again into a narrow street, its trees bare of leaves now, the houses on either side elegant Regency, each with a very small garden before it, steps leading up to doorways topped by equally elegant fanlights. The professor stopped the car and got out to open her door. 'I thought we might lunch at home,' he told her. 'Brontes is anxious to see you again.'

'You live here?' asked Francesca. A silly question, but she had been surprised; it was, she guessed, five minutes away from Mrs Vincent's cottage.

'Yes.' He took her arm and marched her up the

steps as the door was opened by a dignified middle-aged man in a black jacket and pin-striped trousers.

'Ah, Peak. Francesca, this is Peak, who sees that this place runs on oiled wheels. Mrs Peak is my housekeeper. Peak, this is Miss Haley. Show her where she can leave her coat, will you?' He picked up his bag. 'I'll be in the drawing-room, Francesca.'

In the charming little cloakroom concealed beneath the curving staircase, she poked at her hair, added more lipstick and deplored the suit; she had better take off the jacket otherwise it might look as though she were ready to dart out of the house again. Her blouse wasn't new either, but it was ivory silk, laundered and pressed with great care, and the belt around her slender waist was soft leather. Her feet still hurt, but she would be able to ease them out of her shoes again once they were sitting at the table. She went back into the narrow hall and the professor appeared at a half-open door.

'Come and have a drink before lunch.' He held the door wide and Brontes stuck his great head round it, delighted to see her.

The room was long and narrow, with a bay window overlooking the street and a charming Adam fireplace. The chairs were large and deep and well cushioned, and there was a scattering of small lamp tables as well as a handsome bow-fronted display cabinet embellished with marquetry, its shelves filled with silver and porcelain. The professor went to the rent table under the window. He asked, 'Sherry for you? And do sit down.'

She sat, and was aware that mother cat and her kittens were cosily curled up together in one of the easy chairs. She said, 'Oh, they seem very much at home.'

He handed her the sherry. 'Brontes has seen to that; he is their devoted guardian angel.'

She sipped her sherry, very aware of him sitting opposite her, Brontes pressed up against him, both of them watching her. Her tongue, as it sometimes did, ran away with her. 'Do you want to tell me something? Is that why you asked me to lunch?'

'Yes, to both your questions, but it can wait.' He settled back in his great chair. 'Your sister is a bright child; has she any ideas about the future?' It was a casual question and she answered readily enough.

'She's clever; she's set her heart on GCSEs, A levels, and a university.'

'Some discerning young man will snap her up long before then.' He smiled at her. 'And why aren't you married?'

It was unexpected. 'Well, I—I…that is, they weren't the right ones. None of them the right man.'

This muddled statement he received with a gentle smile. 'Have you any messages for Eloise?'

'If you would tell her that Peggy seems happy and is doing well at school and that everything is fine. She hasn't written or phoned, but I expect she's very busy.'

'Undoubtedly,' he agreed gravely. Peak came then to tell them that lunch was ready, and she went with the professor to a smaller room at the back of the house, which overlooked a surprisingly large garden. 'You've got trees, how lovely,' she exclaimed. 'It must look beautiful in the spring.'

They lunched off iced melon, baked salmon in a pastry case and a coffee *bavarois* and, while they ate, the professor kept the conversation quite firmly in his hands; impersonal topics, the kind of talk one might have had with a stranger sharing one's table in a restaurant, thought Francesca peevishly. Back in the drawing-room, drinking coffee from paper-thin cups, she said suddenly, 'I wish you would talk about your work—you looked different at the hospital; it's a side of you that I know nothing about.' She put down her cup. 'I'm sorry, I'm being nosy again.' She looked at her feet, aching in the shoes she longed to kick off. 'Only I'm interested,' she mumbled.

'I have an appointment at half-past two,' he told her. 'I'll drive you back as I go to my rooms, which means that we have half an hour. Do take off those shoes and curl up comfortably.'

'Oh, how did you know? I don't wear them very often and they're a bit tight. You don't mind?'

'Not in the least. What do you want to know about my work, Francesca?'

'Well, I know that you're a professor and a consultant, but are you a surgeon or a physician? You said you went to other hospitals and that you travelled. Why?'

'I'm a surgeon, open-heart surgery valve replacements, by-passes, transplants. Most of my work is at Regent's, but I operate at all the big provincial hospitals if I'm needed. I have a private practice and an out-patients clinic twice a week. I work in Leiden too, occasionally in Germany and the States, and from time to time in the Middle East.'

'Leiden,' said Francesca. 'You said *"tot ziens"* one morning in the park; we looked it up—it's Dutch.'

'My mother is a Dutchwoman; she lives just outside Leiden. I spend a good deal of time there. My father was British; he died two years ago.'

He looked at her, half smiling, one eyebrow raised in a gentle way. The half-smile widened and she thought it was mocking, and went red. He must think her a half-wit with no manners. She plunged into a muddled speech. 'I don't know why I had to be so rude, I do apologise, I have no excuse, if I were you I wouldn't want to speak to me again—'

He said gently, 'But I'm not you, and fortunately I see no reason why I shouldn't speak to you again. For one thing, it may be necessary from time to time. I did tell Eloise that I would keep an eye on Peggy.'

'Yes, of course. I—I expect that you would like to go now.' She sat up straight and crammed her feet back into her shoes and then stood up. 'Thank you for my lunch—it was delicious.'

He appeared not to notice how awkward she felt. Only as he stopped in Cornel Mews and got out to take the key from her and open the door of the cottage did he say, 'We must have another talk some time, Francesca,' and he bent to kiss her cheek as she went past him into the hall.

CHAPTER FOUR

FRANCESCA WAS sitting by the fire, reading to Peggy, when Lucy came in. 'Well, did you have a good lunch? What did you eat?'

Francesca recited the menu.

'Nice—to think I was chewing on liver and bacon… Where did you go?'

'To his house; it's quite close by.'

Lucy flung down her school books and knelt down by the fire. 'Tell me everything,' she demanded.

When Francesca had finished she said, 'He must be very rich. I expect he's clever too. I wonder what his mum's like.'

'How's school?'

'OK.' Lucy dug into a pocket. 'There's a letter for you, but don't take any notice of it; I don't want to go…'

The words were bravely said but palpably not true. A party of pupils was being organised to go skiing two weeks before Christmas. Two weeks in Switzerland with proper tuition and accompanied by teachers. The fare and the expenses totalled a sum which Francesca had no hope of finding.

'Oh, Lucy, I'm so sorry. If it's any consolation I'll

get the money by hook or by crook for next winter.'
She glanced at her sister's resolutely cheerful face.
'All your friends are going?'

'Well, most of them, but I really don't mind, Fran.
We can have a lovely time here, getting ready for
Christmas.'

So nothing more was said about it, although Francesca sat up late, doing sums which, however hard
she tried, never added up to enough money to pay for
Lucy's skiing holiday. There was enough money set
aside for her school fees, of course, but that wasn't to
be touched. She went to bed finally with a headache.

There was no postcard from Mrs Vincent; nor was
there a phone call. Francesca reminded herself that the
professor would be with her, and most likely he would
bring back something for Peggy when he returned.
The child showed no concern at the absence of news
from her mother, although it seemed to Francesca that
she was looking pale and seemed listless; even Tom's
antics were met with only a half-hearted response.
Francesca consulted Mrs Wells. 'I think she should
see a doctor. She isn't eating much either. I wonder
if she's missing her mother...'

Mrs Wells gave her an old-fashioned look. 'I'm not
one for telling tales out of school, but 'er mum never
'as had no time for 'er. Disappointed she was; she so
pretty and charming and Peggy as plain as a pikestaff.
No, you don't need to fret yerself about that, Miss
Haley; little Peggy don't love 'er mum all that much.

She was 'appier when her granny and grandpa came to visit. That was when Dr Vincent was alive—loved the child they did, and she loved them.'

So Francesca had done nothing for a few more days, although Peggy didn't seem any better. She had made up her mind to get a doctor by now. If only the professor had phoned, she could have asked his advice, but he, of course, would be wherever Mrs Vincent was. She fetched Peggy from school, gave her her tea which she didn't want and, as soon as Lucy came home, took the child upstairs to bed. Peggy felt hot and she wished she could take her temperature, but there was a singular lack of first-aid equipment in the house, and she blamed herself for not having attended to that. She sat the child on her lap and started to undress her, and as she took off her clothes she saw the rash. The small, thin back was covered with red spots. She finished the undressing, washed the pale little face, and brushed the mousy hair and tucked the child up in bed. 'A nice glass of cold milk,' she suggested, 'and Lucy shall bring it up to you.'

'Tom—I want Tom,' said Peggy in a small voice. 'I've got a pain in my head.'

'You shall have Tom, my dear,' said Francesca and sped downstairs, told Lucy, and went to the phone. Even if the professor were still away, surely that nice man Peak would have a phone number or, failing that, know of a local doctor.

She dialled the number Mrs Vincent had left in her desk and Peak answered.

'Peak, did Professor Pitt-Colwyn leave a phone number? I need to speak to him—Peggy's ill.'

'A moment, Miss Haley,' and a second later the professor's voice, very calm, sounded in her ear.

'Francesca?'

'Oh, so you are there,' she said fiercely. 'Peggy's ill; there's a rash all over her back and she feels sick and listless. She's feverish, but I can't find a thermometer anywhere and I don't know where there's a doctor and I've not heard a word since Mrs Vincent went away—'

'Peggy's in bed? Good. I'll be with you in about ten minutes.' He rang off and she spent a moment with the unhappy thought that she had been anything but calm and sensible; she had even been rather rude…and he had sounded impassive and impersonal, as though she were a patient to be dealt with efficiently. Though I'm not the patient, she thought in a muddled way as she went back to Peggy and sent Lucy downstairs to open the door for the professor, and then sat down on the side of the bed to hold the tearful child in her arms.

She didn't hear him come in; for such a big man he was both quick and silent. She was only aware of him when he put two hands on her shoulders and eased her away from Peggy and took her place.

He was unhurried and perfectly calm and apparently unworried and it was several minutes before he examined the child, took her temperature and then sat back while Francesca made her comfortable again. 'Have you had chicken-pox?' He glanced at Francesca.

'Me? Oh, yes, years ago; so has Lucy.'

'And so have I, and now so has Peggy.' He took the small, limp hand in his. 'You'll feel better very soon, Peggy. Everyone has chicken-pox, you know, but it only lasts a few days. You will take the medicine Francesca will give you and then you'll sleep as soundly as Tom and in the morning I'll come and see you again.'

'I don't want Mummy to come home—'

'Well, love, there really is no need. Francesca will look after you, and as soon as you feel better we'll decide what is to happen next, shall we?' He kissed the hot little head. 'Lucy will come and sit with you until Francesca brings your medicine. *Tot ziens.*'

Peggy managed a watery smile and said, '*Tot ziens.*'

In the sitting-room Francesca asked anxiously, 'She's not ill, is she? I mean, ill enough to let her mother know? She said she didn't want to be—that is, there was no need to ring her unless there was something serious.'

When he didn't answer she added, 'I'm sorry if I was rude on the phone; I was worried and I thought you were away.'

'Now why should you think that?'

'You said you were going to Cheltenham.'

'As indeed I did go.' He was writing a prescription as he spoke. 'Don't worry, Peggy is quite all right. She has a temperature but, having chicken-pox, that is only to be expected. Get this tomorrow morning and see that she takes it three times a day.' He took a bottle from his bag and shook out a tablet. 'This will dissolve in hot milk; it will make her more comfortable and she should sleep.'

He closed his bag and stood up. 'I'll call in on my way to the hospital in the morning, but if you're worried don't hesitate to phone me; I'll come at once.' At the door he turned. 'And don't worry about her mother. I'll be seeing her again in a day or so and then I can reassure her.'

Francesca saw him to the door and wished him a polite goodnight. If it hadn't been imperative that she should see to Peggy at once, she would have gone somewhere quiet and had a good cry. She wasn't sure why she wanted to do this and there really wasn't time to think about it.

Peggy slept all night and Francesca was up and dressed and giving the little girl a drink of lemonade when the professor arrived. He was in flannels and a thick sweater and he hadn't shaved, and she said at once, 'You've been up all night.'

'Not quite all of it. How is Peggy?'

They went to look at her together and he pronounced himself content with her progress. There were more spots now, of course, but her temperature was down a little and she greeted him cheerfully enough. 'Anything in moderation if she's hungry,' he told Francesca, 'and get the elixir started as soon as you can.'

'Thank you for coming. Lucy's made tea—we haven't had our breakfast yet. You'll have a cup?'

He refused pleasantly. 'I must get home and shower and change; I've an out-patients clinic at ten o'clock.'

She opened the door onto a chilly morning.

'I'll look in some time this evening.' He was gone with a casual nod.

It was late in the afternoon when Francesca had a phone call from Peggy's grandmother in Wiltshire. It was a nice, motherly voice with no hint of fussing. 'Renier telephoned. Poor little Peggy, but we are so glad to know that she is being so well looked after. I suppose you haven't heard from her mother?'

'Well, no, the professor said that he would be seeing her and that there was no need to let her know. Peggy is feeling much better and he is looking after her so well, so please don't be anxious.'

'She's our only grandchild and so like our son. He was Renier's friend, you know. They were at university together and school together—he was best man at their wedding and is godfather to Peggy.'

'Would you like to speak to Peggy? She's awake.

I'll carry her across to the other bedroom; there's a phone there…'

'That would be delightful. Shall I ring off or wait?'

'If you would wait—I'll be very quick…'

The conversation went on for some time, with Peggy on Francesca's lap, talking non-stop and getting too excited. Presently Francesca whispered, 'Look, Peggy, ask Granny if you can telephone her each day about teatime, and if she says ''yes'' say goodbye now.'

A satisfactory arrangement for all parties.

The professor came in the evening, once more the epitome of the well-dressed gentleman. He was coolly polite to Francesca, spent ten minutes with Peggy, who was tired and a little peevish now, pronounced himself satisfied and, after only the briefest of conversations, went away again.

'No need to come in the morning,' he observed, 'but I'll take a look about this time tomorrow.'

The next day he told Francesca that Peggy might get up in her dressing-gown and roam the house. 'Keep her warm, she needs a week or so before she goes back to school. You're dealing with the spots, aren't you? She mustn't scratch.'

The next day he told her that he would be seeing Eloise on the following day.

'How nice,' said Francesca tartly. 'I'm sure you will be able to reassure her. Peggy's granny has been phoning each afternoon; she sounds just like a granny…' A silly remark, she realised, but she went on, 'Peggy's very fond of her.'

'Yes, I know. I shall do my best to persuade Eloise to let her go and stay with her for a few days. You will have to go too, of course.'

'But what about Lucy?'

'I imagine that it could be arranged for her to board for a week or so? Eloise will pay, of course. Would Lucy mind?'

'I think she would love it…but it will be quite an expense.'

'Not for Eloise, and Peggy will need someone with her.'

'What about Tom?'

'I'm sure that her grandmother will make him welcome. I'll let you know.'

He made his usual abrupt departure.

'Most unsatisfactory,' said Francesca to the empty room. She told Lucy, of course, who found it a marvellous idea. 'They have such fun, the boarders—and almost all of my friends are boarders. Do you suppose Mrs Vincent will pay for me?'

'Professor Pitt-Colwyn seemed to think she would. He's going to let me know…'

'Well, of course,' said Lucy airily. 'If they're in love they'll do anything to please each other. I bet you anything that he'll be back in a few days with everything arranged.'

She was right. Several days later he arrived at teatime, just as they were sitting on the floor in front of the fire, toasting crumpets.

Peggy, no longer spotty but decidedly pasty-faced, rushed to meet him.

'Where have you been? I missed you. Francesca and Lucy missed you too.'

He picked her up and kissed her. 'Well, now I'm here, may I have a cup of tea and one of those crumpets? There's a parcel in the hall for you, too.' He put her down. 'Run and get it; it's from your mother.'

'Will you have a cup of tea?' asked Francesca in a hostess voice and, at his mocking smile and nod, went on, 'Peggy seems to be quite well again, no temperature for three days, but she's so pale...'

She came into the room then with the parcel and began to unwrap it without much enthusiasm. A doll—a magnificent creature, elaborately dressed.

'How very beautiful,' said Francesca. 'You must give her a name. What a lovely present from Mummy.'

'She's like all my other dolls and I don't like any of them. I like my teddy and Tom.' Peggy put the doll carefully on a chair and climbed on to the professor's lap. 'I had a crumpet,' she told him, 'but I can have some of yours, can't I?'

'Provided you don't drip butter all over me and Francesca allows it.'

Francesca passed a large paper serviette over without a word, and poured the fresh tea Lucy had made.

That young lady settled herself on the rug before the fire once again and sank her teeth into a crumpet.

'Do tell,' she said. 'Is—?' She caught the professor's eye. 'Oh, yes, of course,' and went on airily, 'Did you have a nice time wherever you went?'

The professor, who had spent exactly twenty-four hours in Birmingham—a city he disliked—only four of which had been in Eloise's company, replied blandly that indeed he had had a most interesting time, as he had a flying visit to Edinburgh and, since heart transplants had often to be dealt with at the most awkward of hours, an all-night session there and, upon his return, another operation in the early hours of the morning at Regent's. Francesca, unaware of this, of course, allowed her imagination to run riot.

She said waspishly, 'I expect a man in your position can take a holiday more or less when he likes. Have another crumpet?'

He took one and allowed Peggy to bite from it before demolishing it.

'There are no more crumpets, I'm afraid,' said Francesca coldly, 'but there is plenty of bread. I can make toast…'

He was sitting back with his eyes closed. 'Delicious—well buttered and spread with Marmite. You know the way to a man's heart, Francesca.'

He opened one eye and smiled at her, but she pretended not to see that and went away to fetch some bread and a pot of Marmite. She put the kettle on again too, foreseeing yet another pot of tea.

The other three were talking about Christmas and laughing a great deal when she got back, and it wasn't until he had at last eaten everything he had been offered that he exchanged a glance with Lucy, who got up at once. 'Peggy! Help me take everything into the kitchen, will you, and we'll wash up? You can have an apron and do the washing; I'll dry.'

Peggy scrambled off the professor's knee. 'You'll not go away?'

'No. What is more, if I'm allowed to, I'll stay until you're in your bed.'

Left alone with him, Francesca cast around in her head for a suitable topic of conversation and came up with, 'Did Mrs Vincent give you any messages for me?'

'None. She thinks it a splendid idea that Peggy should go to her grandmother's for a week or so and that you will go with her. She is quite willing to pay for Lucy to stay at school during that time since she is inconveniencing you. She has asked me to make the arrangements and deal with the travelling and payment of bills and so forth. Oh, and she wishes Mrs Wells to come each day as usual while you're away.'

'Tom Kitten…?'

'He can surely go with you; I can't imagine that Peggy will go without him.'

'No. I'm sure she wouldn't. You reassured Mrs

Vincent about Peggy not being well? She's not worried?'

The professor had a brief memory of Eloise's pretty face turning petulant at the threat of her new, exciting life being disrupted. 'No,' he said quietly. 'She is content to leave Peggy in your charge.'

'When are we to go?'

'Sunday morning. That gives you three days in which to pack and leave everything as you would wish it here. I'll telephone Mrs Vincent and talk to her about it; I know that she will be delighted.'

'It won't be too much work for her?'

'She and Mr Vincent have plenty of help. Besides, they love Peggy.'

'Am I to ask Lucy's headmistress if she can board for a week or two?'

'I'll attend to that as well.'

Lucy and Peggy came back then. 'I've washed up,' piped Peggy importantly, 'and now I'm going to have a bath and go to bed. I'll be so very very quick and if you like you can see where my spots were.'

'I look forward to that,' he assured her gravely. 'In ten minutes' time.'

He went as soon as Peggy, bathed and in her nightgown, had solemnly shown him the faint scars from her spots and then bidden him a sleepy goodnight.

His goodbyes were brief, with the remark that he would telephone some time on Saturday to make final arrangements for Sunday.

Lucy was over the moon; she was popular at school and had many friends and, although she had never said so, Francesca was aware that she would like to have been a boarder, and, as for Peggy, when she was told there was no containing her excitement. Something of their pleasure rubbed off on to Francesca and she found herself looking forward to the visit. The future seemed uncertain: there was still no word from Mrs Vincent, although Peggy had had a postcard from Carlisle. There had been no message on it, merely a scrawled, 'Hope you are being a good girl, love Mummy.'

Francesca's efforts to get Peggy to make a crayon drawing for her mother or buy a postcard to send to her came to nought. She wrote to Mrs Vincent's solicitor, enclosing a letter to her and asking him to forward it. She gave a faithful account of Peggy's progress and enclosed an accurate rendering of the money she had spent from the housekeeping allowance, assured her that the little girl was quite well again and asked her to let her know if there was anything special she wished done. The solicitor replied immediately; he understood from Mrs Vincent that it was most unlikely that she would be returning home for some time and Miss Haley was to do whatever she thought was best for Peggy. It wasn't very satisfactory, but Francesca realised that she would have to make the best of it. At least she could call upon the professor again if anything went wrong, and, now that they were going to stay with Peggy's grandparents for a while, they would surely accept responsibility for the child.

The professor telephoned quite early on Saturday morning; he would take Lucy to her school and at the same time have a word with the headmistress. 'Just to make sure that everything is in order,' he explained in what Francesca described to herself as his soothing voice.

'Should I go with you?' she wanted to know.

'No need. I dare say you've already had a few words with her.'

Francesca, feeling guilty, said that yes, she had. 'Just about her clothes and so on,' she said placatingly, and was answered by a mocking grunt.

He arrived on the doorstep in the afternoon with Brontes sitting on the back seat, greeted her with casual civility, assured Peggy that he would take her to her granny's in the morning, waited while Lucy bade Francesca goodbye at some length and then drove her away, refusing politely to return for tea. 'I'm expecting a call from Eloise,' he explained, watching Francesca's face.

Lucy telephoned in the evening; she sounded happy and any doubts that Francesca might have had about her sister's feeling homesick were swept away. She promised to phone herself when they arrived at Peggy's grandparents' house and went away to finish packing.

The professor arrived in time for coffee which Mrs Wells, who had popped round to take the keys and lock up, had ready. He was in an affable mood, answering Peggy's questions with patience while Brontes brooded in a kindly fashion over Tom. Francesca drank her coffee and had nothing to say, conscious that just having the professor there was all she wanted; he annoyed her excessively at times and she didn't think that he liked her overmuch but, all the same, when he was around she felt that there was no need for her to worry about anything. The future was vague—once Mrs Vincent came home she would be out of work again—but then in the meantime she was saving almost every penny of her wages and she liked her job. Moreover, she had become very fond of Peggy.

Rather to her surprise, she was told to sit in the front of the car. 'Brontes will take care of Peggy,' said the professor. 'Tom can sit in the middle in his basket.'

She stayed prudently silent until they joined the M4 where he put a large, well-shod foot down and allowed the car to slide past everything else in the fast lane. 'Just where are we going?' she asked a shade tartly.

'Oh, dear, did I not tell you? But you do know Wiltshire?' When she nodded he added, 'Just on the other side of the Berkshire border. Marlborough is the nearest town. The village is called Nether Tawscombe. They live in the Old Rectory, a charming old place.'

'You've been there before?'

He laughed shortly. 'I spent a number of school holidays there with Jeff and later, when we were at Cambridge and medical school, we spent a good deal of time there.'

'Then he got married,' prompted Francesca.

'Yes. Eloise was never happy there; she dislikes the country.'

Something in his voice stopped her from saying anything more; she turned round to see how the occupants of the back seat were getting on. Peggy had an arm round Brontes's great neck, she had stuck the fingers of her other hand through the mesh in front of Tom's basket and wore an expression of happiness which turned her plain little face into near prettiness. Francesca, who had had secret doubts about the visit, knew that she had been mistaken.

They arrived at Nether Tawscombe in time for lunch. The one village street was empty under the thin, wintry sunshine, but the houses which lined it looked charming. They got larger as the street went uphill until it reached the church, surrounded by a churchyard and ringed around by fair-sized houses. The Old Rectory was close by; an open gate led to a low, rambling house with diamond-paned windows and a solid front door.

As the professor stopped before it, it was opened

and an elderly man came to meet them. She stood a little on one side until Peggy's excited greetings were over and the two men had shaken hands. She was led indoors while the professor saw to their baggage. The hall was stone-flagged, long and narrow, with a door opening on to the garden at the back of the house at its end. Brontes had made straight for it and had been joined by a black Labrador, who had rushed out of an open doorway as a grey-haired lady, cosily plump, had come into the hall.

Peggy screamed with delight and flung herself at her grandmother, and Mr Vincent said to Francesca, 'Always had a soft spot for each other—haven't had her to stay for a long time. This is delightful, Miss—er…?'

'Would you call me Francesca, please? Peggy does.'

Mrs Vincent came to take her hand then, with a warmth which caused sudden tears to prick her eyelids, for the last few years she had been without that kindly warmth…

That the professor was an old friend and welcome guest was evident: he hugged Mrs Vincent, asked which rooms the bags were to go to, and went up the wide staircase with the air of a man who knew his way about blindfold.

Mrs Vincent saw Francesca's eyes follow him and said comfortably, 'We've known Renier for many years. He and our son were friends; he spent many a school holiday here and Jeff went over to Holland. He's a good man, but I suspect you've discovered that for yourself, Miss...may I call you Francesca?'

'Oh, yes, please. What would you like me to do? Take Peggy upstairs and tidy her for lunch? She's so happy and excited.'

'Yes, dear. You do exactly what you've been doing. We know so little about her day-to-day life now that her father is dead—he brought her here very often, you see.'

No mention of Eloise, reflected Francesca. It wasn't her business, of course. She bore Peggy away upstairs to a couple of low-ceilinged rooms with a communicating door and windows overlooking the wintry garden beyond. After London, even the elegant part of London, it was sheer bliss.

The professor stayed to lunch and she was mystified to hear him say that no, he wasn't going back to London.

'Having a quiet weekend at Pomfritt Cleeve? Splendid,' observed Mr Vincent, and most annoyingly said no more about it.

Renier took his leave soon after lunch, saying goodbye to Francesca last of all, patting her shoulder in an avuncular fashion and remarking casually that he would probably see her at some time. She stood in the hall with everyone else, wishing with all her heart that she were going with him. For that was where she wanted to be, she realised with breathtaking surprise, with him all the time, forever and ever, and, now she came to think about it, she had been in love with him for quite some time, only she had never allowed herself to think about it. Now he was going; not that that would make any difference—he had always treated her at best with friendliness, more often than not with an uninterested politeness. She looked away so that she didn't see him go through the door.

However sad the state of her heart, she had little time to brood over it. Peggy was a different child, behaving like any normal six-year-old would behave, playing endless games with the Labrador and Tom, racing around the large garden with Francesca in laughing pursuit, going for rides on the elderly donkey who lived in the paddock behind the house, going to the shops in Marlborough with her grandmother and Francesca. She had quickly acquired a splendid appetite and slept the moment her small head touched the pillow. A good thing too, thought Francesca, for by bedtime she was tired herself. She loved her days in the quiet village and Mr and Mrs Vincent treated her like a daughter. Sometimes she felt guilty that she should be living so comfortably while Lucy was in London, although she thought that her sister, from all accounts, was as happy as she was herself. They missed each other, but Francesca had the sense to see that it was good for Lucy to learn independence. She tried not to think of the professor too often and she felt that she was succeeding, until after a week or so

Lucy wrote her usual letter and mentioned that he had been to see her at the school and had taken her out to tea. 'To the Ritz, no less!' scrawled Lucy, with a lot of exclamation marks.

The professor, having returned Lucy to her school, went to his home and sat down in his great chair by the fire with Brontes pressed against his knee and mother cat and the kittens asleep in their basket to keep him company. Tea with Lucy had been rewarding and he had made no bones about asking questions, although he had put them in such a way that she hadn't been aware of how much she was telling him. Indeed, she had confided in him that her headmistress had offered her a place in a group of girls from her class going to Switzerland for a skiing holiday. 'But of course I can't go,' she had told him. 'It's a lot of money and Fran couldn't possibly afford it—I mean, we both have to have new winter coats, and if Mrs Vincent comes back we'll have to move again, won't we?'

He had agreed with her gravely, at the same time prising out as much information about the trip as he could. He stroked Brontes's great head. 'I shall have to pay another visit to Eloise,' he told the dog. 'Now how can I fit that in next week?'

Presently he picked up the telephone on the table beside him and dialled a number.

A week, ten days went by. Peggy was so happy that Francesca began to worry about their return; she saw that the child loved her grandparents and they in turn loved her. They didn't spoil her, but she was treated with a real affection which Francesca felt she had never had from her mother. One morning when Peggy had gone off with her grandfather, leaving Francesca to catch up on the washing and ironing of the child's wardrobe, Mrs Vincent came to sit with her in the little room behind the kitchen where the ironing was done. 'You must be wondering why we don't mention Peggy's mother. Oh, I know we talk about her because Peggy must not forget her mother, but you see Eloise never wanted her and when she was born she turned against her—you see she takes after my son, and Eloise was so pretty. She said that her friends would laugh at such an ugly child. It upset Jeff, but she was fortunate—he was a loyal husband; he took Peggy around with him as much as possible and they adored each other. It was a pity that Peggy overheard her mother telling someone one day that she wished the child had not been born. She never told her father, bless the child, but she did tell Mrs Wells, who told me. There is nothing I would like better than to have Peggy to live with us always.'

'Have you suggested it to Eloise?'

'No; you see she will probably marry again and he might like to have Peggy for a daughter.'

Francesca thought Mrs Vincent was talking about the professor. She said woodenly, 'Yes, I dare say that would be very likely.'

It seemed as though it might be true, for the very next day he arrived just as they were sitting down to lunch.

Francesca, going out to the kitchen to ask Bertha, the housekeeper, if she could grill another few chops for their unexpected guest, was glad of her errand: it gave her time to assume the politely cool manner she could hide behind. It was difficult to maintain it, though, for when she got back to the dining-room it was to hear him telling the Vincents that he was on his way to see Eloise. 'I shall be glad of a word with you, sir,' he told Mr Vincent, 'as my visit concerns Peggy, and I think you should know why I am going.'

Francesca ate her chop—sawdust and ashes in her mouth. Afterwards she couldn't remember eating it; nor could she remember what part she took in the conversation during the meal. It must have been normal, for no one looked at her in surprise. She couldn't wait for the professor to be gone, and as though he knew that he sat over coffee, teasing Peggy and having a perfectly unnecessary conversation with Mrs Vincent about the uses of the old-fashioned remedies she used for minor ailments.

He got up at length and went away with Mr Vincent to the study, to emerge half an hour later and, amid a great chorus of goodbyes, take his leave.

This time Francesca watched him go; when next she saw him he would most likely be engaged to Eloise—even married. She was vague about special licences but, the professor being the man he was, she had no doubt that if he wished to procure one at a moment's notice he would find a way to do so.

It was three days later when Mr Vincent remarked to his wife, 'Renier phoned. He has got his way. He's back in London, but too busy to come down and see us for a few days.'

Mrs Vincent beamed. 'Tell me later—how delightful; he must be very happy.' Francesca, making a Plasticine cat for Peggy, did her best to feel happy, because he was happy, and one should be glad to know that someone one loved was happy, shouldn't one? She found it hard work.

He came at the end of the week, walking in unannounced during a wet afternoon. He looked tired; he worked too hard, thought Francesca lovingly, scanning the weary lines on his handsome face. He also looked smug—something she found hard to understand.

CHAPTER FIVE

RENIER HAD HAD LUNCH, he assured Mrs Vincent, before going with Mr Vincent to the study again. When they came back into the sitting-room the older man said, 'Well, my dear, it's all settled. Which of us shall tell Peggy?'

'What?' asked Peggy, all ears. 'Is—is it something nice? Like I can stay here forever?'

'You clever girl to guess,' said Mrs Vincent, and gave her a hug. 'That's exactly what you are going to do—live here with Grandpa and me and go to school every day.'

Peggy flung herself at her grandfather. 'Really, truly? I may stay here with you? I won't have to go back to Mummy? She doesn't want me, you know.'

'Well, darling, your mummy is a very busy person and being on stage is very hard work. You can go and see her whenever you want to,' said Mrs Vincent.

'Shan't want to. Where will Francesca go?'

Francesca went on fixing a tail to another cat and didn't look up. 'If there is no objection, I think it might be a good idea if I took her somewhere quiet and explained everything to her,' said the professor.

He added gently, 'Get your coat, Francesca, and come with me.'

'Now that is a good idea,' said Mrs Vincent. 'Run along, dear; Renier will explain everything to you so much better than we can.'

There was no point in refusing; she fetched her old Burberry and went out to the car with him, to be greeted with pleasure by Brontes, who was roaming the garden. The professor opened the door and stuffed her gently into her seat, got in beside her and, with Brontes's great head wedged between their shoulders, drove off.

'Where am I going?' asked Francesca coldly.

'Pomfritt Cleeve. I have a cottage there. We can talk quietly.'

'What about? Surely you could have told me at Mrs Vincent's house?'

'No, this concerns you as well as Peggy.'

He had turned off the main road into a narrow, high-hedged lane going downhill, and presently she saw a cluster of lights through the gathering dusk. A minute or so later they had reached the village—one street with a church halfway along, a shop or two, and small, old cottages, well maintained—before he turned into another narrow lane, and after a hundred yards or so drove through a propped-open gate and stopped before a thatched cottage of some size. There were lights in the windows and the door was thrown open as she got out of the car, hesitating for a moment, giving Brontes time to rush through the door with a delighted bark, almost knocking down the stout little lady standing there. She said, 'Good doggie,' in a soft, West Country voice and then added, 'Come on in out of the cold, sir, and the young lady. There's a good fire in the sitting-room and tea in ten minutes.'

The professor flung an arm around her cosy person and kissed her soundly. 'Blossom, how very nice to see you again—and something smells delicious.'

He caught Francesca gently by the arm. 'Francesca, this is Blossom, who lives here and looks after the cottage for me. Blossom, this is Miss Haley. Take her away so that she can tidy herself if she wants to, and we'll have tea in ten minutes, just as you say.'

The cottage, decided Francesca, wasn't a cottage really. It might look like one, but it was far too big to warrant such a name, although there was nothing grand about it. The sitting-room to which she was presently shown was low-ceilinged with comfortable chairs and tables dotted around on the polished floor. There was a low table before the fire and sofas on either side of it. She sat opposite her host, pouring tea into delicate china cups and eating scones warm from the oven and, having been well brought up, made light conversation.

However, not for long. 'Let us dispense with the small talk,' said the professor, 'and get down to facts. Eloise is quite happy to allow Peggy to live with her grandparents. She will of course be free to see the child whenever she wishes, but she will remarry very shortly and intends to stay on the stage, so it isn't likely that she will visit Peggy more than once in a while. Mrs Vincent will employ her old nanny's daughter to look after Peggy, so you may expect to leave as soon as she arrives.' Francesca gave a gasp, but he went on, 'Don't interrupt, I have not yet finished. Lucy has been told that she may join a school party going to Switzerland to ski—I have seen her headmistress and she will join the party.'

'Now look here,' said Francesca, and was hushed once more.

'I haven't said anything to you, for I knew that you would refuse to do anything about it. The child deserves a holiday and, as for the costs, you can repay me when you are able.'

'But I haven't got a job,' said Francesca wildly. 'I never heard such arrogance—going behind my back and making plans and arranging things—'

'Ah, yes, as to arrangements for yourself, Eloise is quite agreeable to your remaining at the cottage for a few days so that you can pack your things.'

She goggled at him, bereft of words. That she loved him dearly went without saying, but at the moment she wished for something solid to throw at him. 'You have been busy, haven't you?' she said nastily.

'Yes, indeed I have. I shall drive Lucy over to Zeebrugge to meet the school party there; you would like to come with us, no doubt.'

'How can I? I'll have to look for a job—'

'Well, as to that, I have a proposal to make.' He was sitting back, watching her, smiling faintly.

'Well, I don't want to hear it,' she declared roundly. 'I shan't listen to anything more you may say—'

'Perhaps this isn't the right time, after all. You are cross, are you not? But there is really nothing you can do about it, is there? You will break young Lucy's heart if you refuse to let her go to Switzerland—'

'She had no skiing clothes.'

'Now she has all she needs—a Christmas present.'

She all but ground her teeth. 'And I suppose you're going to get married?'

'That is my intention.'

Rage and despair almost choked her, and she allowed rage to take over.

'I hope you will be very happy.' Her voice was icy and not quite steady.

'I am certain of that.'

'I'd like to go back.' He agreed at once, which was a good thing—otherwise she might have burst into tears. Where was she to go? And there was Lucy to think of when she got back from Switzerland. Would she have time to get a job by then? And would her small hoard of money be sufficient to keep them until she had found work again? There were so many questions to be answered. Perhaps she should have listened to this proposal he had mentioned—it could have been another job—but pride wouldn't allow her to utter another word. She bade Blossom goodbye, complimented her on her scones and got into the car; it smelled comfortingly of leather and, very faintly, of Brontes.

Strangely enough, the great bulk of the professor beside her was comforting too, although she could think of no good reason why it should be.

Back at the Vincent's house after a silent drive, he bade them goodbye, bent his great height to Peggy's hug, observed cheerfully to Francesca that he would be in touch, and left.

She had no idea what he had said to the Vincents, but from what they said she gathered that they understood her to have a settled future, and there seemed no point in enlightening them. Peggy, chattering excitedly as Francesca put her to bed, seemed to think that she would see her as often as she wanted, and Francesca said nothing to disillusion her. The future was her own problem.

She left the Vincents two days later, and was driven back to the mews cottage by Mr Vincent. She hated leaving the quiet village. Moreover, she had grown very fond of Peggy who, even while bidding her a tearful goodbye, was full of plans to see her again, which were seconded by her grandmother. She had responded suitably and kept up a cheerful conversation with her companion as they drove but, once he had left her at the empty house, with the observation that they would be seeing each other shortly, she sat down in the kitchen and had a good cry. She felt better after that, made a cup of tea, and unpacked before starting on the task of re-packing Lucy's cases as well as her own. There had been a brief letter for her before she left the Vincents', telling her that they would be crossing over to Zeebrugge in two days' time, and would she be ready to leave by nine o'clock in the morning and not a minute later?

Mrs Wells had kept the place spotless, and there was a note on the kitchen table saying that she would come in the morning; there was a little ironing and nothing else to do but pack. She was halfway through that when Lucy phoned.

'You're back. Isn't it exciting? I can't believe it's true. I'm coming home tomorrow afternoon. The bus leaves here in the evening, but Renier says he'll take us to Zeebrugge early the next day and I can join the others there. Isn't he a darling?' She didn't wait for Francesca's answer, which was just as well. 'Oh, Fran, I do love being a boarder. I know I can't be, but you have no idea what fun it is. I've been asked to lots of parties at Christmas, too.'

Francesca let her talk. There was time enough to worry over the problem of Christmas; she still had almost three weeks to find a job and somewhere for them to live, too.

'You're very quiet,' said Lucy suddenly.

'I've had a busy day; I'm packing for us both now—I'll do the rest tomorrow. I've got to talk to Mrs Wells, too.'

'I'll help you. You are looking forward to the trip, aren't you?'

'Tremendously,' said Francesca with her fingers crossed. 'See you tomorrow, Lucy.'

By the time Lucy arrived, she had done everything that was necessary. Mrs Wells had been more than helpful, arranging to come early in the morning to take the keys and lock up. The solicitor had been dealt with, she had been to the bank and taken out as much money as she dared, found their passports—unused since they had been on holiday in France with their parents—and, finally, written a letter to Mrs Vincent which she had enclosed in a letter to the solicitor. There was nothing more to do but have a good gossip and go to bed.

The Bentley purred to a halt outside the cottage at precisely nine o'clock, then the professor got out, wished them an affable good-morning, put Francesca's overnight bag and Lucy's case in the boot, enquired as to what had been done with the rest of their luggage—safely with Mrs Wells—and urged them to get in. 'You go in front, Lucy,' said Francesca and nipped into the back seat, not seeing his smile, and resolutely looked out of the window all the way to Dover, trying not to listen to the cheerful talk between the other two.

Five hours later they were in Zeebrugge, driving to the hotel where the rest of the party had spent the night, and it was only then that she realised that she had no idea what was to happen next. There wasn't any time to think about it; the bus was ready to leave. It was only after a hasty goodbye to Lucy, when she was watching the party drive away, that the full awkwardness of the situation dawned upon her. 'Whatever am I going to do?' She had turned on the professor, her voice shrill with sudden fright. 'When is there a boat back?'

He took her arm. 'We are going to my home in Holland for the night. My mother will be delighted to meet you.'

'I must get back—I have to find a job.'

He took no notice, merely urged her gently into the car, got in beside her and drove off.

'This is ridiculous…I've been a fool—I thought we would be going straight back. I'm to spend the night at Mrs Wells's house.'

'We will telephone her.' His voice was soothing as well as matter-of-fact. 'We shall soon be home.'

They were already through Brugge and on the motorway, bypassing Antwerp, crossing into Holland, and racing up the Dutch motorways to Tilburg, Nijmegen and on past Arnhem. The wintry afternoon was turning to an early dusk and, save for a brief halt for coffee and sandwiches, they hadn't stopped. Francesca, trying to make sense of the situation, sat silent, her mind addled with tiredness and worry and a deepseated misery, because once they were back in England there would be no reason to see the professor ever again. The thought cast her in such deep gloom that she barely noticed the country had changed; the road ran through trees and thick shrubbery with a light glimpsed here and there. The professor turned off the road through a gateway, slowed along a narrow, sanded drive and stopped before the house at its end. He leaned over, undid her safety belt, got out and helped her out too, and she stood for a moment, looking at the dark bulk of the house. It was square and solid, its big windows lighted, frost sparkling on the iron balcony above the porch.

She said in a forlorn voice, 'I should never have come with you. I should never have let you take over my life, and Lucy's, too. I'm very grateful for your help; you have been kind and I expect it suited you and Eloise. I can't think why you've brought me here.'

'You wouldn't listen to my proposal at Pomfritt Cleeve,' the professor had come very close, 'I can see that I shall have to try again.' He put his arms around her and held her very close. 'You are a stubborn, proud girl with a beautiful head full of muddled thoughts, and I love you to distraction. I fell in love with you the first time I saw you, and what is all this nonsense about Eloise? I don't even like the woman, but something had to be done about Peggy. Now you will listen, my darling, while I make you a proposal. Will you marry me?'

What with his great arms around her and her heart thumping against her ribs, Francesca hadn't much breath—only just enough to say, 'Yes, oh, yes, Renier,' before he bent to kiss her.

DEAREST EULALIA
by
Betty Neels

CHAPTER ONE

THE two men talking together at the back of the hospital entrance hall paused to watch a young woman cross the vast floor. She was walking briskly, which suggested that she knew just where she was going, but she paused for a moment to speak to one of the porters and they had the chance to study her at their leisure.

She was worth studying: a quantity of dark brown hair framed a beautiful face and the nylon overall she was wearing couldn't disguise her splendid figure.

'Eulalia Langley,' said the elder of the two men, 'runs the canteen in Outpatients. Good at it, too. Lives with her grandfather, old Colonel Langley—your father knew him, Aderik. No money, lives in a splendid house somewhere behind Cheyne Walk. Some family arrangement makes it impossible for him to sell it— has to pass it on to a nephew. A millstone round his neck; Eulalia lives with him, keeps the home going. She's been with us for several years now. Ought to have married by now but I don't suppose there's much chance of that. It's a full-time job here and there isn't much of the day left by the time the canteen shuts down.'

His companion said quietly, 'She's very beautiful,' and then added, 'You say that my father knew Colonel Langley?'

He watched the girl go on her way and then turned to his companion. He was tall and heavily built, and towered over his informative colleague. A handsome man in his thirties, he had pale hair already streaked with grey, a high-bridged nose above a thin mouth and heavy-lidded blue eyes. His voice held only faint interest.

'Yes—during the Second World War. They saw a good deal of each other over the years. I don't think you ever met him? Peppery man, and I gather from what I hear that he is housebound with severe arthritis and is now even more peppery.'

'Understandably. Shall I see more of you before I go back to Holland?'

'I hope you'll find time to come to dinner; Dora will want to see you and ask after your mother. You're going to Edinburgh this evening?'

'Yes, but I should be back here tomorrow—I'm operating and there's an Outpatient clinic I must fit in before I return.'

'Then I'll give you a ring.' The older man smiled. 'You are making quite a name for yourself, Aderik, just as your father did.'

*　　*　　*

Eulalia, unaware of this conversation, went on her way through the hospital to the Outpatients department, already filling up for the morning clinic.

It was a vast place, with rows of wooden benches and noisy old-fashioned radiators which did little to dispel the chill of early winter. Although a good deal of St Chad's had been brought up to date, and that in the teeth of official efforts to close it, there wasn't enough money to spend on the department so its walls remained that particular green so beloved by authority, its benches scuffed and stained and its linoleum floor, once green like the walls, now faded to no colour at all.

Whatever its shortcomings, they were greatly mitigated by the canteen counter which occupied the vast wall, covered in cheerful plastic and nicely set out with piles of plates, cups and saucers, soup mugs, spoons, knives and paper serviettes.

Eulalia saw with satisfaction that Sue and Polly were filling the tea urn and the sugar bowls. The first of the patients were already coming in although the first clinic wouldn't open for another hour, but Outpatients, for all its drawbacks, was for many of the patients a sight better than cold bedsitters and loneliness.

Eulalia had seen that from the first moment of starting her job and since then, for four years, she had fought, splendid white tooth and nail, for the small comforts which would turn the unwelcoming place into somewhere in which the hours of waiting could be borne in some degree of comfort.

Since there had been no money to modernise the place, she had concentrated on the canteen, turning it by degrees into a buffet serving cheap, filling food, soup and drinks, served in brightly coloured crockery by cheerful, chatty helpers.

With an eye on the increasing flow of patients, she sent two of the girls to coffee and went to check the soup. The early morning clinic was chests, and that meant any number of elderly people who lived in damp and chilly rooms and never had quite enough to eat. Soup, even so early in the morning, would be welcome, washed down by strong tea…

One clinic succeeded another; frequently two or more ran consecutively, but by six o'clock the place was silent. Eulalia, after doing a last careful check, locked up, handed over the keys to the head porter and went home.

It was a long journey across the city but the first surge of home-goers had left so she had a seat in the bus and she walked for the last ten minutes or so, glad of the exercise, making her way through the quieter streets down towards the river until she reached a terrace of imposing houses in a narrow, tree-lined street.

Going up the steps to a front door, she glanced down at the basement. The curtains were drawn but she could see that there was a light there, for Jane would be getting supper. Eulalia put her key in the door and opened the inner door to the hall, lighted by a lamp on a side table—a handsome marble-topped nineteenth-century piece which, sadly, her grandfather was unable to sell since it was all part and parcel of the family arrangement...

There was a rather grand staircase at the end of the hall and doors on either side, but she passed them and went through the green baize door at the end of the hall and down the small staircase to the basement.

The kitchen was large with a large old-fashioned dresser along one wall, a scrubbed table at its centre and a Rayburn cooker, very much the worse for wear. But it was warm and something smelled delicious.

Eulalia wrinkled her beautiful nose. 'Toad-in-the-hole? Roasted onions?'

The small round woman peeling apples at the table turned to look at her.

'There you are, Miss Lally. The kettle's on the boil; I'll make you a nice cup of tea in a couple of shakes. The Colonel had his two hours ago.'

'I'll take a cup of tea with me, Jane; he'll be wanting his whisky. Then I'll come and give you a hand.'

She poured her own tea, and put a mug beside Jane. 'Has Grandfather had a good day?'

'He had a letter that upset him, Miss Lally.' Jane's nice elderly face looked worried. 'You know how it is; something bothers him and he gets that upset.'

'I'll go and sit with him for a bit.' Eulalia swallowed the rest of her tea, paused to stroke Dickens, the cat, asleep by the stove, and made her way upstairs.

The Colonel had a room on the first floor of the house at the front. It was a handsome apartment furnished with heavy mahogany pieces of the Victorian period. They had been his grandparents' and although the other rooms were furnished mostly with Regency pieces he loved the solid bulk of wardrobe, dressing table and vast tallboy.

He was sitting in his chair by the gas fire, reading, when she tapped on the door and went in.

He turned his bony old face with its formidable nose towards her and put his book down. 'Lally—jut in time to pour my whisky. Come and sit down and tell me about your day.'

She gave him his drink and sat down on a crossframed stool, its tapestry almost threadbare, and gave him a light-hearted account of it, making much of its lighter moments. But although he chuckled from time to time he was unusually silent, so that presently she asked, 'Something's wrong, Grandfather?'

'Nothing for you to worry your pretty head about, Lally. Stocks and shares aren't a woman's business and it is merely a temporary setback.'

Lally murmured soothingly. Grandfather belonged to the generation which considered that women had nothing to do with a man's world, and it was rather late in the day to argue with him about that.

She said cheerfully into the little silence, 'Jane and

I were only saying this morning that it was a waste of gas and electricity keeping the drawing room open. I never go in there, and if anyone comes to call we can use the morning room…'

'I'll not have you living in the kitchen,' said the Colonel tetchily.

'Well, of course not,' agreed Lally cheerfully, and thought how easy it was to tell fibs once she got started. 'But you must agree that the drawing room takes a lot of time to get warm even with the central heating on all day. We could cut it down for a few hours.'

He agreed reluctantly and she heaved a sigh of relief. The drawing room had been unheated for weeks and so, in fact, had most of the rooms in the house; only her grandfather's room was warm, as was the small passage leading to an equally warm bathroom. Lally wasn't deceitful but needs must when the devil drove…

She went back to the kitchen presently and ate her supper with Jane while they planned and plotted ways and means of cutting down expenses.

It was ridiculous, thought Eulalia, that they had to go on living in this big house just because some ancestor had arranged matters to please himself. Her grandfather couldn't even let it to anyone; he must live in it until he died and pass it on to a nephew who lived on the other side of the world. The family solicitor had done his best but the law, however quaint, was the law. Trusts, however ancient, couldn't be overset unless one was prepared to spend a great deal of money and probably years of learned arguing...

Eulalia ate her supper, helped Jane tidy the kitchen and observed with satisfaction that tomorrow was Saturday.

'I'll get Grandfather into his chair and then do the shopping.'

She frowned as she spoke; pay day was still a week away and the housekeeping purse was almost empty. The Colonel's pension was just enough to pay for the maintenance of the house and Jane's wages; her own wages paid for food and what Jane called keeping up appearances.

What we need, reflected Eulalia, is a miracle.

And one was about to happen.

There was no sign of it in the morning, though. Jane was upstairs making the beds, the Colonel had been heaved from his bed and sat in his chair and Eulalia had loaded the washing machine and sat down to make a shopping list. Breast of chicken for the Colonel, macaroni cheese for Jane and herself, tea, sugar, butter... She was debating the merits of steak and kidney pudding over those of a casserole when the washing machine, long past its prime, came to a shuddering stop.

Usually it responded to a thump, even a sharp kick, but this morning it remained ominously silent.

Extreme measures must be taken, decided Eulalia, and searched for a spanner—a useful tool she had discovered when there was no money for a plumber...

Mr van der Leurs, unaware that he was the miracle Eulalia wished for, paid off his taxi and made his way to the Colonel's house. A man esteemed by the members of his profession, renowned for his brilliant surgery, relentlessly pursued by ladies anxious to marry him, he had remained heart-whole, aware that somewhere on this earth there was the woman he would love and marry and until then he would bury his handsome nose in work. But his patience had been rewarded; one glimpse of Eulalia and he knew that he had found that woman. Now all he had to do was to marry her...

He reached the house and rang the bell and presently the door was opened and Eulalia stood there in a grubby pinny, looking cross. She still had the spanner in her hand, too. He saw that he would need to treat her with the same care with which he treated the more fractious of his small patients.

His 'Good morning' was briskly friendly. 'This is Colonel Langley's house? I wondered if I might visit him? My father was an old friend of his—van der Leurs.' He held out a hand. 'I am Aderik van der Leurs, his son.'

Eulalia offered a hand rather reluctantly. 'Grandfather has talked about a Professor van der Leurs he met years ago…'

Mr van der Leurs watched her face and read her thoughts accurately.

'I'm visiting at St Chad's for a few days,' he told her. 'Mr Curtis mentioned that the Colonel was house-bound with arthritis and might be glad to have a visit. I have called at an awkward time, perhaps…'

He must be all right if Mr Curtis knew him, decided Eulalia.

'I think Grandfather would be pleased to see you. Come in; I'll take you to his room.'

She led him across the hall but before she reached the staircase she turned to look at him.

'I suppose you wouldn't know how to make a washing machine start again?'

He had been wondering about the spanner. He said with just the right amount of doubt in his voice, 'Shall I take a look?'

She led him into the kitchen and Mr van der Leurs gave his full attention to the machine just as though it were one of his small patients on the operating table awaiting his skill. After a moment he took the spanner from her hand, tapped the dial very very gently and rotated it. The machine gave a gurgle and when he tapped it again—the mere whisper of a tap—it came to life with a heartening swish.

Eulalia heaved a sigh of relief. 'Thank you very much. How clever of you, but I dare say you know something about washing machines.' She added doubtfully, 'But you're a doctor.'

He didn't correct her. 'I'm glad I could be of help,' he said, and then stood looking at her with a look of faint enquiry.

She said quickly, 'I'll take you to see Grandfather. He loves to have visitors.'

She took off her pinny and led the way into the hall and up the graceful staircase. It was a cold house—although there were radiators along the walls, none of them gave warmth. Outside the Colonel's door Eulalia stopped. 'I'll bring coffee up presently—you'll stay for that?'

'If I may.'

She knocked and opened the door and then led him into the large room, pleasantly warm with a bright gas fire. There was a bed at one end of the room, bookshelves and a table by the wide window and several comfortable chairs. The Colonel sat in one of them, a reading lamp on the small table beside him, but he looked up as they went in. He eyed Mr van der Leurs for a moment. 'The spitting image of your father,' he observed. 'This is indeed a surprise—a delightful one, I might add.'

Mr van der Leurs crossed the room and gently shook the old hand with its swollen joints. 'A delight for me too, sir; Father talked of you a great deal.'

'Sit down if you can spare an hour. Lally, would

you bring us coffee? You have met each other, of course?'

'Yes, Grandpa, I'll fetch the coffee.'

Mr van der Leurs watched her go out of the room. She wasn't only beautiful, he reflected, she was charming and her voice was quiet. He sat down near the Colonel, noting that the radiators under the window were giving off a generous warmth. This room might be the epitome of warmth and comfort but that couldn't be said of the rest of the house.

Eulalia, going back to the kitchen, wondered about their visitor. He had said that he was at St Chad's. A new appointment? she wondered. Usually such news filtered down to the canteen sooner or later but she had heard nothing. In any case it was most unlikely that she would see him there. Consultants came to Outpatients, of course, but their consulting rooms were at the other end and they certainly never went near the canteen. Perhaps he was visiting to give lectures.

She ground the coffee beans they kept especially for her grandfather and got out the coffee pot and the china cups and saucers, and while she arranged them on a tray she thought about Mr van der Leurs.

He was a handsome man but not so very young, she decided. He had nice blue eyes and a slow smile which made him look younger than he was. He was a big man and tall but since she was a tall girl and splendidly built she found nothing unusual about that.

Indeed, it was pleasant to look up to someone instead of trying to shrink her person.

She found the Bath Oliver biscuits and arranged them on a pretty little plate and bore the tray upstairs and found the two men in deep conversation. The Colonel was obviously enjoying his visitor and she beamed at him as she handed him his coffee and put the biscuits where her grandfather could reach them easily. She went away then, nursing a little glow of pleasure because Mr van der Leurs had got up when she had gone in and taken the tray and stayed on his feet until she had gone.

Nice manners, thought Eulalia as she went downstairs to have her coffee with Jane.

'I heard voices,' observed Jane, spooning instant coffee into mugs.

Eulalia explained. 'And Grandfather was pleased to see him.'

'He sounds all right. I remember his dad; came visiting years ago.'

'He got the washing machine to go again.'

'That's a mercy. Now, Miss Lally, you do your shopping; I'll hang out the washing—see if you can get a couple of those small lamb cutlets for the Colonel and a bit of steak for us—or mince. I'll make a casserole for us and a pie if there's enough...'

Eulalia got her coat from the hall and fetched a basket and sat down at the table to count the contents of her purse. A week to pay day so funds were low.

'It had better be mince,' she said. 'It's cheaper.' And then she added, 'I hate mince...'

She looked up and saw that Jane was smiling—not at her but at someone behind her. Mr van der Leurs was standing in the doorway holding the coffee tray.

'Delicious coffee,' he observed, 'and I was delighted to meet the Colonel.'

Eulalia got up and turned round to face him. 'Thank you for bringing down the tray. This is Jane, our housekeeper and friend.'

He crossed the room and shook hands with her and smiled his slow smile so that she lost her elderly heart to him.

'Miss Lally's just going to do the shopping,' she told him.

'Perhaps I may be allowed to carry the basket?'

And very much to her surprise Eulalia found herself walking out of the house with him and down a narrow side street where there was a row of small shops, old-fashioned and tucked discreetly behind the rather grand houses.

She asked, 'Don't you have to go back to the hospital? I mean, this is kind of you but you don't have to.'

'It's more or less on my way,' said Mr van der Leurs, and since she was too polite to ask where he was going and he had no intention of telling her she made polite small talk until they reached the shops.

The grocer's was small and rather dark but he sold

everything. Mr van der Leurs, without appearing to do so, noted that she bought Earl Grey, the finest coffee beans, Bath Olivers, farm butter, Brie and Port Salut cheese, Cooper's marmalade and a few slices of the finest bacon; and, these bought, she added cheap tea bags, a tin of instant coffee, a butter substitute, sugar and flour and streaky bacon.

It was the same at the butcher's, where she bought lamb cutlets, a chicken breast, lamb's kidneys and then minced beef and some sausages. He hadn't gone into the shop with her but had stood outside, apparently studying the contents of the window. At the greengrocer's he followed her in to take the basket while she bought potatoes and a cabbage, celery, carrots and a bunch of grapes.

'We make our own bread,' said Eulalia, bypassing the baker.

Mr van der Leurs, keeping his thoughts to himself, made light-hearted conversation as they returned to the house. It was evident to him that living was on two levels in the Colonel's house, which made it a sensible reason for him to marry her as quickly as possible. There were, of course, other reasons, but those, like his thoughts, he kept to himself.

At the house he didn't go in but as he handed over the basket he said, 'Will you have lunch with me tomorrow? We might drive out into the country. I find the weekends lonely.'

It was a good thing that his numerous friends in

London hadn't heard him say that. He had sounded very matter-of-fact about it, which somehow made her feel sorry for him. A stranger in a foreign land, thought Eulalia, ignoring the absurd idea; he seemed perfectly at home in London and his English was as good as her own.

'Thank you, I should like that.'

'I'll call for you about eleven o'clock.' He smiled at her. 'Goodbye, Eulalia.'

Jane thought it was a splendid idea. 'Time you had a bit of fun,' she observed, 'and a good meal out somewhere posh.'

'It will probably be in a pub,' answered Eulalia.

She told her grandfather when she carried up his lunch.

'Splendid, my dear; he's a sound chap, just like his father was. I've asked him to come and see me again. He tells me he is frequently in England although he has his home in Holland.'

Eulalia, getting the tea later while Jane had a rest, spent an agreeable hour deciding what she would wear. It was nearing the end of October but the fine weather had held although it was crisply cold morning and evening. She decided on a short jacket, a pleated skirt and a silk jersey top, all of them old but because they had been expensive and well cut they presented an elegant whole. He had said that they would drive into the country, which might mean a pub lunch, but if it were to be somewhere grander she would pass muster…

When he called for her he was wearing beautifully cut tweeds, by no means new but bearing the hallmark of a master tailor, and his polished shoes were hand-made. Even to an untutored eye he looked exactly what he was—a man of good taste and with the means to indulge it. Moreover, reflected Eulalia happily, her own outfit matched his.

He went to see her grandfather, to spend ten minutes with him and give him a book they had been discussing, and then stopped to talk to Jane, who was hovering in the hall, before he swept Eulalia out of the house and into the dark grey Bentley parked on the kerb.

'Is this yours?' asked Eulalia.

'Yes. I need to get around when I'm over here.' He glanced at her. 'Comfortable? Warm enough? It's a lovely morning but there's a nip in the air.'

He took the M4 out of London and turned off at Maidenhead. 'I thought the Cotswolds? We could lunch at Woodstock and drive on from there. A charming part of England, isn't it? You don't need to hurry back?'

'No. Jane likes to go to Evensong but I expect we shall be back long before then. Do you know this part of England well?'

'Not as well as I should like but each time I come here I explore a little more.'

He had turned off the A423 and was driving along country roads, through small villages and the quiet countryside to stop presently at North Stoke, a village by the Thames where they had coffee at a quiet pub. He talked quietly as he drove, undemanding, a placid flow of nothing much. By the time they reached Woodstock, Eulalia was wishing the day would go on for ever.

The Feathers was warm and welcoming, with a pleasant bar and a charming restaurant. Eulalia, invited to choose her lunch, gulped at the prices and then, urged by her companion, decided on lobster patties and then a traditional Sunday lunch—roast beef, Yorkshire pudding, roast potatoes, vegetables…and after that a trifle to put to shame any other trifle. Eulalia finally sighed with repletion and poured the coffee.

'What a heavenly meal,' she observed. 'I shall remember it for years.'

'Good. The Cotswolds are at their best in the autumn, I think.'

He drove to Shipton-under-Wychwood, on to Stow-on-the-Wold and then Bourton-on-the-Water where he obligingly stopped for a while so that she might enjoy its charm and the little river running through the village. At Burford he stopped for tea at a hotel in its steep main street, a warm and cosy place where they sat in a pleasant room by the fire and ate toasted teacakes oozing butter and drank the finest Assam tea.

'This is bliss,' said Eulalia, mopping a buttery mouth. She smiled at him across the little table. 'I've had a heavenly day. Now we have to go back, don't we?'

'I'm afraid so. I'll settle up and see you at the car.'

Eulalia, powdering her beautiful nose, made a face at her reflection.

This has been a treat, she told herself. It isn't likely to happen again and so I mustn't like him too much. Even if I were to meet him at St Chad's it wouldn't be the same; he might not even recognise me. He'll go back to Holland and forget me.

It was already getting dusk and this time Mr van der Leurs took the main roads, travelling at a steady fast pace while they carried on an easy flow of small talk. But for all that, thought Eulalia as they were once more enclosed by the city's suburbs, she still knew almost nothing about him. Not that that mattered since she was unlikely to see him again. She hadn't asked him when he was going back to Holland but she supposed that it would be soon.

At the house, he came in with her. They were met by Jane in the hall.

'You'll have had your tea, but the kettle's boiling if you'd like another cup. The Colonel's nicely settled until supper time. I'm off to church.'

She smiled at them both. 'You've had a nice day?'

'Oh, Jane, it was heavenly.'

'I thought it might be. I'll get my hat and coat.'

'I don't suppose you want more tea?' Eulalia asked Aderik.

'I'd love a cup. While you are getting it may I have five minutes with the Colonel?'

'He'd like that. Do you want me to come up with you?'

'No, no. I know my way. I won't stay more than a few minutes.'

He went up the staircase, tapped on the Colonel's door and, bidden to enter, did so.

The Colonel was sitting in his chair doing a jigsaw puzzle but he pushed it to one side when Mr van der Leurs went in.

'Aderik. You had a pleasant day? Where did you go?'

Mr van der Leurs sat down beside him and gave him a succinct account of the day.

'You found Lally good company? She goes out so seldom. Never complains but it's no life for a girl. I do wonder what will happen to her when I am no longer here. She can't stay here—the place has to go to a nephew. A good chap but married with children.'

'Perhaps I can put your mind at rest about that, sir. I intend to marry Eulalia.'

The Colonel stared at him and then slowly smiled. 'Not wasted much time, have you?'

'I'm thirty-eight. Those years have been wasted romantically. I fell in love with her when I first saw her at St Chad's a day or two ago. I see no reason to waste any more time. You have no objection?'

'Good Lord, no. And your father would have liked her, as I'm sure your mother will.' He paused to think. 'She has no idea of your intentions?'

'None.'

'Well, I'm sure you know how you intend to go about that. You have lifted a load off my mind, Aderik. She's a dear girl and she has a loving heart.'

Mr van der Leurs got up and the Colonel offered a hand. 'You'll stay for supper?'

'No. I think not; enough is as good as a feast. Is that not so?'

The colonel rumbled with laughter. 'You're very like your father. Goodnight, my boy.'

Eulalia was in the kitchen. She and Jane were to have jacket potatoes for their supper but it was hardly a dish to offer to a guest. She hadn't asked him to stay to supper but she expected him to. She made the tea and when he entered the kitchen gave him a worried look.

'Shall we have tea here? Would you like to stay for supper?' She didn't sound at all eager and he hid a smile.

'Thank you but I mustn't stay. I've an appointment this evening. Tea would be fine.'

He drank his tea, waved aside her thanks for her day out, bade her a brisk goodbye and drove himself away. Eulalia shut the door as the Bentley slipped away, feeling hurt and a little peevish. He could at least have waved; it was almost as if he couldn't get away fast enough.

She poured herself another cup of tea. Of course he might be late for his appointment—with a girl? She allowed her imagination to run riot and then told herself sternly to stop being a fool. He was almost a stranger; she had only met him a couple of times; she knew nothing about him... So why was it that she felt so at ease with him, as though she had known him all her life?

If she had hoped to see him at the hospital the next day, she was disappointed. Her journeys into the hospital proper were limited to her visits to the supply department, the general office for requisitioning something for the canteen or taking money from the canteen at the end of the day to one of the clerical staff to lock away, but those trips took her nowhere near the wards and, since she had no idea as to what he actually did, even if she had the opportunity she had no idea where to look for him.

Filling rolls with cheese as the first of the day's patients began to surge in, she told herself to forget him.

Since it was the haematology outpatients clinic the benches were filling up fast. She recognised several of the patients as she poured tea and offered rolls. Anaemia in its many guises took a long time to cure, and if not to cure at least to check for as long as possible...

The clinic was due to start at any moment. She glanced towards the end of the waiting room to the row of consulting rooms and almost dropped the teapot she was filling. Mr van der Leurs, enormous in a white coat, was going into the first room, flanked by two young doctors and a nurse.

'But he's a mister,' said Eulalia to the teapot. 'A surgeon, so why is he at this clinic?' She had picked up quite a bit of knowledge since she had been working at St Chad's, not all of it accurate but she was sure that haematology was a medical field. He had disappeared, of course, and he wouldn't have seen her.

In this she was mistaken.

When the clinic was finally over she was at the back of the canteen getting ready for the afternoon's work and didn't see him leave.

It was six o'clock by the time she had closed the canteen, checked the takings and locked up. She got into her coat, picked up the bag of money and went through to the hospital. The clerk on night duty would lock it away and she would be free to go home. It was a pity that she had seen Mr van der Leurs again, she reflected. It had unsettled her.

She handed over the money and made for the main door. With any luck she wouldn't have to wait too long for a bus and the rush hour was over.

She pushed open the swing doors and walked full tilt into Mr van der Leurs.

He said easily, 'Ah, Eulalia, I was on my way to look for you. I have a book for your grandfather and I wondered if you would like a lift?'

She said slowly, 'I saw you in Outpatients this morning. I thought you were a surgeon—Mr, you know?'

He had taken her arm and was leading her to where the Bentley was parked.

'I am a surgeon, but I do a good deal of bone marrow transplanting and I had been asked to take a look at several patients who might benefit from that.'

He popped her into the car, got in beside her and drove away.

Eulalia said, 'Oh, I see,' which wasn't very adequate as a reply but it was all she could think of, and she answered his casual enquiry as to her day just as briefly; she hadn't expected to see him again and it had taken her by surprise.

He went straight up to the Colonel's room when they reached the house and when he came down again after ten minutes or so she was in the hall. There wasn't a fire in the drawing room. If he accepted her offer of coffee he would have to drink it in the kitchen; the drawing room would be icy...

He refused her offer. 'I'm leaving for Holland in the morning,' he told her, then he smiled down at her, shook her hand, and was gone.

CHAPTER TWO

JANE came to the kitchen door. 'Gone, has he? Well, it was shepherd's pie for supper; I doubt if he would have fancied that. I'll get a tin of salmon in the house; if he comes again, unexpected, like, I can make fish-cakes.'

Eulalia said quietly, 'No need, Jane; he's going back to Holland in the morning.'

'You'll miss him…'

'I don't really know him, but yes, I shall miss him.'

Which was exactly what Mr van der Leurs had hoped for.

She was pouring tea for the thirsty queue towards the end of Thursday's afternoon clinic when she looked up and saw him. She put the teapot down with a thump and hoped that she didn't look as pleased as she felt; he had, after all, bidden her goodbye without a backward glance…

The queue parted for him to watch and listen with interest.

'I'll be outside the entrance,' he told her, smiled impartially at the queue and went on his way.

''E was 'ere last week,' said a voice. 'Looking at my Jimmy—ever so nice 'e was, too.'

'A friend of yours, miss?' asked another voice.

'An acquaintance,' said Eulalia in a voice which forbade confidences of any sort, her colour somewhat heightened. The queue dissolved, the last few patients were called, she began to clear up, and presently, the hall empty, Sue and Polly gone, she closed down for the day.

The clerk kept her talking when she took the money to the office. He was an elderly man and night duty was a lonely job and she was too kind and polite to show impatience while he talked. Perhaps Mr van der Leurs would think that she didn't intend to meet him. She hadn't said that she would, had she? And if it had been a casual offer made on the spur of the moment, he might not wait.

He was there, leaning against the Bentley's bonnet, oblivious of the chilly evening. He opened the door for her as she reached him and got in beside her.

'Could we go somewhere for a cup of coffee? I haven't much time…'

'You can have coffee at home—' began Eulalia, and was cut short by his curt,

'There's a café in the Fulham Road; that is the quickest way.'

She said tartly, 'If you are so pressed for time you had no need to give me a lift.'

He didn't answer but drove through the city. The café he ushered her into was small and half empty. He sat her down at a table away from the other customers, ordered coffee and observed in a matter-of-fact voice, 'This isn't quite what I intended but it will have to do. I got held up.'

The coffee came and Eulalia took a sip. 'I thought you were in Holland.'

'I was; I came over on the fast ferry this afternoon. I must go back on the ferry from Dover in a couple of hours' time.'

'You mean you're only here for an hour or two? Whatever for?'

'I wanted to see you and as I'm going to be away for a few days…'

'But you could have seen me at home or at the hospital.'

'Don't interrupt, Eulalia; there isn't time. It is enough to say that I wanted to see you alone.'

He smiled then and sat back, quite at his ease. 'Will you marry me, Eulalia?'

She opened her pretty mouth and closed it again and stared at him, sitting there asking her to marry him in a manner one would use to ask for the sugar.

'No,' said Eulalia.

He didn't look in the least put out. 'There are a dozen reasons why you should say no. Perhaps you will think about them while I'm away and when I see you again we can discuss them.' He smiled at her. 'I shall see you again, you know, and next time we can talk at our leisure. Now I'm afraid I must take you home.'

Eulalia could think of nothing to say; she tried out several sensible remarks to make in her head but didn't utter them. She could, of course, tell him that she didn't want to see him again but somehow she didn't say so. Later she would think of all kinds of clever replies to make but he wouldn't be there to hear them. And she musn't see him again.

He drove the short distance to the Colonel's house, got out and went with her to the door.

'Well, goodbye,' said Eulalia, and offered a hand.

'Not goodbye; we say *tot ziens*.' He shook her hand briefly and opened the door for her.

As he turned away she asked, 'Where are you going?'

'Albania.'

'But that's… Oh, do take care!'

He stood looking down at her for a moment, his eyes half hidden under their heavy lids. Just for a moment Eulalia had let her heart speak for itself.

Driving down to Dover and once on the other side of the Channel, taking the long road home, Mr van der Leurs allowed his thoughts to dwell on a pleasant future.

October became November and brought cold wind and rain and grey skies, none of which lightened Eulalia's mood. Mr van der Leurs had been gone for a week and she worried about him, and although she told herself that he was old enough and large enough to take care of himself she scanned the papers and listened to the news and wished that there was some way of finding out if he was back home…

The Colonel, expressing a wish to see him again, had to be told.

'He'll be back. Miss him, do you, Lally?'

Arranging his bedside table just so for the night, she admitted that she did, kissed him fondly and bade him sleep well.

The Colonel, waiting for sleep, thought contentedly that he had no need to worry about Lally's future; Aderik would take care of it. He drifted off gently and died peacefully as he slept.

Somehow or other Eulalia got through the next few days. There was a great deal to do—not least the nephew to notify. There were no other family but old friends had to be told, notices printed in *The Times* and *Telegraph*, the bank manager, his solicitor informed, arrangements for the funeral made. The nephew arrived after two days, a middle-aged kindly man who needed to be housed and fed.

There was no question of Eulalia leaving the house until she had made her own arrangements, he told her. He had a wife and four children who would be coming to England shortly but the house was large enough— he had no intention of turning her out of her home. She thanked him, liking him for his concern, and listened politely to his plans. He was an artist of some repute and was delighted to return to London; the house was large enough to house his family in comfort, and there were attics which could be turned into a studio.

His wife and children arrived in time for the funeral so that Eulalia, opening rooms again, getting ready for their arrival, had little time to grieve. After the funeral he would return to sort out his affairs but his wife and children would remain.

Tom and Pam couldn't have been kinder to her, and the children, although circumstances had subdued them, brought the house alive. Somehow, the funeral which she had been dreading turned into a dignified and serene occasion, with the Colonel's old friends gathered there, making themselves known to Tom and Pam, shaking Eulalia by the hand, asking about her job, telling her in their elderly voices that she was a pretty girl and wasn't it time she married.

However, there were still the nights to get through; there was time to grieve then and wonder what the future held for her. She would have to leave the house, of course, despite Pam's kind insistence that she could stay as long as she wanted to. But at least Jane's future was safe; she was to remain as housekeeper.

The Colonel had left Eulalia his small capital—enough to supplement her wages so that she could rent somewhere. But London was expensive; she would have to find somewhere nearer the hospital and even then she would be eating into her bank balance with little chance of saving. Perhaps she should move away from London, find a job in a small town where she could live cheaply…

She was on compassionate leave from her work but she continued to get up early to go down to the kitchen and help Jane. Still in her dressing gown, her hair hanging tangled down her back, she made tea for them both, laid the breakfast table, fed Dickens and cut the bread while Jane made porridge and collected bacon, eggs and mushrooms.

The new owners of the house enjoyed a good breakfast and Jane, now that she had a generous housekeeping allowance, was happy to cook for hearty eaters. After the skimping and saving she and Eulalia had lived with, it was a treat to use her cooking skills once more. And her future was secure. The one thing which troubled her was Miss Lally, brushing aside her worried questions as to where she was to go and how she would manage, assuring her that she would have no trouble in finding a nice little flat and making lots of friends.

She looked across at Eulalia now, a worried frown on her elderly face. She was beautiful even in that elderly dressing gown with her hair anyhow, but she was pale and too thin. She said, 'Miss Lally…' and was interrupted by the front door knocker being thumped.

'Postman's early,' said Eulalia, and went to open it.

Mr van der Leurs stood there, looking larger than ever in the dim light of the porch lamp.

Eulalia stared up at him, burst into tears and flung herself into his arms. He held her close while she sobbed and snuffled into his cashmere overcoat, unheeding of the early morning wind whistling around them. But when she had no more tears, sucking in her breath like a child, he swept her into the house, shut the door and offered her his handkerchief, still with one arm around her.

'Grandfather died,' said Eulalia into his shoulders. 'I'm sorry I've cried all over you but, you see, I didn't know it was you and I was so glad...'

A muddled speech which Mr van der Leurs received with some satisfaction. 'Tell me about it, Eulalia.' He propelled her gently into the kitchen, nodded pleasantly to an astonished Jane and sat Eulalia down at the table.

'You don't object to me coming into your kitchen? Eulalia is rather upset. If I might just stay and hear what has happened...'

'It's a blessing that you've come, sir.' Jane was already pouring boiling water into a teapot. 'You just sit there for as long as you like and don't mind me.'

So he pulled out a chair and sat down beside Eulalia. Nothing would ever dim her beauty, he reflected: tousled hair, pink nose, childish sniffs and wrapped in a garment which he supposed was a dressing gown, cut apparently with a knife and fork out of a sack. He asked quietly, 'When did the Colonel die, Eulalia?'

She gave a final sniff and sipped some tea and told him. Her voice was watery but she didn't cry again and he didn't interrupt her. Only when she had finished he said gently, 'Go and get dressed, Eulalia. Tell Tom that you are going out to have breakfast with me and will be back later.'

When she hesitated he added, 'I'm sure Jane thinks that is a good idea.'

Jane said at once, 'Just what she needs—to get away from us all for a bit, talk about it, make a few plans.'

She gave Mr van der Leurs a sharp look and he smiled. 'Just so, Jane!'

Lally went to the door. She turned round when she reached it. 'You won't go away?'

He got up and opened the door for her. 'No, I won't go away, but don't be long; I'm hungry.'

A remark which made everything seem perfectly normal. Just as it seemed perfectly normal to find the Bentley outside. It was only as they were driving through the early morning traffic that Eulalia asked, 'How long have you been back?'

'I got to Schiphol late last night, went home and got the car and took the late night ferry from Ostend.'

'But you haven't been to bed. You haven't got to go to St Chad's and work...?'

'No. No, I wanted to see you.'

She said faintly, 'But don't you want to get some sleep?'

'Yes, but there are several things I want to do first. We'll go to Brown's and have breakfast.'

It seemed that he was known there. The doorman welcomed them with a cheerful 'Good morning', summoned up someone to park the car and held the door open for them. It was quiet, pleasantly warm inside and for the moment free of people. They sat at a table by a window and an elderly waiter assured them that the porridge was excellent and did they fancy kedgeree?

It wasn't until they were eating toast and marmalade and another pot of coffee had been brought that Mr van der Leurs made any attempt at serious conversation. Only when she asked him how long he would be in London did he tell her that he would be returning to Holland that evening.

When she protested, 'But you can't—you've not been to bed; you must be tired,' he only smiled.

One or two people had come to eat their breakfasts, exchanging polite 'Good mornings' and opening their newspapers. Eulalia leaned across the table, anxious not to be heard.

'Why have you brought me here?'

'To eat breakfast,' he said promptly, and smiled when she said crossly,

'You know that isn't what I mean.'

He said, suddenly serious, 'You know that if I had known about the Colonel I would have come at once?'

'Yes. I don't know quite how I know that, but I do.'

'Good. Eulalia, will you marry me?'

'You asked me once already…'

'In somewhat different circumstances. Your grand-father knew of my intentions and thought it was a good idea.'

She stared at him. 'After I told you I wouldn't…'

'Yes.'

'You mean you were going to ask me again?'

'Of course.' He sounded matter-of-fact. 'Shall we go for a walk and talk about it?'

When she nodded, he added, 'I'll book a table for lunch here. I'll drive you back on my way to the ferry afterwards.'

It was as if he had lifted all her worries and doubts onto his own shoulders, she reflected.

They walked to Hyde Park. There were few people there: dog owners and joggers and a few hardy souls who had braved the chilly November morning. Mr van der Leurs hardly spoke and Eulalia, busy with her chaotic thoughts, hardly noticed. They had walked the length of the Serpentine before he said, 'It is high time that I married, Eulalia, but until I met you I hadn't given it much thought. I need a wife—a professional man does—but I want a friend and a companion too, someone sensible enough to see to my home, to be a hostess to my friends, and cope with the social side of my life. You know nothing of me but if we marry you may have all the time you wish for to get to know me.'

Eulalia said gravely, 'But doesn't love come into it?'

'Later, and only if you wish it...'

'You mean you would be quite happy to have me as—as a friend until I'd got used to you?'

He hid a smile. 'Very neatly put, Eulalia; that is just what I mean. And now let us look at the practical side. You have no home, no money and no prospects, whereas I can offer you a home, companionship and a new life.'

He stopped walking and turned her round to face him. 'I promise you that I will make you happy.'

She looked up into his face. 'I believe you,' she told him, 'but have you considered that you might meet a woman you could fall in love with?'

'Yes, I have thought about that too. I am thirty-eight, my dear; I have had ample time in which to fall in love a dozen times—and out again.'

'I've never been in love,' she told him. 'Oh, I had teenage crushes on film stars and tennis players but I never met any young men once I'd left school and gone to live with Grandfather. I know almost everyone at St Chad's. But I'm just the canteen lady; besides, I'm twenty-seven.'

Mr van der Leurs restrained himself from gathering

her into his arms and hugging her. Instead he said, 'It
is obvious to me that we are well suited to each other.'

He took her arm and walked on. Since he was obviously waiting for her to say something, Eulalia said,
'You asked me to marry you. I will.'

And she added, 'And if it doesn't work out you
must tell me...'

He stopped once more and this time took her in his
arms and kissed her gently, a very light, brief kiss.
He said, 'Thank you, Eulalia.'

They walked on again with her arm tucked under
his. Presently he said, 'I shall be away for several days
after which I can arrange for a day or so to be free.
Would you consider marrying by special licence then?
I know it is all being arranged in a rush and in other
circumstances I wouldn't have suggested it. But I can
see no good reason for you to remain any longer than
you must at Tom's house. I'm sure he would never
suggest that you should leave before you are ready
but you can't be feeling too comfortable about it.'

'Well, no, I'm not. Tom is very kind and so is Pam
but I'm sure they'll be glad to see me go. I shall miss
Jane...'

'Is she also leaving? She may come with you, if
you wish.'

'Tom has asked her to stay as housekeeper and she
has agreed. She's lived there for years.'

They were retracing their steps. She glanced up at
him and saw how tired he was. She said warmly, 'I'll

be ready for whatever day you want us to marry. Must I do anything?'

'No… I'll see to everything. If you would give me the name of your local clergyman and his church, as soon as everything is settled I'll let you know.' He added, 'It will be a very quiet wedding, no brides-maids and wedding gown, no guests…'

'I wouldn't want that anyway. It would be a sham, wouldn't it? What I mean is we're marrying for…' She sought for words. 'We're not marrying for the usual reasons, are we?'

He reflected that his reasons were the same as any man in love but he could hardly say so. He said merely, 'I believe that we shall be happy together. And now let us go back and have our lunch…'

They had the same table and the same waiter—a dignified man who permitted himself a smile when Mr van der Leurs ordered champagne.

'The lobster Thermidor is to be recommended,' he suggested.

So they ate lobster and drank champagne and talked about this and that—rather like a married couple who were so comfortable in each other's company that there was no need to say much. Eulalia, spooning Charlotte Russe, felt as though she had known Aderik all her life, which was exactly what he had intended her to think. She liked him and she trusted him and in time she would love him but he would have to have patience…

He drove her back to the house presently and spent ten minutes talking to Tom before leaving. He bade Eulalia goodbye without wasting time and drove away, leaving her feeling lonely and all of a sudden uncertain.

'What you need,' said Pam, 'is a cup of tea. We're delighted for you—Tom and I would never have turned you out, you know, but you're young and have your own life and he seems a very nice man. I'm sure you'll be happy. What shall you wear?'

'Wear?'

'For the wedding, of course.'

'I haven't any clothes—I mean, nothing new and suitable.'

'Well, I don't suppose you'll need to buy much; your Aderik looks as though he could afford to keep a wife. Tom told me that his uncle has left you a little money. Spend it, dear; he would have wanted you to be a beautiful bride.'

'But it'll be just us…'

'So something simple that you can travel in and wear later on. You go shopping tomorrow; he might be back sooner than you think and you must be ready.'

So the next morning Eulalia went to the bank and, armed with a well-filled purse, went shopping. It wasn't just something in which to be married that she needed; she was woefully short of everything. She went back at the end of the day, laden with plastic bags, and there were still several things which she must have. But she was satisfied with her purchases: a wool coat with a matching crêpe dress in grey and a little hat in velvet to go with them, a jersey dress, and pleated skirt and woolly jumpers and silk blouses, sensible shoes and a pair of high-heeled court shoes to go with the wedding outfit.

Tomorrow she would get a dressing gown and undies from Marks & Spencer. The question of something pretty to wear in case Aderik took her out for an evening was a vexatious one. She had spent a lot of money and there wasn't a great deal left, not sufficient to buy the kind of dress she thought he might like—plain and elegant and a perfect fit. She had seen such a dress but if she bought it it would leave her almost penniless and she had no intention of asking Aderik for money the moment they were married.

This was a tricky problem which was fortunately solved for her. Tom and Pam gave her a cheque for a wedding present, explaining that they had no idea what to give her. 'I'm sure Mr van der Leurs has everything he could possibly want, so spend it on yourself, Lally.'

It was a handsome sum, more than enough to buy the dress, and what was left over she could spend on something for Aderik and tell him it was from Tom and Pam.

Trying the dress on, Eulalia smiled at her reflection in the long mirror. It was exactly right; the colour of old rose, silk crêpe, its simple lines clinging to her splendid shape in all the right places. Perhaps she would never wear it; she had no idea if Aderik had a social life but it would be there, hanging in her wardrobe, just in case...

She displayed it to Tom, Pam and Jane, and packed it away in the big leather suitcase which had belonged to her grandfather. She was quite ready now. Aderik hadn't phoned or written but she hadn't expected him to do so. He was a busy man; he had said that he would let her know when he was coming and it never entered her head to doubt him.

He phoned that evening, matter-of-fact and casual. He would be with her in two days' time and they were to marry on the following morning and travel back to Holland that evening. 'You are well?' he wanted to know. 'No problems?'

'No, none, and I'm quite ready. The Reverend Mr Willis phoned to say he was coming to see me this evening. I don't know why.'

'I asked him to. I don't want you to have any doubts, Eulalia!'

'Well, I haven't, but it will be nice to talk to him. I've known him a long time.'

'I'll see you shortly. I'm not sure what time I'll get to London.'

'I'll be waiting. You're busy? I won't keep you. Goodbye, Aderik.'

She could have wished his goodbye to have been a little less brisk…

Mr Willis came that evening; they had known each other for a number of years and it pleased her that he was going to marry them. 'I would have liked to have met your future husband before the wedding, Lally, but in the circumstances I quite understand that it is not possible. We had a long talk over the phone and I must say I was impressed. You are quite sure, aren't 'you? He has no doubts but perhaps you have had second thoughts?'

'Me? No, Mr Willis. I think we shall be happy together. Grandfather liked him, you know. And so do I…'

'He will be coming the day after tomorrow? And I understand you will be returning to Holland on the day of the wedding?'

'Yes, it all seems rather a scramble, doesn't it? But he has commitments at the hospital which he must keep and if we don't marry now, in the next day or so, he wouldn't be free for some time. Tom and his wife have been very kind to me but you can understand that I don't want to trespass on their hospitality for longer than I must.'

'Quite so. Both you and Mr van der Leurs are old enough not to do anything impetuous.'

Eulalia agreed, reflecting that buying the rose-pink dress had been impetuous. She didn't think that Mr van der Leurs had ever been impetuous; he would think seriously about something and once he had decided about it he would carry out whatever it was in a calm and unhurried manner…

Mr Willis went away presently after a little talk with Tom, and Eulalia went upstairs and tried on the pink dress once more…

Mr van der Leurs arrived just before midnight. Tom and Pam had become worried when he didn't arrive during the day but Eulalia was undisturbed. 'He said he would be here today, so he'll come. It may be late, though. You won't mind if I stay up and see him? We shan't have time to talk in the morning.'

So she sat in the kitchen with Dickens for company and everyone else went to bed. She had the kettle singing on the Aga and the coffee pot keeping warm. If he was hungry she could make sandwiches or make him an omelette. The house was very quiet and she had curled up in one of the shabby armchairs, allowing her thoughts to wander.

She had lived with the Colonel ever since she had been orphaned, gone to school, lived a quiet life, had friends, gone out and about until her grandfather had lost most of his money. It had been tied up in a foreign bank which had gone bankrupt. He had then been stricken with arthritis of such a crippling nature that there was little to be done for him. It was then that she had found a job. She supposed that if Aderik hadn't wanted to marry her she would have stayed there for the rest of her working life, living in a bed-sitter, unwilling to accept Tom's offer of help.

'I'll be a good wife. It will be all right once I know more about him. And we like each other.' She addressed Dickens, sitting in his basket, and he stared at her before closing his eyes and going to sleep again.

He opened them again at the gentle knock on the door and Eulalia went to open it.

Mr van der Leurs came in quietly, dropped a light kiss on her cheek and put down his bag and his overcoat. 'I've kept you from your bed, but I couldn't get away earlier.'

'I wasn't sleepy. Would you like a meal? Come into the kitchen.'

'Coffee would be fine. I won't stay; I just wanted to make sure that everything was all right.'

She was warming milk. 'Have you got somewhere to stay?'

'Brown's. I'll be at the church at eleven o'clock. I've booked a table at Brown's for all of us afterwards. I arranged that with Tom. We can collect your luggage from here later and be in plenty of time for the evening ferry.'

'And when we get to Holland will you be able to have a few days' holiday?'

'A couple of days. You won't see a great deal of me, Eulalia, but as soon as it's possible I'll rearrange my work so that I can be home more often.'

They sat opposite each other at the table, not saying

much. She could see that he was tired and she was pleasantly sleepy. Presently he got up, put their mugs tidily in the sink and went with her to the door, put on his coat and picked up his bag. Then he stood for a minute, looking down at her.

He had no doubts about his feelings for her; he had fallen in love with her and he would love her for ever. Now all he needed was patience until she felt the same way.

He bent and kissed her, slowly and gently this time. 'Sleep well, my dear.'

She closed the door behind him and went up to her room and ten minutes later was asleep, her last thoughts happy ones.

She was wakened by Jane with a breakfast tray.

'Brides always have breakfast in bed, Miss Lally, and Mrs Langley says you are to eat everything and no one will disturb you until you're dressed and ready.'

So Eulalia ate her breakfast and then, since it was her wedding day, took great pains with her hair and her face before getting into the dress and coat, relieved to see that they looked just as nice as they had done when she had bought them. And finally, with the little hat crowning her head, she went downstairs.

They were all there, waiting for her, ready to admire her and wish her well, and presently Pam and Jane and the children drove off to the church, leaving Eulalia and Tom to wait until it was time for him to get his own car from the garage and usher her into the back seat.

'Why can't I sit in the front with you?' asked Eulalia.

'Brides always sit in the back, Lally...'

The church was dimly lit, small and ancient and there were flowers. That much she noticed as they reached the porch. She clutched the little bouquet of roses which Aderik had sent that morning and took Tom's arm as they walked down the aisle to where she could see Mr Willis and Aderik's broad back. There was another man there too. The best man, of course. She dismissed him as unimportant and kept her eyes on Aderik. If only he would turn round...

He did, and gave her a warm, encouraging smile which made everything perfectly all right, and since there was nothing of the pomp and ceremony of a traditional wedding to distract her thoughts she listened to every word Mr Willis said and found them reassuring and somehow comforting. She wondered if Aderik was listening too and peeped up into his face. It was calm and thoughtful, and, reassured, she held out her left hand so that he could slip the ring on her finger.

Leaving the church with him, getting into the Bentley with him, she touched the ring with a careful finger, remembering the words of the marriage service. She had made promises which she must keep...

Mr van der Leurs glanced at her serious face. 'The

advantage of a quiet wedding is that one really listens, don't you agree?'

'Yes. I—I liked it.'

'And you looked delightful; I am only sorry that we have to hurry away so quickly. You still have to meet my best man—an old friend, Jules der Huizma. We see a good deal of each other. He's married to an English girl—Daisy—you'll meet her later and I hope you'll be friends.'

'Do they live near you? I'm not sure where you do live...'

'Amsterdam but I was born in Friesland and my home is there. When I can arrange some free time I'll take you there to meet my family.'

'It's silly really, isn't it? I mean, we're married and I don't know anything about you.'

'True, but you know me, don't you, Eulalia? And that's important.'

She nodded. 'I feel as if I've known you for a very long time—you know? Like very old friends who don't often meet but know how the other one is feeling.'

Mr van der Leurs knew then that he had his heart's desire, or most of it. Perhaps he wouldn't have to wait too long before Eulalia fell in love with him. He would leave no stone unturned to achieve that.

The luncheon party at Brown's hotel was all that a wedding breakfast should be—champagne, lobster patties, chicken à la king, sea bass, salads, red onion tartlets, garlic mushrooms in a cream sauce and then caramelised fruits and ice cream and finally the wedding cake. When it was cut and Eulalia and Aderik's health had been drunk, he made a speech, gave brief thanks and offered regret that they couldn't stay longer and enjoy their friends' company. Then the best man, wishing them well, said he was delighted that he would see more of them in the future.

He seemed nice, thought Eulalia, and wondered why his Daisy wasn't with him—she must remember to ask…

Then it was time to go. She was kissed and hugged and Jane cried a little for they had been through some difficult years together. 'But I'll be back to see you,' said Eulalia. 'Aderik is often over here and I shall come with him.'

She turned and waved to the little group as they drove away. She was leaving a life she knew for an unknown future.

CHAPTER THREE

THEY travelled over to Holland on the catamaran from Harwich and were driving through the outskirts of Amsterdam before midnight. The crossing had been choppy and Eulalia was glad to be on dry land again. The lights of the city were welcoming and she felt a surge of excitement. They hadn't talked much, though Aderik had pointed out the towns they bypassed, but there was no way of seeing them in the dark night.

They had talked about the wedding and he had promised that he would show her as much as possible of Amsterdam before he went back to his usual working day. Now he said, 'I live in the centre of the city; we're coming to a main street—Overtoom—which leads to one of the main squares—Leidseplein—and a little further on I'll turn right onto the Herengracht; that's one of the canals which circle the old part of the city. The house is in a quiet street just off the canal and has been in my family for many years.'

There was plenty to see now. The streets were still bustling with people, cafés were brightly lighted, there were trams and buses and cars. Mr van der Leurs turned into a street running beside a canal bordered by trees and lined with tall narrow houses with steep gables and important-looking front doors.

Eulalia, wide awake by now despite the lateness of the hour, said happily, 'Oh, it's like a painting by Pieter de Hooch...'

'True enough since they might have been painted by him. They knew how to build in those days; all these houses are lived in still.'

He crossed a bridge and turned into a narrow street beside another, smaller canal also lined with trees and a row of gabled houses. The street was short and there was another bridge at its end, too small for cars, spanning yet another canal. It was very quiet, away from the main streets with only the bare trees stirring in the night wind, and as he stopped before the last house Eulalia asked, 'Is this where you live?'

'Yes. Are you very tired? I think that Ko and Katje will be waiting up for us.'

She assured him that she was wide awake as he opened her door and they crossed the street to his front door—a handsome one with an ornate transom above it—and it was now flung open wide as they mounted the two steps from the pavement.

Eulalia hadn't known what to expect. Aderik had scarcely mentioned his home, and she had supposed that it would be a solid, comfortable house, the kind of house she imagined a successful man might live in. But this was something different. She was ushered in and the door was shut behind them before Mr van der Leurs spoke, and that in his own language to the stout, middle-aged man who had admitted them. Then he took her arm. 'Eulalia, this is Ko, who runs our home with his wife. Come and meet everyone.'

She shook hands with Ko who welcomed her in English and then shook hands with his wife, Katje, as stout as her husband, beaming good wishes which Aderik translated. Then there was Mekke, young and buxom, adding her good wishes in hesitant English, and lastly Wim, a small, wizened man 'who has been in the family for as long as I can remember', said Mr van der Leurs. 'He drives the car when I'm not around and sees to the garden.' He looked around him. 'Where is Humbert?'

They had taken the precaution, explained Ko, of putting him in the garden in case *mevrouw* was nervous of dogs.

Aderik looked at her. 'Are you nervous of dogs, Eulalia?'

'No, I like them. May he not come in and meet me? He must be wanting to see you again.'

Ko had understood her and trotted off through a door at the back of the hall.

'*Koffie?*' asked Katje, and trotted after him, taking Mekke and Wim with her.

Mr van der Leurs turned Eulalia round, unbuttoned her coat and cast it on one of the splendid chairs flanking a console table worthy of a museum.

'Then come and meet Humbert.'

He opened a door and led her into a high-ceilinged room with an ornate plaster ceiling, tall narrow windows and a wide fireplace with a great hood above it. There was a splendid fire burning in the fire basket below, adding its light to the sconces on the walls hung with crimson silk. It was a magnificent room and Eulalia stood in the doorway and gaped at it.

But she wasn't allowed to stand and stare. 'This way,' said Aderik, and crossed the floor to another door at the end of the room, opposite the windows. This led to a little railed gallery with steps down to another room. A library, she supposed, for its walls were lined with shelves filled with books and there were small tables and comfortable chairs. But she had no chance to do more than look around her; the room led into a conservatory with a profusion of greenery and elegant cane furniture, and that opened onto the garden, which was narrow and high-walled and surprisingly large.

The dog that rushed to meet them was large too, a great shaggy beast who gave a delighted bark and hurled himself at his master. Then, at a word from Aderik the dog offered a woolly head for her to scratch. Mr van der Leurs switched off the outside lights and closed the door to the garden, then led the way back to the library, through another door in the further wall. Here there was a veritable warren of small rooms until he finally opened the last door which brought them back into the hall.

'Tomorrow,' he assured her, 'you will be given a leisurely tour of the house. You must be tired; come and have a drink and something to eat and Katje will take you to your room.'

The Stoelklok in the hall chimed the hour as they went back into the drawing room where, on a small table by the fire, Ko was arranging a tray of coffee and a plate of sandwiches. Eulalia, half asleep now but excited too, drank her coffee, and, suddenly discovering that she was hungry, ate several sandwiches.

'What time do you have breakfast?'

'Since I am free tomorrow and we have all day before us, would half past eight suit you?'

She nodded. 'What time do you usually breakfast?'

'Half past seven. I walk to the hospital. If I have a list it starts at half past eight. If you would rather have your breakfast in bed that can easily be arranged.'

'I've only ever had breakfast in bed this morning and I like getting up early…'

'Splendid.' He got up and tugged the bell-pull by the fireplace and when Katje came said, 'Sleep well, my dear. I'll see you at breakfast.'

Eulalia got up, longing now for her bed. She lifted her face for his kiss, quick and light on her cheek, and followed Katje up the oak staircase to the landing above. It was ringed by several doors and another staircase but Katje led her to the front of the house and opened a door with something of a flourish.

The room was already lighted and heavy brocade curtains were drawn across the windows. There was a pale carpet underfoot and a Georgian mahogany and satinwood four-poster flanked by mahogany bedside tables faced the windows between which was a satinwood table with a triple mirror. There was a tapestry-covered stool before it and there were two Georgian armchairs on either side of a mahogany tallboy.

Eulalia caught her breath at the room's beauty as Katje bustled past her and opened the door in a wall, revealing a vast closet; she could see her few clothes hanging forlornly there; someone had unpacked already. Another door led to a bathroom, which Katje crossed to open yet another door, revealing a second room, handsomely furnished but simple.

Katje trotted back, smiling and nodding, and went away. Eulalia lost no time in undressing and bathing before tumbling into bed. The splendid room must be explored thoroughly but not tonight. She was asleep as her head touched the pillow.

She woke as Mekke was drawing back the curtains; the girl wished her a good morning and put a tea tray beside her. She said in English, 'Breakfast soon, *mevrouw*,' and went away. There was an ornate green enamel and gilt clock on the tallboy striking eight o'clock as she drank her tea.

Eulalia nipped from her bed and dressed quickly in a skirt, blouse and sweater, wasted time hanging out of the window in the cold morning air to view the quiet street outside and the canal beyond, then hurried downstairs. The house was alive with cheerful, distant voices and Humbert's deep bark as she reached the hall, uncertain where to go.

Aderik opened a door and then crossed the hall to her, kissed her cheek and wished her a good morning. 'You slept well? Come and have breakfast.'

He ushered her into a small room, very cosy with a small table laid ready for them, and Humbert came prancing to have his head scratched and grin at her.

Eulalia found her voice. 'What a dear little room. Did I see it last night?'

'We came through it but I doubt whether you saw it; you were asleep on your feet, weren't you?'

He smiled at her and pulled out a chair for her before sitting down himself. 'There's tea or coffee; you must let Ko know which you prefer to have.' He added kindly, 'It's all strange, isn't it? But you'll soon find your feet.'

Eulalia said slowly, 'I have the feeling that I shall wake up presently and find that none of this is happening.'

She buttered toast. 'It all happened so quickly...'

'Indeed it did, but now you can have all the time you want to adjust—it is merely that you will be doing it after we are married and not before. I imagine that you would have given your future a good deal of thought if we had waited to marry. You may still do so, Eulalia, and I hope that if you have doubts or problems you will tell me.'

'Yes, I will but I shan't bother you more than I

must for you must be very occupied. What else do you do besides operating?'

'I have an outpatients clinic once a week, ward rounds, private patients at my consulting rooms, consultations—and from time to time I go over to St Chad's and occasionally to France or Germany.'

He saw the look on her face. 'But I am almost always free at the weekends and during the week there is the odd hour...'

Waiting for Eulalia in the hall presently, he watched her coming down the stairs. She was wearing a short jacket and no hat; a visit to a dress shop would have to be contrived; a warm winter coat was badly needed and some kind of a hat. It was obvious to him that his dearest Lally was sorely in need of a new wardrobe. He said nothing; he was a man who had learned when to keep silent. In answer to her anxious enquiry he merely assured her that Humbert had had a long walk before breakfast.

'We will come home for lunch and take him for a walk in one of the parks,' he suggested. 'But now I'll show you something of Amsterdam.'

Mr van der Leurs loved his Amsterdam; his roots went deep for a long-ago ancestor had made a fortune in the Indies—a fortune which his descendants had prudently increased—and built himself the patrician house in the heart of the city. The house in which he had been born and grown to manhood. He had left it for long periods—medical school at Leiden, years at

Cambridge, a period of Heidelburg—but now he was firmly established in his profession, making a name for himself, working as a consultant at St Chad's, travelling from time to time to other countries to lecture or examine or attend a consultation.

He wanted Eulalia to love Amsterdam too and, unlike the tours arranged for sightseers, he walked her through the narrow streets away from the usual sights. He showed her hidden canals away from the main *grachten*, old almshouses, houses built out beside the canals so that their back walls hung over the water. He showed her churches, a street market, the flower barges loaded down with colour, gave her coffee in a crowded café where men were playing billiards and the tables were covered with red and white checked cloths, and then wove his way into the elegant streets where the small expensive dress shops were to be found.

Before one of those plate-glass windows he paused. 'The coat draped over that chair...it would suit you admirably and you will need a thick topcoat; it can be so cold here in the winter. Shall we go inside and see if you like it?'

He didn't wait for her to answer but opened the door. Five minutes later Eulalia and he returned to the pavement and this time she was wearing the coat. It was navy blue cashmere and a perfect fit, while on her head was a rakish little beret. The jacket, the friendly saleslady had promised, would be sent to the house.

Eulalia stood in the middle of the pavement, regardless of passers-by. 'Thank you, Aderik,' she said. 'It's the most beautiful thing I've ever possessed.' Her eyes searched his quiet face. 'I—I haven't many clothes and they're not very new.' She looked away for a moment and then gave him a very direct look. 'I hope you're not ashamed of me?'

Mr van der Leurs realised the danger ahead. He said in a matter-of-fact voice, 'You look elegant in anything you wear, my dear, and you are beautiful enough to wear a sack and still draw interested glances. And no, I am not ashamed of you, but I don't want you catching cold when all that are needed are warmer clothes.'

He took her arm and walked on. 'I think that you must get a few things before winter really sets in.'

Put like that, it seemed a sensible suggestion. He glanced down at her face and saw with satisfaction the look of delighted anticipation on it.

They went back to a main street and caught a tram. It was in two sections and both of them were packed. Eulalia stood with his arm around her, loving every minute of it, and then scrambled off when they reached the point where the street intersected the Herengracht. They walked back home from there so that she could find her way back on her own.

They lunched in the small room where they had

breakfasted with Humbert sitting between them, happy now that they were home, knowing that presently he would be taken for a walk.

They went to Vondel Park, a long walk which took them past the Rijksmuseum and through a tangle of small streets to the park. Here Humbert raced to and fro while they walked the paths briskly in the teeth of a cold wind.

'Tomorrow we will take the car,' said Mr van der Leurs cheerfully, 'so that you may get a glimpse of Holland. This is not the time of year to see it, of course, but the roads will be empty and we can cover a good deal of ground. You know of St Nikolaas, of course? You must see him with Zwarte Piet riding through the streets. It was once a great day but now we celebrate Christmas much as you do in England. All the same, we exchange small presents and the children have parties.'

He turned her round smartly and started the walk back to the park's gates. 'And after St Nikolaas there will be parties and concerts and the hospital ball and the family coming for Christmas.'

'The family?' asked Eulalia faintly. 'You have a large family?'

'Mother, brother and sisters, nieces and nephews, scattered around the country.'

'You didn't tell me. Do they know you have married me?'

'Yes, and they are delighted. I should have mentioned it; it quite slipped my mind.'

She didn't know whether to laugh or be angry. 'But you should have told me; I might have changed my mind...'

'No, no. You married me, not my family. You'll like them. We don't see much of each other but we like each other.'

'This is a ridiculous conversation,' said Eulalia severely.

He tucked her hand under his arm. 'Yes, isn't it? Let us go home for tea and then I must do some work, much though I regret that. You can make a list of your shopping while I'm doing that and I'll tell you where the best shops are.'

They had tea in the drawing room by the fire—English tea and crumpets.

'Can you get crumpets here?' asked Eulalia, licking a buttery finger.

'There is a shop which sells them, I believe. We don't, as a nation, have afternoon tea, only if we go to a café or tea room.'

'Am I going to find life very different here?'

He thought for a moment. 'No, I think not. You will soon have friends, and there are any number of English living here. I shall take you to the hospital and introduce you to my colleagues there and their wives will invite you for coffee.'

'Oh—but not before I've got some new clothes...'

'No, no. In any case I shall be away for a couple of days next week; I have to go to Rome.'

'Rome? To operate?'

'To examine students. Ko will take care of you.'

He had sounded casual and for some reason she felt hurt. Surely she could have gone with him or he could have refused to go?

An unreasonable wish, she realised.

He went away to his study presently and she found pencil and paper and made a list of the clothes she might need. The list got longer and longer and finally she became impatient with it and threw it on the table by her chair. What was the use of making a list if she had no idea of how much money she could spend?

She curled up in her chair and went to sleep. It had been an active day and, besides that, her thoughts were in a muddle.

When she awoke Aderik was sitting on a nearby chair with Humbert pressed close to him, reading the list.

He glanced at her and finished his reading. 'You will need more than two evening frocks and a good handful of what my sisters call little dresses. There will be coffee mornings and tea parties. You'll need a raincoat and hat—there's a Burberry shop.'

He took out his pen and added to the list. 'If you'd rather not go alone Ko will go with you, show you where the best shops are and wait while you shop.'

'The best man,' said Eulalia. 'You said he had a wife—Daisy…'

'They had a son two weeks ago. When I get back from Rome we'll go and visit them. I dare say she will go shopping with you if you would like that.'

'If she could spare the time, I would.'

'We will have a day out tomorrow, if you would like that, but will you come to church with me after breakfast?'

'Yes, of course I will. Is it that little church we pass on the way here?'

'Yes; there is service at nine o'clock. I think you may find it not so very different from your own church.'

Eulalia, standing beside him in the ancient, austere little church, reflected that he was quite right. Of course she couldn't understand a word but somehow that didn't matter. And afterwards the *dominee* and several people gathered round to meet her, making her feel instantly at home. That Aderik was well liked and respected among the congregation was obvious, and it struck her anew how little she knew about him.

They went back home for coffee and then, with Humbert on the back seat, set off on their tour.

Mr van der Leurs, a man of many parts, had planned the day carefully. He took the road to Apeldoorn and then by side roads to Zwolle and then north for another twenty miles to Blokzijl, a very small town surrounding a harbour on the inland lakes of the region. It was hardly a tourist centre but the restaurant by the lock was famous for its food. He parked the car and as Eulalia got out she exclaimed, 'Oh, how Dutch! Look at the ducks and that little bridge over the lock.'

She beamed up at him. 'This is really Holland, isn't it?'

'Yes. In the summer there are yachts going to and fro and it can be crowded. Would you like to have lunch here?'

'Oh, yes, please…'

They had a table in a window overlooking the lock in a room half full of people, and Eulalia, with one eye on the scene outside, discovered that she was hungry and ate prawns, grilled sole and Charlotte Russe with a splendid appetite, listening to Aderik's gentle flow of conversation, feeling quietly happy.

They didn't hurry over their meal but presently they drove on, still going north in the direction of Leeuwarden, driving around the lakes and then to Sneek and Bolsward before bypassing Leeuwarden and crossing over to North Holland on the other side of the Ijsselmeer. The dyke road was almost empty of traffic, just over eighteen miles of it, and Mr van der Leurs put his well-shod foot down. Eulalia barely had time to get her bearings before they were on land again, and making for Alkmaar.

They stopped for tea then but they didn't linger

over it. 'I'm going to take the coast road as far as Zandvoort. If it's not too dark we'll take a look at the sea.'

The road was a short distance from the sea but very soon he turned off to Egmond aan Zee, a small seaside town, very quiet now that it was winter. He parked the car and together they went down to the beach. It was dusk now, with a grey sky and a rough sea. Eulalia could see the sands stretching away north and south into the distance. 'You could walk for miles,' she said, then added, 'I like it; it's lonely…'

'Now it is. In the summer the beach is packed.'

He took her arm. 'Come, it will be dark very soon. We'll be home in half an hour.'

It was quite dark by the time they got home, to sit by the fire and then eat their supper while Aderik patiently answered her questions about everything she had seen during the day.

It was lovely, she reflected, sitting there in the beautiful drawing room with Aderik in his chair and Humbert sprawled between them. Despite the grandeur of the room, she felt as though she belonged. She was sleepy too and presently he said, 'Go to bed, my dear; we've had quite a long day.'

'When do you have to go tomorrow?'

'I must leave the house by half past seven.'

'May I come and have breakfast with you? You won't mind if I'm in my dressing-gown?'

'That would be delightful. Shall I tell Mekke to call you at seven o'clock?'

'Yes, please, and thank you for a lovely day.' They went to the door together. 'I feel as though I've been here for years and years.' She gave a little laugh, 'That's silly, isn't it? We've only been married a couple of days.'

He smiled and kissed her cheek. 'Sleep well.'

The house was quiet when she went down in the morning but there were lights on in the dining room and a shaded lamp in the hall. She slid into her chair opposite Aderik, wished him 'Good morning' and told him not to get up. She was wearing the same worthy dressing gown, he saw at once, and her hair was hanging down her back and she was flushed with sleep and very beautiful. He hoped it wouldn't be too long before she fell in love with him...

She asked about his trip and he answered her briefly, promising to phone her that evening. When he got up to go his goodbye was cheerful and brief; nothing of his longing to stay with her showed in his face, which was very calm. She had been happy with him during their two days together: he had seen that in her expressive face—now she would be alone and have time to think about them and realise how happy they had been—and miss him.

It was a gamble, and Mr van der Leurs wasn't a gambling man. But he had faith in his own judgement and a great deal of patience.

He said, 'Ko will take care of you,' and kissed her swiftly, leaving her standing in the hall feeling quite lost.

But not for long. When she came down presently, dressed and ready for the day ahead, Ko was waiting for her. He handed her an envelope and went away to fetch some coffee and she sat down and opened it. There was a great deal of money inside. There was a note too from Aderik. 'Buy as much as you want; if you need more money, ask Ko who will know where to get it.'

She began counting the notes. It seemed like a fortune; she would have to make another list and plan what she could buy. Whatever she did buy would have to be of the best quality. Her coat was of the finest cashmere and she guessed expensive, but Aderik hadn't quibbled over its price. Whatever she bought must match it. She stowed the money away carefully and, seen on her way by a fatherly Ko, left the house.

Years of penny-pinching had taught her to be a careful shopper and that stood her in good stead now, as she stifled an impulse to enter the first elegant boutique she saw and buy everything which might take her fancy. Instead she sought out some of the bigger stores, inspecting their windows, and presently chose one bearing a resemblance to one of the fashion houses in London and went inside.

She had made a wise choice; the underwear department had everything a well-dressed girl would want. She choked over the prices but even though Aderik was never likely to see her purchases she would feel right. And there was no reason why he shouldn't see a dressing gown—she bought a pink quilted silk garment almost too charming to keep hidden in the bedroom and added it to the pile of silk and lace.

When she had paid for them and asked for them to be delivered to the house, there was still a great deal of money left…

Aderik had told her to buy a Burberry. She found the shop, bought it and added a matching rain hat, paid for those too and arranged to have them delivered. With the bit firmly between her teeth, she went in search of the boutique where Aderik had bought her coat.

The saleslady recognised her at once. She was alone? she enquired of Eulalia. 'Perhaps *mevrouw* is looking for something special to wear of an evening, ready for the festive season?'

'Well, yes, but first I'd like to see some dresses for the day. Thin wool or jersey?'

'I have just the thing.' The saleslady raised her voice and said something unintelligible to a young girl hovering at the back of the boutique, who sped away and returned presently with several dresses.

'A perfect size twelve,' said the saleslady in her more or less fluent English, 'and a figure to make other women envious, *mevrouw*. Try this jersey dress, such a good colour—we call it mahogany—very simple in cut but elegant enough to wear later in the day.'

An hour later, Eulalia left the boutique, considerably lighter in purse but possessed of a jersey dress, a cashmere twin set, a tweed suit, its skirt short enough to show off her shapely legs, a dark red velvet dress which she was advised could be worn on any occasion after six o'clock, and a pleated skirt, all of which would be delivered to the house. She had tried on several evening gowns too, uncertain which to buy. It was the saleslady who suggested that perhaps she might like to return when it was convenient and bring her husband with her.

Eulalia had agreed although she doubted if he would have the time or the inclination to go with her, but at least she could describe them to him and he could advise her.

She went home for her lunch then; tomorrow was another day and she needed to sit down quietly and check her list and count her money. But first of all after lunch she would put on her coat again and go with Ko and Humbert to Vondel Park and walk there for an hour while Humbert nosed around happily.

There weren't many people about when they got there for it was cold and the day was closing in but she enjoyed it; Ko had ready answers to all her questions, giving gentle advice, telling her a little about the household's routine.

'And Katje hopes that you will come to the kitchen when you wish; she is anxious that you should know everything. You have only to say when you wish it.'

'I'd like that very much, Ko. When is the best time? I mean, Katje has her work to do.'

'That is thoughtful of you, *mevrouw*. Perhaps in the afternoon after lunch?'

'Tomorrow? You will be there, Ko, to translate…?'

'Naturally, *mevrouw*. Now it is time for us to return.'

The parcels and boxes had been delivered while they had been in the park; Eulalia had her tea by the fire and then went upstairs and unpacked everything and put them in drawers and cupboards. She would go to bed early, she decided, and try on everything then.

It was as she was sitting in the drawing room with Humbert pressed up against her that she began to feel lonely. The excitement of shopping had kept her thoughts busy all day but now she wished that Aderik was there. Even if he was working in his study, just to know that he was at home would be nice. They really got on very well, she reflected. Of course they had to get to know each other, and since it seemed that he was away from home a good deal that may take some time. In the meantime she must learn her way around and be the kind of wife he wished for. He would be home again tomorrow—late in the evening, he had said, but she would wait up for him as any good wife would.

He phoned later that evening and she gave a sigh of relief at the sound of his voice.

'You have had a happy day?' he wanted to know.

She told him briefly. It would have been nice to have described her shopping to him in some detail but after a day's work he might not appreciate that. 'I've had a lovely day and Ko took me and Humbert to Vondel Park this afternoon. Have you been busy?'

'Yes. I shall have to stay another day, I'm afraid. I'll ring you tomorrow and let you know at what time I'll be home.'

She tried to keep the disappointment out of her voice. She said, 'Take care, won't you?'

'Yes, and you too. *Tot ziens.*'

It was raining the next morning but that couldn't dampen Eulalia's determination to do some more shopping. In the Burberry and the little hat she went in search of boots and shoes. She had seen what she wanted on the previous day in a shop in the Kalverstraat—boots, soft leather with a sensible heel, and plain court shoes, black, and, since she could afford it, brown as well. She would need more than these but the boots were expensive and she needed gloves...

Her purchases made, she went into a café and ordered coffee and then walked home, getting lost on the way. Not that she minded; she was bound to miss her way until she had lived in Amsterdam for some time. She had a tongue in her head and everyone seemed to speak English...

After lunch she went to the kitchen and sat down at the big scrubbed table with Ko and Katje. It was a room after her own heart, with a flagstone floor, old-fashioned wooden armchairs on either side of the Aga and a great wooden dresser with shelves loaded with china. There were cupboards too and Katje showed her the pantry, the boot room and the laundry and a narrow staircase behind a door in the wall.

It was a delightful room, and she sat there feeling very much at home, realising that it was her home now.

The afternoon passed quickly, looking into cupboards with Katje, going round the house once more, examining piles of linen stacked in vast cupboards, being shown where the keys of the house were kept, the wine cellar, the little room where Ko kept the silver locked up.

She had her tea presently, had a long telephone talk with Tom and Pam and then had her dinner. Aderik had said that he would phone and she went back to the drawing room to wait for his call. When he did ring it was almost eleven o'clock and he had little to say, only that he would be home in the late afternoon.

Eulalia put the phone down feeling let down and then she told herself that she was being a fool. Aderik had probably had a hard day; the last thing he wanted to do was to listen to her chatter. And he was coming home tomorrow.

Just before she slept she decided to wear the jersey dress. 'It will really be very nice to see him again,' she muttered sleepily. 'I hope he feels the same about me.'

She woke in the night with the terrible thought that he might not like having her for his wife after all but in the sane light of morning she had forgotten it.

CHAPTER FOUR

It WAS wet and cold and very windy in the morning. Eulalia was glad that she had done all the shopping she had planned to do and needed little persuasion from Ko to stay indoors. She peered out at the dismal weather and hoped that Aderik would have a good journey home. It was a pity that he hadn't told her if he was likely to arrive earlier. She got into the jersey dress, did her face with extra care and arranged her hair just so before going to the library to wander round its shelves with Humbert for company. She drank her coffee, going every now and then to look out of the window to see if the Bentley was outside.

There was still no sign of it as she ate her lunch and since sitting around waiting was pointless she set off to explore the house again. This time she went to the very top floor and discovered the attics—two rooms under the gabled roof with tiny windows back and front. They were filled with tables and chairs, old pictures, boxes of china and glass and long-forgotten children's toys. There were great leather trunks too; she hauled on their lids and discovered dresses of a bygone age carefully wrapped in tissue paper.

Someone had left a pinny hanging on a door and

she put it on for the rooms were dusty and sat down on one of the trunks to examine a large box filled with toys, while Humbert, bored, went to sleep on a pile of rugs.

Mr van der Leurs, coming silently into his house, got no further than the hall before Ko came to meet him, took his coat and his overnight case and offered him coffee or a meal. He wanted neither but took his briefcase to his study and asked, '*Mevrouw* is home? It seems very quiet…'

'She was in the library but I believe she went upstairs.' He added, 'Humbert was with her—devoted he is, already.'

Mr van der Leurs went up the staircase; for such a big man he was light on his feet and quiet. He paused on the landing for his ear had caught a faint sound from somewhere above him. He went on up to the next floor and then opened the small door in a wall which led to the narrow stairs to the attics. It was cold up there, for which reason Eulalia had closed the door at the top of the stairs, and as he opened it Humbert hurled himself at him. Mr van der Leurs stood for a moment, the great dog in his arms, staring over his head at Eulalia, getting to her feet, hampered by the armful of dolls she was holding. She put them down carefully, beaming at him.

'Aderik, you're home…' She took off the pinny. 'I meant to be sitting in the drawing room looking welcoming, only you didn't come so I came up here to pass the time and now I'm a bit dusty.'

Words which brought a gleam to his eye but all he said was, 'How very nice you look; is that a new dress?' He crossed the room and kissed her, a friendly kiss conveying nothing of his feelings. 'How delightful it is to be home again.'

'It's almost tea time but would you like a meal? Did you have a good flight and was the visit to Rome successful?'

'Shall we have tea round the fire and I'll tell you about my trip?'

'Oh, please. I'll just put these dolls back...'

They went back down to the drawing room with Humbert at their heels and found Ko arranging the tea tray before the fire. Since Katje had a poor opinion of the meals Mr van der Leurs was offered when he was away from home, there was a splendid selection of tiny sandwiches, hot crumpets in their lidded dish, currant bread and butter and a Madeira cake—Katje considered that she made the finest Madeira cake in Amsterdam.

Over tea and for an hour or more after, he told her where he had been and why, what he had done and where he had stayed. Listening to his quiet voice gave her the pleasant feeling that they had been married for years, completely at ease with each other and like any other married couple.

'I don't need to go to hospital today,' said Aderik.

'Would you like to meet Daisy? Jules will probably be at home too.'

'Yes, please. Jules looked very nice and I'd like to meet Daisy.'

The der Huizmas lived less than ten minutes' walk away and it was bright and cold. Walking through narrow streets, crossing canals by narrow bridges with Humbert walking sedately beside them, Eulalia asked, 'They don't mind Humbert coming too?'

'No, they have a dog—Bouncer; he and Humbert are the greatest of friends.'

As they mounted the steps to the front door Eulalia saw that the house was very similar to Aderik's but she had no time to look around before the door was opened.

'Joop,' Mr van der Leurs greeted the severe-looking man, who stood aside so that they might enter. 'We're expected? Eulalia, this is Joop who runs the house with Jette, his wife.

'My wife, Joop.'

Eulalia offered a hand and watched the severe elderly face break into a smile before he led the way across the hall to a door which was flung open before they reached it.

The girl who came to meet them was small, with no pretensions to good looks, but her smile was lovely.

Aderik gave her a hug and kissed her soundly.

'Daisy, I've brought Eulalia as I promised.' He turned to greet Jules who had followed his wife.

Daisy took Eulalia's hand. 'You're as beautiful as Aderik said you were. I do hope we shall be friends…'

'I'm sure we shall.' Eulalia was kissed in her turn by Jules who took her coat and hat and urged her into the drawing room. All this while Humbert had been sitting, quivering with impatience, and once in the room he went to greet the rather odd-looking dog who came trotting to meet him. 'Bouncer,' explained Daisy.

Jules added, 'A dog of many ancestors but devoted to all of us as well as Humbert. Come and sit by the fire and tell us what you have been doing since you arrived.'

They talked over their coffee and biscuits and then the two men went to Jules's study and the dogs with them.

'So now shall we go and see Julius? He's three weeks old today. He'll be asleep because I've just fed him. Jules's sister's nanny came to help me for a while but I want to look after him myself—and Jules is marvellous with him.'

She led the way upstairs into a large airy room. There was an elderly woman sitting in a chair knitting who smiled and nodded at them as they went in to bend over the cot.

Julius was sleeping, a miniature of his father, and

Daisy said, 'Isn't he gorgeous? We had to call him Julius after Jules's father but it's a nice name, don't you think?'

'Just right for him; he's a lovely boy. You must be so proud of him.'

Eulalia looked at the sleeping baby, thinking she would like one just like him...

Perhaps in a while Aderik would become fond of her—she knew he liked her otherwise he wouldn't have married her, but he treated her as a dear friend and that wasn't the same. He hadn't mentioned love—it was she who had done that and his answer had been almost casual.

Later, on their way back to the house, Eulalia said, 'They're happy, aren't they? Jules and Daisy—how did they meet?'

'Daisy came to Amsterdam to see about some antiques and fell into a canal, and Jules fished her out—they had met in England at her father's antiques shop but I imagine her ducking started the romance.'

'He must love her very dearly—I mean, I don't suppose Daisy looked too glamorous...'

He said evenly, 'I don't imagine that glamour has much to do with falling in love.'

'Well, no, but I should think it might help...'

Next morning they had breakfast together and he left the house directly they had finished, saying he wasn't sure when he would be home. She decided she would go to the shops and get something to do—

knitting or tapestry work. Until she knew some people time would hang heavily on her hands. Of course when Aderik had the time he would introduce her to his family and friends...

A question which was partly settled when he got home that evening.

'It will be the feast of St Nikolaas in a day or two,' he told her. 'You will have seen the shops... St Nikolaas comes to the hospital and perhaps you would like to come and see him? It would be a good opportunity for you to meet some of my colleagues there with their wives and children. It's something of an occasion, especially for the children.'

'I'd like that. What time does he come?'

'Eleven o'clock. I'll come and fetch you about half past ten.' He smiled at her. 'I think you'll enjoy it. The day after tomorrow.'

She saw him only briefly the next day for he left the house directly after breakfast. It was evening before he came home and then after dinner he went to his study. When, feeling peevish, she went to wish him goodnight he made no effort to keep her talking.

At breakfast he reminded her to be ready when he came for her.

'You are sure you want me to come?' She sounded tart and he looked up from the letter he was reading to stare at her.

'Quite sure,' he told her mildly. 'Everyone's looking forward to meeting you.'

Which she decided wasn't a very satisfactory answer.

But she took care to be ready for him and she had taken great pains with her appearance—the new coat, one of the new dresses, the little hat just so on her dark hair, good shoes and handbag. She hoped that she looked exactly as the wife of a respected member of the medical profession should look.

It seemed that she did for when Aderik came into the house he gave her a long, deliberate look and said quietly, 'I'm proud of my wife, Lally.'

She said breathlessly, 'Oh, are you really, Aderik? What a nice thing to say. I'm feeling a bit nervous.'

'No need.' He spoke casually, popped her into the car and drove to the hospital.

Its forecourt was filled with people, mostly children. He parked in the area reserved for the senior consultants and took her into the vast foyer through a side door. There was a crowd round the entrance but there were small groups of people standing and chatting at the back. Eulalia reminded herself that she was no longer the canteen lady and took comfort from Aderik's hand under her elbow and found herself shaking hands with the hospital director and his wife and then a seemingly endless succession of smiling faces and firm handshakes. And Daisy was there with Jules.

'Hello, you do look nice. What did you think of the director and his wife?'

'Friendly; he looks awfully nice and kind and so does his wife.'

'They are. You do know that she is English?' And at Eulalia's surprised look Daisy added, 'Husbands do forget things, don't they? She came over here to nurse, oh, years ago, and they got married and they're devoted to each other. They've got four children, three boys and a girl. Her name's Christina. She's forty-five. She gives lovely dinner parties and we all like her very much.'

She beamed at Eulalia. 'You will be very happy here and Aderik is a dear. We're all so glad that he's found you. You will get asked out a lot, you know.'

The men had joined them and everyone was moving forward to get a good view. St Nikolaas was approaching; they could hear the children shouting and clapping and a moment later Eulalia saw him seated on his white horse, in his bishop's robes, riding into the forecourt with his attendant, Zwarte Piet, running beside him, the sack into which he would put all the naughty children over his shoulder.

The noise was terrific as he got off his horse and stood in the forecourt, an impressive figure who presently addressed his audience in a long speech. Eulalia didn't understand a word but she found it fascinating and when he had finished clapped and cheered as loudly as anyone there.

St Nikolaas came into the foyer then, making his stately way towards the children's wards. He paused

to speak to the director, nodded graciously to everyone as he passed and disappeared into one of the lifts
with the director and his wife.

Aderik took her arm. 'He will be about half an hour
and then he comes back to the courtyard and throws
sweets to the children there. We're going to have
lunch now—another opportunity for you to get to
know everyone.'

He glanced down at her happy face. 'Enjoying it?'

'Oh, yes. Does he go anywhere else?'

'The other hospitals in Amsterdam. Of course there
is a St Nikolaas in every town and village. It's a great
occasion for the children for he leaves presents for
them by the fireplace in their homes and if a grown-
up finds a gift by his plate he mustn't ask who it is
from but thank St Nikolaas for it. Now if you're ready
we'll go and have lunch.'

A buffet had been set up in the consultants' room,
a vast apartment furnished solidly with a great deal
of brown leather and dark wood. Chairs and tables
had been set up and everybody fetched their food and
found places to sit with friends.

Mr van der Leurs piled a plate of food for Eulalia,
settled her at a table with Daisy, the casualty officer's
wife and two younger doctors, promised to be back
shortly and went away. The doctors were friendly,
only too pleased to tell her about St Nikolaas and
Zwarte Piet, and she began to enjoy herself.

Presently they were joined by an older man who

introduced himself as Pieter Hirsoff, one of the anaes-
thetists. He was charming to Eulalia and she responded rather more warmly than she realised. It was
pleasant to be chatted up... When he suggested that
she might like to see one of the many museums in the
city, she agreed readily. 'But not the Rijksmuseum,'
she told him. 'Aderik has promised to take me there.'

'I know just the right one for you—a patrician
house furnished just as it was when it was first built.
It's on one of the *grachten*. Suppose I come for you
tomorrow afternoon? I'm sure you will enjoy it.'

He excused himself then and Eulalia joined in the
general talk, wondering where Aderik had got to.

He came presently with Jules. They had been up to
their wards, they explained, and St Nikolaas was
about to leave.

'I'll drive you home,' he told Eulalia, 'but I must
come back here for a while.'

Daisy said quickly, 'Come back with us, Eulalia,
and have tea. Jules has to come back here and I'd
love a gossip. Aderik can fetch you when he's finished
here.'

So Eulalia went back to the der Huizmas' and had
tea with Daisy and talked about the morning's events.
Baby Julius was brought down to be fed and then lay
placidly sleeping on Eulalia's lap while they discussed
Christmas.

'We go to Jules's family home and so do the rest

of his family. It's great fun. I dare say you'll go to Aderik's family. You haven't met them yet?'

'No. There wasn't much time to arrange anything before we married and Aderik doesn't have much free time.'

'Oh, well,' said Daisy comfortably. 'You'll see them all at Christmas. Now you've met everyone at the hospital you'll make lots of friends, but I hope we'll be friends, real friends, you and me.'

It was later that evening as Eulalia and Aderik sat together after dinner that she told him she was going to spend the afternoon with Dr Hirsoff.

Mr van der Leurs had been reading his paper, but now he put it down.

'Which museum are you going to?' He sounded only mildly interested, and when she told him he said, 'Ah, yes, an interesting place. You liked him?'

'Yes. He's very amusing and easy to talk to.' She looked up sharply. 'You don't like him?'

'My dear girl, what has that to do with it? You are free to choose your friends and I would never stand in your way. We are both, I trust, sensible people, tolerant of each other's tastes and wishes. I hope you will have a very pleasant afternoon.'

He turned a page and returned to his reading, leaving her seething although she had no idea why she was put out. She knew that their marriage wasn't quite like the normal matrimonial state but surely he should show some interest, concern even, in the friends she made.

Pieter Hirsoff came for her after lunch and, since Aderik had phoned to say that he wouldn't be home until the evening and she had spent the morning painstakingly discussing household matters with Katje and Ko, Eulalia was quite ready to enjoy his company. And he was good company, guiding her expertly through the museum and then suggesting that they might have a cup of tea before he drove her home. He took her to a large hotel on the Leidseplein and ordered tea and cakes, and it wasn't until she told him that she would like to go home that he put a hand over hers on the table and smiled across it at her.

'Eulalia, we must meet again. This afternoon has been delightful. We are two lonely people, are we not? My wife doesn't care to live in Amsterdam and Aderik is so engrossed in his work, I doubt if he is home as often as he might be.'

She was too surprised to speak for a moment. She might be twenty-seven years old but there hadn't been much chance to gain worldly experience behind the canteen counter... She quelled a desire to lean over and box his ears; that would never do! He was a colleague of Aderik's. She said in a matter-of-fact voice, 'I'm sorry you're lonely, but I'm not; I'm very happy. Aderik is a marvellous husband and I love living here. I know I shall make lots of friends—his friends too— and I'm sure you'll be one of them. It was kind of you to take me out and I've enjoyed it but now I really must go home.'

'I hope Aderik knows what a treasure he's married.' They were walking to the car. 'I'm a persistent man, Eulalia.'

In the car she said, 'You're being silly now. Aderik and I have only been married for little more than a week; can you not understand that life for us is perfect?'

Which wasn't quite true but surely she would be forgiven for the lie so that she could convince the man? She had thought she liked him, but now she wasn't so sure…

Mr van der Leurs didn't get home until almost dinner time. He came into the drawing room with Humbert, who had gone into the hall to meet him, and bade Eulalia a cheerful hello.

'Did you enjoy your afternoon with Hirsoff?' he wanted to know.

'Since you ask,' said Eulalia tartly, 'I didn't.'

He handed her a drink and asked, still cheerfully, 'Oh? Why not?'

'He got a bit, well, a bit intense…'

'What did you expect? You're a beautiful young woman. It's only logical that he would chat you up.'

She tossed off her sherry. 'What a simply beastly thing to say. And if you knew that he was that kind of a man, why didn't you tell me not to go out with him?'

He had picked up the first of his letters and slit the envelope carefully before he answered.

'When we married—before we married—I told you that you might have all the time you needed to get to know me and settle into your new life. I hope by now that you know that I meant what I said. The fact that we are married and like each other enough to live together doesn't mean that I have any right to dictate to you.'

'You mean that you would never interfere in anything I might want to do or with the friends that I might make?'

'That is what I mean.'

'You don't mind?' she began angrily, and was interrupted by Ko telling them that dinner was served.

After that there was no chance to go on talking about it. Mr van der Leurs, keeping his thoughts to himself, rambled on about this and that, making it impossible for Eulalia to argue with him. After dinner he told her that he had some phone calls to make and it was an hour or more before he came back to sit by the fire with Humbert at his feet.

Eulalia sat with her newly bought tapestry frame before her, stabbing the needle in and out of the canvas, regardless of the havoc she was making. They were quarrelling, she reflected, or rather she was trying to quarrel; Aderik was being most annoyingly placid. She wondered what she would have to do to ruffle that smooth manner. She couldn't think of anything at the moment so she bade him a chilly good-night and went to bed, her dignified exit rather spoilt by the kiss he dropped on her cheek as he opened the door for her.

She took a long time to go to sleep. She would have liked someone to confide in but the only person who would have done nicely was Aderik and he, she had to admit, seemed placidly indifferent, rather like an elder brother who didn't want to be bothered but was tolerant of her.

And how absurd, she reflected, half asleep by now, discussing her doubts and worries with the very person who was causing them.

An opinion that was strengthened at breakfast the next morning; Aderik was his usual amiable self but quite clearly he had neither the time nor the inclination to enter into a serious discussion.

He handed her an envelope addressed to them both. 'An invitation to the Christmas ball in a week's time. The invitation was delayed until we returned here but it was taken for granted that we would accept. Send a note to Christina ter Brandt, will you? It's a grand affair…'

'I haven't a dress…'

'Then we will go and buy one. Tomorrow directly after lunch.'

He was looking through his post. 'There are several invitations to dine and here's a letter for you inviting you to have coffee with Christina…'

He added warmly, 'You'll like her: everyone does.'
He got up. 'I must go—I've a full day ahead of me
so don't expect me until this evening. Why not do
some Christmas shopping? Perhaps you can think of
something to give Katje—and Mekke is getting engaged. I'll see to Ko.'

'And your family?'

'I'll take a morning off and we'll go shopping together.'

He kissed her cheek swiftly as he went.

Leaving her with a great deal to think about. His
family would come to stay at Christmas, he had told
her that, but somehow she hadn't thought any more
about it. Now Christmas was less than three weeks
away; there would be presents to buy and Katje to
consult about meals and rooms. She choked back indignation; he had told her so little…

She sought out Ko. 'Christmas,' she said urgently.
'People will be coming to visit. How long do they
stay, Ko? And do we have a tree and holly and give
presents?'

He assured her that they did. Christmas, he told her
in his careful English, had at one time been a rather
solemn occasion, more a church festival, while St
Nikolaas had been a more important feast. But
Holland had adopted many English customs so that
there would be turkey and Christmas pudding,
a Christmas tree and decorations and the giving of
presents.

'You will wish to consult with Katje, *mevrouw*, and decide on menus and beds for the guests. It will be a relief for *mijnheer* that he has you here to oversee the preparations.'

That evening after dinner, sitting comfortably together, it seemed a good time to her to broach the subject of Christmas.

'There is a great deal I need to know,' she began firmly, 'and I would like you to tell me.'

Mr van der Leurs put down his newspapers, the very picture of an attentive husband. 'Such as?'

'Well, your family. How many are coming to stay and for how long?' A sudden surge of indignation made her voice shrill. 'I know nothing about them.' She added pettishly, 'Probably they won't like me.'

Mr van der Leurs, at his most reasonable, observed, 'How can you say that when you haven't met them?' He saw that she was put out and added in a quite different voice, 'My mother is the kind of mother one hugs and kisses and who offers a cosy shoulder if one wants comforting. My sisters are younger than I am; Marijka is twenty-eight, married and has two children—boys. Lucia is thirty, married, also, with two girls and a boy. Paul is the youngest, twenty-three, in his last year at Leiden. He falls in and out of love so often I've given up trying to remember their names.'

He smiled then. 'Contrary to your expectations, they will like you and you will like them. They will come on Christmas Eve and Katje will be able to ad-

vise you as to where they will sleep and so on. I'll
get a free morning and we'll go shopping together for
presents. I believe that you will find it a Christmas
very much like the celebrations in England.'

She had the lowering feeling that she had been
making a fuss about nothing but there was still something. 'I have to buy a dress for the ball...'

'Tomorrow afternoon,' he reminded her placidly.

Not a very satisfactory conversation, she reflected;
somehow she still felt that she had been making a fuss
about nothing.

She went round the house in the morning with
Katje, deciding which rooms should be made ready
for their guests. There was time enough before
Christmas but she wanted everything to be perfect...

Aderik was home punctually for lunch and while
she went to put on her outdoor things he took
Humbert for a brisk walk.

'And we'll walk too,' he told her. 'It's cold but dry
and quicker than taking the car. Where do you want
to go first?'.

'The boutique where you bought my coat; there
were some lovely dresses...'

She spent a blissful hour trying on one gown after
another. It was hard to decide and she wanted to wear
a dress which Aderik would like. Finally she was left
with a choice between a pearl-grey chiffon which fitted perfectly but was perhaps not quite grand enough,
and a pale pink taffeta with a square neckline, tiny

cap sleeves and a wide skirt. She tried them on again in turn and stood rather shyly while Aderik studied her.

'Have them both,' he decided.

While the saleswoman had gone to supervise their packing, Eulalia said in a whisper, 'But we're only going to one ball...'

'There will be others,' he said. He had got up from the elegant little chair and was wandering around, to stop by a stand upon which a russet velvet dress had been artfully thrown. 'Now, I like that. Will you try it on?'

The saleslady was already at his elbow. 'It is *mevrouw's* size and a perfect colour for her.'

So Eulalia was swept back behind the silk curtains and helped into the velvet dress and, studying her reflection in the long mirror, had to admit that she really looked rather nice in it...

'But when will I wear it?' she wanted to know as they gained the street once more.

'Christmas Day. Now come and help me choose something for my mother...'

Eulalia had coffee with Christina ter Brandt on the following morning. The ter Brandts lived in a large house in a tree-lined road on the outskirts of den Haag. Aderik had told her that when they were first married Duert ter Brandt had been director of the main hospital there but the last few years had seen him holding the same position in Amsterdam. It was more than half an hour's drive between the two cities but neither of them wished to leave their home in den Haag and Duert enjoyed driving.

Aderik had driven her there, going first to the hospital and coming back for her during the morning, and she had worried that he was wasting his time.

'Not when I'm with you, Lally,' he had told her quietly, 'but it might be a good idea if we were to look around for a car for you. Can you drive?'

'No. We never had a car.'

'Then you shall have lessons. I like to drive you myself but there may be occasions when that's not possible.'

He had stayed only a few minutes at the house and Christina had told him that she would be going into Amsterdam to have lunch with Duert and would see Eulalia safely home.

Eulalia enjoyed her morning; Christina was the kind of person one could confide in. Not that she did that but she was sure if she ever needed help or advice Christina would give it without fuss. And during the course of the morning she offered tidbits of information about the small everyday problems Eulalia had encountered.

'Of course Aderik will have told you a great deal but men do tend to overlook the small problems— tipping and tram fares and whether to wear a long or short dress; that kind of thing.'

Which reminded Eulalia to ask about the ball.

'Quite an event,' said Christina. 'Long dresses and any jewellery you can lay hands on...' She glanced quickly at Eulalia's hands, bare save for her wedding ring. 'It's all rather dignified and stately but great fun. You have met quite a few of the wives at the hospital? You'll meet a lot more but you'll only need to smile and murmur. You're rather a nine days' wonder, you know. Aderik's family are coming for Christmas? They always do; they're all delightful so don't worry about meeting them.'

Christina poured more coffee. 'What do you think of the shops in Amsterdam?' she asked, and the conversation moved on.

She drove Eulalia back presently. 'I don't suppose Aderik will be back for lunch? It's been fun meeting you; you must come again and perhaps we can meet Daisy one morning here and have coffee?'

She drove away and Eulalia, warmed by her friendliness, had her lunch and then sat down to write Christmas cards and make a painstaking list of people for whom she would need to buy presents.

It seemed a good idea to go shopping the next day. Aderik would be away until mid-afternoon but if she had an early lunch she would have time to do at least some of her shopping—the children's presents, perhaps.

She went down to breakfast ready to tell him, to find that he had left the house in the early hours of the morning. An emergency, Ko told her, but he hoped to be home during the afternoon, probably around four o'clock.

So after lunch she set out with her list and a nicely filled purse. She felt at home in the city now although she was familiar only with the main streets. That morning, while she had been in the kitchen, she had told Katje that she was going shopping; it was surprising how well they understood each other as long as they kept their conversation to basics. Mekke had been there too, helping them out when they reached an impasse. Her English was only a smattering but she was quick to understand and quick to learn.

When Eulalia had mentioned that she wanted to buy toys for the children she had told Eulalia where to go: a large store near the Central Station. *Mevrouw* must take a tram to the station and then walk; the shop was close by and she would find all the toys she could wish for there. She had even drawn a map to make finding it easy.

Eulalia clutched it as she walked to the Leidsestraat and got into a tram. It took her a few minutes to find the street Mekke had written down and when she reached the shop it was packed with people so that it took her longer than she expected to find just what she wanted.

The final purchases made, she glanced at her watch. Aderik would be home in a short while and she wanted to be there. She joined the surge of people leaving the store and started walking briskly, confident of her direction.

She had been walking for several minutes when it dawned on her that she was in a street she didn't know. Somehow she must have missed a turning. Not a serious matter, she told herself, and turned to walk back the way she had come. It was a narrow street and there were few people in it and no shops.

She stopped the first person coming towards her and asked the way; her Dutch was negligible but 'Central Station' and an arm waved enquiringly should be enough. It seemed that it wasn't; she tried two more people and was about to try again when the faint drizzle became a downpour. She was brushed aside; no one wanted to hang around answering questions in such weather...

There was no shelter and she could hardly knock on a door, while to try and find her way on her own was a waste of time... She wasn't the Colonel's granddaughter for nothing; she walked on until she saw a telephone box.

It took time to find the right coins and decipher the instructions, and, although there was no one about, the street outside, its lights almost obscured by the rain, looked menacing. She dialled and heard Aderik's voice.

'It's me. I'm lost and it's raining...'

He was reassuringly calm. 'Do you know the name of the street?'

'No, it's dark and—and empty.'

Mr van der Leurs, stifling a panic which astonished him, became all at once briskly reassuring.

'You're in a phone box? Tell me the number on the dial. Did you tell anyone where you were going?'

'Yes, Mekke. To a big toy shop near the station...'

'Stay where you are, Lally. I'll be with you very shortly.'

'I'm sorry to be a nuisance...' Her voice had a decided squeak.

'You've been very sensible, my dear; just stay where you are.'

Mr van der Leurs went into the hall and found Ko. 'Ask Mekke to come here, will you?'

When she came, he asked, 'Mekke, this shop you suggested *mevrouw* should visit—which street?' And when she told him he went on, 'And is there another entrance?'

'Yes, *mijnheer*, at the back of the shop.' She put her hand to her mouth. '*Mevrouw* has lost herself?'

'Only temporarily. Do you know the street? Is there a phone box in it?'

'Yes. Turn left as you leave the shop.'

Mr van der Leurs nodded, whistled to Humbert and went out to his car. The streets were jammed with traffic but he knew a number of back ways...

He slid to a halt by the phone box and got out, opened its door and took Eulalia in his arms.

'My poor dear, you're wet and cold...'

'I was getting frightened too,' muttered Eulalia into his shoulder. 'I don't know why I got lost...'

'There was another entrance at the back of the shop—a natural mistake.'

He gathered up her parcels and shoved her gently into the car. 'Humbert's in the back.'

The car was warm and comfortable and Humbert pushed his woolly head against her shoulder. Eulalia supposed it was relief which made her want to cry. She sniffed away the tears and Aderik, without looking at her, said cheerfully, 'Dry clothes and tea and then you can show me what you have bought.'

CHAPTER FIVE

BACK at the house, Aderik pulled off her wet gloves, took off her coat and gave it to a hovering Ko and tossed her hat into a chair while Katje and Mekke, both talking at once, urged her to get into something warm.

'I'm only a bit wet,' protested Eulalia, and shivered.

'You appear half drowned. Go and get into something dry; your feet are sopping. And don't be long; I want my tea.'

So she went up to her room with an emotional Mekke in attendance, declaring in a mixture of English and Dutch that it was all her fault; she should never have told *mevrouw* to go to that shop. If *mevrouw* caught cold she would never forgive herself...

Ten minutes later Eulalia went back downstairs. Mekke had taken away her wet shoes and damp skirt and she had got into a jersey dress, brushed her hair and done her face, none the worse for her soaking. She had been frightened; she hoped that Aderik hadn't noticed that...

But of course he had.

He was standing with his back to the fire, his hands

in his pockets and Humbert lolling beside him, while Ko arranged the tea things on a small round table between the two armchairs drawn up to the blaze.

Eulalia heaved a sigh of contentment; it was lovely to be home and she told him so. 'I'll be more careful next time,' she told him earnestly.

'It's easy to get lost,' he said easily, 'but you will soon find your way around. I must arrange for you to have lessons in Dutch so that you can ask the way. There are parts of Amsterdam where English might not be understood. I'm sorry that you got so wet...'

She had hoped that he might have said more than that; that it had been sensible of her to phone, a word of praise for her good sense and lack of panic, but he began a casual conversation about Christmas, dismissing the whole thing as trivial, reflected Eulalia pettishly.

Mr van der Leurs, watching her expressive face from under his eyelashes, thought his own thoughts and presently asked her if she would like to go shopping with him in the morning. 'I'm free until two o'clock; we might get the family presents bought. You found what you wanted for the children?'

'Yes. I hope they'll do; I mean, I haven't seen the children yet, have I? I don't know what they like.'

He didn't answer that but asked abruptly, 'Are you happy, Eulalia?'

She was too surprised to say anything for a moment. She put down the toasted teacake she was on the point of eating and licked a buttery finger. She said composedly, 'Yes, I am happy. Why do you ask, Aderik?'

'When I asked you to marry me I promised that you could have all the time you needed to get to know me and adjust to a new way of life. Ours was hardly a traditional marriage, was it? There should be time to reflect on the future together before becoming man and wife and I gave you no time for that. You may have regrets or doubts. And I think that you like me well enough to tell me if that is the case?'

She said thoughtfully, 'I don't think I ever had any doubts or regrets. Perhaps I should have thought about it more...but I feel at home here although it's much grander than I had expected. And I miss Grandfather...but we get on well together, don't we? And in a little while, as soon as I've learnt to speak Dutch and become the kind of wife you want...'

'You are the kind of wife I want, Lally. Stay just as you are. Learn to speak Dutch by all means, but don't change.'

He got up and pulled her gently to her feet. 'And now that you are quite certain that you are happy here with me I think that it is time we became engaged!'

He had put his arm around her shoulders and she stared up at him.

'Engaged? But we are married!'

'So now we will be engaged as well.'

He took a little box out of his pocket and opened

it. There was a ring inside—diamonds in an old-fashioned gold setting. 'My grandmother's ring—I had it altered to fit your finger.'

He picked up her hand and slipped it above her wedding ring and, before she could speak, bent and kissed her. A gentle, slow kiss which left her with a surge of delight, so unexpected that she lost her breath.

'Oh,' said Eulalia, and kissed him back.

Mr van der Leurs' arms tightened around her for a moment, then he let her go. 'Sealed with a kiss,' he said lightly. 'Now tell me, have you any ideas about these presents?'

Eulalia sat down again, feeling vaguely disappointed, telling herself that she had no reason to be; hadn't Aderik just given her a most beautiful ring? And the kiss—she refused to think about that for the moment. It hadn't been like the other brief kisses he had given her—brief tokens of affection; it had left her feeling unsettled.

Mr van der Leurs, sitting in his chair, Humbert's great head resting on his knee, watched her face, and because he loved her so deeply he guessed her thoughts and was satisfied. A little more time and a lot more patience, he reflected.

They went shopping in the morning and Eulalia, at Aderik's quiet direction, bought silk scarves, exquisite handbags, gloves as supple as velvet, earrings for his mother, thin gold bangles for his sisters, books for his brother, before having a cup of coffee while they decided what to get Katje, Ko and Mekke. Soft fleece-lined slippers for Ko, whose elderly feet would be glad of them at the end of the day, and silk-lined gloves for Katje. As for Mekke—a quilted dressing gown in one of the bright colours she loved...

They went home, well pleased with their purchases, and after an early lunch Aderik left for the hospital, leaving Eulalia sitting at the little writing desk in the small sitting room, carefully writing Christmas cards from the list he had given her. It was a long list, prudently updated from year to year so that all she had to do was copy names and addresses. Tomorrow, she decided, she would buy presents to send to England; the cards she had already sent. And she still had to find a present for Aderik.

The days passed surprisingly quickly, with last-minute presents to buy, Humbert to take for walks, and rather anxious preparations for the ball, now only a day or two away. And Aderik was seldom home before the early evening. So it was all the more delightful when she went down to breakfast on the morning before the day of the ball to be told that he was free until the afternoon and would she like to see more of Amsterdam?

'Not a museum; we'll save those for when we have hours of leisure. Suppose we just walk round some of the older streets? Most of them have little antique or book shops and the small houses are worth seeing.'

It was a day for walking: a cold blue sky, frost underfoot and the city bustling with preparations for Christmas. But the small streets to which Aderik led the way were quiet. The small gabled houses had their doors shut, spotless curtains shrouding their gleaming windows. From time to time they met a housewife, basket on arm, going to the shops, and exchanged good mornings, and they stopped frequently to look in the shop windows.

Eulalia found them fascinating—book shops galore and antiques shops, some with their goods spread out on the narrow pavement. Aderik bought her a small china bowl, patterned in the lavender colour, which was the first Delftware. It had a small chip and a hair-line crack yet was none the less expensive, but since she didn't know the price and Mr van der Leurs paid without comment she accepted it with delight.

It was as they were on their way back, going down a narrow lane with a few shops and rather shabby cottages, that Eulalia stopped suddenly before a window. There was a kitten sitting in a cage there, a puny little creature with huge eyes. Attached to the cage was a card with 'Goedkoop' written on it.

Eulalia tugged at Aderik's sleeve. 'How could any-one be so callous?' she demanded. 'Writing "cheap" on that card, just as though the little creature is fit for nothing. And supposing no one wants him? He'll just die.'

Mr van der Leurs looked down at her furious face, flushed with rage, her eyes flashing. She looked so beautiful he could hardly keep his hands off her. He said, 'We want him; he's just the companion Humbert will enjoy.'

The smile she gave him was his reward. 'You'll buy him? I'll look after him; he won't be a nuisance…'

He opened the door and its old-fashioned bell tinkled rustily and an elderly man came through the curtain at the back of the shop. Eulalia couldn't understand what was said; the man sounded apologetic and had a great deal to say while Aderik listened silently. Presently he handed the man some notes and the kitten was fetched out from the window, removed from his cage and transferred to the inside of Aderik's topcoat, and they were ushered out of the shop with some ceremony.

'Oh, Aderik, thank you. I'm sure he'll grow into a splendid cat. That horrible man…'

'He had a so-called pet shop there but is moving away. He sold the animals he had, and the shop, but this small creature for some reason wasn't sold, so he put it in the window as a last hope before being drowned.'

He added, 'Don't be sad; he's going to be our family pet and he's too small to remember his unhappy start. We'll cut through here; there's a shop in the next street where we can buy him a basket and anything else he needs.'

Eulalia was struggling not to cry. She had no reason to do so; the kitten was safe, Aderik had dealt with the unhappy little episode with instant calm; for some reason she realised that was why she wanted to cry. And that was absurd. He was a man of unfailing kindness. She might not know him very well yet but of that she was sure. And she trusted him…

Back at the house the kitten was laid on a clean towel, given warm milk and gently examined. He was in poor shape but Aderik thought that with good food and tender loving care he had a good chance of growing into a handsome cat. All the same, he would take him to the vet when he got home later in the day. So the kitten was settled in the basket Aderik had bought for him, lined with paper and a blanket, before the warm hearth. Humbert, at first doubtful and puzzled, came and sat beside him and presently, to their delight, the kitten crawled out of his basket and curled up between Humbert's paws.

Mr van der Leurs was late home; the bone marrow transplant he had done that afternoon had had unexpected complications and he would have to go back to the hospital later on. Nevertheless he took the kitten to the vet before he sat down to his dinner.

'Nothing wrong with him,' he assured Eulalia.

'He's had his injections and a thorough overhaul; all he needs now is feeding up and warmth.'

'And to be loved,' said Eulalia. 'And he must have a name—an important one to make up for an unhappy start. Something grand…'

They were sitting in the drawing room with Humbert lying on Aderik's feet and the kitten half buried against the great dog's furry chest.

'Ferdinand,' said Eulalia, 'and we can call him Ferdie. Oh, Aderik, I'm so glad you saved him.'

'He's made himself at home; I hear that Katje is mincing chicken and keeping milk warm on the Aga and obviously Humbert is pleased to have him.'

He got up carefully from his chair. 'I have to go back to the hospital. I'll say goodnight, Lally, and see you at breakfast. Ko will see to Humbert and Ferdie.'

He brushed her cheek with a quick kiss, a brief salute which left her feeling lonely. 'How can I possibly feel lonely?' asked Lally of her two companions.

And indeed she had no leisure to feel lonely; the next day was spent attending to Ferdie's needs, taking Humbert for a walk and then getting down to the serious business of dressing for the ball. She had decided on the pink taffeta and when she was finally dressed she had to admit that she really looked rather nice. She had taken pains with her face and her hair, and the fine cashmere shawl which she had had the forethought to buy made a warm and dramatic wrap against the cold night. There remained nothing for her to do but go down to the drawing room and wait for Aderik.

He was late, she thought worriedly; perhaps there had been an emergency which would hold him up for hours, and they might have to miss the first part of the evening, even the whole evening. She sat there trying not to fidget in case it creased her dress, thinking how much she had been looking forward to the ball. She hadn't been to a dance for a long time; she had always refused invitations to the annual dance at St Chad's; she couldn't afford a dress for one thing and for another she had been afraid that no one would dance with the canteen lady... But now she had the right clothes and a husband to partner her, and she very much wanted to dance with Aderik.

She glanced at the clock once more, heard voices in the hall and just had time to compose her features into serenity as the door opened and Aderik came in.

Annoyingly unhurried. Eulalia bit back wifely admonishments to hurry up and change, smiled as though time were of no importance at all, and said, 'Hello, Aderik. Would you like a drink before you change?'

He had shut the door and was leaning against it looking at her.

'Eulalia, you leave me speechless. I was prepared to see an impatient virago hissing at me to hurry up and change and did I know the time? Instead of which I find a charming vision in pink offering me a drink!'

He crossed the room and pulled her to her feet. 'You look beautiful and that is a most becoming gown.' He held her away so that he could study her at his leisure. 'My enchanting wife,' he said quietly and then dropped her hands and added briskly, 'Give me fifteen minutes,' and was gone...

He was as good as his word and returned the epitome of a well-dressed man with time on his hands.

Eulalia said uncertainly, 'You won't leave me alone, will you?'

He hid a smile. 'No, Lally, although I think that you will have more partners than you will be able to cope with. Shall we go?' When she got up and picked up her wrap, he added, 'Just a moment,' and took a long box from an inner pocket. 'I have never given you a wedding present, have I?'

He took the double row of pearls from the box and fastened it round her neck and bent to kiss her. 'I wanted you to feel free, Lally...'

She knew what he meant; he had wanted her to marry him without any strings attached. She said simply, 'Thank you, Aderik. You are so good to me and thank you for that too.'

She turned to look in the gilt wood mirror above a wall table and put a hand up to touch the pearls. 'They're very beautiful.'

The ball was being held in the assembly hall of the hospital and the place was packed. The ter Brandts

were standing by the doors, shaking hands and exchanging greetings as the guests arrived. Christina
kissed Eulalia and said warmly, 'You look lovely;
Aderik must be so proud of you. He'll be lucky to
have more than two or three dances with you. Daisy
and Jules are here already; it's quite a crush but you'll
find them when the dancing stops.'

She turned to Aderik and Duert kissed Eulalia's
cheek. 'I shall want a dance with you later,' he told
her.

They joined the dancers then—they were playing a
waltz and she gave herself up to the delight of dancing; it was as though she and Aderik had danced together all their lives and for a moment she was oblivious of anything but his arm around her and her feet
following his of their own volition. But presently he
said, 'There are many people here whom you met
when you came to see St Nikolaas, but you won't
remember all of them.'

He was greeting other couples as they danced and
she hastened to nod and smile too, feeling shy. When
the dance ended and a rather pompous man and his
wife approached them, Aderik said, 'You remember
Professor Keesman, Eulalia? And his wife?'

Eulalia murmured politely and Mevrouw Keesman
said kindly, 'You have met so many new faces, it
must be difficult for you. You must come and visit
me soon—after Christmas perhaps? I should like that.'

Eulalia barely had time to thank her before

Professor Keesman danced her off into a slow foxtrot. He was a short stout man and she discovered quickly that he was self-important too, impressing upon her the high rank of his position in the hospital. She listened politely, making appropriate replies when necessary, thinking that Aderik never boasted about his work, nor did Duert, and she suspected that they were just as important as the professor. She hoped that Aderik wasn't a close friend of the Kessmans; she much preferred Duert and Jules.

But if she didn't much care for the professor there were any number of guests there who professed to be close friends of Aderik. She didn't lack for partners and from time to time she would find him at her elbow introducing her to one or other of them and claiming her for a dance.

They had supper with Daisy and Jules and half a dozen couples who obviously knew each other well and Eulalia got up from the supper table with enough invitations to fill her days for weeks to come. And when they went back into the ballroom Aderik whisked her onto the dance floor.

'Now we can dance together until the end,' he told her. 'My duty dances are done and you have had partners tumbling over each other to get at you; now we can behave like an old married couple and dance together.'

'Oh, yes, please,' said Eulalia. 'I feel so comfortable with you and I've run out of polite small talk!'

'But you are enjoying yourself? You have been much admired.'

'I've had a lovely time. I did my best to behave like a consultant's wife. I hope I didn't let you down. I mean, not remembering names and not being amusing or witty.'

She felt his arm tightening round her. 'My dear Eulalia, do not, I beg you, try to change in any way. You are delightful as you are, restful and soft-voiced and with the happy knack of knowing when to talk and when to keep silent.'

In other words, reflected Eulalia, dull. It was a depressing thought but if that was what he wanted in a wife then she would endeavour to be just that.

Somehow—she wasn't sure why—the pleasures and the excitement of the evening had evaporated. Which was absurd. She had had partners and compliments and there had been young women of her own age only too ready to make friends.

She watched Daisy and Jules dancing together and had a sudden pang of envy. And the ter Brandts, no longer in their first youth but obviously devoted… But of course they're in love, thought Eulalia wistfully.

The ball wound to a close and the guests began a leisurely departure, calling goodnights, stopping to chat with friends before going out into the cold night.

Back home, Aderik said, 'Shall we have a warm

drink before we go to bed? Katje will have left something ready for us.'

The kitchen was cosy and neither Humbert nor Ferdie did more than open an eye as they went in.

'Hot cocoa?' suggested Eulalia, and fetched mugs from the dresser and the plate of sandwiches she had asked Katje to make. 'Supper seems a long while ago,' she observed. 'I asked Katje to make them with ham and there's cold chicken...'

'Bless you for being a thoughtful housewife,' said Aderik, and took a huge mouthful before sitting down at the table opposite her. 'What a pleasant way to end the evening.'

He smiled at her. 'And you looked lovely, Lally. I am a very much envied man.'

She thanked him gravely. 'I've never been to a grand ball before; it was exciting.' She put down her mug. 'I think I'll go to bed.'

He got up and went to the door with her. 'Shall we go and buy the Christmas tree in the morning? I've private patients to see in the afternoon but otherwise I'm free.'

'Oh, yes—and a little one for Katje and Ko and Mekke?'

'Of course. We'll go into the country. Goodnight, Lally.'

She went to her bed feeling deprived. A goodnight kiss would have set the seal on the evening.

*   *   *

It was mid-morning before they set out. Humbert had to have his walk, Ferdie needed to be fed and brushed and made much of and Katje needed to discuss what they should have for dinner that evening…

'We'll have lunch out,' said Aderik. 'I need to be back soon after one o'clock.'

He drove out of Amsterdam and took the road to Hilversum, some twenty miles away, and then turned off the main road into a narrow country lane running between flat fields. There was wooded country ahead of them and when they reached it there was a small village, well hidden from the road.

Aderik parked by a small farm at the edge of the village and they got out and walked across the yard and round the back to find an old man surrounded by Christmas trees in all shapes and sizes. He shouted a greeting to Mr van der Leurs and came to shake hands and then shake Eulalia's. He had a great deal to say, too, in his gruff old voice, nodding and shaking his head and then leading them among the trees. They chose a splendid one for the house and a small one for the kitchen and Eulalia wandered off, leaving Aderik to pay and talk to the man. Presently he joined her.

'The trees will be delivered in two days' time. They'll be in tubs and his son will bring them and carry them into the house.'

'He'll need a tip? How much do I give him?'

'Ten guilden—I've paid for transport…'

'And a cup of coffee,' said Eulalia, very much the housewife.

Christmas was near now; Eulalia's days were filled wrapping presents, deciding on menus with Katje—a hilarious business with Ko patiently translating the more complicated remarks, although he was quick to tell her that her Dutch was improving each day. And then there was Humbert needing a walk even on a wet day, and Ferdie, still puny but beginning to look more like a kitten should.

There was Daisy to visit too and new-found friends phoning and Christina coming for coffee. Life was perfect, Eulalia told herself, ignoring the thought that all the same there was something not quite right... Perhaps it was because she didn't see much of Aderik: an hour or two in the evening, a brief half-hour at breakfast.

It was Christina who told her that he had agreed to take several teaching rounds. 'And I can't think why,' she added. 'Duert told him that they could be fitted in after the New Year so that he could be free instead of staying at the hospital in the afternoons.' She didn't say any more because she had seen the look on Eulalia's face. Had they quarrelled? she wondered, and dismissed the idea as absurd, sorry that she had said it.

Eulalia tried to forget about it. Aderik had his reasons for wanting to fill his days with work and when he was home he was as kind and friendly to her as he always was—only he was so seldom home…

She told herself she was worrying about nothing and flung herself into the final arrangements for the arrival of their guests.

Paul arrived first on the day before Christmas Eve, breezing into the house just before lunch, clapping Ko on the back, kissing Katje and Mekke, hugging Eulalia, demanding to know where Aderik was. He was almost as tall as his brother and very like him in looks, bubbling over with good spirits.

'I'm not supposed to be here until this evening, am I? But I couldn't wait to meet you. You're even more beautiful than Aderik said. Am I in my usual room? Is lunch at half-past twelve? I'm famished.'

Eulalia liked him. When he was ten years older he would be just like Aderik.

'How much longer will you be in Leiden?' she asked over lunch.

'Another year. I'm qualified but I want to specialise. I'd like to go to England, work in a hospital there and get some experience. Of course I'll never reach the heights Aderik has—he's top of the tree. I only hope I'll be half as good.'

They took Humbert for his walk presently and soon after they got back Aderik came home in time to greet the rest of his family, his arm around Eulalia as he introduced her to his mother who was unexpectedly small and plump with grey hair pulled severely back from a kind face, to his sisters, tall and good-looking, and their husbands and five children.

'It is too bad,' said Mevrouw van der Leurs, 'that you should have to meet all of us at once, and more so since Aderik tells me that you have no family. But we welcome you most warmly, Eulalia, and hope that you will adopt us as your own.' Eulalia, hugged and kissed and made much of, reflected that this was going to be a wonderful Christmas.

And so it was. The children were small enough to believe in Father Christmas and the old house rang with their small voices, and after tea everyone helped decorate the tree, glittering with baubles and with a magnificent fairy doll topping it, and then they all went to the kitchen while Katje and Ko decorated the smaller tree with the children's help.

Since it was Christmas time dinner was served earlier than usual so that the children could stay up for it, and Eulalia, looking round the table, thought how marvellous it was to belong to such a happy family. She caught Aderik's eye, sitting at the head of the table, and beamed at him, and he smiled back briefly as he turned to speak to his mother.

For a moment she felt chilled. But it was impossible to be downcast; Paul took all her attention and when they got up from the table she went upstairs with Lucia and Marijka and helped them put the children to bed. Afterwards they sat and talked over coffee and the delicious little biscuits Katje had made.

Mevrouw van der Leurs declared that she was tired and would go to bed—the signal for everyone else to do the same. Eulalia, kissed goodnight and complimented on the delicious dinner and pleasant evening, was left alone with Aderik, and she asked anxiously, 'Was it really all right? Just as you wanted it?'

'It was perfect, Eulalia.'

'Oh, good. Your mother is a darling, isn't she? And your sisters and brother and the children.' She gave a small sigh. 'They're all so happy.'

'Does that mean that you're not, Lally?'

'No, no, of course not. I was only thinking that I've missed so much. Although Grandfather and Jane were always so good to me.' She added sharply, 'I'm not whinging…'

'No, no; I never thought you were. I'm glad that you do like the family—your family as well as mine.'

'Well, I think it's very nice of them not to mind that you married me in such a hurry.' She got up. 'I'm going to bed. Will you make sure that Ferdie's comfortable when you take Humbert to his basket?'

He went to open the door for her. 'I'm going to the hospital in the morning but I'll be back for lunch. Would you like to go to the midnight service at the English church?'

'Oh, yes. Daisy told me about it. All of us?'

'No, just you and me. The family will go to morning service which will give us the chance to put the presents round the tree.'

Her eyes shone. 'It's like a fairy-tale Christmas,' she told him, and leaned up to kiss his cheek.

Mr van der Leurs went back to his chair. In fairy tales, he reflected, the prince always won the hand of the princess. Which was what he intended to do.

Christmas Eve passed in a happy bustle: last-minute talks with Katje, walking with Paul and the children and Humbert while Lucia and Marijka saw to the children's presents, Ferdie to feed and play with, chatting to her mother-in-law over coffee and then Aderik coming home and the house alive with children's voices. But all five had an early supper and were put to bed and dinner was a leisurely meal with easy talk and a lot of laughter.

The house was quiet when Aderik and Eulalia went out to the car. It was bitterly cold but there were stars and half a moon casting its icy light. The city was thronged with people and although the shops were long since shut their lighted windows rivalled the lighted Christmas trees in the squares. The church was in a small enclosure off Kalverstraat, surrounded by a ring of old houses, and was already almost full. Eulalia saw Christina and Duert ter Brandt almost at once, and then Daisy and Jules.

There was a Christmas tree and holly and flowers and a choir. It was all so English and she felt tears prick her eyelids. The congregation burst into the opening carol and after a moment she joined in.

It took some time to leave the church once the service was over, there were so many people to exchange good wishes with. The streets were quieter now and the shop windows dark, but as they reached the house she could see a glimmer of light through the transom over the door and inside it was warm and very welcoming.

'Coffee in the kitchen if you would like it,' she told Aderik, and went ahead of him to fill the mugs and get it ready.

He came into the kitchen presently, took the mugs from her and set them on the table. 'Happy Christmas, Lally. I'm cheating and giving you your present while we are alone together.'

It was earrings, gold and diamonds with a pearl drop.

Eulalia looked up at him. 'Aderik—they are so very beautiful; I've never seen anything as lovely. Thank you over and over again; you are so good and kind to me.' She kissed his cheek. 'May I try them on now?'

She slipped the hooks into her ears and went to look in the small looking-glass by the dresser, turning this way and that, her eyes shining.

It would be so easy, he thought, watching her, to play on her happiness and gratitude, but that wasn't what he wanted. If she came to love him it had to be of her own free will...

'Could I wear them to breakfast?'

He laughed then. 'Well, perhaps lunch would be a better choice. What dress are you wearing?'

'The russet velvet you chose.' She beamed at him as she sat down to drink her coffee. 'I'm so happy I could burst,' she told him, and presently, her coffee drunk, she wished him goodnight and went off to bed, still wearing the earrings.

Everyone was up early in the morning and breakfast was eaten to a chorus of seasonal greetings. The children could hardly eat for excitement and were presently borne away to church, leaving Aderik and Eulalia to collect up the presents and arrange them round the tree. They went to the kitchen first with the gifts for Katje, Ko and Mekke. Wim was there too, shaking hands and having a great deal to say to Eulalia, who didn't understand a word but made up for that by smiling a lot and looking interested. He was profuse in his thanks for the box of cigars and the envelope Mr van der Leurs gave him and went to sit by the Aga, for he was to spend the day there, joining in the festivities.

The presents arranged, Aderik took Humbert for his walk and Eulalia fetched Ferdie to sit in his little basket in the drawing room and then everyone was back from church to drink coffee.

Eulalia had decided that their traditional Christmas dinner should be eaten at midday so that the children could join in before the presents were handed out. She had taken great pains with the table and on her way upstairs went to check that everything was just so. It looked magnificent with the white damask cloth, silver and sparkling glass. She had made a centrepiece with holly and Christmas roses and gold ribbon and the napkins were tied with red ribbon. She went to her room then, got into the russet velvet dress and fastened the pearls, put in the earrings and went back to the drawing room.

That night curled up in her bed, waiting for sleep, Eulalia re-lived the day. It was one that she would always remember for it had been perfect. Christmas dinner had been a success; the turkey, the Christmas pudding, the mince pies, the wines and champagne had all been praised. And as for the presents, everyone had declared that everything they had received was exactly what they wanted.

She closed her eyes to shut out the thought that she and Aderik had had no time to be together, had exchanged barely a dozen words. If she hadn't been so sleepy she might have worried about that.

In Holland, she had discovered, there wasn't a Boxing Day but a second Christmas Day, only the names were different. The day was spent looking at presents again, going for a walk, playing games with the children and having friends in for drinks in the evening. She spent it being a good hostess, making endless light conversation with Aderik's friends and their wives, trying out her fragmented Dutch on her sisters-in-law, being gently teased by Paul and all the while wishing for Aderik's company.

Everyone went home the next day and the house was suddenly quiet, for Aderik had gone to the hospital in the early morning. She had slipped down to sit with him while he had breakfast but there was no time for a leisurely talk.

'I shall probably be late home,' he'd told her, getting up to leave. 'I've a list this morning and a clinic in the afternoon.'

She mooned around the house with Humbert padding beside her and Ferdie tucked under one arm. 'I do miss them all,' she told Humbert, and then changed that to, 'I do miss Aderik.'

It was nearly lunchtime when Ko came looking for her. He looked so anxious that she said, 'Ko, what's the matter? Are you ill?'

'*Mevrouw*, there has been a message from the hospital, from the director. There has been an explosion in one of the theatres and I am to tell you not to worry.'

'Aderik,' said Eulalia—and, thrusting Ferdie at Ko, flew past him and into the hall, to drag on an elderly mac she kept for the garden. She dashed out of the house, racing along the narrow streets, oblivious of the cold rain and the slippery cobbles. If he's hurt, I'll die, she told herself. She said loudly, 'Oh, Aderik,

I love you. I think I always have and now perhaps it's too late and how silly of me not to know.'

She glared at a solitary woman standing in her way and pushed past her. She was sopping wet and bedraggled when she reached the hospital and the porter on duty gave her a shocked look and started towards her, but she flew past him and belted up the stairs to the theatre unit. She had to pause then for the place was thronged with firemen and police and porters carrying away equipment. They were all too busy to notice her. She edged her way through, looking for someone who would know where Aderik was. He might even now be being treated for injuries—or worse, said a small voice in the back of her head.

She was dodging in and out of the various side rooms and then saw the main theatre at the end of the corridor, its doors off the hinges, everything in it twisted and smashed. She slithered to a halt and almost fell over when Aderik said from somewhere behind her, 'My dear, you shouldn't be here.'

She turned on him. 'Why didn't you tell me, phone me? You must have known I'd be half out of my mind. You could have been hurt—killed. I'm your wife.' She burst into tears. 'And it doesn't matter to you but I love you and I really will not go on like this.'

She stopped, aware that she was babbling, that that was the last thing she had meant to say to him. She wiped a hand across a tear-stained cheek and muttered, 'I didn't mean to say that.' She gave a great sniff and said in a small polite voice, 'I hope you haven't been hurt.'

Mr van der Leurs wasted a moment or so looking at her—hair in wet streamers, a tear-smeared face, in an old mac fit for the refuse bin and thin slippers squelching water. And so beautiful…!

He removed the wet garment from her and took her into his arms.

'My darling,' he said gently, 'why do you suppose I married you?'

'You wanted a wife.' She sniffed again.

'Indeed I did. You. I fell in love with you the moment I set eyes on you at St Chad's. I knew that you didn't love me, but I was sure that if I had patience you would find that you love me too.'

'You never said…' mumbled Eulalia.

'I cherished the thought that you would discover it without any help from me.'

His arms tightened around her. 'I'm going to kiss you,' he said.

'Oh, yes, please,' said Eulalia.

They stood there, the chaos around them forgotten, watched by silent onlookers: firemen, doctors, police and porters and the odd nurse, all of them enjoying the sight of two people in love.

A CHRISTMAS PROPOSAL
by
Betty Neels

CHAPTER ONE

THE girl standing in a corner of the crowded room hardly merited a second glance; she was small, with light brown hair strained back into an unfashionable bun, a face whose snub nose and wide mouth did nothing to redeem its insignificance, and she was wearing an elaborate shrimp-pink dress. But after his first glance the man standing across the room from her looked again. Presently he strolled over to stand beside her. His 'Hello' was pleasant and she turned her head to look at him.

She answered him politely, studying him from large brown eyes fringed by curling lashes. Looking at her eyes, he reflected that one soon forgot the nose and mouth and dragged-back hair. He smiled down at her. 'Do you know anyone here? I came with friends—I'm staying with them and was asked to come along with them. A birthday party, isn't it?'

'Yes.' She looked past him to the crowded room, the groups of laughing, gossiping people waving to each other with drinks in their hands, the few couples dancing in the centre. 'Would you like me to introduce you to someone?'

He said in his friendly way, 'You know everyone here? Is it your birthday?'

'Yes.' She gave him a quick surprised look and bent her head to examine the beaded bodice of her dress.

'Then shouldn't you be the belle of the ball?'

'Oh, it's not my party. It's my stepsister's—that pretty girl over by the buffet. Would you like to meet Clare?'

'The competition appears too keen at the moment,' he said easily. 'Shouldn't you be sharing the party, since it's your birthday too?'

'Well, no.' She had a pretty voice and she spoke matter-of-factly. 'I'm sure you'd like to meet some of the guests. I don't know your name...'

'Forgive me. Hay-Smythe—Oliver.'

'Bertha Soames.' She put out a small hand and he shook it gently.

'I really don't want to meet anyone. I think that perhaps I'm a little on the old side for them.'

She scrutinised him gravely—a very tall, strongly built man, with fair hair thickly sprinkled with grey. His eyes were grey too, and he had the kind of good looks which matched his assured air.

'I don't think you're in the least elderly,' she told him.

He thanked her gravely and added, 'Do you not dance?'

'Oh, I love to dance.' She smiled widely at him, but as quickly the smile faded. 'I—that is, my stepmother asked me to see that everyone was enjoying themselves. That's why I'm standing here—if I see anyone on their own I make sure that they've got a drink and meet someone. I really think that you should…'

'Definitely not, Miss Soames.' He glanced down at her and thought how out of place she looked in the noisy room. And why, if it was her birthday, was she not wearing a pretty dress and not that ill-fitting, over-elaborate garment? 'Are you hungry?'

'Me? Hungry?' She nodded her head. 'Yes, I missed lunch.' Her eyes strayed to the buffet, where a number of people were helping themselves lavishly to the dainties upon it. 'Why don't you…?'

Dr Hay-Smythe, hard-working in his profession and already respected by older colleagues, a man who would never pass a stray kitten or a lost dog and who went out of his way to make life easy for anyone in trouble, said now, 'I'm hungry too. Supposing we were to slip away and have a meal somewhere? I don't imagine we should be missed, and we could be back long before this finishes.'

She stared at him. 'You mean go somewhere outside? But there isn't a café anywhere near here—besides…'

'Even Belgravia must have its pubs. Anyway, I've my car outside—we can look around.'

Her eyes shone. 'I'd like that. Must I tell my stepmother?'

'Certainly not. This door behind you—where does it lead? A passage to the hall? Let us go now.'

'I'll have to get my coat,' said Bertha when they were in the hall. 'I won't be long, but it's at the top of the house.'

'Haven't you a mac somewhere down here?'

'Yes, but it's very old...'

His smile reassured her. 'No one will notice in the pub.' He reflected that at least it would conceal that dreadful dress.

So, suitably shrouded, she went out of the house with him, through the important front door, down the imposing steps and onto the pavement.

'Just along here,' said the doctor, gesturing to where a dark grey Rolls-Royce was parked. He unlocked the door, popped her inside and got in beside her. As he drove off he asked casually, 'You live here with your parents?'

'Yes. Father is a lawyer—he does a lot of work for international companies. My stepmother prefers to live here in London.'

'You have a job?'

'No.' She turned her head to look out of the window, and he didn't pursue the subject but talked idly about this and that as he left the quiet streets with their stately houses and presently, in a narrow street bustling with people, stopped the car by an empty meter. 'Shall we try that pub on the corner?' he suggested, and helped her out.

Heads turned as they went in; they made an odd couple—he in black tie and she in a shabby raincoat—but the landlord waved them to a table in one corner of the saloon bar and then came over to speak to the doctor.

'Ain't seen yer for a while, Doc. Everything OK?'

'Splendid, thank you, Joe. How is your wife?'

'Fighting fit, thanks to you. What'll it be?' He glanced at Bertha. 'And the little lady here? A nice drop of wine for her?'

'We're hungry, Joe…'

'The wife's just this minute dished up bangers and mash. How about that, with a drop of old and mild?'

Dr Hay-Smythe raised an eyebrow at Bertha, and when she nodded Joe hurried away, to return presently with the beer and the wine and, five minutes later, a laden tray.

The homely fare was well cooked, hot and generous. The pair of them ate and drank in a friendly silence until the doctor said quietly, 'Will you tell me something about yourself?'

'There's nothing to tell. Besides, we're strangers; we're not likely to meet again.' She added soberly, 'I think I must be a little mad to be doing this.'

'Well, now, I can't agree with that. Madness, if at all, lies with people who go to parties and eat too much and drink too much and don't enjoy themselves. Whereas you and I have eaten food we enjoy and are content with each other's company.' He waited while

Joe brought the coffee he had ordered. 'Being strangers, we can safely talk knowing that whatever we say will certainly be forgotten.'

'I've never met anyone like you before,' said Bertha.

'I'm perfectly normal; there must be thousands exactly like me.' He smiled a little. 'I think that perhaps you haven't met many people. Do you go out much? The theatre? Concerts? Sports club? Dancing?'

Bertha shook her head. 'Well, no. I do go shopping, and I take my stepmother's dog out and help when people come for tea or dinner. That kind of thing.'

'And your sister?' He saw her quick look. 'Stepsister Clare—has she a job?'

'No—she's very popular, you see, and she goes out a great deal and has lots of friends. She's pretty—you must have seen that...'

'Very pretty,' he agreed gravely. 'Why are you unhappy, Bertha? You don't mind my calling you Bertha? After all, as you said, we are most unlikely to meet again. I'm a very good listener. Think of me as an elder brother or, if you prefer, someone who is going to the other side of the world and never returning.'

She asked, 'How do you know that I'm unhappy?'

'If I tell you that I'm a doctor, does that answer your question?'

She smiled her relief. 'A doctor! Oh, then I could talk to you, couldn't I?'

His smile reassured her.

'You see, Father married again—oh, a long time ago, when I was seven years old. My mother died when I was five, and I suppose he was lonely, so he married my stepmother.

'Clare was two years younger than I. She was a lovely little girl and everyone adored her. I did too. But my stepmother—you see, I've always been plain and dull. I'm sure she tried her best to love me, and it must be my fault, because I tried to love her, but somehow I couldn't.

'She always treated me the same as Clare—we both had pretty dresses and we had a nice nanny and went to the same school—but even Father could see that I wasn't growing up to be a pretty girl like Clare, and my stepmother persuaded him that it would be better for me to stay at home and learn to be a good house-wife…'

'Was Clare not a partner in this, too?'

'Well, no. She has always had lots of friends—I mean, she hadn't time to be at home very much. She's really kind to me.' She laid a hand on a glimpse of pink frill which had escaped from the raincoat. 'She gave me this dress.'

'You have no money of your own?'

'No. Mother left me some, but I—I don't need it, do I?'

The doctor didn't comment on that. All he said was, 'There is a simple solution. You must find a job.'

'I'd like that, but I'm not trained for anything.' She added anxiously, 'I shouldn't have said all that to you. Please forget it. I have no right to complain.'

'Hardly complaining. Do you not feel better for talking about it?'

'Yes, oh, yes. I do.' She caught sight of the clock and gave a little gasp. 'Heavens, we've been here for ages…'

'Plenty of time,' said the doctor easily. 'I dare say the party will go on until midnight.' He paid the bill and stowed her in the Rolls once more, then drove her back and went with her into the house. Bertha shed the raincoat in the hall, smoothed the awful dress and went with him into the vast drawing room. The first person to see them was her stepmother.

'Bertha, where have you been? Go at once to the kitchen and tell Cook to send up some more vol-au-vents. You're here to make yourself useful—'

Mrs Soames, suddenly aware of the doctor standing close by, became all at once a different woman. 'Run along, dear.' She spoke in a quite different voice now, and added, 'Don't be long—I'm sure your friends must be missing you.'

Bertha said nothing, and slipped away without a glance at the doctor.

'Such a dear girl,' enthused Mrs Soames, her massive front heaving with pseudo maternal feelings, 'and such a companion and help to me. It is a pity that she is so shy and awkward. I have done my best—' she managed to sound plaintive '—but Bertha is an intelligent girl and knows that she is lacking in looks and charm. I can only hope that some good man will come along and marry her.'

She lifted a wistful face to her companion, who murmured the encouraging murmur at which doctors are so good. 'But I mustn't bother you with my little worries, must I? Come and talk to Clare—she loves a new face. Do you live in London? We must see more of you.'

So when Bertha returned he was at the other end of the room, and Clare was laughing up at him, a hand on his arm. Well, what did I expect? reflected Bertha, and went in search of Crook the butler, a lifelong friend and ally; she had had a good supper, and now, fired by a rebellious spirit induced by Dr Hay-Smythe's company, she was going to have a glass of champagne.

She tossed it off under Crook's fatherly eye, then took a second glass from his tray and drank that too. Probably she would have a headache later, and certainly she would have a red nose, but since there was no one to mind she really didn't care. She wished suddenly that her father were at home. He so seldom was…

People began to leave, exchanging invitations and greetings, several of them saying a casual goodbye to Bertha, who was busy finding coats and wraps and mislaid handbags. Dr Hay-Smythe was amongst the first to leave with his party, and he came across the hall to wish her goodbye.

'That was a splendid supper,' he observed, smiling down at her. 'Perhaps we might do it again some time.'

Before she could answer, Clare had joined them. 'Darling Oliver, don't you dare run off just as I've discovered how nice you are. I shall find your number in the phone book and ring you—you may take me out to dinner.'

'I'm going away for some weeks,' he said blandly. 'Perhaps it would be better if I phoned you when I get back.'

Clare pouted. 'You wretched man. All right, if that's the best you can do.'

She turned her head to look at Bertha. 'Mother's looking for you…'

Bertha went, but not before putting out a small, capable hand and having it shaken gently. Her, 'Goodbye Doctor,' was uttered very quietly.

It was after Bertha had gone to her bed in the modest room on the top floor of the house that Mrs Soames went along to her daughter's bedroom.

'A successful evening, darling,' she began. 'What do you think of that new man—Oliver Hay-Smythe? I was talking to Lady Everett about him. It seems he's quite well-known—has an excellent practice in Harley Street. Good family and plenty of money—old money...' She patted Clare's shoulder. 'Just the thing for my little girl.'

'He's going away for a while,' said Clare. 'He said he'd give me a ring when he gets back.' She looked at her mother and smiled. Then she frowned. 'How on earth did Bertha get to know him? They seemed quite friendly. Probably he's sorry for her—she did look a dowd, didn't she?'

Clare nibbled at a manicured hand. 'She looked happy—as though they were sharing a secret or something. Did you know that he has a great deal to do with backward children? He wouldn't be an easy man... If he shows an interest in Bertha, I shall encourage him.' She met her mother's eyes in the mirror. 'I may be wrong, but I don't think he's much of a party man—the Paynes, who brought him, told me that he's not married and there are no girlfriends—too keen on his work. If he wants to see more of Bertha, I'll be all sympathy!'

The two of them smiled at each other.

Dr Hay-Smythe parted from his friends at their house and took himself off to his flat over his consulting rooms. Cully, his man, had gone to his bed, but there was coffee warm on the Aga in the kitchen and a covered plate of sandwiches. He poured himself a mug of coffee and sat down at the kitchen table, and the Labrador who had been snoozing by the Aga got up sleepily and came to sit beside him, ready to share his sandwiches. He shared his master's thoughts too, chewing on cold roast beef and watching his face.

'I met a girl this evening, Freddie—a plain girl with beautiful eyes and wearing a truly awful frock. An uninteresting creature at first glance, but somehow I feel that isn't a true picture. She has a delightful voice—very quiet. She needs to get away from that ghastly stepmother too. I must think of something...'

Bertha, happily unaware of these plans for her future, slept all night, happier in her dreams than in her waking hours.

It was two days later that the doctor saw a way to help Bertha. Not only did he have a private practice, a consultancy at two of the major hospitals and a growing reputation in his profession, he was also a partner in a clinic in the East End of London, dealing with geriatrics and anyone else who could not or would not go to Outpatients at any of the hospitals.

He had spent the evening there and his last patient had been an old lady, fiercely independent and living on her own in a tiny flat near the clinic. There wasn't a great deal he could do for her; a hard working life and old age were taking their toll, but she stumped around with a stick, refusing to go into an old people's home, declaring that she could look after herself.

'I'm as good as you, Doctor,' she declared after he had examined her. 'But I miss me books—can't read like I used to and I likes a good book. The social lady brought me a talking book, but it ain't the same as a real voice, if yer sees what I mean.' She added, 'A nice, quiet voice…'

He remembered Bertha then. 'Mrs Duke, would you like someone to come and read to you? Twice or three times a week, for an hour or so?'

'Not if it's one of them la-de-da ladies. I likes a nice bit of romance, not prosy stuff out of the parish mag.'

'The young lady I have in mind isn't at all like that. I'm sure she will read anything you like. Would you like to give it a try? If it doesn't work out, we'll think of something else.'

'OK, I'll 'ave a go. When'll she come?'

'I shall be here again in two days' time in the afternoon. I'll bring her and leave her with you while I am here and collect her when I've finished. Would that suit you?'

'Sounds all right.' Mrs Duke heaved herself out of her chair and he got up to open the door for her. 'Be seeing yer.'

The doctor went home and laid his plans; Mrs Soames wasn't going to be easy, a little strategy would be needed…

Presently he went in search of Cully. Cully had been with him for some years, was middle-aged, devoted and a splendid cook. He put down the silver he was polishing and listened to the doctor.

'You would like me to telephone now, sir?'

'Please.'

'And if the lady finds the time you wish to visit her unacceptable?'

'She won't, Cully.'

Cully went to the phone on the wall and the doctor wandered to the old-fashioned dresser and chose an apple. Presently Cully put back the receiver.

'Five o'clock tomorrow afternoon, sir. Mrs Soames will be delighted.'

The doctor took a bite. 'Splendid, Cully. If at any time she should ring me here, or her daughter, be circumspect, if you please.'

Cully allowed himself to smile. 'Very good, sir.'

The doctor was too busy during the next day to give much thought to his forthcoming visit; he would have liked more time to think up reasons for his request, but he presented himself at five o'clock at Mrs Soames' house and was shown into the drawing room by a grumpy maid.

Mrs Soames, encased in a vivid blue dress a little too tight for her ample curves, rose to meet him. 'Oliver, how delightful to see you—I'm sure you must be a very busy man. I hear you have a large practice.' She gave rather a shrill laugh. 'A pity that I enjoy such splendid health or I might visit your rooms.'

He murmured appropriately and she patted the sofa beside her. 'Now, do tell me why you wanted to see me—' She broke off as Clare came into the room. Her surprise was very nearly real. 'Darling, you're back. See who has come to see us.'

Clare gave him a ravishing smile. 'And about time, too. I thought you were going away.'

'So did I.' He had stood up when she'd joined them, and he now took a chair away from the sofa. 'A series of lectures, but they have been postponed for a couple of weeks.'

Clare wrinkled her nose enchantingly. 'Good; now you can take me out to dinner.'

'A pleasure. I'll look in my appointments book and give you a ring, if I may. I was wondering if you have any time to spare during your days? I'm looking for someone who would be willing to read aloud for an hour or two several times a week to an old lady.' He smiled at Clare. 'You, Clare?'

'Me? Read a boring book to a boring old woman? Besides, I never have a moment to myself. What kind of books?'

'Oh, romances…'

'Yuk. How absolutely grim. And you thought of me, Oliver?' She gave a tinkling laugh. 'I don't even read to myself—only *Vogue* and *Tatler*.'

The doctor looked suitably disappointed. 'Ah, well, I dare say I shall be able to find someone else.'

Clare hesitated. 'Who is this old woman? Someone I know? I believe Lady Power has to have something done to her eyes, and there's Mrs Dillis—you know, she was here the other evening—dripping with diamonds and quite able to afford half a dozen companions or minders or whatever they're called.'

'Mrs Duke lives in a tiny flat on her own and she exists on her pension.'

'How ghastly.' Clare looked up and caught her mother's eye. 'Why shouldn't Bertha make herself useful? She's always reading anyway, and she never does anything or goes anywhere. Of course—that's the very thing.'

Clare got up and rang the bell, and when the grumpy maid came she told her to fetch Miss Bertha.

Bertha came into the room quietly and stopped short when she saw Dr Hay-Smythe.

'Come here, Bertha,' said Mrs Soames. 'You know Dr Hay-Smythe, I dare say? He was at Clare's party. He has a request to make and I'm sure you will agree to it—something to keep you occupied from time to time. Perhaps you will explain, Oliver.'

He had stood up when Bertha had come into the room, and when she sat down he came to sit near her. 'Yes, we have met,' he said pleasantly. 'I came to ask Clare to read to an old lady—a patient of mine—whose eyesight is failing, but she suggested that you might like to visit her. I believe you enjoy reading?'

'Yes, yes, I do.'

'That's settled, then,' said Mrs Soames. 'She's at your disposal, Oliver.'

'Would you like to go to this lady's flat—say, three

times a week in the afternoons—and read to her for an hour or so?'

'Yes, thank you, Doctor.' Bertha sounded politely willing, but her eyes, when she looked at him, shone.

'Splendid. Let me see. Could you find your way to my rooms in Harley Street tomorrow afternoon? Then my secretary will give you her address. It is quite a long bus ride, but it won't be too busy in the afternoon. Come about two o'clock, will you? And thank you so much.'

'You'll have a drink, won't you?' asked Mrs Soames. 'I must make a phone call, but Clare will look after you. Bertha, will you go and see Cook and get her list for shopping tomorrow?'

The doctor, having achieved his purpose, sat for another half-hour, drinking tonic water while Clare drank vodka.

'Don't you drink?' She laughed at him. 'Really, Oliver, I should have thought you a whisky man.'

He smiled his charming smile. 'I'm driving. It would never do to reel into hospital, would it?'

'I suppose not. But why work in a hospital when you've got a big practice and can pick and choose?'

He said lightly, 'I enjoy the work.' He glanced at his watch. 'I am most reluctant to go, but I have an appointment. Thank you for the drink. I'll take you out to dinner and give you champagne at the first opportunity.'

She walked with him to the door, laid a pretty little

hand on his arm and looked up at him. 'You don't mind? That I don't want to go to that old woman? I can't bear poverty and old, dirty people and smelly children. I think I must be very sensitive.'

He smiled a little. 'Yes, I am sure you are, and I don't mind in the least. I am sure your stepsister will manage very well—after all, all I asked for was someone to read aloud, and she seems to have time on her hands.'

'I'm really very sorry for her—her life is so dull,' declared Clare, and contrived to look as though she meant that.

Dr Hay-Smythe patted her hand, removed it from his sleeve, shook it and said goodbye with beautiful manners, leaving Clare to dance away and find her mother and gloat over her conquest.

As for the doctor, he went home well pleased with himself. He found Clare not at all to his taste but he had achieved his purpose.

It was raining as Bertha left the house the following afternoon to catch a bus, which meant that she had to wear the shabby mackintosh again. She consoled herself with the thought that it concealed the dress she was wearing—one which Clare had bought on the spur of the moment and disliked as soon as she'd got home with it.

It was unsuitable for a late autumn day, and a wet one, being of a thin linen—the colour of which was quite brilliant. But until her stepmother decided that Bertha might have something more seasonal there was nothing much else in her wardrobe suitable for the occasion, and anyway, nobody would see her. The old lady she was to visit had poor eyesight...

She got off the bus and walked the short distance to Dr Hay-Smythe's rooms, rang the bell and was admitted. His rooms were elegant and restful, and the cosy-looking lady behind the desk in the waiting room had a pleasant smile. 'Miss Soames?' She had got up and was opening a door beside the desk. 'The doctor's expecting you.'

Bertha hadn't been expecting him! She hung back to say, 'There's no need to disturb him. I was only to get the address from you.'

The receptionist merely smiled and held the door wide open, allowing Bertha to glimpse the doctor at his desk. He looked up then, stood up and came to meet her at the door.

'Hello, Bertha. Would you mind waiting until I finish this? A few minutes only. Take this chair. You found your way easily?' He pushed forward a small, comfortable chair, sat her down and went back to his own chair. 'Do undo your raincoat; it's warm in here.'

He was friendly and easy and she lost her shyness and settled comfortably, undoing her raincoat to reveal the dress. The doctor blinked at its startling colour as he picked up his pen. Another of Clare's castoffs, he supposed, which cruelly highlighted Bertha's nondescript features. Really, he reflected angrily, something should be done, but surely that was for her father to do? He finished his writing and left his chair.

'I'm going to the clinic to see one or two patients. I'll take you to Mrs Duke and pick you up when I've finished. Will you wait for me there?' He noticed the small parcel she was holding. 'Books? How thoughtful of you.'

'Well, Cook likes romances and she let me have some old paperbacks. They may please Mrs Duke.'

They went out together and the receptionist got up from her desk.

'Mrs Taylor, I'm taking Miss Soames with me. If I'm not back by five o'clock, lock up, will you? I've two appointments for this evening, haven't I? Leave the notes on my desk, will you?'

'Yes, Doctor. Sally will be here at six o'clock…'

'Sally is my nurse,' observed the doctor. 'My right hand. Mrs Taylor is my left hand.'

'Go on with you, Doctor,' said Mrs Taylor, and chuckled in a motherly way.

Bertha, brought up to make conversation when the occasion warranted it, worked her way painstakingly through a number of suitable subjects in the Rolls-Royce, and the doctor, secretly amused, replied in his kindly way, so that by the time he drew up in a shabby street lined with small terraced houses she felt quite at ease.

He got out, opened her door and led the way across

the narrow pavement to knock on a door woefully in need of a paintbrush. It was opened after a few moments by an old lady with a wrinkled face, fierce black eyes and an untidy head of hair. She nodded at the doctor and peered at Bertha.

'Brought that girl, 'ave yer? Come on in, then. I could do with a bit of company.' She led the way down the narrow hall to a door at the end. 'I've got me own flat,' she told Bertha. 'What's yer name?'

'Bertha, Mrs Duke.'

The doctor, watching her, saw with relief that she had neither wrinkled her small nose at the strong smell of cabbage and cats, nor had she let her face register anything other than friendly interest.

He didn't stay for more than a few minutes, and when he had gone Bertha, bidden to sit herself down, did so and offered the books she had brought.

Mrs Duke peered at their titles. 'Just me cup of tea,' she pronounced. 'I'll 'ave *Love's Undying Purpose* for a start.' She settled back in a sagging armchair and an elderly cat climbed onto her lap.

Bertha turned to the first page and began to read.

CHAPTER TWO

BERTHA was still reading when the doctor returned two hours later. There had been a brief pause while Mrs Duke had made tea, richly brown and laced with tinned milk and a great deal of sugar, but Bertha hadn't been allowed to linger over it. She had obediently picked up the book again and, with a smaller cat on her own knees, had continued the colourful saga of misunderstood heroine and swashbuckling hero.

Mrs Duke had listened avidly to every word, occasionally ordering her to 'read that bit again', and now she got up reluctantly to let the doctor in.

'Enjoyed yourselves?' he wanted to know.

'Not 'arf. Reads a treat, she does. 'Artway through the book already.' Mrs Duke subsided into her chair again, puffing a bit. 'Bertha's a bit of all right. When's she coming again?'

He looked at Bertha, sitting quietly with the cat still on her knee.

'When would you like to come again?' he asked her.

'Whenever Mrs Duke would like me to.'

'Tomorrow? We could finish this story…'

'Yes, of course. If I come about the same time?'

'Suits me. 'Ere, give me Perkins—like cats, do you?'

'Yes, they're good company, aren't they?' Bertha got up. 'We'll finish the story tomorrow,' she promised.

In the car the doctor said, 'I'll bring you over at the same time and collect you later. I want to take a look at Mrs Duke; she's puffing a bit.'

'Yes—she would make tea and she got quite breathless. Is she ill?'

'Her heart's worn out and so are her lungs. She's turned eighty and had a very hard life. She refuses to go into hospital. You have made her happy reading to her—thank you, Bertha.' She smiled and he glanced at her. 'You didn't find the smells and the cats too much for you?'

'No, of course not. Would she be offended if I took a cake or biscuits? I'm sure Cook will let me have something.'

'Would you? I think she would be delighted; she's proud, but she's taken to you, hasn't she?'

He reflected with some surprise that he had rather taken to Bertha himself...

'Could we settle on which days you would like to visit Mrs Duke? I'll bring you tomorrow, as I've already said, but supposing we say three times a week? Would Monday, Wednesday and Friday suit you? Better still, not Friday but Saturday—I dare say that will help her over the weekend. I'll give you a lift on Wednesdays and Saturdays and on Mondays, if you will come to my rooms as usual, there will be someone to take you to Mrs Duke.'

'I'll go any day you wish me to, but I must ask my stepmother... And I can get a bus—there's no need...'

'I go anyway. You might just as well have a lift. And on Mondays there is always someone going to the clinic—I'm one of several who work there.'

'Well, that would be nice, if you are sure it's no trouble?'

'None whatsoever. Is your stepmother likely to object to your going?'

'I don't think so.' Bertha paused. 'But she might not like me going with you...' She spoke matter-of-factly.

'Yes. Perhaps you are right. There is no need to mention that, is there?'

'You mean it will be a kind of secret between us?'

'Why not?' He spoke lightly and added, 'I'm taking your stepsister out to dinner tomorrow evening. She is a very popular girl, isn't she?'

Which somehow spoilt Bertha's day.

Two weeks went by and autumn showed signs of turning into winter. Mrs Soames had decided that Bertha, since she went out so seldom, needed no new dresses; Clare had several from last year still in perfect condition. A little alteration here and there and they would be quite all right for Bertha, she declared, making a mental note that she would have to buy something new for the girl when her father returned in a month's time.

So Bertha, decked out more often than not in a hastily altered outfit of Clare's—lime-green and too wide on the shoulders—went on her thrice-weekly visits to Mrs Duke: the highlights of her week. She liked Wednesdays and Saturdays best, of course, because then she was taken there by the doctor, but the young man who drove her there on Mondays was nice too. He was a doctor, recently qualified, who helped out at the clinic from time to time. They got on well together, for Bertha was a good listener, and he always had a great deal to say about the girl he hoped to marry.

It had surprised Bertha that her stepmother hadn't objected to her reading sessions with Mrs Duke, but that lady, intent on finding a suitable husband for Clare, would have done a good deal to nurture a closer friendship with Dr Hay-Smythe. That he had taken Clare out to dinner and accepted an invitation to dine with herself, Clare and a few friends she took as a good sign.

Clare had looked her best at the dinner party, in a deceptively simple white dress. Bertha had been there, of course, for there had been no good reason for her not to be, wearing the frightful pink frock again— quite unsuitable, but really, when the girl went out so seldom there was no point in buying her a lot of clothes.

Dr Hay-Smythe had been a delightful guest, Mrs Soames had noted, paying court to her darling Clare and treating Bertha with a friendly courtesy but at the same time showing no interest in the girl. Very satisfactory, Mrs Soames had reflected, heaving such a deep sigh that her corsets creaked.

It was at the end of the third week on the Saturday that Mrs Duke died. Bertha had just finished the third chapter of a novel that the old lady had particularly asked her to read when Mrs Duke gave a small sigh and stopped breathing.

Bertha closed her book, set the cat on her lap gently on the ground and went to take the old lady's hand. There was no pulse; she had known there wouldn't be.

She laid Mrs Duke's hands tidily in her lap and went into the tiny hall to where the doctor had left a portable phone, saying casually that she might need it and giving her a number to call. She hadn't thought much about it at the time, but now she blessed him for being thoughtful. She dialled the number—the clinic—and heard his quiet voice answer.

'Mrs Duke.' She tried to keep her voice steady. 'Please would you come quickly? She has just died…'

'Five minutes. Are you all right, Bertha?'

'Me? Yes, thank you. Only, please come…' Her voice wobbled despite her efforts.

It seemed less than five minutes until he opened the door and gave her a comforting pat on the shoulder as he went past her into the living room to examine Mrs Duke. He bent his great height over her for a few minutes and then straightened up.

'Exactly as she would have wished,' he said. 'In her own home and listening to one of her favourite stories.'

He looked at Bertha's pale face. 'Sit down while I get this sorted out.'

She sat with the two cats crouching on her lap—they were aware that something wasn't quite right—while he rang the clinic, and presently a pleasant elderly woman came and the doctor picked up Mrs Duke and carried her into her poky bedroom.

'I'll take you home,' he told Bertha. 'It's been a shock. I'm sorry you had to be here.'

'I'm not. I'm glad. If Mrs Duke didn't know anything about it... The cats—we can't just leave them.' She stroked their furry heads. 'I'd have them, only I don't think my stepmother...'

'I'll take them. There's room for them at my flat and Freddie will enjoy their company—my dog.'

'Mrs Duke would be glad of that; she loved them.' Bertha put the pair gently down and got to her feet. 'I could go by bus. I expect there's a lot for you to do.'

'Time enough for that. Come along.' He glanced at his watch. 'You need a cup of tea.'

'Please don't bother.' Two tears trickled slowly down her cheeks. 'It doesn't seem right to be talking about tea...'

'If Mrs Duke were here it would be the first thing that she would demand. Be happy for her, Bertha, for this is exactly what she wished for.'

Bertha sniffed, blew her nose and mopped up her tears. 'Yes, of course. Sorry. I'll come now. You're sure about the cats?'

'Yes. Wait while I have a word with Mrs Tyler.' He went into the bedroom and presently came out of it again, and whisked Bertha into the car.

He stopped the car in a side-street close to Oxford Street and ushered her into a small café where he sat her down at a table, ordered a pot of tea and took a seat opposite her.

'There is no need to say anything to your step-mother for the moment. It so happens that a nursery school I know of needs someone to read to the chil-dren. Would you consider doing that? The times may be different, but I'm sure I can explain that to Mrs Soames. Will you leave it to me? You will want to come to the funeral, won't you? Will you phone my rooms—tomorrow evening? Can you do that?'

'Well, I take my stepmother's dog for a walk every evening—I could go to the phone box; it's not far...'

'Splendid.' His smile was kind. 'Now, drink your tea and I'll take you home.' He added casually, 'I don't think there is any need to say anything to your stepmother about your change of job or Mrs Duke's death, do you?' He gave her a sidelong glance. 'I can explain that it will suit everyone concerned if the times are changed.'

'If you wouldn't mind. I don't think my stepmother would notice. I mean…'

'I know what you mean, Bertha.' His quiet voice reassured her.

The funeral was to be on Wednesday, she was told when she telephoned the following evening on her walk, and if she went as usual to the doctor's rooms she would be driven to Mrs Duke's flat. 'And as regards Monday,' went on the doctor, 'come at the usual time and I'll take you along to the nursery school so that you can meet everyone and arrange your hours.'

As she went back into the house she met Clare in the hall, dressed to go out for the evening. She twirled round, showing off the short silky frock.

'Do you like it, Bertha? It shows off my legs very well, doesn't it? It's a dinner party at the Ritz.' She smiled her charming smile. 'I might as well have as much fun as possible before I settle down and become a fashionable doctor's wife.'

She danced off and Bertha took the dog to the kitchen. Was that why the doctor was being so kind to her, finding her work to fill her empty days? To please Clare, with whom he was in love? Well, who wouldn't be? reflected Bertha. Clare was so very pretty and such fun to be with.

She was surprised that her stepmother had had no objection to her changing the hours of her reading, but the doctor, driving her to the funeral, observed that there had been no trouble about it. 'Indeed, Mrs Soames seemed pleased that you have an outside interest.'

It was a remark which surprised Bertha, since her stepmother had evinced no interest in her comings and goings. It was a thought which she kept to herself.

A surprisingly large number of people were in the church. It seemed that Mrs Duke while alive had had few friends, but now even mere acquaintances crowded into the church and returned to her flat, filling it to overflowing while her nephew, a young man who had come from Sheffield with his wife, offered tea and meat-paste sandwiches.

Bertha, in the habit of making herself useful, filled the teacups and cut more bread and listened to the cheerful talk. Mrs Duke was being given a splendid send-off, and there had been a nice lot of flowers at the funeral.

'Aunty left her bits and pieces to me,' said her nephew, coming into the kitchen to make another pot of tea, 'as well as a bit in the Post Office. She 'as two cats too—I'll 'ave ter 'ave 'em destroyed. We've got a dog at home.'

'No need. Dr Hay-Smythe has taken them to his home.'

'Up ter 'im. 'E did a good job looking after Aunty.'

The doctor came in search of her presently. 'I think we might leave—I'll get someone to take over from you. Did you get a cup of tea?'

She shook her head. 'It doesn't matter.'

He smiled. 'It's a powerful brew. Wait there while I get someone…'

Mrs Tyler came back with him. 'Off you go, dearie. Everyone'll be here for another few hours and you've done more than your fair share. It was good of you and the doctor to come.'

'I liked Mrs Duke,' said Bertha.

'So did I. She'd have enjoyed this turn-out.'

'Are you expected home?' asked the doctor as he drove away.

'My stepmother and Clare are at a picture gallery and then going to have drinks with some friends. I expect you're busy—if you'd drop me off at a bus stop…'

'And then what will you do?' he wanted to know.

'Why, catch a bus, of course,' said Bertha in her practical way. 'And have a cup of tea when I get home.'

'Someone will have it ready for you?'

'Well, no. Crook's got the afternoon off and so has Daisy—she's the housemaid—and Cook will have her feet up—her bunions, you know.'

'In that case we'll have tea at my place.'

'It's very kind of you to ask me, but really you don't have to be polite. I've taken up a lot of your time, and you must have an awful lot to do.'

He spoke testily. 'Bertha, stop being so apologetic. If you don't wish to have tea with me say so. If not, come back with me and discuss the funeral over tea and toast.'

She said indignantly, 'I'm not being apologetic.' Her voice rose slightly. 'I don't care to be—to be…'

'Pitied? The last thing you can expect from me, my girl.'

He stopped outside his rooms and got out to open her door. She looked up at him as she got out and found herself smiling.

Cully had the door open before they had reached it. He was introduced to Bertha and offered her a dignified bow before opening the sitting-room door.

'We would like tea, Cully,' said the doctor. 'Earl Grey and hot buttered toast—and if you can find a few cakes?'

'Certainly, sir. Shall I take the young lady's coat?'

He shuddered inwardly at the sight of the garish dress, but his face was inscrutable; he had until now had a poor opinion of any young ladies his master had brought home from time to time for the occasional drink or lunch, but this one was different, never mind the horrible garment she was wearing. He glided away to arrange cakes on a plate. Made by himself, of course. He didn't trust cakes bought in a shop.

Bertha, happily unaware of Cully's thoughts, went into the sitting room with the doctor to be greeted by Freddie before he went to his master's side.

'How very convenient,' said Bertha, 'having your home over your consulting rooms. I didn't know you lived here.'

She gently rubbed Freddie's head and looked around her. The room was very much to her taste—a pleasing mixture of comfortable chairs and sofas and antique wall cabinets, lamp-tables, a magnificent Georgian rent table under the window and a giltwood mirror over the fireplace. That was Georgian too, she was sure.

She gave a little sigh of pleasure. 'This is a beautiful room,' she told him gravely.

'I'm glad you like it. Do sit down.' He offered her a small bergère, with upholstery matching the mulberry brocade curtains, and took an armchair opposite her. When her eyes darted to the long-case clock as it chimed the hour of four, he said soothingly, 'Don't worry. I'll see that you get back home before anyone else.'

Cully came in then with a laden tray. He sat everything out on a low table between them and slid away, but not before he had taken a good look at Bertha— nicely contrived from under lowered lids. His first impressions had been good ones, he decided.

Bertha made a good tea; she was hungry and Cully's dainty sandwiches and little cakes were delicious. Sitting there in the quiet, restful room with the doctor, whom she trusted and thought of as a friend, she was content and happy, and if their conversation dealt entirely with the visits she was to make to the nursery school she had no quarrel with that. She had been reminded so often by her stepmother and Clare that she was a dull companion and quite lacking in charm that she would have been surprised if the doctor had been anything else but briskly businesslike.

She was to go each morning from eleven o'clock until half past twelve, if that suited her, he told her, and she agreed at once. It might be a bit awkward sometimes, if she was needed to take the dog out or to go to the shops on some errand for her stepmother, but she would worry about that if and when it happened; there was no need to tell him.

'There are any number of books there; the children are various ages—two years to around four or five. You do understand that you need only read to them? There are plenty of helpers to do the necessary chores.'

'I think I shall like it very much.' Bertha smiled. 'Every day, too...'

He took her home presently, waiting until she had gone inside and then poked her head round the front door to tell him that no one was home.

* * *

Beyond telling Bertha how fortunate she was that Dr Hay-Smythe had found her something to do, her step-mother asked no questions. It was inconvenient that Bertha had to go each morning, of course, but since he was almost a friend of the family—indeed, almost more than that—she complied. 'Clare is quite sure that he's in love with her, so of course we would wish to do anything to oblige him in any way.'

So on Monday morning Bertha set off to go to the doctor's rooms. She was to go there first, he'd told her. The nursery school wasn't far from them and she would be shown the way and introduced to the matron who ran the place. She wasn't to feel nervous about going, for Matron already knew that she would be coming.

Mrs Taylor was at the rooms and greeted her with a friendly smile. 'Just a minute while I get Dr Hay-Smythe—he's in the garden with that dog of his.' She picked up the phone as she spoke, and a few minutes later he came in.

'I'll walk round with you, Bertha.' He glanced at his watch. 'I've time enough.'

She went with him down into the street and skipped along beside him to keep up.

'You can take a bus to the corner,' he told her. 'Go straight there after today.'

He turned down a narrow street and then turned again into a cul-de-sac lined with narrow, rather shabby houses. Halfway down he mounted the steps to a front door, rang the bell and then walked in.

The hall was rather bare, but the walls were a cheerful yellow and there was matting on the floor and a bowl of flowers on a table against the wall. The woman who came to meet them was small and stout with a jolly face and small bright eyes. She greeted the doctor like an old friend and looked at Bertha.

'So you're to be our reader,' she said, and shook hands. 'We are so glad to have you—we need all the help we can get. Come and see some of the children.'

She opened the door into a large, airy room full of children and several younger women. 'Of course, you won't be reading to them all,' she explained, 'but I've picked out those who will understand you, more or less. They love the sound of a voice, you know...'

They were in the centre of the room now with children all around them. 'We have children with special needs—three who are blind, several who had brain damage at birth and quite a few physically disabled...'

The doctor was watching Bertha's face. It showed surprise, compassion and a serene acceptance. Perhaps it had been unkind of him not to have told her, but he had wanted to see how she would react and she had reacted just as he had felt sure she would—with kindness, concern and not a trace of repugnance.

She looked at him and smiled. 'I'm going to like coming here,' she told him. 'Thank you for getting me the job.' She turned to the matron. 'I do hope I'll do…'

'Of course you will, my dear. Come along and take your jacket off and we'll get you settled.'

Bertha put out a hand to the doctor. 'I dare say I shan't see you again—well, perhaps when you come to see Clare, but you know what I mean. I can't thank you enough for your kindness.'

The doctor shook her hand in his large, firm one. 'Probably we shall see each other here occasionally. I come quite often to see the children.'

He went away then, and Bertha was led away by the matron, introduced to the other helpers and presently began to read to the circle of children assembled round her chair. It was an out-of-date book—an old fairy tale collection—and she started with the first story.

It wasn't going to be straightforward reading; she was interrupted frequently by eager little voices wanting her to read certain parts again, and some of them needed to have parts of the story explained to them, but after a time she got the hang of it and by half past twelve she and the children understood each other very well. She would do better tomorrow, she promised herself, going home to a solitary lunch, since her stepmother and Clare were out.

Within a few days Bertha had found her feet. It was a challenging job but she found it rewarding; the children were surprisingly happy, though sometimes difficult and frequently frustrated. They were lovable, though, and Bertha, lacking love in her own home, had plenty of that to offer.

At the end of two weeks she realised that she was happy, despite the dull life she led at home. Her stepmother still expected her to run errands, walk the dog and fetch and carry for her, so that she had little time to call her own. She was glad of that, really, as it gave her less time to think about Dr Hay-Smythe, for she had quickly discovered that she missed him.

She supposed that if Clare were to marry him—and, from what her stepsister said occasionally, Bertha thought that it was very likely—she would see him from time to time. He had been to the house once or twice, and Clare would recount their evenings together at great length, making no attempt to hide the fact that she had made up her mind to marry him.

When Bertha had asked her if she loved him, Clare had laughed. 'Of course not, but he's exactly what I want. Plenty of money, a handsome husband, and a chance to get away from home. Oh, I like him well enough…'

Bertha worried a lot about that; it spoilt her happiness. Dr Hay-Smythe wasn't the right husband for Clare. On the other hand, being in love with someone wasn't something one could arrange to suit oneself, and if he loved Clare perhaps it wouldn't matter.

It was towards the middle of the third week of her

visits to the nursery school that Clare unexpectedly asked her to go shopping with her in the afternoon. 'I've some things I simply must buy and Mother wants the car, and I hate taxis on my own. You'll have to come.'

They set out after lunch, and since it had been raining, and was threatening to do so again, Crook hailed a taxi. Clare was in good spirits and disposed to be friendly.

'It's time you had something decent to wear,' she said surprisingly. 'There's that jersey two-piece of mine—I never liked it; it's a ghastly colour—you can have that.'

'I don't think I want it if it's a ghastly colour, Clare. Thank you all the same.'

'Oh, the colour is ghastly on *me*. I dare say you'll look all right in it.' She glanced at Bertha. 'You'd better take it. Mother won't buy you anything until Father gets home, and he's been delayed so you'll have to wait for it.'

Bertha supposed that the jersey two-piece wouldn't be any worse than the lime-green outfits and there was no one to see her in it anyway. She wondered silently if there would ever be a chance for her to earn some money. She was a voluntary worker, but if she worked longer hours perhaps she could ask to be paid? She wouldn't want much.

The idea cheered her up, so that she was able to stand about patiently while Clare tried on dresses and then finally bought a pair of Italian shoes—white kid with high heels and very intricate straps. Bertha, watching them being fitted, was green with envy; she had pretty feet and ankles, and Clare's were by no means perfect. The shoes were on the wrong feet, she reflected in a rare fit of ill-humour.

The afternoon had cleared. Clare gave Bertha the shoes to carry and said airily that they would walk home. 'We can always pick up a taxi if we get tired,' she declared. 'We'll cut through here.'

The street was a quiet one, empty of traffic and people. At least, it was until they were halfway down it. The elderly lady on the opposite pavement was walking slowly, carrying a plastic bag and an umbrella, with her handbag dangling from one arm, so she had no hands free to defend herself when, apparently from nowhere, two youths leapt at her from a narrow alleyway. They pushed her to the ground and one of them hit her as she tried to keep a hand on her bag.

Clare stopped suddenly. 'Quick, we must run for it. They'll be after us if they see us. Hurry, can't you?'

Bertha took no notice. She pushed away Clare's hands clinging to her arm, ran across the street and swiped at one of the youths with the plastic bag containing Clare's new shoes. It caught him on the shins and he staggered and fell. She swung the bag again, intent on hitting the other youth. The bag split this time and the shoes flew into the gutter.

Confronted by a virago intent on hurting them, the pair scrambled to their feet and fled, dropping the lady's handbag as they went. Short of breath and shaking with fright, Bertha knelt down by the old lady.

'My purse—my pension…' The elderly face was white with fear and worry. It was bruised, too.

'It's all right,' said Bertha. 'They dropped your handbag. I'll get it for you. But, first of all, are you hurt?'

Before the old lady could answer, Clare hissed into Bertha's ear, 'My shoes—my lovely new shoes. You've ruined them. I'll never forgive you!'

'Oh, bother your shoes,' said Bertha. 'Go and bang on someone's door and get an ambulance.'

Just for once, Clare, speechless at Bertha's brisk orders, did as she was told.

She was back presently, and there were people with her. Bertha, doing her best to make the old lady as comfortable as possible, listened with half an ear to her stepsister's voice.

'Two huge men,' said Clare, in what Bertha always thought of as her little-girl voice. 'They ran at this poor lady and knocked her down. I simply rushed across the street·and hit them with a shopping bag— one of them fell over and they ran away then.' She gave a little laugh. 'I've never been so scared in my life…'

'Very plucky, if I might say so,' said a voice.

Another voice asked, 'You're not hurt, young lady? It was a brave thing to do.'

'Well, one doesn't think of oneself,' murmured Clare. 'And luckily my sister came to help me once the men had gone.'

The old lady stared up at Bertha's placid face. 'That's a pack of lies,' she whispered. 'It was you; I saw you…' She closed her eyes tiredly. 'I shall tell someone…'

'It doesn't matter,' said Bertha. 'All that matters is that you're safe. Here is your handbag, and the purse is still inside.'

She got to her feet as the ambulance drew up and the few people who had gathered to see what was amiss gave her sidelong glances with no sign of friendliness; she could read their thoughts—leaving her pretty sister to cope with those violent men… Luckily there were still brave girls left in this modern day and age of violence…

Bertha told herself that it didn't matter; they were strangers and never likely to see her again. She wondered what Clare would do next—beg a lift from someone, most likely.

There was no need for that, however.

By good fortune—or was it bad fortune?—Dr Hay-Smythe, on his way from somewhere or other, had seen the little group as he drove past. He stopped, reversed neatly and got out of his car. Clare, with a wistful little cry, exactly right for the occasion, ran to meet him.

CHAPTER THREE

'OLIVER!' cried Clare, in what could only be described as a brave little voice. 'Thank heaven you're here.' She waved an arm towards the ambulancemen loading the old lady onto a stretcher. 'This poor old woman—there were two enormous men attacking her. She's been hurt—she might have been killed—but I ran as fast as I could and threw my bag at them and they ran away.'

The onlookers, gathering close, murmured admiringly. 'Proper brave young lady,' said one.

'Oh, no,' Clare said softly. 'Anyone would have done the same.' She had laid a hand on the doctor's arm and now looked up into his face.

He wasn't looking at her. He was watching the stretcher being lifted into the ambulance. The old lady was saying something to Bertha, who had whipped a bit of paper and pencil from her bag and was writing something down.

He removed Clare's hand quite gently. 'I should just take a look,' he observed.

He spoke to the ambulance driver and then bent over the old lady, giving Bertha a quick smile as he did so. 'Can I help in any way? I'm told there's nothing broken, but you had better have a check-up at the hospital.'

The shrewd old eyes studied his face. 'You're a doctor? Don't you listen to that girl's tale. Not a word of truth in it. Seen it with my own eyes—tried to run away, she did. It was this child who tackled those thugs—twice her size too.' She gave a weak snort of indignation. 'Mad as fire because her shoes had been spoilt. Huh!'

'Thank you for telling me. Do we have your name? Is there anyone who should be told?'

'This young lady's seen to that for me, bless her. Gets things done while others talk.'

'Indeed she does.' He took her hand. 'You'll be all right now.'

He went back to the driver and presently, when the ambulance had been driven away, he joined Bertha. 'Let me have her name and address, will you? I'll check on her later today. Now I'll drive you both home.'

Clare had joined them. 'What was all that about? You don't need to bother any more; she'll be looked after at the hospital. I feel awfully odd—it was a shock…'

'I'll drive you both back home. I dare say you may like to go straight to bed, Clare.'

Clare jumped into the car. 'No, no—I'm not such a weakling as all that, Oliver. I dare say Bertha would like to lie down for a bit, though—she was so frightened.' She turned her head to look at Bertha on the back seat, who looked out of the window and didn't answer.

The doctor didn't say anything either, so Clare went on uncertainly, 'Well, of course, it was enough to scare the wits out of anyone, wasn't it?'

No one answered that either. Presently she said pettishly, 'I had a pair of new shoes—wildly expensive— they've been ruined.' Quite forgetting her role of brave girl, she turned on Bertha. 'You'll have to pay for them, Bertha. Throwing them around like that—' She stopped, aware that she had let the cat out of the bag. 'What was the good of flinging the bag at those men when they had already run away?'

'I'm sure you can buy more shoes,' said the doctor blandly. 'And what is a pair of shoes compared with saving an old lady from harm?'

He glanced in his mirror, caught Bertha's eye and smiled at her, and lowered an eyelid in an unmistakable wink.

It gave her a warm glow. Never mind that there would be some hard words when she got home; she had long since learned to ignore them. He had believed the old lady and she had the wit to see that he wouldn't mention it—it would make it so much worse for her and would probably mean the end of her job at the nursery school. If any special attention from him were to come to Clare's or her stepmother's notice, they would find a way to make sure that she never saw him again…

The doctor stopped the car before their door, and Clare said coaxingly, 'Take me out to dinner this evening, Oliver? I do need cheering up after all I've just gone through. Somewhere quiet where we can talk?'

He had got out to open her door and now turned to do the same for Bertha. 'Impossible, I'm afraid. I've a meeting at seven o'clock which will last for hours—perhaps at the weekend…'

He closed the car door. 'I suggest that you both have an early night. If there is any news of the old lady I'll let you have it. I shall be seeing her later this evening. Bertha, if you will give me her address, I'll see that her family are told.'

She handed it over with a murmured thank-you, bade him goodbye and started up the steps to the door, leaving Clare to make a more protracted leave-taking—something which he nipped in the bud with apparent reluctance.

Clare's charm turned to cold fury as they entered the house. 'You'll pay for this,' she stormed. 'Those shoes cost the earth. Now I've nothing to wear with that new dress…'

Bertha said matter-of-factly, 'Well, I can't pay for them, can I? I haven't any money. And you've dozens of shoes.' She looked at Clare's furious face. 'Are they really more important than helping someone in a fix?' She wanted to know. 'And what a lot of fibs you've told everyone. I must say you looked the part.'

She stopped then, surprised at herself, but not nearly as surprised as Clare. 'How dare you?' Clare snapped. 'How dare you talk to me like that?'

'Well, it's the truth, isn't it?' asked Bertha placidly. 'But, don't worry, I shan't give you away.'

'No one would believe you...'

'Probably not.' Bertha went up to her room, leaving Clare fuming.

The full weight of her stepmother's displeasure fell upon her when she went downstairs presently. She was most ungrateful, careless and unnaturally mean towards her stepsister, who had behaved with the courage only to be expected of her. Bertha should be bitterly ashamed of herself. 'I had intended to take you to a charity coffee morning at Lady Forde's, but I shall certainly not do so now,' she finished.

Bertha, allowing the harsh voice to wash over her head, heaved a sigh of relief; the last time she had been taken there she had ended up making herself useful, helping Lady Forde's meek companion hand round the coffee and cakes. She looked down at her lap and didn't say a word. What would be the use?

She would have been immensely cheered if she had known of the doctor's efforts on her behalf. There had to be a way, he reflected, sitting in his sitting room with Freddie at his feet, in which he could give Bertha a treat. It seemed to him that she had no fun at all—indeed, was leading an unhappy life.

'She deserves better,' he told Freddie, who yawned. 'Properly dressed and turned out, she might stand a chance of attracting some young man. She has beautiful eyes, and I don't know another girl who would have held her tongue as she did this afternoon.'

It was much later, after Cully had gone to his bed and the house was quiet, that he knew what he would do. Well satisfied, he settled Freddie in his basket in the kitchen and went to bed himself.

The doctor waited another two days before calling at Mrs Soames's house. He had satisfied himself that Bertha was still going to the nursery. Matron had been enthusiastic about her and assured him that there had been no question of her leaving, so he was able to dispel the nagging thought that her stepmother might have shown her anger by forbidding her to go.

He chose a time when he was reasonably sure that they would all be at home and gave as his excuse his concern as to whether the two girls had got over their unfortunate experience. All three ladies were in the drawing room—something which pleased him, for if Bertha wasn't there, there was always the chance that she would hear nothing of his plans.

Mrs Soames rose to meet him. 'My dear Oliver, most kind of you to call—as you see, we are sitting quietly at home. Dear Clare is somewhat shocked still.'

'I'm sorry to hear it,' said the doctor, shaking Clare's hand and giving Bertha a smiling nod. 'Perhaps I can offer a remedy—both for her and for Bertha, who must also be just as upset.'

Mrs Soames looked surprised. 'Bertha? I hardly think so. She isn't in the least sensitive.'

The doctor looked grave and learned. He said weightily, 'Nevertheless, I think that both young ladies would benefit from my plan.'

His bedside manner, reflected Bertha, and very impressive and effective too, for her stepmother nodded and said, 'Of course. I bow to your wisdom, Oliver.'

'Most fortunately I am free tomorrow. I should be delighted if I might drive them into the country for the day, away from London. To slow down one's lifestyle once in a while is necessary, especially when one has had a shock such as Clare had.' He looked at Bertha. 'And I am sure that Bertha must have been upset. I haven't had the opportunity to ask her—'

'There's no need,' Clare interrupted him hastily. 'I'm sure she needs a break just as I do. We'd love to come with you, Oliver. Where shall we go?'

'How about a surprise? Is ten o'clock too early for you?'

'No, no. Not a minute too early.' Clare was at her most charming, and then, as he got up to go, she said suddenly, 'But of course Bertha won't be able to go with us—she reads to old ladies or something every morning.'

'Tomorrow is Saturday,' the doctor reminded her gently. 'I doubt if she does that at the weekends.' He glanced at Bertha. 'Is that not so, Bertha?'

Bertha murmured an agreement and saw the flash of annoyance on Clare's face. All of a sudden she was doubtful as to whether a day spent in the company of Clare and the doctor would be as pleasant as it sounded.

After he had gone, Clare said with satisfaction, 'You haven't anything to wear, Bertha. I hope Oliver won't feel embarrassed. It's a great pity that you have to come with us. You could have refused.'

'I shall enjoy a day out,' said Bertha calmly, 'and I shall wear the jersey two-piece you handed down to me. I'll have to take it in…'

Clare jumped up. 'You ungrateful girl. That outfit cost a lot of money.'

'It's a ghastly colour,' said Bertha equably, and went away to try it on. It was indeed a garment which Clare should never have bought—acid-yellow, and it needed taking in a good deal.

'Who cares?' said Bertha defiantly to the kitchen cat, who had followed her upstairs, and began to sew—a tricky business since her eyes were full of tears. To be with the doctor again would be, she had to admit, the height of happiness, but she very much doubted if he would feel the same. He was far too

well-mannered to comment upon the two-piece—
probably he would be speechless when he saw it—
but it would be nice to spend a day with him wearing
an outfit which was the right colour and which fitted.

'I suppose I am too thin,' she observed to the cat,
pinning darts and cobbling them up. The sleeves were
a bit too long—she would have to keep pushing them
up—and the neck was too low. Clare liked low necks
so that she could display her plump bosom, but
Bertha, who had a pretty bosom of her own, stitched
it up to a decent level and hoped that no one would
notice.

Dr Hay-Smythe noticed it at once, even though half-
blinded by the acid-yellow. An appalling outfit, he
reflected, obviously hastily altered, for it didn't fit
anywhere it should and the colour did nothing for
Bertha's ordinary features and light brown hair. He
found that he was full of rage at her treatment, although he allowed nothing of that to show. He wished
her good morning and talked pleasantly to Mrs
Soames while they waited for Clare.

She came at last, with little cries of regret at keeping him waiting. 'I wanted to look as nice as possible
for you, Oliver,' she said with a little laugh. And indeed she did look nice—in blue and white wool, simply cut and just right for a day in the country. She
had a navy shoulder-bag and matching shoes with

high heels. The contrast between the two girls was cruel.

The doctor said breezily, 'Ah, here you are at last. I was beginning to think that you had changed your mind!' He smiled a little. 'Found someone younger and more exciting with whom to spend the day.'

This delighted Clare. 'There isn't anyone more exciting than you, Oliver,' she cooed, and Bertha looked away, feeling sick and wishing that the day was over before it had begun.

Of course Clare got into the seat beside Oliver, leaving him to usher Bertha into the back of the car where Freddie, delighted to have company, greeted her with pleasure.

Clare, turning round to stare, observed tartly, 'Oh, you've brought a dog.' And then said, with a little laugh, 'He'll be company for Bertha.'

'Freddie goes wherever I go when it's possible. He sits beside me on long journeys and is a delightful companion.'

'Well, now you have me,' declared Clare. 'I'm a delightful companion too!'

A remark which the doctor apparently didn't hear.

He drove steadily towards the western suburbs, apparently content to listen to Clare's chatter, and when he was finally clear of the city he turned off the main road and slowed the car as they reached the countryside. They were in Hertfordshire now, bypassing the towns, taking minor roads through the woods and fields and going through villages, peaceful under the morning sun. At one of these he stopped at an inn.

'Coffee?' he asked, and got out to open Clare's door and then usher Bertha and Freddie out of the car.

The inn was old and thatched and cosy inside. The doctor asked for coffee, then suggested, 'You two girls go ahead. I'll take Freddie for a quick run while the coffee's fetched.'

The ladies' was spotlessly clean, but lacked the comforts of its London counterparts. Clare, doing her face in front of the only mirror, said crossly, 'He might have stopped at a decent hotel—this is pretty primitive. I hope we shall lunch somewhere more civilised.'

'I like it,' said Bertha. 'I like being away from London. I'd like to live in the country.'

Clare didn't bother to reply, merely remarking as they went to join the doctor that the yellow jersey looked quite frightful. 'When I see you in it,' said Clare, 'I can see just how ghastly it is!'

It was an opinion shared by the doctor as he watched them cross the bar to join him at a table by the window, but nothing could dim the pleasure in Bertha's face, and, watching it, he hardly noticed the outfit.

'The coffee was good. I'm surprised,' said Clare. 'I mean, in a place like this you don't expect it, do you?'

'Why not?' The doctor was at his most genial. 'The food in some of these country pubs is as good or better than that served in some of the London restaurants. No dainty morsels in a pretty pattern on your plate, but just steak and kidney pudding and local vegetables, or sausages and mash with apple pie for a pudding.'

Clare looked taken aback. If he intended giving her sausages and mash for lunch she would demand to be taken home. 'Where are we lunching?' she asked.

'Ah, wait and see!'

Bertha had drunk her coffee almost in silence, with Freddie crouching under the table beside her, nudging her gently for a bit of biscuit from time to time. She hoped that they would lunch in a country pub—sausages and mash would be nice, bringing to mind the meal she and the doctor had eaten together. Meeting him had changed her life...

They drove on presently into Buckinghamshire, still keeping to the country roads. It was obvious that the doctor knew where he was going. Bertha stopped herself from asking him; it might spoil whatever surprise he had in store for them.

It was almost noon when they came upon a small village—a compact gathering of Tudor cottages with a church overlooking them from the brow of a low hill.

Bertha peered and said, 'Oh, this is delightful. Where are we?'

'This is Wing—'

'Isn't there a hotel?' asked Clare. 'We're not going

to stop here, are we?' She had spoken sharply. 'It's a bit primitive, isn't it?' She saw his lifted eyebrows. 'Well, no, not primitive, perhaps, but you know what I mean, Oliver. Or is there one of those country-house restaurants tucked away out of sight?'

He only smiled and turned the car through an open wrought-iron gate. The drive was short, and at its end was a house—not a grand house, one might call it a gentleman's residence—sitting squarely amidst trees and shrubs with a wide lawn before it edged by flowerbeds. Bertha, examining it from the car, thought that it must be Georgian, with its Palladian door with a pediment above, its many paned windows and tall chimneystacks.

It wasn't just a lovely old house, it was a home; there were long windows, tubs of japonica on either side of the door, the bare branches of Virginia creeper rioting over its walls and, watching them from a wrought-iron sill above a hooded bay window, a majestic cat with a thick orange coat. Bertha saw all this as Clare got out, the latter happy now at the sight of a house worthy of her attention and intent on making up for her pettishness.

'I suppose we are to lunch here?' she asked as the doctor opened Bertha's door and she and Freddie tumbled out.

His 'yes' was noncommittal.

'It isn't a hotel, is it?' asked Bertha. 'It's someone's home. It's quite beautiful.'

'I'm glad you like it, Bertha. It is my home. My mother will be delighted to have you both as her guests for lunch.'

'Yours?' queried Clare eagerly. 'As well as your flat in town? I suppose your mother will live here until you want it for yourself—when you marry?' She gave him one of her most charming smiles, which he ignored.

'Your mother doesn't mind?' asked Bertha. 'If we are unexpected...'

'You're not. I phoned her yesterday. She is glad to welcome you—she is sometimes a little lonely since my father died.'

'Oh, I'm sorry.' Bertha's plain face was full of sympathy.

'Thank you. Shall we go indoors?'

The house door opened under his hand and he ushered them into the wide hall with its oak floor and marble-topped console table flanked by cane and walnut chairs. There was a leather-covered armchair in one corner too, the repository of a variety of coats, jackets, walking sticks, dog leads and old straw hats, giving the rather austere grandeur of the hall a pleasantly lived-in look. The doctor led the way past the oak staircase with its wrought-iron balustrade at the back of the hall and opened a small door.

'Mother will be in the garden,' he observed. 'We can go through the kitchen.'

The kitchen was large with a vast dresser loaded

with china against one wall, an Aga stove and a scrubbed table ringed by Windsor chairs at its centre. Two women looked up as they went in.

'Master Oliver, good morning to you, sir—and the two young ladies.'

The speaker was short and stout and wrapped around by a very white apron. The doctor crossed the room and kissed her cheek.

'Meg, how nice to see you again.' He looked across at the second woman, who was a little younger and had a severe expression. 'And Dora—you're both well? Good. Clare, Bertha—this is Meg, our cook, and Dora, who runs the house.'

Clare nodded and said, 'hello,' but Bertha smiled and shook hands.

'What a heavenly kitchen.' Her lovely eyes were sparkling with pleasure. 'It's a kind of haven…' She blushed because she had said something silly, but Meg and Dora were smiling.

'That it is, miss—specially now in the winter of an evening. Many a time Mr Oliver's popped in here to beg a slice of dripping toast.'

He smiled. 'Meg, you are making my mouth water. We had better go and find my mother. We'll see you before we go.'

Clare had stood apart, tapping a foot impatiently, but as they went through the door into the garden beyond she slipped an arm through the doctor's.

'I love your home,' she told him, 'and your lovely old-fashioned servants.'

'They are our friends as well, Clare. They have been with us for as long as I can remember.'

The garden behind the house was large and rambling, with narrow paths between the flowerbeds and flowering shrubs. Freddie rushed ahead, and they heard his barking echoed by a shrill yapping.

'My mother will be in the greenhouses.' The doctor had disengaged his arm from Clare's in order to lead the way, and presently they went through a ramshackle door in a high brick wall and saw the greenhouses to one side of the kitchen garden.

Bertha, lingering here and there to look at neatly tended borders and shrubs, saw that Clare's high heels were making heavy weather of the earth paths. Her clothes were exquisite, but here, in this country garden, they didn't look right. Bertha glanced down at her own person and had to admit that her own outfit didn't look right either. She hoped that the doctor's mother wasn't a follower of fashion like her step-mother.

She had no need to worry; the lady who came to meet them as the doctor opened the greenhouse door was wearing a fine wool skirt stained with earth and with bits of greenery caught up in it, and her blouse, pure silk and beautifully made, was almost covered by a misshapen cardigan of beige cashmere as stained as the skirt. She was wearing wellies and thick gardening gloves and looked, thought Bertha, exactly as the doctor's mother should look.

She wasn't quite sure what she meant by this, it was something that she couldn't put into words, but she knew instinctively that this elderly lady with her plain face and sweet expression was all that she would have wanted if her own mother had lived.

'My dear.' Mrs Hay-Smythe lifted up her face for her son's kiss. 'How lovely to see you—and these are the girls who had such an unpleasant experience the other day?'

She held out a hand, the glove pulled off. 'I'm delighted to meet you. You must tell me all about it, presently—I live such a quiet life here that I'm all agog to hear the details.'

'Oh, it was nothing, Mrs Hay-Smythe,' said Clare. 'I'm sure there are many more people braver than I. It is so kind of Oliver to bring us; I had no idea that he had such a beautiful home.'

Mrs Hay-Smythe looked a little taken aback, but she smiled and said, 'Well, yes, we're very happy to live here.'

She turned to Bertha. 'And you are Bertha?' Her smile widened and her blue eyes smiled too, never once so much as glancing at the yellow jersey. 'Forgive me that I am so untidy, but there is always work to do in the greenhouse. We'll go indoors and have a drink. Oliver will look after you while I tidy myself.'

They wandered back to the house—Clare ahead

with the doctor, his mother coming slowly with Bertha, stopping to describe the bushes and flowers that would bloom in the spring as they went, Freddie and her small border terrier beside them.

'You are fond of gardening?' she wanted to know.

'Well, we live in a townhouse, you know. There's a gardener, and he comes once a week to see to the garden—but he doesn't grow things, just comes and digs up whatever's there and then plants the next lot. That's not really gardening. I'd love to have a packet of seeds and grow flowers, but I—I don't have much time.'

Mrs Hay-Smythe, who knew all about Bertha, nodded sympathetically. 'I expect one day you'll get the opportunity—when you marry, you know.'

'I don't really expect to marry,' said Bertha matter-of-factly. 'I don't meet many people and I'm plain.' She sounded quite cheerful and her hostess smiled.

'Well, as to that, I'm plain, my dear, and I was a middle daughter of six living in a remote vicarage. And that, I may tell you, was quite a handicap.'

They both laughed and Clare, standing waiting for them with the doctor, frowned. Just like Bertha to worm her way into their hostess's good books, she thought. Well, she would soon see about that.

As they went into the house she edged her way towards Mrs Hay-Smythe. 'This is such a lovely house. I do hope there will be time for you to take me round before we go back.' She remembered that

that would leave Bertha with Oliver, which would never do. 'Bertha too, of course...'

Mrs Hay-Smythe had manners as beautiful as her son's. 'I shall be delighted. But now I must go and change. Oliver, give the girls a drink, will you? I'll be ten minutes or so. We mustn't keep Meg waiting.'

It seemed to Bertha that the doctor was perfectly content to listen to Clare's chatter as she drank her gin and lime, and his well-mannered attempts to draw her into the conversation merely increased her shyness. So silly, she reflected, sipping her sherry, because when I'm with him and there's no one else there I'm perfectly normal.

Mrs Hay-Smythe came back presently, wearing a black and white dress, which, while being elegant, suited her age. A pity, thought Bertha, still wrapped in thought, that her stepmother didn't dress in a similar manner, instead of forcing herself into clothes more suitable to a woman of half her age. She was getting very mean and unkind, she reflected.

Lunch eaten in a lovely panelled room with an oval table and a massive sideboard of mahogany, matching shield-back chairs and a number of portraits in heavy gilt frames on its walls, was simple but beautifully cooked: miniature onion tarts decorated with olives and strips of anchovy, grilled trout with a pepper sauce and a green salad, followed by orange cream soufflés.

Bertha ate with unselfconscious pleasure and a

good appetite and listened resignedly to Clare tell her hostess as she picked daintily at her food that she adored French cooking.

'We have a chef who cooks the most delicious food.' She gave one of her little laughs. 'I'm so fussy, I'm afraid. But I adore lobster, don't you? And those little tartlets with caviare…'

Mrs Hay-Smythe smiled and offered Bertha a second helping. Bertha, pink with embarrassment, accepted. So did the doctor and his mother, so that Clare was left to sit and look at her plate while the three of them ate unhurriedly.

They had coffee in the conservatory and soon the doctor said, 'We have a family pet at the bottom of the garden. Nellie the donkey. She enjoys visitors and Freddie is devoted to her. Shall we stroll down to see her?'

He smiled at Bertha's eager face and Freddie was already on his feet when Clare said quickly, 'Oh, but we are to see the house. I'm longing to go all over it.'

'In that case,' said Mrs Hay-Smythe in a decisive voice, 'you go on ahead to Nellie, Oliver, and take Bertha with you, and I'll take Clare to see a little of the house.' When Clare would have protested that perhaps, after all, she would rather see the donkey, Mrs Hay-Smythe said crisply, 'No, no, I mustn't disappoint you. We can join the others very shortly.'

She whisked Clare indoors and the doctor stood up.

'Come along, Bertha. We'll go to the kitchen and get a carrot…'

Meg and Dora were loading the dishwasher, and the gentle clatter of crockery made a pleasant background for the loud tick-tock of the kitchen clock and the faint strains of the radio. There was a tabby cat before the Aga, and the cat with the orange coat was sitting on the window-sill.

'Carrots?' said Meg. 'For that donkey of yours, Master Oliver? Pampered, that's what she is.' She smiled broadly at Bertha. 'Not but what she's an old pet, when all's said and done.'

Dora had gone to fetch the carrots and the doctor was sitting on the kitchen table eating a slice of the cake that was presumably for tea.

'I enjoyed my lunch,' said Bertha awkwardly. 'You must be a marvellous cook, Meg.'

'Lor' bless you, miss, anyone can cook who puts their mind to it.' But Meg looked pleased all the same.

The donkey was in a small orchard at the bottom of the large garden. She was an elderly beast who was pleased to see them; she ate the carrots and then trotted around a bit in a dignified way with a delighted Freddie.

The doctor, leaning on the gate to the orchard, looked sideways at Bertha. She was happy, her face full of contentment. She was happily oblivious of her startling outfit too—which was even more startling in the gentle surroundings.

Conscious that he was looking at her, she turned her head and their eyes met.

Good gracious, thought Bertha, I feel as if I've known him all my life, that I've been waiting for him…

Clare's voice broke the fragile thread which had been spun between them. 'There you are. Is this the donkey? Oliver, you do have a lovely house—your really ought to marry and share it with someone.'

CHAPTER FOUR

THEY didn't stay long in the orchard—Clare's high-heeled shoes sank into the ground at every step and her complaints weren't easily ignored. They sat in the conservatory again, and Clare told them amusing tales about her friends and detailed the plays she had recently seen and the parties she had attended.

'I scarcely have a moment to myself,' she declared on a sigh. 'You can't imagine how delightful a restful day here is.'

'You would like to live in the country?' asked Mrs Hay-Smythe.

'In a house like this? Oh, yes. One could run up to town whenever one felt like it—shopping and the theatre—and I dare say there are other people living around here…'

'Oh, yes.' Mrs Hay-Smythe spoke pleasantly. 'Oliver, will you ask Meg to bring tea out here?'

After tea they took their leave and got into the car, and were waved away by Mrs Hay-Smythe. Bertha waved back, taking a last look at the house she wasn't likely to see again but would never forget.

As for Mrs Hay-Smythe, she went to the kitchen, where she found Meg and Dora having their own tea.

She sat down at the table with them and accepted a cup of strong tea with plenty of milk. Not her favourite brand, but she felt that she needed something with a bite to it.

'Well?' she asked.

'Since you want to know, ma'am,' said Meg, 'and speaking for the two of us, we just hope that the master isn't taken with that young lady what didn't eat her lunch. High and mighty, we thought—didn't we, Dora?'

'Let me put your minds at rest. This visit was made in order to give the other Miss Soames a day out, but to do so it was necessary to invite her stepsister as well.'

'Well, there,' said Dora. 'Like Cinderella. Such a nice quiet young lady too. Thanked you for her lunch, didn't she, Meg?'

'That she did, and not smarmy either. Fitted into the house very nicely too.'

'Yes, she did,' said Mrs Hay-Smythe thoughtfully. Bertha would make a delightful daughter-in-law, but Oliver had given no sign—he had helped her out of kindness but shown no wish to be in her company or even talk to her other than in a casual friendly way. 'A pity,' said Mrs Hay-Smythe, and with Flossie, her little dog, at her heels she went back to the greenhouse, where she put on a vast apron and her gardening gloves and began work again.

* * *

The doctor drove back the way they had come, listening to Clare's voice and hardly hearing what she was saying. Only when she said insistently, 'You will take me out to dinner this evening, won't you, Oliver? Somewhere lively where we can dance afterwards? It's been a lovely day, but after all that rural quiet we could do with some town life...'

'When we get back,' he said, 'I am going straight to the hospital where I shall be for several hours, and I have an appointment for eight o'clock tomorrow morning. I am a working man, Clare.'

She pouted. 'Oh, Oliver, can't you forget the hospital just for once? I was so sure you'd take me out.'

'Quite impossible. Besides, I'm not a party man, Clare.'

She touched his sleeve. 'I could change that for you. At least promise you'll come to dinner one evening? I'll tell Mother to give you a ring.'

He glanced in the side-mirror and saw that Bertha was sitting with her arm round Freddie's neck, looking out of the window. Her face was turned away, but the back of her head looked sad.

He stayed only as long as good manners required when they reached the Soameses' house, and when he had gone Clare threw her handbag down and flung herself into a chair.

Her mother asked sharply, 'Well, you had Oliver all to yourself—is he interested?'

'Well, of course he is. If only we hadn't taken Bertha with us…'

'She didn't interfere, I hope.'

'She didn't get the chance—she hardly spoke to him. I didn't give her the opportunity. She was with his mother most of the time.'

'What is Mrs Hay-Smythe like?'

'Oh, boring—talking about the garden and the Women's Institute and doing the flowers for the church. She was in the greenhouse when we got there. I thought she was one of the servants.'

'Not a lady?' asked her mother, horrified.

'Oh, yes, no doubt about that. Plenty of money too, I should imagine. The house is lovely—it would be a splendid country home for weekends if we could have a decent flat here.' She laughed. 'The best of both worlds.'

Bertha, in her room, changing out of the two-piece and getting into another of Clare's too-elaborate dresses, told the kitchen cat, who was enjoying a stolen hour or so on her bed, all about her day.

'I don't suppose Oliver will be able to withstand Clare for much longer—only I mustn't call him Oliver, must I? I'm not supposed to have more than a nodding acquaintance with him.' She sat down on the bed, the better to address her companion. 'I think that is what I must do in the future, just nod. I think about him too much and I miss him…'

She went to peer at her face in the mirror and nodded at its reflection. 'Plain as a pikestaff, my girl.'

Dinner was rather worse than usual, for there were no guests and that gave her stepmother and Clare the opportunity to criticise her behaviour during the day.

'Clare tells me that you spent too much time with Mrs Hay-Smythe…'

Bertha popped a morsel of fish into her mouth and chewed it. 'Well,' she said reasonably, 'what else was I to do? Clare wouldn't have liked it if I'd attached myself to Dr Hay-Smythe, and it would have looked very ill-mannered if I'd just gone off on my own.'

Mrs Soames glared, seeking for a quelling reply. 'Anyway, you should never have gone off with the doctor while Clare was in the house with his mother.'

'I enjoyed it. We talked about interesting things— the donkey and the orchard and the house.'

'He must have been bored,' said her stepmother crossly.

Bertha looked demure. 'Yes, I think that some of the time he was—very bored.'

Clare tossed her head. 'Not when he was with me,' she said smugly, but her mother shot Bertha a frowning look.

'I think you should understand, Bertha, that Dr Hay-Smythe is very likely about to propose marriage to your stepsister…'

'Has he said so?' asked Bertha composedly. She

studied Mrs Soames, whose high colour had turned faintly purple.

'Certainly not, but one feels these things.' Mrs Soames pushed her plate aside. 'I am telling you this because I wish you to refuse any further invitations which the doctor may offer you—no doubt out of kindness.'

'Why?'

'There is an old saying—two is company, three is a crowd.'

'Oh, you don't want me to play gooseberry. I looked like one today in that frightful outfit Clare passed on to me.'

'You ungrateful—' began Clare, but was silenced by a majestic wave of her mother's hand.

'I cannot think what has come over you, Bertha. Presumably this day's outing has gone to your head. The two-piece Clare so kindly gave you is charming.'

'Then why doesn't she wear it?' asked Bertha, feeling reckless. She wasn't sure what had come over her either, but she was rather enjoying it. 'I would like some new clothes of my own.'

Mrs Soames's bosom swelled alarmingly. 'That is enough, Bertha. I shall buy you something suitable when I have the leisure to arrange it. I think you had better have an early night, for you aren't yourself... The impertinence...'

'Is that what it is? It feels nice!' said Bertha.

She excused herself with perfect good manners and

went up to her room. She lay in the bath for a long time, having a good cry but not sure why she was crying. At least, she had a vague idea at the back of her head as to why she felt lonely and miserable, but she didn't allow herself to pursue the matter. She got into bed and the cat curled up against her back, purring in a comforting manner, so that she was lulled into a dreamless sleep.

Her mother and Clare had been invited to lunch with friends who had a house near Henley. Bertha had been invited too, but she didn't know that. Mrs Soames had explained to their hosts that she had a severe cold in the head and would spend the day in bed.

Bertha was up early, escorting the cat back to her rightful place in the kitchen and making herself tea. She would have almost the whole day to herself; Crook was to have an afternoon off and Cook's sister was coming to spend the day with her.

Mrs Soames found this quite satisfactory since Bertha could be served a cold lunch and get her own tea if Cook decided to walk down to the nearest bus stop with her sister. The daily maid never came on a Sunday.

All this suited Bertha; she drank her tea while the cat lapped milk, and decided what she would do with her day. A walk—a long walk. She would go to St James's Park and feed the ducks. She went back upstairs to dress and had almost finished breakfast when

Clare joined her. Bertha said good morning and she got a sour look, which she supposed was only to be expected.

It was after eleven o'clock by the time Mrs Soames and Clare had driven away. Bertha, thankful that it was a dull, cold day, allowing her to wear the lime-green which she felt was slightly less awful than the two-piece, went to tell Crook that she might be late for lunch and ask him to leave it on a tray for her before he left the house and set out.

There wasn't a great deal of traffic in the streets, but there were plenty of people taking their Sunday walk as she neared the park. She walked briskly, her head full of daydreams, not noticing her surroundings until someone screamed.

A young woman was coming out of the park gates pushing a pram—and running across the street into the path of several cars was a small boy. Bertha ran. She ran fast, unhampered by high heels and handbag, and plucked the child from the nearest car's wheels just before those same wheels bowled her over.

The child's safe, she thought hazily, aware that every bone in her body ached and that she was lying in a puddle of water, but somehow she felt too tired to get up. She felt hands and then heard voices, any number of them, asking if she were hurt.

'No—thank you,' said Bertha politely. 'Just aching a bit. Is that child OK?'

There was a chorus of 'yes', and somebody said

that there was an ambulance coming. 'No need,' said Bertha, not feeling at all herself. 'If I could get up…'

'No, no,' said a voice. 'There may be broken bones…'

So she stayed where she was, listening to the voices; there seemed to be a great many people all talking at once. She was feeling sick now…

There were no broken bones, the ambulanceman assured her, but they laid her on a stretcher, popped her into the ambulance and bore her away to hospital. They had put a dressing on her leg without saying why.

The police were there by then, wanting to know her name and where she lived.

'Bertha Soames. But there is no one at home.'

Well, Cook was, but what could she do? Better keep quiet. Bertha closed her eyes, one of which was rapidly turning purple.

Dr Hay-Smythe, called down to the accident and emergency department to examine a severe head injury, paused to speak to the casualty officer as he left. The slight commotion as an ambulance drew up and a patient was wheeled in caused him to turn his head. He glanced at the patient and then looked again.

'Will you stop for a moment?' he asked, and bent over the stretcher. It was Bertha, all right, with a muddy face and a black eye and hair all over the place.

He straightened up. 'I know this young lady. I'll wait while you take a look.'

'Went after a kid running under a car. Kid's OK but the car wheel caught her. Nasty gash on her left leg.' The ambulanceman added, 'Brave young lady.'

Dr Hay-Smythe bent his great height again. 'Bertha?' His voice was quiet and reassuring. She opened the good eye.

'Oliver.' She smiled widely. 'You oughtn't to be working; it's Sunday.'

He smiled then and signalled to the men to wheel the stretcher away. It struck him that despite the dirt and the black eye nothing could dim the beauty of her one good eye, its warm brown alight with the pleasure of seeing him again.

There wasn't too much damage, the casualty officer told him presently—bruising, some painful grazes, a black eye and the fairly deep gash on one leg. 'It'll need a few stitches, and there's a good deal of grit and dirt in the wound. She'd better have a whiff of anaesthetic so that I can clean it up. Anti-tetanus jab too.'

He looked curiously at his companion; Dr Hay-Smythe was a well-known figure at the hospital, occasionally giving anaesthetics and often visiting the patients in his beds on the medical wards. He was well liked and respected, and rumour had it that he was much in demand socially; this small girl didn't seem quite his type…

Dr Hay-Smythe looked at his watch. 'If you could see to her within the next half-hour I'll give a hand. It'll save calling the anaesthetist out.'

Bertha, getting stiffer with every passing minute and aware of more and more sore places on her person, had her eyes closed. She opened the sound one when she heard his voice.

'You have a cut on your leg, Bertha,' he told her. 'I'm going to give you a whiff of something while it's seen to, then you will be warded.'

'No, no, I must go back home. Cook might wonder where I am.'

'Only Cook?' he gueried gently.

'Crook's got a half-day and my stepmother and Clare have gone to Henley to lunch with friends. There's no need to bother Cook; her sister's there.'

'Very well, but you are to stay here, Bertha. I'll see that your stepmother knows when she returns. Now, how long ago is it since you had your breakfast?'

'Why ever do you want to know? About eight o'clock.'

'Purely a professional question. No, close your eyes; I'm going to give you an injection in the back of your hand.' He turned away and spoke to someone she couldn't see and presently, eyes obediently shut, she felt a faint prick. 'Count up to ten,' he said, his voice reassuringly casual.

She got as far as five.

When she opened her eyes again she was in bed—a corner bed in a big ward—and the casualty officer and Dr Hay-Smythe were standing at the foot of it.

'Ah, back with us.' He turned away for a moment while two nurses heaved her up the bed, rearranged a cradle over her leg and disappeared again.

He studied her thoughtfully; anywhere else she would have minded being stared at like that, but here in hospital it was different; here he was a doctor and she was just another patient.

'Can I go home soon?' she asked.

It was the last place he wished her to go. She looked very small, engulfed in a hospital gown far too large for her, with her face clean now but pale and the damaged eye the only colour about her. Her hair, its mousy abundance disciplined into a plait, hung over one shoulder.

He said after a moment, 'No, you can't, Bertha. You're in one of my beds and you'll stay here until I discharge you.' He smiled suddenly. 'This is Dr Turner, the casualty officer who stitched you up.' And as another young man joined them he went on, 'And this is the medical officer who will look after you—Dr Greyson. I'll go and see your stepmother this afternoon and she will doubtless arrange to send in whatever you need.'

He offered a hand and she took it and summoned

up a smile. 'Thank you for all your trouble. I hope I haven't spoilt your day.'

She closed her eyes, suddenly overcome by sleep.

Dr Hay-Smythe waited until the late afternoon before calling at the Soameses' house—too late for tea and too early for drinks—since he had no wish to linger there. He was admitted by Cook, since Crook was still enjoying his half-day, and ushered into the drawing room, where Mrs Soames and Clare were sitting discussing the lunch party. They greeted him eagerly, bored with each other's company.

'Oliver!' Clare went to meet him. 'How lovely—I was just wondering what I would do with the rest of this dull day, and you're the answer.'

He greeted her mother before replying, 'I'm afraid not. I have to return to the hospital very shortly. I have come to tell you that Bertha has had an accident—'

'The silly girl,' interposed Mrs Soames.

'She saved the life of a small boy who had run into the street in front of a car.' His voice was carefully expressionless. 'She is in hospital with a badly cut leg and severe bruising, so she must stay there for a few days at least. Would you take her whatever is necessary when you go to see her?'

'You've seen her?' Clare's voice was sharp.

'Yes. I happened to be in the accident and emergency department when she was admitted. She is in very good hands. I'll write down the name of the ward for you—there is no reason why you shouldn't visit her this evening.'

'Quite impossible, Oliver. I've guests coming for dinner.' Mrs Soames uttered the lie without hesitation. 'And I can't allow Clare to go. She is so sensitive to pain and distressing scenes; besides, who knows what foul germs there are in those public wards? She *is* in a public ward?'

'Yes. Perhaps you would ask one of your staff.' He paused, and then went on silkily, 'Better still, if you could give me whatever is needed, I will take it to Bertha.'

This suggestion met with the instant rejection he had expected. 'No, no!' cried Mrs Soames. 'Cook shall go with Bertha's things, and at the same time make sure that she has all she wants. The poor child!' she added with sickening mendacity. 'We must take good care of her when she comes home.'

She gave Clare a warning glance so that the girl quickly added her own sympathy. 'I hope she comes home soon.' Clare sounded wistfully concerned. 'I shall miss her.'

As indeed she would, reflected the doctor. There would be no one to whom she might pass on her un-suitable clothes. She was wearing a ridiculous outfit now, all frills and floating bits; he much preferred Bertha in her startling lime-green. Indeed, upon fur-ther reflection he much preferred Bertha, full-stop.

He took his leave presently and went back home to

fetch Freddie and take him for a long walk in Hyde Park. And that evening, after he had dined, he got into his car once more and drove to the hospital. Visiting hours were long over and the wards were quiet, the patients drinking their milk or Ovaltine and being settled down for the night. Bertha was asleep when, accompanied by the ward sister, he went to look at her.

'Someone came with her nightclothes and so on?' he wanted to know.

'Oh, yes, Doctor. The family cook—a nice old soul. Gave her a large cake in a tin too, and said she would come again and that if she couldn't come someone called Crook would.'

'Ah, yes, the butler.'

'Has she no family?'

'A stepmother and a stepsister and a father who at present is somewhere in the States. He's a well-known QC.'

Sister looked at him. There was nothing to see on his handsome features, but she sensed damped-down rage. 'I'll take good care of her, Doctor,' she said.

He smiled at her then. 'Good—and will you be sure and let me know before she goes home?'

Bertha, after a refreshing sleep, felt quite herself in the morning. True, she was still stiff and sore, and it was tiresome only having the use of one eye, but she sat up and ate her breakfast and would have got out of bed armed with towel and toothbrush if she hadn't been restrained.

The leg must be rested, she was told. The cut had been deep and very dirty, and until it had been examined and re-dressed she would have to remain in her bed.

There was plenty to keep her interested, however. The elderly lady in the bed next to hers passed half an hour giving her details of her operation, most of them inaccurate, but Bertha listened enthralled until Sister came down the ward with a Cellophaned package.

'These have just come for you, Bertha. Aren't you a lucky girl?'

It was a delicate china bowl filled with a charming mixture of winter crocuses.

'There's a card,' prompted Sister.

Bertha took it from its miniature envelope. The writing on it was hard to read. 'Flowers for Bertha', it said, and then the initials 'O.H-S.'

Sister recognised the scrawl. 'Just the right size for your locker top,' she said breezily, and watched the colour flood into Bertha's pale face. Who'd have thought it? the sister asked herself, sensing romance.

There were visitors later—the small boy whom she had saved led into the ward by his mother and bearing a bunch of flowers. The mother cried all over Bertha and wrung her hand and, very much to Bertha's embarrassment, told everyone near enough to listen how Bertha had saved her small son from being run over.

'Killed, he would have been—or crippled for life. A proper heroine, she is.'

That evening Crook came, bearing more flowers and a large box of chocolates from Cook and the daily and the man who came to do the garden each week.

'Is everything all right at home, Crook?' asked Bertha.

'Yes, Miss Bertha. I understand that there is a letter from your father; he hopes to return within the next few weeks. Mrs Soames and Miss Clare have been down to Brighton with friends; they are dining out this evening.'

'I'm not sure how long I am to stay here, Crook...'

'As long as it takes you to get quite well, Miss Bertha. You're not coming home before.'

He got up to go presently, with the promise that someone would come to see her again.

'Thank you for coming, and please thank the others for the chocolates and flowers. It's so kind of them and I know how busy you all are, so I won't mind if none of you can spare the time to visit. You can see how comfortable I am, and everyone is so friendly.'

On his way out, Sister stopped him. 'You come from Mrs Soames's household? Is she coming to see Miss Soames? She must wish to know about her injuries and I'd like to advise her about her convalescence.'

'Mrs Soames is most unlikely to come, Sister. If you will trust me with any details as to the care of Miss Bertha when she returns home, I shall do my utmost to carry them out,' said Crook.

When Dr Hay-Smythe came onto the ward later that evening, as she was going off duty, Sister paused to talk to him and tell him and the medical officer, who had come to do an evening round, what Crook had told her. 'I'll keep her as long as possible, but I'm always pushed for beds. And although I know you have beds in this ward, doctor, it is a medical unit and Bertha's a surgical case.'

'A couple more days, Sister?' He glanced at the young doctor with him. 'Turn a blind eye, Ralph? At least until the stitches come out. If she goes home too soon she'll be on that leg all day and ruin the CO's painstaking surgery. How is she, by the way?'

'A model patient; she's next to Mrs Jenkins—a thrombosis after surgery—and she's delighted to have such a tolerant listener.' She glanced at the doctor. 'She was delighted with your flowers, doctor.'

'Good. May I see Miss Arkwright for a moment? She wasn't too good yesterday.'

Miss Arkwright was at the other end of the ward from Bertha, but she could see Dr Hay-Smythe clearly as he went to his patient's bedside. She was feeling sleepy, but she kept her eye open; he would be sure to come and say goodnight presently. Only he didn't.

After a few minutes he went away again without so much as a glance in her direction.

Bertha discovered that it was just as easy to cry with one eye as two.

The next few days were pleasant enough—the nurses were friendly, those patients who were allowed up came to sit by her, bringing their newspapers and reading out the more lurid bits, since her eye, now all the colours of the rainbow and beginning to open again, was still painful. Cook came too, this time with a bag of oranges.

Everything was much as usual, she told Bertha comfortably, omitting to mention that Mrs Soames's temper had been worse than usual and that Clare was having sulking fits.

'That nice doctor what she's keen on—always asking 'im ter take 'er out, she is, and 'im with no time to spare. 'E's taking 'er out to dinner this evening, though.'

Bertha stayed awake for a long time that night, listening to the snores and mutterings around her, the occasional urgent cry for a bedpan, the equally urgent whispers for tea. She closed her eyes each time the night nurse or night sister did her round and she heard the night sister say quietly, 'She'll have to go home in a couple of days; she's only here as a favour to Dr Hay-Smythe.'

Bertha lay and thought about going home. She had

no choice but to do so for she had no money. It would mean seeing Clare and Oliver together, and she wasn't sure if she could bear that.

I suppose, she reflected, with the clarity of mind which comes to everybody at three o'clock in the morning, that I've been in love with him since he came over to me and asked me if it was my birthday. I'll have to go away… Once Father's back home, perhaps he'll agree to my training for something so that I can be independent. I'll have my own flat and earn enough money to be able to dress well and to go to the hairdresser and have lots of friends… She fell into an uneasy doze.

She was allowed out of bed now, and later the next day Staff Nurse took out alternate stitches.

'I'll have the rest tomorrow,' she said briskly. 'Don't run around too much; it's not quite healed yet. I expect you'll be going home in a day or two now.'

Bertha told Crook that when he came that afternoon. 'Please don't tell anyone, will you? I wouldn't want to upset any plans…'

They both knew Mrs Soames wasn't likely to change any plans she had made just because Bertha was coming home.

Dr Hay-Smythe came to see her that evening. 'You're to go home the day after tomorrow. I'll take you directly after lunch. You feel quite well?'

'Yes, thank you, I'm fine. Some of the stitches are out and it's a very nice scar—a bit red…'

'You won't see it in a few months. Will you be able to rest at home?'

'Oh, of course,' said Bertha airily. 'I can sit in the drawing room. But I don't need to rest, do I? I'm perfectly well. I know my eye's still not quite right, but it looks more dramatic than it is.'

He sat down on the side of the bed. 'Bertha, my mother would like you to go and stay with her for a week or two, perhaps until Christmas. How would you like that?'

Her eyes shone. 'Oh, how kind of her. I'd have to ask my stepmother first…'

He found himself smiling at her eager face. The few days in hospital had done her good; she had a pretty colour and she looked happy. He took her hand in his, conscious of a deep contentment. He had cautioned himself to have patience, to give her time to get to know him, but he had fallen in love with her when he had first seen her and his love had grown over the weeks. She was the girl he had been waiting for, and somehow or other he had managed to keep close to her, despite the dreadful stepmother and the tiresome Clare. He wouldn't hurry her, but after a few days he would go home and tell her that he loved her in the peace and quiet of the country.

He said now, 'We have to talk, Bertha. But not here.'

The ward was very quite and dim. He bent and kissed her gently and went away. Mrs Jenkins, feigning sleep and listening to every word, whispered, 'Now go to sleep, ducks. Nothing like a kiss to give you sweet dreams.'

The next day Oliver realized that he would have to see Mrs Soames before taking Bertha home. There was bound to be unpleasantness and he wanted that dealt with before she arrived. Not that he intended to tell her that he was in love with Bertha and was going to marry her, only that his mother had invited her to stay for a short time.

Mrs Soames gushed over him and then listened to his plans, a smile pinned onto her face. He was surprised at her readiness to agree with him that a week or so's rest was necessary for Bertha, but, thinking about it later, he concluded that it might suit her and Clare to have Bertha out of the way—she would be of no use to them around the house until her leg was quite healed. All the same, he had a feeling of unease.

CHAPTER FIVE

OLIVER'S feeling of unease was justified. Mrs Soames, left to herself, paced up and down her drawing room, fuming. Bertha had gone behind her back and was doing her best to put a spoke in Clare's wheel. The wretched girl! Something would have to be done.

Mrs Soames, by now in a rage, spent some time thinking of the things she would like to do to Bertha before pulling herself together. Anger wasn't going to help. She must keep a cool head and think of ways and means. She heard Clare's voice in the hall and went to the door and called for her to come to the drawing room.

'Presently,' said Clare, who was halfway up the stairs. 'I've broken a fingernail and I must see to it at once...'

Something in her mother's voice brought her downstairs again.

'What's the matter?'

'Oliver has been here. Bertha is to come home tomorrow and his mother has invited her to stay with her for a couple of weeks.' Mrs Soames almost choked with fury as she spoke. 'The ungrateful girl— going behind our backs. She's cunning enough—

she'll have him all to herself if she goes to his home.'
She looked thoughtful. 'I wonder—Clare, get me the
telephone directory.'

His receptionist was still at his rooms, and, in answer to Mrs Soames's polite enquiry, said that she
was afraid that Dr Hay-Smythe wouldn't be seeing
new patients during the coming week. 'And he will
be going on holiday the following week. But I could
book you for an appointment in three weeks' time.'

Mrs Soames put down the phone without bothering
to answer.

'He's going on holiday in a week's time—he'll go
home, of course, and they'll have a whole week together. We have this week to think of something,
Clare.'

Clare poured them each a drink and sat down.
'She'll have to go away—miles away. Now, who do
we know…?'

'She'll have to go immediately—supposing he calls
to see her?'

'We can say she's spending the weekend with
friends.' Clare sat up suddenly. 'Aunt Agatha,' she
said triumphantly. 'That awful old crow—Father's elder sister, the one who doesn't like us. We haven't
seen her for years. She lives somewhere in the wilds
of Cornwall, doesn't she?'

'Perfect—but will she have Bertha to stay? Supposing she refuses?'

'She doesn't need to know. You can send Bertha

there—tell her that Aunt Agatha isn't well and has asked if she would go and stay with her.'

'What are we to say? Bertha may want to see the letter…'

'No letter. A phone call.' Clare crowed with laughter. 'I'd love to see her face when Bertha gets there.' She paused to think. 'We'll have to wait until Oliver has brought her home and then pack her off smartly. Do you suppose that he's interested in her? It's ridiculous even to think it. Why, Bertha's plain and dull— it's not possible. Besides, he's taken me out several times…'

'He will again, darling,' said Mrs Soames. She smiled fondly at her daughter; she could rest assured that Clare would get her way.

Bertha was ready and waiting when the doctor came for her. Her leg was still bandaged and her cheek under the black eye was grazed, but all he saw was the radiance of her smile when she saw him. He held down with an iron will a strong desire to gather her into his arms and kiss her, and said merely, 'Quite ready? The leg is comfortable? I can see that the eye is better.'

'I'm fine,' declared Bertha—a prosaic statement, which concealed her true feelings. 'It's very kind of you to take me home.'

He only smiled, waiting while she said goodbye to

Sister and the nurses; she had already visited each bed to shake hands with its occupant.

He carried on a gentle, rambling conversation as he drove her home and as he drew up before the door he said, 'I'm coming in with you, Bertha.' Mrs Soames had seemed pleasant enough, but he still had an uneasy feeling about her.

Mrs Soames and Clare were both there, waiting for them. Clare spoke first.

'Bertha, are you quite better? Ought you to rest?' She gave a small, apologetic smile. 'I'm sorry I didn't come and see you—you know how I hate illness and dreary hospitals. But I'll make it up to you.'

Bertha, recognising this as a deliberate act to put her stepsister in a good light, murmured back and replied suitably to her stepmother's enquiries, which gave Clare the opportunity to take the doctor aside on the pretext of enquiring as to Bertha's fitness.

'Is she all right to walk about? Not too much, of course. We'll take good care of her.' She smiled up into his face. 'It is so kind of your mother to have her to stay. Will you be going to your home too?'

He looked down at her, his face bland. 'I shall do my best.' He got up from the sofa where they were sitting. 'I must go. I have several patients to see this afternoon.' He crossed the room to where Bertha was in uneasy conversation with her stepmother. 'I will come for you in three days' time, Bertha. Mrs Soames, I'm sure you'll take good care of her until then.' He shook hands then turned to Bertha. 'I hope to get away at half past twelve— will you be ready for me then?'

'Yes—yes, thank you.'

'Don't try and do too much for a few days.'

No one could fault the way in which he spoke to her—a detached kindness, just sufficiently friendly. Only his eyes gleamed under their lids.

Bertha's stepmother, once the doctor had gone, was so anxious to make sure that Bertha had everything she wanted, wasn't tired, wasn't hungry, or didn't wish to lie down on her bed that Bertha was at pains to discover what had brought about this change of heart.

She wasn't the only one. Crook, going back to the kitchen after he had served dinner, put down his tray and said darkly, 'Depend upon it, this won't last— there's madam begging Miss Bertha to have another morsel and is she comfortable in that chair and would she like to go to bed and someone would bring her a warm drink. Poppycock—I wonder what's behind it?'

Apparently nothing; by the end of the second day Bertha's surprise at this cosseting had given way to pleased relief, and Crook had to admit that Mrs Soames seemed to have had a change of heart. 'And not before time,' he observed.

Bertha went to bed early. She had packed her bag with the miserable best of her wardrobe, washed her hair and telephoned the nursery school to tell the matron that she would be coming back after Christmas if they still wanted her. Since her stepmother was showing such a sympathetic face, Bertha had told her that she was no longer reading to an old lady but to a group of children.

'Why didn't you tell me this?' Mrs Soames strove to keep the annoyance out of her voice.

'I didn't think that it was important or that you would be interested.'

Mrs Soames bit her tongue and summoned up a smile. 'Well, it really doesn't matter, Bertha. I'm sure it is very worthwhile work. Oliver arranged it for you, I expect?'

Bertha said that yes, he had, and didn't see the angry look from her stepmother.

Clare, when told of this, burst into tears. 'You see, Mother, how she has been hoodwinking us all this time. Probably seeing him every day. Well, she'll be gone when he comes. Is it all arranged?'

It was still early morning when Bertha was roused by her stepmother. 'Bertha, I've just had a phone call from your aunt Agatha. She's not well and asks for you. I don't think she's desperately ill, just needs someone there other than the servants. She has always been fond of you, hasn't she? She begged me to ask you to go as soon as possible, and I couldn't refuse.'

'I'm going to Mrs Hay-Smythe today, though…'

'Yes, yes, I know. But perhaps you could go to your aunt just for a day or two.'

'Why must I go? Why should she ask for me?'

'She's elderly—and she's always been eccentric.' Mrs Soames, sensing that she was losing the battle, said with sudden inspiration, 'Suppose you go today? I'll phone her doctor and see if he can arrange for someone to stay with your aunt, then you can come straight back. A day's delay at the most. Your father would want you to go.'

'Oliver expects me to be ready—'

'Write him a note and I'll explain. Believe me, Bertha, if Clare could go in your place she would, but you know how your aunt dislikes her.'

Bertha threw back the bed clothes. 'Very well, but I'm coming back, whatever arrangements are made.'

'Well, of course you are. Get dressed quickly and I'll find out about trains.'

Mrs Soames went away to tell Clare that their plan was working so far. 'I told her that I was finding out about the next train.' She glanced at the clock. 'I've just time to dress and drive her to Paddington. She can have breakfast on the train.' She turned at the door. 'Bertha's writing a note for Oliver. Get rid of it before he comes—and not a word to the servants. I'll see them when I get back. I don't mean to tell them where she has gone.'

An hour later, sitting in the train, eating a breakfast she didn't want, Bertha tried to sort out the morning's happenings. It didn't occur to her that she had been tricked; she knew that her stepmother didn't like her, but that she would descend to such trickery never crossed her mind. She had written to Oliver—a careful little note, full of apologies, hoping that he wouldn't be inconvenienced and hoping to see his mother as soon as she could return.

Clare had read it before she'd torn it into little pieces.

The train journey was a lengthy one. Bertha, eating another meal she didn't want, thought about Oliver. He would have been to her home by now, of course, and been told about her sudden departure. She wished she could have written a longer letter, but there hadn't been time. She could think of nothing else, her head full of the whys and wherefores of something she couldn't understand. It was a relief when Truro was reached at last and she got out to change to a local train, which stopped at every station until it stopped, at last, at her destination.

The village was small and she remembered it well from visits when she was a child. Miss Soames lived a mile or two away from the narrow main street, and Bertha was relieved to see a taxi in the station yard. She had been given money for her expenses—just sufficient to get her to her aunt's house—and since her stepmother had pointed out that there was no point in getting a return ticket as she herself would drive down and fetch Bertha she had accepted the situation willingly enough. Her head full of Oliver, nothing else mattered.

Her aunt's house looked exactly the same as she remembered it—solid and rather bleak, with a splendid garden. Bertha toiled up the path with her suitcase and knocked at the door.

After a moment it was flung open and Miss Agatha Soames, majestic in a battered felt hat and old and expensive tweeds, stood surveying Bertha.

'Well, upon my word. Why are you here, gel?'

Bertha, not particularly put out by this welcome, for her aunt was notoriously tart, said composedly that her stepmother had sent her. 'She told me that you were ill and needed a companion and had asked for me urgently.'

Miss Soames breathed deeply. 'It seems to me from the look of you that it is you who needs a companion. Your stepmother is a vulgar, scheming woman who would be glad to see me dead. I am in the best of health and need no one other than Betsy and Tom. You may return home.' She bent a beady eye on Bertha. 'Why have you a black eye? She actually sent you here to me?'

'Yes, Aunt Agatha.' Awful doubts were crowding into Bertha's tired head.

Miss Soames snorted. 'Then she's up to something. Wants you out of the way in a hurry. Been upsetting the applecart, have you? Poaching on that Clare's preserves, are you?'

When Bertha's cheeks grew pink, she said, 'Took a fancy to you instead of her, did he? Well, if he's got any sense he will come after you.'

Bertha shook her head. 'No, I don't think so. He doesn't know where I am—I didn't tell him.'

'They won't tell him either. But if he's worth his salt he'll find you. Love him?'

'Yes, Aunt Agatha. But he doesn't think of me like that, though he's a kind man.'

'We will see.' Miss Soames thrust the door wide open and said belatedly, 'Well, come in. Now you're here you'd better stay. Where's your father?'

'I'm not exactly sure, but he's coming home soon.'

Aunt Agatha said, 'Pah!' and raised her voice. 'Betsy, come here and listen to this.' Betsy came so quickly that Bertha wondered if she had been standing behind the door.

'No need to tell, I heard it all. Poor lamb. I'll get the garden room ready and a morsel of food. The child looks starved—and look at that eye! A week or two here with good food and fresh air is what she needs.'

During the next few days that was what Bertha got. Moreover, her aunt ordered Tom to bring the elderly Rover to the front door and she and Bertha were driven into Truro, where she sailed in and out of various shops buying clothes for her niece.

When Bertha protested, she said, 'I'll not have a niece of mine wearing cast-off clothes which are several sizes too big and quite unsuitable. I shall speak to your father. Don't interfere, miss.'

So Bertha thanked her aunt and got joyfully into skirts and blouses and dresses which fitted her slender person and were made of fine material in soft colours. If only Oliver could see her now. She had talked to her aunt about what she should do and that lady had said, 'Do nothing, gel. Let your stepmother wonder, if she can be bothered to do so. You are not to write to her nor are you to telephone. You will stay here until this doctor finds you.'

'He won't,' said Bertha. 'He'll never find me...'

'Have you never heard of the proverb "Love finds a way"? I have great faith in proverbs,' said Aunt Agatha.

Oliver had presented himself at half past twelve exactly to collect Bertha, and had been shown into the drawing room. Mrs Soames had come to meet him.

'Oliver, thank heaven you have come. I tried to get you on the phone, but there was no answer.'

She'd found his calm unnerving.

'Bertha!' she'd exclaimed. 'She must be ill—that accident. She got me out of bed early this morning and insisted on being driven to Euston Station. I begged her to stay, to phone you, to wait at least until you came. She was quite unlike herself—so cold and determined.'

'You did as she asked?' His voice had been very quiet.

'What else could I do? She wouldn't listen to reason.'

'She had money? Did she say where she was going?'

'I gave her what I had. She told me that she was going to an aunt—a relation of her mother's, I believe, who lives somewhere in Yorkshire. I begged her to tell why she wanted to leave us and I reminded her that she was to visit your mother—she said she would write to you.' Mrs Soames managed to squeeze out a tear. 'I really don't know what to do, Oliver. Clare is terribly upset.'

Oliver sounded quite cheerful. 'Why, I suggest that we wait until one or other of us gets a letter. She is quite capable of looking after herself, is she not?'

'Yes, of course. Will you come this evening so that we three can put our heads together? Dinner, perhaps?'

'Not possible, I'm afraid, Mrs Soames.' He spoke pleasantly, longing to wring the woman's neck. There was something not right about the story she had told him. He would get to the bottom of it if it took him weeks, months…

'The whole thing is fishy,' he told Freddie as he drove away. Someone somewhere would know where

Bertha had gone; he would send Cully round later with some excuse or other and he could talk to Crook—both he and Cook were obviously fond of Bertha, and in the meanwhile he would see if the nursery school knew anything.

'Gone?' asked Matron. 'Without a word to anyone? I find that hard to believe. Why, she telephoned not a day or two ago to say that she would be coming back after Christmas, when she had had a short holiday.'

Oliver thanked her. It hadn't been much help, but it was a start.

Cully's visit had no success, either. Crook was disturbed that Bertha had gone so unexpectedly, but he had no idea where she might be. Certainly there was an aunt of hers somewhere in the north of England, and the master had a sister living, but he had no idea where.

The doctor phoned his mother and sat down to think. Mrs Soames had been very glib, and he didn't believe a word of what she had said, but there was no way of getting her to tell the truth. To find this aunt in Yorkshire when he had no idea of her name or where she lived was going to be difficult. Her father's sister—unmarried, Crook had said—was a more likely possibility. He went to bed at last, knowing what he would do in the morning.

Mr Soames QC was well-known in his own profession. The doctor waited patiently until a suitable hour the next morning and then phoned his chambers.

'No,' he was told. 'Mr Soames is still in the States. Would you like to make an appointment at some future date?'

The doctor introduced himself. 'You are his chief clerk? So I can speak freely to you? I am a friend of the Soames family and there is a personal matter I should like to attend to—preferably with Mr Soames. Failing that, has he a relation to whom I could write? This is a family matter, and Mrs Soames is not concerned with it.'

'Dr Hay-Smythe? You have a practice in Harley Street. I remember that you were called to give evidence some time ago.'

'That is so. You would prefer me to come and see you?'

'No. No, that won't be necessary. Mr Soames has a sister living in Cornwall. I could give you her address.' The clerk sounded doubtful.

'I will come to your chambers to collect it, and if you wish to let Mr Soames know of my request, please do so.'

It was impossible to go down to Cornwall for at least two days; he had patients to see, a ward round at the hospital, an outpatients clinic, and then, hours before he intended to leave, an urgent case. So, very nearly

a week had passed by the time he got into his car with
Freddie and began the long drive down to Cornwall.

It was already later than he had intended; he had
no hope of reaching Miss Soames's house at a reasonable hour. He drove steadily westward, Freddie
alert beside him, and stopped for the night at Liskeard
in an old friendly pub where he was given a hearty
supper before going to his room, which was low-
ceilinged and comfortable. Since Freddie had behaved
in a very well-bred manner he accompanied his master, spreading his length across the foot of the bed.

'This is definitely not allowed,' Oliver told him.
'But just this once, since it is a special occasion. I
only hope that Bertha's aunt likes dogs.'

Freddie yawned.

They were on their way again after breakfast—bacon, mushrooms freshly picked, fried bread, a sausage
or two and egg garnished with a tomato. A meal to
put heart into a faint-hearted man—something which
the doctor was not. In an hour or so he would see his
Bertha again, beyond that he didn't intend to think for
the moment. He whistled as he drove and Freddie, no
lover of whistling, curled his lip.

It was shortly after ten o'clock when Betsy carried the
coffee tray into Miss Soames's sitting room, which
was small and pleasant, overlooking the wide stretch
of garden at the back of the house. Bertha was out
there, walking slowly, her hair in a plait over one

shoulder, and wearing one of the pretty winter dresses which Miss Soames had bought for her.

Her aunt, peering over her spectacles at her, observed, 'The girl's not pretty, but there's something about her... Takes after our side of the family, of course.' She poured her coffee. 'Leave the child for the moment, Betsy. She's happy.'

Betsy went away, but she was back again within a minute.

'There's an 'andsome motor car coming up to the door...'

Miss Soames sipped her coffee. 'Ah, yes, I was expecting that. Show the gentleman in here, Betsy, and say nothing to Bertha.'

The doctor came in quietly. 'Miss Soames? I apologise for calling upon you unexpectedly. I believe that Bertha is staying with you?' He held out a hand. 'Oliver Hay-Smythe.'

She took the hand. 'What kept you, young man?' she wanted to know tartly. 'Of course, I knew that you would come, although Bertha is sure that she will never see you again.'

He followed her gaze out of the window; Bertha looked very pretty, and his rather tired face broke into a smile.

'I told her that if a man was worth his salt he would find her even if he had to search the world for her.' She gave him a level gaze. 'Would you do that, Doctor?'

'Yes. I do not quite understand why she is here. I think that her stepmother wanted her out of the way. That doesn't matter for the moment, but it took me some time to discover where she was.'

'You have driven down from London? What have you done with your patients?'

He smiled. 'It took a good deal of organising, but I'd planned a holiday this week.'

'You'll stay here, of course.' She looked over his shoulder. 'What is it, Betsy?'

'There's a dog with his head out of the car window.'

'Freddie. Might I allow him out? He's well-mannered.'

'Get the beast, Betsy,' commanded Miss Soames, and when Freddie, on his best behaviour, came into the room, she offered him a biscuit.

'Well, go along, young man. There's a door into the garden at the back of the hall.'

Freddie, keeping close to his heels, gave a pleased bark as he saw Bertha, and she turned round as he bounded towards her. She knelt and put her arms round his neck and watched Oliver crossing the lawn to her. The smile on her face was like a burst of sunshine as she got slowly to her feet. He saw with delight that she had a pretty colour in her cheeks and a faint plumpness which a week's good food had brought about. Moreover, the dress she was wearing revealed the curves which Clare's misfits had so successfully hidden.

He didn't say anything, but took her in his arms and held her close. Presently he spoke. 'I came as soon as I could, my darling. I had to find you first...'

'How?' asked Bertha. 'Who...?'

'Later, my love.' He bent his head and kissed her.

Bertha, doing her best to be sensible, said, 'But I want to know why my stepmother sent me here— she'll be so angry when she finds out.'

'Leave everything to me, dear heart. You need never see her or Clare again if you don't want to. We'll marry as soon as it can be arranged. Would you like Christmas Eve for a wedding?'

He kissed her again, and eventually, when she had stopped feeling light-headed, she said, 'You haven't asked me—you haven't said—'

'That I love you?' He smiled down at her. 'I love you, darling Bertha. I fell in love with you the moment I clapped eyes on you in that hideous pink dress. Will you marry me and love me a little?'

She reached up to put her arms round his neck. 'Of course I'll marry you, dear Oliver, and I'll love you very much for always. Will you kiss me again? Because I rather like it when you do.'

Aunt Agatha, unashamedly watching them from her chair, took out her handkerchief and blew her nose,